GANG OF WAR

My H&K's ready, and the wire's humming, ready to pop anything that threatens me. I carefully push open the lounge door and scan the room. Drek everywhere—chip carriers, empty flash-pak food containers, beer cans, the usual—piled on the two low tables and the handful of chairs. On the couch is a figure—and it's so bundled up in coats, stained blankets, and the lounge's curtains that I can't even tell what sex it is. And it's snoring, but it sounds more like someone trying to breathe through scuba gear clogged with porridge. I feel smothered just hearing it.

I move across the room using the H&K's flash-suppressor, I push the fold of curtain back from the figure's head so I can see the face. It's Paco, and he looks like drek. His skin's not so much white as a faint tinge of blue, and his lips are cracked and peeling, showing fissures here and there so deep they're down to pink meat. There's thick, yellow-white mucus trailing from his nose. I know why his breathing's got that underwater sound to it—his lungs must be full of the drek.

His puffy eyes blink, then slowly open. They're so bloodshot I can barely see any white at all. They roll blindly for a moment then settle on my face.

"Help me," he says, and his voice is a tortured, horrible, bubbling thing. "I got the bug, 'mano. I think I'm gonna die."

DARING ADVENTURES

SHADOWRUN

LONE WOLF

Nigel D. Findley

A ROC BOOK

ROC
Published by the Penguin Group
Penguin Books USA Inc., 375 Hudson Street,
New York, New York 10014, U.S.A.
Penguin Books Ltd, 27 Wrights Lane,
London W8 5TZ, England
Penguin Books Australia Ltd, Ringwood,
Victoria, Australia
Penguin Books Canada Ltd, 10 Alcorn Avenue,
Toronto, Ontario, Canada M4V 3B2
Penguin Books (N.Z.) Ltd, 182–190 Wairau Road,
Auckland 10, New Zealand

Penguin Books Ltd, Registered Offices:
Harmondsworth, Middlesex, England

First published by Roc, an imprint of Dutton Signet,
a division of Penguin Books USA Inc.

First Printing, February, 1994
10 9 8 7 6 5 4 3 2 1

Series Editor: Donna Ippolito
Cover: Romas Kukalis
Interior Illustrations: Joel Biske

 REGISTERED TRADEMARK—MARCA REGISTRADA

To Fred,
my favorite (as yet) unpublished novelist

Live with wolves, howl like a wolf.

—Russian proverb

BOOK ONE

1

Another fragging raid. And, typically, at the worst possible time.

We're in one of the warehouses owned by the Cutters—the small one way the hell and gone out east of Lake Meridian—loading crates of Czech assault rifles into the back of a GMC Bulldog truck for transshipment to points south. I'm not supposed to know the rifles' final destination, but I make it my business to know what I'm not supposed to. Call it fragging survival. So, anyway, this shipment's earmarked for some hotheads down in Sioux Nation who apparently have some minor bitch with the local government that they think only high-velocity ammunition will solve. Just the kind of drek that's business as usual for the Cutters. And, as far as I can figure, it always has been, even from their early days as just a local gang in Los Angeles back eighty years or so. The Cutters don't do high-volume in the arms biz (you want to outfit an army, you go see the Mafia, the yaks, or some friendly government), but they do pride themselves on quality. Take the crated assault rifles that are doing such a number on my lower back: top quality vz 88Vs that fell off the back of a truck in Brno, or some fragging place, and somehow found their way to 144th Avenue Southeast. Of course, the Cutters are into hundreds of other kinds of biz as well—from drugs and chips to kidnapping and extortion to (I drek you not) freelance security work for the occasional corp. And that, of course, is why I am where I am.

Which, at the moment, happens to be grunting and wrestling with eighty-plus kilos of ordnance in a wooden crate apparently tailor-made to send stiletto-sized slivers right through the palms and fingers of my work gloves. The slag holding up the other end of my crate—Fraser, a malnourished ork with ratty dreadlocks—doesn't seem to mind, but mainly because he's under the wire. His midbrain is con-

stantly hooked to a signal from a simsense deck, but it's one set for the lowest possible intensity. Not enough to cut him off entirely from reality, but definitely enough to color his every perception of the real world. Hell, for all I know, the same slivers that are driving me crazy could be making *his* hands feel like he's got a good hold on Honey Brighton's luscious yams.

There are four other guys humping crates with us: Piers and Lucas, Paco and En. (I don't envy Paco, having to keep up with En, who pops methamphetamines for breakfast.) All but Fraser are humans, which means we're struggling with the limitations of human muscle (except for En, who either doesn't know or care). Why didn't the big bosses send along a couple of trolls to help out? The huge trog everyone calls Box could have tucked a crate under each arm and then fragging *run* to the truck.

The six of us in the grunt squad aren't the only ones sent to the warehouse, of course. We've got three spotters out, plus Katrina, our driver. She leaning against the Bulldog's front end, staring off at nothingness and looking much too scrawny to carry the rack that fills out her kevlar T-shirt. A real space-case, that Katrina.

Of course, it isn't nothingness she's staring at. A fiber-optic line as thin as one of her greasy hairs runs from her datajack to the truck's comm panel, where some repeaters are pulling in signals from the warehouse's surveillance cameras. When Ranger and the others assigned us out here to pick up the ordnance, they gave us the spotters plus our own eyes, and that was it. But once I got aboard and realized what the Bulldog's onboard electronics were capable of, I felt smug as hell as I set Katrina to watching out for our sorry asses. Great idea.

Too bad it didn't work worth a frag.

One moment everything's chill, then the next there's gunfire from outside, and Katrina's down like she's been pole-axed.

Panic stations. I drop my end of the crate—not worrying about Fraser on the other end—and sprint toward Katrina. Nothing personal there, but knowing what took her down might make a big difference in the minutes to come.

She's flat out, maybe dead, but still in one piece. No holes, no missing meat, no blood. Either somebody sent something nasty through the circuits to her datajack or else there's a mage kicking around. If it's a mage, we're hosed big-time because we don't have any magic of our own to fight back with. If it's something technological, it's probably a "tingler" sending enough of an overvoltage through the surveillance systems to overload Katrina's filters—and maybe Katrina too.

And then everyone's running around like a fragging elven fire drill. Fraser's hopping around on one foot screaming a blue streak while everyone else is hauling out their weapons and looking for cover.

As for me, I just hunker down next to Katrina and scope things out. If you don't know where the threat's coming from, running like a spooked rat is as likely to take you straight into the guns of the bad guys as it is to save your hoop. Besides, I want to see if I can figure out who's hitting us.

There are plenty of candidates. Neither the Mafia nor the yaks would bother to harass the Cutters, but we're always butting heads against some of the Seoulpa rings. The Cutters are tougher than the other local gangs—except for the Ancients, maybe—which scares off some, but makes others occasionally want to take their shots at the biggest kid on the block. So it could be any of a dozen interested parties.

More gunfire from around the back of the warehouse, and the other boys of the grunt squad are suddenly finding new cover. I don't bother: the Bulldog will cover me from a number of angles, and if push comes to frag, I can always hide under it, or inside it.

Another burst of fire, this time from yet another angle and accompanied by a scream. Somebody's down, and from the direction of the sound, I'd guess it's one of our spotters. Cursing almost as fiercely as Fraser, I pull out my SMG. The feather-touch of the wire in my brain tells me the skillwires are pulling data from the skillsoft plugged into the socket at the back of my neck. My palm tingles, and some normally unused part of my brain lights up as the gun's circuitry synchs up with the tech in my head. Instead of merely holding a gun, I now feel like the weapon's a living part of me. Like, at last my arm is whole again, or some such drek. Data floods into my mind as the smartgun and my skillsoft do their digital handshaking. Heckler & Koch 227-S, recoil-suppression active, silencer at nominal one hundred percent effectiveness—as if it matters—twenty-eight rounds in the clip, one in the pipe.

And that's the problem. I've got one spare clip and that's it. Same with Fraser and the rest of the boys: maybe a hundred and fifty rounds between us. Hell, we're not supposed to get into a scrap; that's what the muscleboys outside are for. If anything, we're overarmed to handle the one or two leakers we thought we might run into. Well, that's all changed now, for fragging sure. Another frantic burst of firing, another howl—this one wailing on for a while before cutting off sharply. Sounds like the hardboys are taking a pasting. I look around at my "command," which is what these sorry scroffs have suddenly become. They're all hunkered down with ordnance out, the red dots of sighting lasers tracking everywhere, even over each other. It's just getting better and better.

But, hold the phone, you say. What about all those dandy Czech assault rifles? Well, maybe it's true that we've got three or four ARs each, but bullets we ain't got. The ammo that was supposed to be the other half of the Sioux shipment is stored somewhere else. (Don't ask me why; some perverted extension of "range safety," I guess.) So unless we feel like using the rifles as clubs, all those crates full of ARs don't mean squat.

To my right, Piers sprays a long burst into the shadows just under the roof at the far end of the warehouse. Bullets spatter and spark off all the metal up there, and I think for a moment he's seeing things. But fragged if there isn't a squawk and then a dark shape tumbling from the catwalk to crash-splat into some cargo boxes below. Lucas—a few ticks late, as usual—hoses down the spot where the figure isn't anymore.

So they're up top, too, whoever they are. When I heard the first shots, I figured some other gang. When Katrina went down, I upped the ante to someone serious, a first-tier gang. Possibly the Ancients or a squad of Seoul men. Now I'm not so sure. Whoever they are, their tactics are good, and they're showing more discipline than the typical gang. I'm starting to get a bad feeling about this.

Sudden panic. I can see all the boys, all five of them. That means they're all on the same side of the Bulldog as me. Which means . . .

Staying low, with my head down at about knee-level, I

duck around the front of the truck. Someone sees the movement. Muzzle-flashes flare in the dark corner, and bullets tear into the truck's bodywork. I respond with a controlled, three-round burst, but it's more an attempt at suppression fire to keep their heads down than in hopes of hitting anything. Meanwhile the tech in my head is predicting impact points, recording ammunition expended, and measuring wear and tear on the silencer. Then I duck back as the Bulldog undergoes more drastic depreciation.

Frag, things are definitely not looking good. And then they suddenly look even worse as Fraser goes over sideways, his throat torn away. Lucas pops up like he's on springs and fires back in the direction of the incoming mail. I hear a grunt of pain from the shadows. It doesn't sound like a kill, but maybe somebody got slowed down.

I scramble to the rear of the truck for a look around that way. All I can see are shadows every fragging where among the crates and shipping cases and piles of odds and sods. There are lights, of course, hanging from the girders and catwalks near the roof, but not many, not enough. For about the hundredth time, I wish I'd gone for the full-meal deal and had my eyes enhanced while the surgeon already had me opened up installing the skillwires. Thermo, or even just low-light, would be a lifesaver at the moment. Wouldn't it be a hoot if the thing that got me killed right now was a little queasiness over eye surgery?

Muzzle-flashes from the darkness, and then I'm sucking dust on the floor. The Bulldog gets remodeled again as I roll under it. I cap off another three-round burst, blind, into the darkness. A figure moves, and for the first time I can see who we're up against.

Blue combat armor with yellow trim, helmet with semimirrored macroplast face-shield, matte-black shock gloves. Stun baton on the web belt, bandolier with extra clips, and an H & K submachine gun in the mitts. A Lone Star Fast Response Team trooper. Oh boy, just fragging marvelous.

Bullets chew up the cargo case next to the FRTer, then whoever's shooting at him walks the burst into his chest. The trooper's armor stops the light rounds, but by pure luck a ricochet tags the visor release on his helmet. Up snaps the macroplast shield, and for an instant I can see the slag's face. Then there's no face anymore, just a spray of red.

Down he goes, and I send three more rounds over the top of his body. "Got one!" I yell, just in case any of the boys are listening. Then I scrabble back out the other side of the Bulldog.

Lone Star. Fragging wonderful. Whatever happened to interdepartmental communication, tell me that? Some parts of the Star know not to dick with certain Cutters operations, and why. But why didn't Officer Friendly—may he rest in peace—and his little friends get the word? Probably some kind of internecine rivalry between the Organized Crime (Gang) task force and some other little personal empire within the corporation. That drek happens all the time within the Cutters, so why should the Star be any different?

Now the Bulldog rocks under the impact of another kind of report—a full-throated boom this time rather than the high-pitched ripping of SMG fire. I know enough about Lone Star equipment and tactics to know what it is. If this is a typical FRT squad, there's one guy out there with a Mossberg CMDT combat auto-shotgun; if it's a double squad, there are two of those beauties roaming around.

Time to leave. Right now. The shotgun blast came from the right side of the truck, the passenger side. So I scramble out from under the driver's side. Fire comes from above, hosing down the ground in front of me. Trideo shows to the contrary, it's surprisingly difficult to fire accurately from a higher elevation. I return fire in the rough direction of the muzzle-flashes. Little chance of actually hitting anything, which is fine by me, but there's nothing more disruptive to a gunman's concentration than a bullet past the ear. When Katrina went down, she fell against the driver's side door, shutting it. The cargo door's still open, though—with a crate of ARs half-in half-out—so that's the way I dive into the Bulldog.

The CMDT shotgun put a hole big enough to stick my head through in the truck's right side, and individual pellets have punched finger-size holes in the other side. SMG rounds continue to clatter and spang off the vehicle's exterior as I scramble over three crates of useless ordnance into the driver's compartment. Another burst stars and frosts the windshield while I'm tearing Katrina's fiber cable out of the control panel to enable the conventional controls.

"Mount up!" I scream, hitting the starter and hoping the boys can hear me over the gunfire.

The engine lights up instantly, thank the gods; this is no time to have to call the Motor Club. I slip the automatic transmission into gear, tromping on the brake with my left foot while pushing the gas pedal to the floor. Hardware complains, and the torque of the big turbocharged engine tilts the truck a couple of degrees to the left. More rounds spatter off the armor. Ducking down low, I slap at the row of switches for the lights. Lots of lights, and big lights, all over the Bulldog. Christ knows how many millions of candlepower or lumen-feet or whatever, but enough to light up an area the size of a football field brighter than noon. Anyone looking even near the truck is going to be flash-dazzled inside this dimly lit warehouse. Don't quote me on this, but I think the lighting rig kicks out enough photons to overload even flare compensation in cybereyes.

Weapons open up all around the warehouse, a continuous burst of reflex fire, but nothing so much as grazes the truck. Trying to fire into the lights must be a bitch, but I'd say the effort doesn't seem to be worth squat.

I can smell something start to cook—it's not a great idea to hold a brake-stand for very long even if your engine isn't turbocharged—but I've got to give the boys at least a few more seconds. Even with my eyes streaming from the almost blinding reflection of the Bulldog's fragging lights, I can see movement among the cargo boxes. In one of my mirrors I spot little Piers on his feet and sprinting for the truck. Then there's a triple boom, and he doesn't so much go down as rupture when a three-round burst from the auto-shotgun slams into him.

En and Paco are on the move too. I don't see Lucas at all, and I sure as frag don't have time to send out a search party. Paco's got his head down and he's hauling hoop for the Bulldog's open door. Running into the truck's lights has got to be blinding him, but there's nothing I can do about that. Bullets chew up the concrete floor around him, but I don't think anything scores.

En's halfway to the truck too, but the drugs in his system don't seem to understand about self-preservation. He puts on the brakes, turns and empties his SMG in one long burst—god knows at what. Answering fire comes back from all over. His head snaps back, something sprays out the back of his neck, and that's the end of En.

I hear Paco slam into the back of the truck, and then I hear him scrambling in. "Go, Larson!" he croaks.

I go. I know I'm leaving friendlies behind—Katrina's still alive, I think, and who knows what happened to Lucas?—but I don't have much choice. I release the brakes, and we're off, fast and wild. I'm hoping whatever it is that just fell out the back of the truck is the crate of rifles and not Paco, but I'm too busy fighting the wheel as the truck fishtails wildly and almost gets away from me. I aim the Bulldog roughly down one of the lanes between high stacks of crates, but don't quite get it right, and I almost go out the side window as we sideswipe something. Bullets are thudding into the bodywork all around, but not much is getting through. Then the truck bucks like it got butted in the rear by a juggernaut, and the lower rear-right corner of the cargo bay is just fragging *gone*. The CMDT scores again. I don't know if it was just a lucky shot, or if the fragger with the combat gun is going for the tires. If so, we're in trouble. The Bulldog's got runflat tires, but run-shredded they're not.

Wall ahead. I hang a skidding, squealing right, and we're running parallel to the long side of the warehouse. Not particularly where I want to be. At the next lane I hang another right.

And there's an FRT trooper standing directly in my path. For an instant he's frozen there in the lights looking like he's facing down an Angel of the Lord, then he's flinging himself aside. I think I tag his boot-heel as we go by. I flip him the finger, even knowing he won't see it. (Probably won't see anything but afterimage for the next couple of minutes.) A hard left, and we're heading down the centerline of the building. The big up-and-over door's right ahead—closed, of course—so I push the pedal to the metal again and brace for impact. I hear Paco yelp as he sees what's coming, and I second the emotion. The door looms up, reflecting entirely too much of our own light back into my face.

We hit the door at sixty klicks or so, and through we go. The only thing that keeps me in my seat is my death-grip on the wheel. Something goes squish-pop in my left wrist and it feels like someone's set fire to my thumb, but I've got other things to worry about. My cargo, for one. Paco and a couple of crates of rifles come forward at high speed, and suddenly I have to deal with company in the driver's compartment. Some of the metal from the door's still plastered across the front of the Bulldog so I can't see squat, and we're still taking fire from somewhere. We bounce off something—the way this night's going, it's probably a fragging Citymaster, or maybe a panzer—but at least the impact removes the metal blocking my view. (The windshield, too, but you can't have everything.)

Now I can see where I am, and I don't like it. The warehouse parking lot's full of Lone Star patrol cars, all with their pretty lights flashing and sparking. From the number of vehicles, I'd guess we're dealing with at least two FRT squads. (Two-plus combat guns. Glad I didn't know that earlier.) Figures scurry around as we tear out onto 144th Avenue, and a couple of cars are firing up for the pursuit.

Time to make a call. I reach for the radio, but Paco distracts me with a "Whafuck?" or some other pithy comment. He's already dazed by his abrupt visit to the front of the truck, and not tracking well, so I cold-cock him. Then I place my call. I suppose my radio manner is a little lacking in professionalism, but—to quote the sleeping Paco—Whafuck?

It takes a while, but eventually the message filters through channels to the right ears. The lights and sirens on our ass turn off, and we're alone on the streets of Kent.

About fragging time, too.

2

Ranger, the Cutters' war boss, isn't happy, but then he rarely is. He claims to be third-generation Cutters, which makes him a real rarity, a gang member whose father and grandfather both managed to live long enough to have kids. Or maybe he's just lying through his teeth, with the smart money on the bulldrek side of the equation. He's sitting in his "office," actually a sparsely furnished room upstairs in the Cutters' Ravenna safehouse, on Thirty-sixth Avenue Northeast, a block from the Calvary Cemetery. He's got his Doc Marten drek-stompers up on a table, and he's giving me and Paco the evil eye out from under his heavy black monobrow.

"Three crates," he bitches. "Three fragging crates out of a dozen, that's all you bring back. Plus you lose us eight soldiers, and the warehouse is blown. Good night's work, Larson."

"They can't trace any of the drek in the warehouse back to us," I point out reasonably. The Cutters, like all first-tier gangs, learned long ago the wonders of shells, fronts, and holding companies.

"Frag the trace," he barks. He pounds a fist down on the table and his half-kilo of bracelets and bangles clatter like scrap metal. "The Star's going to suspect, and they're going to be watching the place, right?" I nod. He's right, that's just what the Star's going to do. "So you blew us the warehouse, drekhead," he finishes.

Sometimes the tech in my head seems to know I'm mad before I do. This is one of those times. I feel the touch of the wire, feel the i-face reaching out for the circuitry of my H & K (which, of course, is somewhere else). And I realize the wire would like to kill Ranger, and so would I.

But I bite back on the sudden anger. Out the corner of my

eye I see Paco shifting from foot to foot. He's not mad, he's embarrassed or scared, and that just seems to fan my anger.

Somehow I keep it under control, though. "What were we supposed to do?" I ask, as coolly as I know how. "There was no tail on us. We set out the watchers, and I had Katrina jacked into the surveillance system. There was no sign of trouble." I shrug. "Then suddenly we're dealing with *two* Lone Star FRT squads. Eight of us against ... what? ... twenty of them?" Twenty-four, actually, according to Lone Star SOP, but not a smart thing to mention. "They've got armor and heavy weapons, we've got fragging popguns." The anger's building, so I bite back on it again. "The way I see it, we're lucky we made it out with even three crates and the Bulldog."

Ranger looks away. He knows I'm right, but he's got to have someone to blame. If me and my team didn't frag it up, then it will look like he was at fault for not sending enough troops or for fragging up in security. He knows I'm not going to back down and be the convenient little scapegoat, and he hates me for it. Well, tough drek and cry me a fragging river. "So how the frag do we fulfill the weapons order, tell me that?" he carps.

"We don't," I answer simply. "Tell the . . ."—I almost say "the Sioux," which would lead to considerable ugliness— " . . . tell the clients tough drek. Or just tell them to keep it in their pants for a couple of weeks while we make another connection." I shrug again. "And it's not our concern anyway, is it?" I ask. "Let the slags in biz development eat the loss. It's their action."

Ranger clouds up again, and I realize that somehow the Sioux deal is actually *his* action, and the hose-up has cost him bad—money or rep, or maybe both. Which is interesting. The Cutters are compartmentalized. There's a ... well, call it a "division"—since some of the members like pretending the gang's a corp anyway—that handles business deals like the Czech rifles. The war boss and his soldiers provide security, but it's kind of like interdepartmental loans of resources. Normally, Ranger wouldn't give a flying frag about the loss of the rifles or the warehouse, and he would simply write off the loss of Fraser, En, and the rest as business-as-usual attrition of his personal empire.

So why does he give a frag? Were the Sioux hotheads supposed to use those ARs for something besides a little lighthearted antigovernment terrorism? Something that's important to Ranger as the Cutters war boss? I could guess, but guessing isn't my job—it's *knowing*. Knowing, and passing the word to the right people.

Ranger's still glowering and fragging near gnashing his teeth, and my wire still wants to kill him. So I tell him, "Look, chummer, if it'll make you feel any better to hear me say I'm sorry, well, frag, I'm sorry. Mea maxima culpa and all that horsedrek. But remember I got three crates of rifles, the Bulldog, and two able-bodied solders"—I indicate me and Paco—"out of a fragging untenable position. If you think anybody else could have done a better job against a double FRT squad, then I'd like to hear about it."

Again I'm telling the truth, and again Ranger purely doesn't want to hear it. But he can't call me on it, and that makes him even madder. Sure, I could have toadied and kissed hoop, but where's the percentage in that? Ranger hates me anyway—I've known that for a while—so brown-nosing wouldn't buy me anything on that front, and it'd lose me respect from Paco. This way, I've edged Ranger a hair closer to doing something terminal to me, while making sure as frag Paco's going to tell his chummers how Rick Larson stood up to the war boss and made him eat it. And that's going to buy me bolshoi face among the troops. Looks like a bargain to me.

"Anything else?" I ask, shading my voice into that gray area between confidence and insolence.

"Get the frag out of my sight," Ranger barks, and I guess there isn't.

Outside in the hall, I feel Paco wants to say something. I stop and turn to him. He's a young guy. Thin, stands just shy of two meters, and has jet black hair. When wearing his tough face, he could be in his mid-twenties, but I happen to know he's only seventeen or so. Hard little cobber for all that. From what I hear, he grew up in the barrios of East L.A., started running with the local Latino gangs and earned his three dots—tattooed in the saddle between left thumb and forefinger—when he was eleven. Then he graduated to the South Central Cutters a year later. He came up here to Seattle two years ago. Nobody knows why and Paco won't talk about it, but he's been carving out a niche for himself ever since. With five years in the Cutters, he's one of the veterans. Give him ten years and he'll be war boss . . . if he lives that long.

But right now he wants to say something. "Yeah?" I ask.

He won't meet my eyes. "Just wanted to say thanks, 'mano," he mumbles. "For not leaving."

I wave it off. "Zero that," I tell him. His gratitude embarrasses me—he may have capped a dozen people, like his rep says, but in some ways he's still a kid. We walk in silence a few more steps, heading for the stairway down. Then I say conversationally, "Ranger's sure got his pecker in a knot about those rifles. Almost like he's on the line for something."

Paco picks up on it right away. He grins like a jackal. "Be kinda nice to know why, huh, 'mano?" he says quietly. "Always good to have an edge."

I shrug, but inside I'm smiling. Sharp kid. He got the point immediately. He thinks I'm angling to finesse Ranger, and that I'm after some kind of leverage. Let him think that. He also thinks he's in my debt, and probably figures he can pay it off by finding out what Ranger's percentage was in the Sioux deal. A win-win deal: he frees himself of a debt to me, and I learn what I want to know with no risk to my personal skin. I wish it always worked that way.

I check my watch, not surprised to see how late it is. Just past 0400. I'm scragged to the bone and my mouth tastes like something died in there. What I want most in the world at this moment is a bed—even an empty one—but there's still biz to be done, still an unspoken agreement to seal with Paco. I slap the ganger on the shoulder. "It's Miller time."

"Echo that," he grins.

3

I've never been to a full-on Cutters council of war before, and it's got Ranger totally bent to see me at this one. I'm nominally one of his boys, a mere lieutenant whose only job should be to liase between the street monsters of the Cutters' rank and file, and him and the other rarefied upper echelons of the gang. But lately I've been.... moonlighting, you could call it, working with other high-ups in the hierarchy, generally making myself as indispensable as possible. I started off slow with the social chameleon drek, something that always came easy even before my extensive training. Whenever you meet someone import, the general idea is to feed back exactly what that person wants to see or hear. If the cobber likes people who show they've got big brass ones, I lay on the bravado and the machismo. If he likes people who think before they act, I hit him with a well thought-out plan for avoiding Lone Star entanglements on certain operations. Etcetera etcetera drekcetera. From there it's just a matter of doing gofer work for them when they need it—no job too large, no job too small—until they come to trust me and eventually depend on me as a kind of unofficial advisor. That's how I worked my way up to become one of Ranger's lieutenants. Once there, and at least partially secure in my position, I was free to branch out.

So that's how I come to be here in the "ops room" of the Cutters. Ranger would probably rather lose his left nut then see me here, but the war boss doesn't have the juice to contradict Vladimir and the Deer shaman Springblossom—two Cutters top dogs who specifically requested my presence.

The ops room is in the basement of the Cutters' biggest safe house—the one on South 164th Street, right under the final approach for the transPacific suborbitals. It's a dark and stuffy place with no ventilation to clear away the smoke from Springblossom's super king-size Menthol Ultra-Js—

which she chain-smokes to "feel the spirits." Yeah, right. The way I feel just from breathing her side-stream smoke, it's a wonder anybody can make a sensible decision down here.

The centerpiece of the room is a corp-style board-room table—a real high-tech model whose mahogany top is inset with flatscreen displays and datajack sockets at each place, tri-D display facilities, and enough number-crunching horsepower to put an Ultra-VAX to shame. Fragged if I know how the Cutters got their hands on this baby—the tech alone would cost nearly a mil, not to mention what mahogany must go for these days. (That's right. Real wood, not macroplast veneer.)

All the movers and shakers in the Seattle Cutters are sitting around the table. Blake the big boss at the head, with Vladimir at his right hand and Springblossom smoking her brains out at his left, and Ranger sitting opposite him and looking generally slotted off. Filling the rest of the seats are Musen the accountant, Fahd of biz development, a real hardcase name of Cain (I had him tagged as outside talent, maybe a shadowrunner on contract or some such drek), plus a few more I don't recognize. Standing along the walls are the lesser lights who have some reason to be here but don't warrant a seat at the table. Me, for one, and Blake's personal Praetorian guard—including Box the troll looking like a nightmare out of the unexpurgated Brothers Grimm—plus a couple of other toadies.

Anyway, Vladimir's got the floor at the moment. He's wearing a suit, for frag's sake, and looks more like a European banker than a ganger. With his quiet, reasonable voice and perpetually calm, placid manner, you might even mistake him for a wuss. But good old Vladimir has more blood on his hands than anyone else sitting at that table—with the possible exception of Blake—and he's always ready to add to his score of kills. But, of course, only if it makes good business sense.

"I disagree with the war boss," he's saying calmly. "We stand to gain nothing from war with the Ancients at this point in time, to say nothing of the potential risks. A war would be costly for both sides, and might . . . hmm, bleed off enough assets to encourage one or more of the Seoulpa rings to try to take advantage of the situation." He shrugs and brushes an invisible fleck of dust off his cuff. "In any case, the Ancients have done nothing to warrant a declaration of war at this time."

Fahd, who looks like a rabid weasel, shoots back, "They took out one of our fragging transfer depots, isn't that enough? Five thousand units of beetle chips—that's two point five mil street value, gone." Musen nods agreement, but shows some hesitancy. He agrees with the figures, but not with Fahd's conclusions.

Vladimir shrugs again. "Stipulated," he says carefully. "Yet intelligence hints that the Ancients weren't aware the depot was ours, and would probably have chosen another target had they been. Correct?" He looks at me for confirmation.

"That's right," I tell the table. Vladimir thinks I've got mondo contacts on the street and in the shadows, and he's come to trust my "intelligence estimates" on a lot of subjects. (That'd change right quick if he found out that most of my contacts are within the Star, but fragged if I'm going to *let* him find out.)

"Bulldrek," Ranger snarls, ready to spit venom, and the battle lines are drawn. Ranger and Fahd are for war; Vladimir and Musen are against it. Springblossom's been feeling the spirits so much her eyes aren't focused, so she's a null. As for Cain, the way his cold eyes are flicking around makes him look like he's just sitting back and enjoying the show, maybe even contemplating taking side bets on the outcome. Box just wants to tear somebody's head off, but, then, Box always just wants to tear somebody's head off. The others are staying well out of it—smart of them—and boss-man Blake is showing slightly less emotion than the mahogany tabletop.

And me? From the looks Ranger and Fahd are throwing me, I must have planted myself firmly in Vladimir's camp by confirming his fix on the situation. Fragging marvelous.

Vladimir looks down the table at Ranger, and you can almost feel the room's temperature suddenly drop a dozen degrees. He holds that long, piercing look for ten seconds or more, then lets a faint and oh-so-supercilious smile twist his lips. "If you say so," he says mildly, and Ranger goes red then white, like he's been accused of hoopfragging devil rats. But old Vladimir doesn't care, he just goes on, "To reiterate, I believe that outright war with the Ancients would be counterproductive to our best interests." He looks around the table, as if soliciting comments. Nobody seems to have any they want to utter at the moment—except for Ranger, of course, who's saying it all with his eyes.

Vladimir nods as though he's made his point. "Yet," he continues, "we have lost money. I would propose approaching the leadership of the Ancients with a comprehensive statement of our losses." He turns his cool gaze on Musen. "Two point five million nuyen. Is that correct?"

Musen nods, his prominent Adam's apple bobbing up and down like he's trying to swallow a racquetball. "Plus structural damage in the sum of five hundred twenty-one thousand. Plus the expenditure of four personnel assets." He means dead Cutters. "The adjusted total would be"—for a moment his eyes seem to roll back in their sockets as he accesses his headware— "three million one hundred two thousand nuyen. Conservatively." I wonder how the four "expended personnel assets" would feel if they knew that Musen was valuing their lives at just over twenty-two K nuyen each.

"Three point one million, then." Vladimir accepts the correction equably. "Considerably less than the cost of outright war, I would submit. For both the Cutters *and* the Ancients. Yes, I think a war would cost us both considerably more when one takes into account the lost revenue and assets, and the impairment of our ability to capitalize on new business opportunities during the rebuilding phase." He smiles—I think that's what he's doing—his lips forming a thin straight line. "I believe the leadership of the Ancients will see reason."

"What about our rep?" Ranger grates. "What are the other gangs going to think when they see the Ancients hitting us hard and we don't hit back?" He sneers at Vladimir, who merely raises an eyebrow, and I feel the sudden urge to go hide behind Box. But Ranger just rags on. "What are the Seoulpa rings going to think when they see us hurt, and then they see us mincing on over to present the dandelion-eaters with a fragging *bill*? And what are they going to *do*?"

"What they will do," Vladimir replies, his urbane voice in frightening contrast to the killing look in his eyes, "is nothing. They will see us still on good terms with the Ancients, not distracting and weakening ourselves in a foolish war. They will see us strong and ready to repulse any moves they might make against us. If we declare war, on the other hand, they will see us reassigning to the battle lines the very resources that have so far dissuaded them from moving against us."

Perfectly logical, but too much of the time logic is to Ranger what red cloth is to a bull. The war boss is on his feet now and drawing a big breath to say something that's going to get him in real trouble with Vladimir. Go to it, Ranger, say I.

But Blake cuts him off. Not by telling him to stuff it, not even by holding up a cautioning hand. No, he merely raises the forefinger of his right hand, which is resting flat on the table. The finger moves maybe a centimeter, but it's enough to cut Ranger off in mid-rant. That's power for you. That's also Blake.

He waits quietly while Ranger swallows whatever he was going to say and sits himself back down. Then he looks around the table. For a moment Blake reminds me of sims I've seen of lions in the wild, before they all died out. He's got the same air of indolence and latent violence as a big cat looking out over the savanna. Or something. It helps that he's a big man—nearly a full two meters tall and built like an urban brawl banger—but that's not all of it. I've never seen him move fast, and if his broad, handsome face—a couple of shades darker than the mahogany table—were any more placid, any medico would probably declare him dead on the spot. There's just something about him that radiates power, pure and simple. I've seen people with big brass ones clanging between their legs, people who were death on two feet, walk into the same room with Blake, and suddenly look like they wanted to roll over onto their backs and whine like wolves submitting to the pack leader. Yeah, that's Blake.

Almost in slow motion he scans the faces of the people at the table, shifting his eyes from one to the next. When his gaze settles on someone, that individual seems to shrink visibly. Not Springblossom, because she probably doesn't notice, and not Vladimir. But everyone else, which sure as frag includes Ranger.

Then Blake turns that laser gaze on me, and again I want to hide behind Box. "You're Larson, right?" he asks in a voice like velvet and midnight.

I have to think about it for a moment, then nod.

"And you confirm what Vladimir has said? About the Ancients not knowing the depot was ours?"

"That's what the street says," I tell him, and my voice sounds like a kid's in my own ears. "I scoped it with a bunch of sources, and they all corroborate it," I babble on. He nods his acknowledgment, and I shut the frag up.

Blake looks at Vladimir, and Vladimir raises one eyebrow a hair. Then Blake's eyes are back on me. "I'd like to hear your opinion, Larson," he says. "Do we go to war or not?"

And suddenly every fragging eye in the place is on me— some surprised, some curious, two differentially dilated, and some with looks that could kill. I try to think of something to say, but the only thing that keeps running through my head is Paco's comment from the night before—*Whafuck?*— and somehow that doesn't seem appropriate. "Well, I . . . ," I stammer, and then stall.

But Blake's still looking at me, so I mentally give my head a shake. Rick Larson, zero defects. "No war," I croak.

"Ranger disagrees," Blake points out.

"Ranger's wrong," I say.

Not a politic comment, I guess. Ranger's on his feet, his cheeks so flushed he looks like he's hemorrhaging, and I'm suddenly a scapegoat for all the anger he doesn't have the cojones to direct at Vladimir or Blake. "What the frag do you know about it, you snot-nosed punk?"

The wire's different today—I've slotted an escrima chip instead of one for my H & K smartgun—but it still wants to kill Ranger. And that's my excuse for snapping back, "More than you, drekhead." My hand slips into my jacket pocket. No firearms at councils—a rule applying even to bodyguards like Box (not that he needs firearms)—and some electronics I shouldn't be carrying tell me that the ops room has hardware built into the door frame to detect smuggled holdouts.

Null sweat, though. Chem-sniffers and metal detectors don't pick up my "click-stick," a collapsible baton like the Jap cops use. It's made of a modified densiplast that's as dense as iron and lets it pack some heft, but it's totally non-magnetic. Collapsed, the stick's a cylinder about twelve centimeters long, and just the right diameter for a comfortable grip. Snap your wrist and it extends with a triple click out to about thirty centimeters, with enough mass in the bulbous tip to crack bone.

Ranger clouds up even more, growling something that sounds suspiciously like Whafuck, and then lunges. His big right hand whips behind his back, re-emerges with a composite blade, his own nonmetallic holdout.

I reach for the wire, and the brutal simplicity of escrima fills my mind. It's from the Philippines, escrima is, and I wouldn't classify it as a martial art because there's nothing artistic about it. There are no forms, no formal rules or competitions. It's about as brutal and pragmatic as the military-style hand-to-hand taught at the Academy, but it's better for my needs because it assumes your opponent's armed. Apart from the balisong "butterfly" knife, the only weapon it teaches you to use is a short stick or wand—the kind of "weapon of opportunity" you can pick up just about anywhere—which just happens to be about the same size as my click-stick. What a coincidence.

As Ranger lunges, out comes my click-stick. Snap the wrist, clickity-click and I'm ready for action. I want to growl out something chill, something like, "Okay, sunshine, let's see what you've got," but I don't have anywhere near enough time.

He comes in low, aiming to drive the blade straight toward my gut, one of the toughest knife-moves to stop. I leap back half a meter, catch his wrist in the vee formed by my left wrist and the click-stick in my right hand, deflecting his thrust past my left side. (*Just* past: I feel the blade tug at my shirt.) Then I snap a quick backhanded shot at his head with the baton. The sharp crack as the stick hits Ranger's forehead echoes in the room, and blood sprays from his scalp. For an instant he's frozen, eyes defocused, wide open. It'd be so easy to drive the tip of the baton into his throat, shatter the hyoid bone and rupture his larynx, then just stand back and watch him die. Easy and, in the grand scheme, probably a very smart move.

But at the moment probably not the best *political* move. Killing during a council is somewhat frowned upon, and hardly the best way to win friends and influence people. So instead of the throat, I jab the baton into his solar plexus, but nowhere near as hard as I want to. He says whoof, sits down abruptly—missing his chair by a meter, so sorry—and ceases to pay attention to the proceedings.

Out of the corner of my eye I see something like a leather-covered wall coming up on my flank. "It's chill," I tell Box quickly, stepping back out of striking range of Ranger. As coolly as I can manage, I crack the baton tip against the ferrocrete wall of the ops room to release the ferrules, then collapse it and slip it back into my pocket. Hands nice and visibly empty, I turn back to Blake. "You were saying?" I ask.

For an instant the big man's lips move in what could almost be a smile. His laser-beam gaze is steady on my face. He was expecting something like this, I realize. He orchestrated the whole thing as a kind of test. But a test for who: for me or for Ranger? If for me, did I pass or fail? Fail for goading Ranger, or pass for dropping him? Who the frag knows?

"I was saying, you vote against war," Blake says coolly as though nothing at all's gone down. "Why?"

"Too expensive," I shoot back. "Too high a cost, too little return."

"What about rep?" Fahd snarls.

I could be politic here, but something—maybe it's the look in Blake's eyes—tells me that's not the way to play it. Time for a risk, maybe. If I win, I'm into the inner councils, suddenly increasing my value exponentially. "What about it?" I fire back. "Your way, the rep we get is that we're stupid for wading into a costly war we could have avoided." Fahd the weasel's face goes white, and I know I've made another enemy. Busy day. I consider stopping there, but whafuck? "You want to stroke your ego," I tell Fahd directly, "go beat the drek out of someone who's not going to bloody your nose. Cut a deal with the Ancients, like Vladimir says, but go butt heads with the Eighty-Eights." I name one of the local Chinese-style triads. "They've been getting too frisky anyway."

And there are Blake's laser eyes burning into my skull again, and I feel like he's counting my fillings or sifting through my brain. For an instant I'm drek-scared that maybe he's a shaman or a hermetic who can actually read my mind. But I put that one aside immediately. If Blake could do that, he'd have done so already, and I'd be suffering from a nine-millimeter migraine right about now.

The silence stretches painfully, and I feel the irrational urge to babble just to fill time. But before I lose it, Blake nods slowly. "The Eighty-Eights," he muses, "yes. An object lesson to others, hmm?" He smiles at Vladimir, who nods too. "You've got a free hand to approach the Ancients leadership about compensation," Blake tells his advisor. "It's your baby."

Then the leader turns to Fahd, and the weasel seems to shrink back from the boss' speculative gaze. Again the silence stretches, then Blake taps the table top with a forefinger—a major display of emotion for him. "There will be no reprisals against the Ancients," he says firmly. "None. I'll hold you responsible for telling that to *him*." He gestures to the still-unconscious Ranger. "But, I want some raids against the Eighty-Eights. Hit them hard, hurt them. And make sure the street knows who's doing it. Tell him that, too."

The gang boss pauses, and this time there's no mistaking the faint smile. "And tell him I think he should use Larson here as a major asset," he adds.

From the way Fahd is looking at me, I can imagine just how that message is going to get presented to Ranger. I keep my face expressionless as I glance at Blake. The question I asked myself earlier is suddenly much more important. Which one of us is he trying to test? Because the way things are working out, one of us isn't going to make it out of this alive.

And that seems to be just what Blake has in mind.

4

The meet's set to go down at the Coffee Bon, one of the high-tone kissaten—Japanese-style coffeehouses—that have recently begun to spring up in Seattle's downtown core. The CB's probably the most profitable, and the most prestigious, right in the middle of the corporate sector, just across the street from the Yamatetsu HQ at Fifth and Pike. The decor's just the right weird, kind of a retro view of the future—how somebody in 1954 predicted 2054 would look, or some such drek. Lots of mirror-flash, lots of high tech masquerading as low tech masquerading as high tech, if you know what I mean. The background music, if you can call it that, is all randomly synthesized tones, supposedly monitored by some kind of algorithm that selects for combinations that would be pleasant to the (meta)human ear. Yeah, right. At least the coffee's good—real coffee, not soykaf—but then, for fifteen-plus nuyen a cup, it oughtta be. No free refills, either.

The meets always go down in different places, and I never know who my contact's going to be. There's no schedule either, because a schedule could be predicted. Sometimes I go for two, three weeks without checking in with anyone. That's why they call this deep cover, I guess. The Star uses a couple of different channels to get word to me—and vicey versey—but the best is also the simplest. Among the Cutters, I've got a rep as a kind of techno-wonk. Other soldiers spend their spare time getting brain-fried, getting laid, or getting into fights. I do my share of that—the requirements of my cover, not because I enjoy it, ha!—but I spend at least some time every day logging onto UCAS Online, this big public bulletin board service on the Matrix. (I'm a nullhead—no datajack, just my chipjacks—so I use a low-cost, palm-size computer.) UOL has a drekload of chill features, but the big selling point's the massive message base. Lots of slags from all over the continent—even some from

Europe sometimes—log on to connect with special interest groups or real-time online free-for-alls about anything and everything. With so much message traffic, it's easy to slip a coded message into the data stream. Nothing tricky—it doesn't need to be—and nothing that resembles a code in any way. You'd really have to know what you're looking for to spot the kind of messages we exchange. (Frag, sometimes I miss them myself; I've hosed a couple of meets that way, but sometimes that's the price you got to pay.) The message telling me to show up at the Coffee Bon today read like a typical neo-anarchist rant against the monopoly on the news media—badly argued, badly spelled, and badly out of date.

So that's how come I'm jandering into the place just before the hour when the junior suits start drifting out of the skyrakers to deplete their expense accounts over lunch. I don't belong in the CB; every head that turns to look at me, every lip that twists in scorn, every voice that hesitates momentarily, tells me that. I'm obviously from the wrong side of the tracks, and that makes me dangerous and suspect. I don't wear Zoé, Mortimer of London, Gucci, or Bally, sateen or synthsilk. My fashion tends more to Skulz, Doc Marten, synthleather, and kevlar. Of course, nobody's going to point that out to me. The current political climate considers dress codes "elitist" (except on actual megacorp turf, of course, where anything goes and you might as well protest the law of gravity). As long as I'm not packing ordnance, illegal armor, or restricted cyberware—at least nothing the tech drek in the doorway can pick up—nobody can tell me I don't belong. That won't stop every slot in the place from trying to communicate that concept without saying it outright, however. Any other gangers in the area might wonder why I'm even bothering, except that I've carefully built up a rep for hanging in suit bars and restaurants just for the pleasure of slotting people off.

I jander in, give the slag behind the big espresso machine the old stare-down, and sashay toward the back of the place. I see my contact at once. She's at the bar, sitting on one of those retro-nuevo chairs that must have been designed by a frustrated proctologist. She used to be a chummer (and more than that for one weekend at the Mayflower Plaza Hotel that I'd like never to forget, thank you) when we were both back in Milwaukee, going through the local Lone Star Academy together, and then again while I was learning the streets and

how to work them. Ever since we both got transferred out
west, I know she's carved out a niche for herself in the data
management side of the Organized Crime division of the
Star. Her name's Catherine Ashburton, likes to be called Cat,
and she's drop-dead gorgeous, always was, always will be.
Petite's the word, I guess: stands not much more than a meter and a half, weighs about fifty and most of that's in her
rockets. Straight, short, copper-colored hair, the kind of
color that makes you think she'd look hot in emerald green.
But instead she always wears cranberry or certain shades of
pink, and looks like she just stepped out of a fashion-trid ti-
tle sequence. Today her eyes are a deep violet.

Cat's dressed exactly like a member of one of the schools
of brightly colored secretaries that flit around the skyrakers
at lunch and after work, trying to avoid-attract the barracuda
managers. An ice-maiden, unapproachable, unless your
monthly pay's eight-K nuyen or up. Then she'll be all titters
and smiles and unspoken invitations. Me, on the other hand,
the only way I could get eight-K nuyen in a month would be
to sell my folks into slavery, then hit big in the lottery. She
sees me strolling her way and freezes up.

So I of course swing myself onto the stool right next to
her and give her the once-over, copper top to stiletto heels.
"Double espresso," I snap to the counterman without taking
my eyes off the sweetmeat next to me. Cat plays it perfectly.
Everything about her shows her internal turmoil—terrified
of the street monster beside her, yet equally scared that moving or reacting at all might provoke me. For an instant I
catch her violet eyes, and I see the flash of cool amusement.
She's enjoying this, getting out of the office and into the
field. And, who knows? Maybe deep down she doesn't mind
seeing me again.

My espresso arrives. The barista running the machine is
working at top speed, getting my order out fast so I'll
leave. I knock back the little cup of bitter coffee and push
the empty toward the counterman. "Another," I tell him.

I give Cat another top-to-tail scan and a feral street grin
while I'm getting ready for the exchange. These meets have
two purposes. First, I hand over my report of what's gone
down with the Cutters since the last one, and second, I pick
up new instructions from my superior officers. Instructions?
Actually, they're usually limited to something like, "Keep
your head down and keep reporting." Maybe it's surpris-

ing in this age of high tech and high expectations that a
physical meet's the way to go, but it makes sense if you
think about it.

First off, as I said, I'm a nullhead, a non-decker. (If I had
the tech, training, and inclination to punch deck, everything
would be different.) That limits what I can do in the Matrix.
Just because some of the Cutters soldiers think I'm a techno-
wonk, that doesn't mean I'm actually any good at it. It's just
that I look fragging brilliant next to their computer-illiteracy.
About all I'm good for is logging onto UOL and posting ar-
gumentative messages, however. The Cutters do have their
own deckers, of course—a couple working for Musen the
accountant, one or two in Fahd's biz development empire,
and another one or two working directly for Blake. I can't
prove it, but I strongly suspect a couple of them sometimes
monitor what I do when I'm online. No surprise. Blake
would be a fool not to keep watch on a communication
channel like that.

So, filing reports and receiving orders over the net isn't
smart. Physical meets sound dangerous—and sometimes
they are—but not if you do them right. First point:
whoever's on the other end of the meet—Cat today—I don't
talk to them about what's going down. They're not my con-
duit, just my postman.

On the way over to the CB, I "dictated" my report inside
my head, dumping it onto a datachip slotted into one of my
jacks. Before I went into the kissaten, I pulled the chip and
stashed it in a small carrier cylinder not much bigger than a
toothpick, and I've got it palmed now. My orders are on a
similar chip stashed somewhere on Cat's person. All we've
got to do is make the switch.

Isn't this dangerous? Well, yeah, but some risks you've
just got to take. Also, I've done some things to cover myself. First off, the chip holding my report and the one with
my orders are disguised as "jolts," those illegal simsense-
analogs that you can slot like a datasoft but that give you a
thirty-minute high before erasing themselves. Somebody
would have to know just what they were looking for to recognize that my chips contain anything other than simsense
files. Then they'd have to break the security encoding and
sidestep a wiz little virus that erases all data at the slightest
provocation. When I get my orders, I slot the chip and
download the data directly into my headware, erasing the

chip at the same time. No, not just erase: overwrite with ones, then overwrite with zeroes, then with ones again. The big-domes in the Star's technical research division assure me that nothing can pull traces of data off the chip after that. (I suppose somebody could read the data right out of my headware memory using SQUIDs, but that's a real high-tech process and how likely is it that I'd sit still for it? Null.)

So that's my cover, and it's a fragging good one. Sure, I'm the one came up with it, but that's still the objective opinion of one of the Star's best undercover assets. If the Cutters ever catch me at one of these meets, my cover is that I'm feeding the monkey on my back—a secret jolt habit. Why don't I buy my chips through the Cutters' own distribution network? Because I don't want the higher-ups to know I've got a weakness, chummer. You scan that, don't you? It's a good rationalization, based on one of the great principles of (meta)human psychology. Don't try to convince people you're innocent. It's much easier to make them believe you're guilty of a lesser offense. (It also gives the soldiers doing the pinch a little extra incentive to let me be. They know something I don't want made public, and you're just not (meta)human if you don't relish having leverage against someone.)

My second espresso arrives, and I knock that one back too. This time I toss the empty to the barista. He catches it, but doesn't seem to know what to do with it. I lean close to Cat, drape an arm round her shoulder, and grab a quick feel of her rockets. She stiffens up and shakes herself free, but by that time the chip carrier with my report is down her cleavage. She's a better actor than I expected. The face she turns to me is white and tight-lipped with fury. But the glint of amusement is still in those impossibly violet eyes, and a little more than amusement maybe. Who knows, maybe she remembers that weekend at the Mayflower too? Stranger things have happened.

Now I stroke her thigh, and she grabs my hand in a surprisingly tight grip, forcing it away from her. I feel something tiny and hard pushed into my hand, and I quickly palm it. Exchange made, and the show we're putting on is guaranteed to have everyone looking away uncomfortably.

"Fragging ice-maiden, aren't you, slitch?" I snarl. "You don't know what you're missing."

"I'd rather jam with a devil rat," she hisses back. Nice line.

"Could be arranged," I tell her, which draws from her the faintest hint of a wink. Interesting. I'd like to pursue the matter, but now's not the time, here's not the place. Which is too fragging bad.

I swing off the chair and jander away. I see the counterman trying to get up the juice to tell me I owe him money, so I shoot back over my shoulder, "It's on her tab," and I'm out onto the street. A Lone Star bike cop cruises by slowly, giving me the once-over. I grin at him, pull back the sides of my jacket to show I'm not carrying heat. He scowls and rides on.

Surprise, surprise, it's not raining, and there's even a patch of blue sky about the size of my thumbnail. All in all, this day's not shaping up so bad.

5

By the time I've got my bike out of hock from the Washington Athletic Club parkade and ridden to my doss on Northeast Sixtieth Street in Ravenna—a convenient few blocks from the Cutters' safe house—I've slotted the chip Cat passed me, downloaded the contents, and scanned them. Didn't take me long. Predictably, my orders are: "Keep your head down and keep reporting." (Am I psychic or what?) There's nothing specific the Star wants me to watch for, and if they know about anything strange coming up, they don't see fit to warn me. I mentally trigger the utility that triple-overwrites and wipes the chip, and I eject it from my jack. I don't even bother to use the chip carrier, just let it fall out onto the road as I ride.

In contrast, my report—the one that got to nestle between Cat's cushions, lucky fragging chip—should give whoever's authorized to read it something to think about. First there's a rundown on the Sioux assault rifle scam. (Paco came through with the background on that, and was slotted off that it wasn't anything deep and dark I could use against Ranger. It turns out the war boss had loaned money and assets to Musen to swing the deal. Why didn't the biz honcho have his own assets to invest? Well, there hangs a tale, priyatel, but one that doesn't matter much to me or my superiors.) Then there's an update on the decision to approach the Ancients for restitution. If the Star has an agent as high up in the Ancients as I am in the Cutters, they can manipulate this situation in whatever nasty direction their little hearts desire. And then there's a warning about raids on the Eighty-Eights, and ditto if the Star's got a deep-cover agent there.

Then comes the fun stuff, basically a two-megapulse rant about bureaucracies and communication breakdowns and how they can frag up the best policies and strategies. All "for the good of the force," of course, but mainly driven by my own crankiness at almost getting geeked by my "brothers in arms" in the FRT squads. Eminently understandable, I figure.

And that about covers the level of communication I have with my superiors. Sometimes I feel kind of like a fire-and-forget weapon. The Star went to a frag of a lot of trouble setting up my background when they transferred me from Milwaukee. (Oh, sure, I'd done undercover work before—lots of undercover work—and I'm fragging good at it, but I'd never done anything this long-term and deep. Frag, joining the ruling cadre of a major first-tier gang. It still loosens my bowels to think about it.)

I still don't know how they built my story so deep and so impenetrable. All I know is that the first couple of months I was scared drekless that some underpaid, overworked, under-motivated, hung-over Lone Star clerk had missed something vital that would end up getting me scragged—I couldn't help remembering that the Star's computer system had once sent me three statements for overdue parking tickets in Milwaukee . . . in the sum of 0.00. But it's been almost eighteen months now and, if anything, my cover only seems more bulletproof, but I still sometimes wake up in a cold sweat waiting for the Mexican frag-up.

After all that effort—the Star's and mine—I'm in place and making my reports, but my superiors sometimes don't seem to pay much attention. I think it's only twice that I've actually been told to pay attention to something specific, and that just doesn't seem like the most efficient use of me as a resource. Of course, during the two times I'm talking about, the drek was fragging near running down my legs while I was trying to ferret out what the Star wanted. From a theoretical standpoint, they should give me more guidance. But, from a personal point of view, I'm much happier this way, and much more likely to live to collect my pension.

To hell with that drek anyway. Chewing it through now's probably just a way of distracting myself from the fact that the blue sky I saw over downtown has turned out to be as dependable as a politician's promise and that the hard rain's started up again. By the time I reach Ravenna and find a good place for my bike, I'm soaked to the fragging skin. My apartment's in a building called the Wenonah, a low-rise that's about twice as old as I am. It used to be painted, I think, but the solvent they call rain in Seattle has seen to that. The building's just bare concrete now, stained and pitted and streaked with pigeon-drek. (Query: With so many other species going out forever, how the frag do those flying rats people call pigeons manage to hang on? End of digression.) I jander up the stairs to the front door, push it open.

The Wenonah used to be a "security building," and the notice to that effect is still bolted to the wall over what used to be the intercom panel. Of course, the panel's been stripped, lo, these many months now, with all the electronic hardware peeled out and probably sold. Doesn't matter worth a drek anyway. About the same time the intercom panel went west, somebody took a shotgun and blew the locking mechanism out of the door. The property management company responsible for the place keeps promising they'll replace it Real Soon Now.

I swing up the stairs, superstitiously stepping around the stain where one of my erstwhile neighbors bled out after a minor difference of opinion with his girlfriend. Making my way down the dark and narrow hallway toward the back, I hear music coming from inside my doss even before I get close enough to see that the door's open a crack. My H & K's in my hand and I'm reaching for the wire, moving forward as quiet as a ghost, ready to make my grand entrance and deliver a three-round lesson on the sanctity of private property.

But then I listen to the music rather than just hear it, and I know who's inside my place. The song—and I use the word loosely—is "Scrag 'em All" by Darwin's Bastards, one of the more in-your-face bands on the trog-rock scene. If you didn't know this drek was supposed to be music, you'd probably mistake "Scrag 'em All" for the noise of street repairs around the sprawl.

I engage the safety on the H & K, but don't slip it back in the holster. Can't be too friendly here. Then I stride up to my door, push it gently with a boot, and step to the side. Just in case. I don't really expect trouble, but now's not the time to start any bad habits.

As the door swings open, the only offensive force that comes through the opening is more of Darwin's Bastards, now grinding their way into a trog-rock cover of "Stairway to Heaven". Scary stuff. In some ways, a burst of autofire would have been more comforting. But I don't let my face show any reaction as I move into the doorway.

The first thing I see is drek strewn everywhere—over the

floor, over what little furniture there is, and heaped in the corner. It looks like someone's tossed the place or maybe set off a grenade in the middle of the room. Basically just the way I left it.

Someone's sprawled in my single armchair—formerly the home of a pile of laundry that's been pushed onto the floor. Bart is his name—Big Bad Bart to his friends—"that trog bastard" to everyone else (the overwhelming majority). He's a big, bloated ork standing a touch over two meters and massing one thirty-five if he's a gram. He's got a big sagging gut that looks like it's sitting on his lap, and jowls big and heavy enough to stop a punch to his larynx. Sure, Bart's a tub of lard, and it would be easy to dismiss him because of it. But I've seen him move, and he's stronger and faster on his feet than his flabby bulk would make you think.

He smiles up at me from the chair, and I'm glad I haven't eaten. Bart's one of those orks who seems to consider tooth decay a badge of honor. His protruding fangs are yellowed and chipped, and the rest of his teeth are black. His breath could knock over a devil rat at five paces.

And since we're on the topic of Bart's odious personal habits, let's talk about Darwin's Bastards. I'm egalitarian and open-minded when it comes to musical preference. Even though I'd probably rather listen to a jet engine spooling up than sit through an album by DB or Trollgate, if Bart wants to listen to that poisonous trash, it's chill with me. My kick is that he likes to inflict it on the world. He's always got his Sony ChipMan deck hanging from his belt, but instead of listening to the so-called "music" through earphones, trode rig, or datajack, he sets the deck to narrowcast to a pair of Bose MicroVox speakers built into the rigid shoulder-boards of his jacket. With the volume usually cranked up to brain-melting, trying to carry on a conversation with the slag turns into an exercise in lip-reading.

Big Bad Bart and I aren't on the best of terms. Never have been, and recent developments seem to be conspiring to make sure we never will be. The fat pig apparently hoop-kissed his way up the hierarchy of Cutters soldiers until he became one of Ranger's more trusted lieutenants. When I showed up in the sprawl, my faked background marking me as a real "comer" in the gang scene, Bart decided I was a threat to him and all his progress. He never made any moves against me, though; by the time he'd figured things out, I'd already ingratiated myself with enough of the big bosses to make fragging me too big a risk. But he sure as frag nuzzled up even closer to Ranger's hoop.

That's ancient history. Now? If Bart was once concerned that I was angling to be Ranger's protégé, it doesn't seem to be bothering him anymore. Don't get me wrong. Ranger would never confess that I'd whipped his hoop in the council meeting. But drek like that spreads through the gang faster than gossip in a retirement-village bridge club.

It'll also have made the rounds that I'm boss-man Blake's fair-haired boy at the moment, and that—probably—protects me from harassment and direct retribution. Unless it can be disguised as something else, of course.

So, I snarl at Bart, "What the frag do you want?" My H & K's by my side, handshaking happily with the wire in my brain. The tech reassures me just how fast I could bring the gun up and squeeze the trigger if I have to, and estimates how much of Bart would be blown into the upholstery of my armchair.

Bart smiles, and I can imagine the wave of halitosis rolling slowly across the room toward me. "War council," he says—or that's what I think he says.

"Yeah?" I ask. "So what you doing here, priyatel?" The word's Russian for "friend," but I know my tone changes the meaning to something very different. "Never heard of a fragging phone?"

He shrugs, and his jowls wobble. Darwin's Bastards are screaming something about being a rock and not rolling, and the accompaniment sounds like a car being disassembled by an autocannon. The wire informs me that, yes, I could blow the ChipMan off his belt—probably—without doing more than lacerating the rolls of fat he calls a waist. Tempting idea, but maybe I'll save it for a later date. "Ranger wanted me to deliver the invitation in person," he says. He looks at the watch on a sausage-sized finger. "You're gonna be late." And then he grins, like that's been the idea all along.

"Then what you sitting on your hoop for?" I demand. "Let's go."

6

We ride the couple of blocks from the Wenonah to the Cutters' place by the cemetery. Bart's hog—a 2052 Gaz-Niki White Eagle—is almost ten years newer than my Harley Scorpion, but its owner apparently takes no more care of it than he does of himself. The bloated ork cruises along behind me, the clattering blast of the Eagle's badly tuned engine fitting perfectly with the percussion part of DB's "Bloody Day Coming". We park the bikes out back, then jander into the safe house.

The "war council" is going down in the basement, and it's already underway when we swing in the door. There are a dozen or so soldiers there—like Paco, all young, all tough. I've worked with most of them before, and get on well with the majority of those. Seeing a couple of fists raised in greeting, I shoot back a chill grin. Ranger's up front—not giving the briefing, surprisingly—and the look he gives me would strip paint. All the seats are taken, so I lean against the room's back wall. Bart follows me in and, wonder of wonders, kills the soundtrack.

It's a tough little biff named Kirsten who's giving the briefing. She's using a portable projection display with a subnotebook computer, throwing an image of the screen display up on the far wall. At the moment, the display is showing a map of the Hyundai pier, a segment of the docks down around Pier 42 where that weird multicorp firefight went down last November. The cross-hairs cursor is settled on one of the "temporary" warehouses across Marginal Way from the piers, right under the Alaskan Way viaduct. (They were "temporary" when the city built them to handle an interim undercapacity in 2034 or so, but the city never replaced them with anything better.) I know the place she's rattling on about. It's right in the shadow of the Kingdome, a depot and sometime meeting place for the triad called the Eighty-Eights.

Kirsten grates on about asset distributions, primary and secondary objectives, but I just tune her out. All that milspeak comes down to one statement: go visit the Eighty-Eights and frag them up. Simple. No matter what the war boss or his designate—Kirsten, in this case—has to say about it, whoever's actually leading the raid has total discretion over how to use his "assets" and what to choose as objectives. Much as the Cutters might want to pretend otherwise, the gang isn't an army and doesn't have anywhere near the level of command and control of a professional outfit like the Star.

So that frees up my mind to worry about more pressing problems. My continued survival, for one, a subject very close to my heart.

Ranger would like to see me gutted. That's obvious and—after the gang council where I dropped him—inevitable. Yet Ranger, like Bart, has to recognize the fact that Blake apparently has his eye on me, for whatever reason. Geeking me without damn good reason would not be conducive to continued good health. Or something.

Oh, Ranger could easily arrange for someone to scrag me. An up-and-comer inside the Cutters might do it for brownie points with the war boss, and outside talent isn't that expensive in a buyer's market like Seattle. But no matter how theoretically unattributable Ranger makes the kill, there's always the chance the blame will find its way back to him and the word get out that he had me fried. A route that would be a definite risk.

But there's a much simpler, much more certain route he could take that dates all the way back to that early example of science fiction, the Bible. I can't remember which Biblical figure did it, or why, but one of them sent an enemy out to the wars, put him in the front line, and got him geeked that way. (The Bible doesn't say if the cobber behind the plot also arranged for someone in the second line to get careless with his spear, but that's the play I'd have used if it were me setting it up.)

And so, all in all, it doesn't come as any surprise when I hear Kirsten announce, "Larson, you're leading Team A. Bart's got Team B."

I shoot a glance over at Big Bad Bart, and he's giving me

one of those dentist-frightening smiles of his. He knows
what I'm thinking, and I know he knows, and he knows I
know it. Suddenly I feel a tingling in my back, right between
my shoulder blades, and the meaning is inescapable. As far
as Ranger and Bart are concerned, I've got a target painted
over my spine.

Night again, and we're rolling through the streets of Seattle in another Bulldog van to what's sure as frag going to be
another shoot-out in another warehouse. Whoever said,
"Life's just one damn thing after another" doesn't know
squat. Life's the same damn thing over and over again.

The Bulldog's packed to the gunwales with the "heavies"
from both Team A and Team B. That's ten gang-bangers—
including Bart, who bulks enough for two. Everybody's
wearing whatever armor they've got and bristling with assorted offensive weaponry, with all of us jammed into a win-
dowless box designed for eight. A couple of the younger
gangers are talking quietly, carrying on a tough-chill conversation to prove to each other, themselves, and anybody else
who cares that they're cool as ice and smooth as silk. But
the more experienced soldiers know. We can smell the tension, a kind of low-grade funk that you never really forget.
Some of Team A are checking their weapons again. Paco,
my lieutenant on this one, is toying with one of the grenades
hanging from his bandolier—a nervous habit that doesn't
make me feel any better. Bart seems to be asleep.

A button-transceiver burbles inanities in my ear. Both
teams have sent two bike "scouts" ahead to scope out the
target, and the team leaders—me and Bart—are in constant
contact with our scouts. I don't know about Bart's people,
but mine seem to figure they're not doing their jobs if they
aren't keeping me apprised—in exquisite detail—of the
whole lot of nothing that's going down across from Pier 42.
It's real tempting to cut them off—except I'm sure as frag
that the moment I do, they'll babble something I really
should know, and I'll miss it.

I give my people one last scan. Apart from Paco, I've got
Jaz, a classic example of Cutters street muscle (big and not
overly bright). Also Marla, who claims to be a Snake shaman, but seems to consider nine-mil ammo her fetish of
choice. And then there's the musclebound ork everyone just
calls Doink. I've never worked directly with Doink before,

but I know that the others are steady and dependable. Plus, they like me personally—or I think they do—which makes me feel a little better. Not because I'm insecure around people who don't like me, but more because they'd be less likely to go along with Ranger's plan to off me—I hope.

And Team B? I know them, too: Sydney with her cherished grenade launcher; Fortunato and Jack "the Hammer," some of the gang's younger blood; and Zig the dwarf cradling his Remington Roomsweeper like it's a baby. I've worked with a couple of them, and shot the drek and boozed it up with the rest. Like with my own team, I figure they're probably not in on any plan to cut me down from behind.

But then they don't need to be, not with Big Bad Bart in on the game. Propped up in a corner of the van, snoring his fat head off, he's packing an Enfield AS7 drum-fed assault shotgun—a big, brutal motherfragger of a weapon that looks no bigger than a popgun in his hands. The Mossberg CMDT combat gun—which the Star FRT used to pulp little Piers and remodel my van a couple of nights back—is more lethal, but not by much. If Bart takes a shot at me, I'll be too busy getting torn to shreds to notice the difference. So the name of that tune is not to let him into a position where he can take that shot.

Bart and I—with our chosen lieutenants Paco and Sydney—talked out our tactics before putting the teams into the van. Or maybe "tactics" isn't the right term for a battle plan that boils down to "drive through the fence, jump out, and blow drek up real good". My (limited) experience with the Eighty-Eights told me not to expect much security at the temporary warehouse, and the scout reports back that up. (Unless—and here's a nasty thought—Ranger leaked details of the raid, and now they're waiting for us with everything they've got. That would sure as drek take me out, but it'd also cost him nine more valuable assets, including Bart. No, the cost would be just too high.) The goal's a quick in-and-out—maximum impact, maximum shock value, minimum personnel exposure. And that means personal explosives. That's why everyone's packing a half-dozen grenades. If we do it right, we'll be back in the Bulldog and on the road again before the echoes have died away—and before whatever Eighty-Eights happen to be there know just what's going down.

A new voice in my button transceiver—the driver. "We're

at King and Marginal." I tap my earpiece, sending a beep of confirmation back to her. Out the corner of my eye I see Bart do the same thing. His eyes are still closed, but he's definitely awake now.

Less than a minute. I feel the Bulldog start to accelerate. "Lock and load," I tell my people—unnecessarily, probably, but I always love saying that. The inside of the van echoes with metallic snicks and clacks. I pull my H & K from its shoulder-holster, and let wire and weapon get reacquainted.

"Point one," the driver says, and now I hear her voice both in my earpiece and through the van's intercom. "Hang on, boys and girls."

I brace myself as the Bulldog swerves hard to the left and accelerates again. A jolt and a crash of metal against the body-panels, and we're through the gate. I'm almost flung out of my seat as the driver jams on the brakes and we skid to a stop. "Go!" I snap. The two side doors of the modified Bulldog fly open, and we pour out—Team A out the left side, Team B out the right.

The warehouse is straight ahead of me, about twenty meters away. The two windows I can see are dark, the only light coming from above the door that must lead to the office. Parked out in front is a flash new targa-top Westwind 2000. (Looks like members of the Eighty-Eights make more money than the Cutters.) The Westwind severely depreciates in value as Sydney pumps a grenade into it—crack-WHUMP—a friendly invitation for whoever's in the warehouse to come out and play, I guess. I turn away from the flames, and wave Team A around the left side of the warehouse. Paco takes point, with the others following close behind him, and I trail along at the rear.

Just as we round the corner, a door bursts open and out pelt three armed figures. Paco and Jaz open up with their SMGs, and the targets basically disappear in clouds of blood and tissue. It's over before the three Eighty-Eights can cap off a single round, and before Doink even knows there's a fight on. The sound of gunfire comes from around the front of the building, and I realize the triad's sent forces out that way too. This is where it gets dicey as far as I'm concerned. Once the bullets start to fly, all Bart has to do is sit back and wait for the best time to take his shot at me. Again there's that strong tingling between my shoulder blades.

The three deceased Eighty-Eights neglected to shut the door behind them, so Paco dive-rolls in, and I hear his SMG stuttering away inside. Jaz and the others follow him, and again I'm ass-end Charley.

This warehouse is a lot smaller than the Cutters' Lake Meridian facility, and it's nowhere near as claustrophobic—none of those high-stacked crates that turn the place into a labyrinth of walls and alleys. There's still a drekload of cover, however, and the handful of small lights make the place about as bright as a moonlit city street. There aren't any colors, and few details, but the light should be enough to spot movement.

Like that over there. I spin to the left and up comes my H & K. But before I can even bring the gun to bear, the running figure—another Eighty-Eight, presumably—gets chopped down by someone else. From somewhere to my right—the warehouse office where Team B was headed, I'd guess—there's the distinctive ripping sound of a Uzi III on full-auto. A hostile, obviously—none of our guys were packing Uzis. Then the whole fragging place echoes with the brutal ba-ba-bam! of Bart's auto-shotgun, and the Uzi doesn't speak again.

The sound of that fragging shotgun on burst-fire brings back too many bad memories of my last visit to a warehouse, and in my mind's eye I see little Piers getting blown out of all human shape. Way down deep in my heart of hearts (or maybe half a meter lower in my contracting scrotal sack) I know that good old Bart has one of those three-round bursts earmarked for me. That he'll grease me—preferably from behind, so there's no chance of me reacting—and then claim that the light was deceptive or that I wandered into his killing zone or some drek. Translation: Oops, better luck next reincarnation. Not particularly satisfying, from my point of view.

So the trick is to hunker down somewhere where I can see trouble coming and do something about it. I look around, look up ... Ah, perfect.

Mounted on the wall near me is a ladder leading up (presumably) to the overhead catwalks. About ten meters off the ground, right next to the ladder, there's a rusting metal light fixture bolted to the wall. Like the other lights dotted around the warehouse, it's not bright enough to illuminate the floor well.

But it *is* bright enough to dazzle someone looking directly into it. And that's all that matters.

Quickly, before I have time to think it through and get
scared, I scurry over to the ladder and clamber up. For the
first few moments I feel hideously exposed, but that's just irrational fear talking. Then I'm ten meters up, right next to
the metal housing of the light. I can feel its heat on my bare
skin. I feel more exposed than ever, but I know that's not the
case at all. Anybody looking my way will see only the light.
I turn around, hanging on with my left hand and settling the
H & K in my right.

This is an incredible vantage point, I realize. With low
piles of crates and other similar drek providing cover, I can
still see over a lot of it. In the first few seconds I spot a couple of Eighty-Eights hiding from the marauding Cutters. I
could cap them both if I wanted to, but I don't. It'd only
draw attention to me, which is the last thing I want. I can
also see members of Team A—namely Paco and Doink—
doing their sweep.

And there's Bart. He's come out of the office area, and
he's moving forward slowly near the wall. Hanging from its
broad suspension harness, shock pad firmly against his right
hip, the auto-shotgun is at the ready. Even mounted on a suspension harness, the AS7 is big and bulky enough to make
most people clumsy. Not Bart; he's big and bulky himself,
and strong enough to lug the killer weapon around like it
weighed no more than a feather. I've got to take that into account, as well as the fact that he's probably strong enough to
ride out the recoil of multiple bursts. For all I know, he
might have jiggered the gun so it's capable of full autofire.
Not at all a pleasant thought. I lose sight of him for a moment behind an abnormally high pile of crates, and my stomach twists with sudden fear. Maybe he knows where I am,
and he's moving in for a clean shot . . . But then the big brutal muzzle pokes out into the open again, followed by Bart
himself, and I breathe a little easier.

Part of me wants to cap him right now. The wire tells me
I can put a burst right on the money, all five rounds impact-
ing within a centimeter of his ugly ear before he even knows
what's happening. But then my years of drek-sucking cop
training get in the way: lethal force only in response to direct threats and all that jazz. Who knows? Maybe I'm wrong
about Bart wanting to grease me, and taking him down before I'm sure is just plain premeditated murder (yes, officer,
I'll come quietly). Below, the bloated ork pivots slowly and

his shotgun comes to bear on something. My eyes follow his intended line of fire.

It's Paco. Continuing his sweep, the young ganger has just cleared a crate that's marked as machine parts. I see his head move slightly and I know he picked up Bart in his peripheral vision. I also know he's labeled the ork as "friendly," and decided to ignore him. Bart moves the shotgun to follow, and I know what's going to happen. The ork's "mandate" isn't to drop only me, but anyone who's personally loyal to me as well.

"Paco, break!" I scream, and not a millisecond too soon. The younger ganger reacts like he's chipped to the max, flings himself forward and down into the cover of some macroplast shipping cases.

The assault shotgun roars, the burst disintegrating the crate where Paco was standing an instant before. The ganger might have caught the periphery of the shot pattern, and almost certainly got hit by what was left of the crate, but odds are he lived through it. Not through any fault of Bart's, of course.

I bring my H & K to bear, putting the sighting dot on the ork's temple. "You're out of here," I say.

But before I can pull the trigger, he's coming around, bringing the AS7 up into line. Faster than I've ever seen him move, faster than anyone has a *right* to move. He pulls the trigger and the big motherfragging gun roars again.

Too soon, an instant too soon. The light next to me, the metal housing, and a good chunk of the wall explode into shrapnel. Splinters of metal lash my bare hands and face. Instinctively I bring up my right hand—my gun hand—to shield my eyes, an instant too late to do any good. Then I have to bring my H & K back into line.

I've got enough time to make it good this time around. Bart had to swing the shotgun's shock pad off his hip when he spun to take a shot at me, so he didn't have the pad to absorb any of the recoil when he fired. Strong as he is, he's not strong enough to stop an AS7 on burst-fire riding way the frag up and off-line. And strong as he is, it's not enough to wrestle the gun back onto target before a five-round burst of nine-mil smashes his skull wide open.

"Scrag 'em all," I mutter as I clamber down the ladder, trying to control the sudden shaking in my hands and the wrenching in my gut.

7

And to think I'd been concerned about how to deal with Ranger. Elementary, my dear Watson, and all that drek. I didn't even have to lift a finger.

With Big Bad Bart's brains blasted, I let the rest of Teams A and B geek the other Eighty-Eights and have fun with their grenades while Paco and I slipped outside for a quick discussion. It took all the jam I had to suppress my reaction—the shakes, the nausea, the sense of absolute fragging *wrongness*—that comes every time I've had to kill someone. (Every time? Well, to be honest, priyatel, that's *both* times—including Bart.) Anyway, I was sure that showing such a reaction would probably diminish me in Paco's eyes, something decidedly counterproductive at the moment. So I bit back on everything, shoving it into the old emotional gunnysack where my nightmares go looking for raw material.

Predictably, Paco wasn't hyped to the max to learn that Ranger had put both him and me beyond salvage, and I didn't even have to voice the idea that the war boss' useful days were over. But Paco was also smart enough to realize that, satisfying though it might be, marching up to Ranger and putting a bullet in his gut wasn't the best way to handle the matter. All I had to do was remind the younger ganger that Ranger always rode his big BMW Blitzen super-bike everywhere, and that the war boss seemed sadly negligent when it came to mechanical maintenance. A satanic grin spread across Paco's face and he told me, "The gumbás a corpse. Count on it."

The matter resolved itself nicely the next day. The explosive charge Paco wired into the Blitzen's ignition was big enough to take care of the immediate problem, but small enough not to cause too much collateral damage. The concussion shook the Ravenna safe house and broke a few windows, with both Paco and I on hand to rush outside with the other shocked gangers and swear vengence against whatever rival outfit had done the dirty deed. Ranger was out of the way, and the last things that went through his mind were his cojones.

And that, of course, left a nice opening in the Cutters hierarchy. Can't have a gang without a war boss. Not in Seattle, and particularly not in 2054. Blake had to replace Ranger and he had to do it now. No, not now, *right* now. In an ideal world, I'd have gotten the nod, called up from the ranks to sit on the council of the high and mighty. Yeah, right. I can think of lots of words to describe the world, and "ideal" isn't one of them.

Instead, Blake called in a marker from the boss of the Cutters' Atlanta "chapter," and within twenty-four hours of Ranger's last ride, there was a new hoop in Ranger's chair. Bubba, his nickname was—I drek you not; fragging *Bubba*—a red-necked Georgia cracker who also happened to be ork. (Considering the way a lot of good ol' boys view the metaraces, it's surprising Bubba managed to avoid lynching himself. Or is that too cynical?) To my eternal surprise, I found myself both liking and respecting the newcomer after talking to him for a while. Even though his accent made him sound like his IQ was in the room-temperature range—and yes, we're talking Celsius here—he turned out to be smart as a whip, aggressive but willing to listen to people more familiar with the scoop going down in Seattle. I could almost get to like him.

Even though I didn't get the war boss slot, there must be more of a turnover in the ranks than I thought. Or, at least, that's the way I interpret it when I get called in to talk to big-boss Blake a couple of days after the explosion.

Blake's in his private quarters on the upper floor of the Sea-Tac safe house, the one on South 164th Street. Box the troll is standing watch outside the door, his asymmetrical head ducked forward but still brushing against the ceiling. He doesn't ask me my business or do the "friend-or-foe" crap; he just reaches behind him and opens the door when he sees me coming down the hall. I jander on past him, flipping him a mock salute, then I'm into one of Blake's private residences.

I don't know what I expected—or if I really expected anything in particular—but I'm still surprised. The place is light, airy-looking—tans and off-whites. I guess you could describe the decor as "pseudo-African". There's some strange kind of woven carpet on the floor, a deer pelt—or maybe it's real antelope—on one wall, and a couple of brutal-looking short thrusting spears on another. Assegai, you'd probably call them. It sounds weird, I know, but none of it's overdone or artificial. With the few people who ever come up here, the setup can't possibly be for the purpose of impressing others. I suppose Blake must like it. I find myself wondering again about his background. He's never pushed the Afro-American thing at all. He's black, but so what? Since goblinization, skin pigmentation doesn't mean as much as it used to. Does all this drek come from a single African country or is it some kind of pan-African hodgepodge? Got me hangin', chummer.

Anyway, there's Blake himself, sprawled almost bonelessly in a big tan armchair. Sitting on the floor beside him, long legs tucked under her, is an unbelievably gorgeous woman—black as night, with eyes so big and soft you could fall right in and drown. I hardly give her a glance, though, because my attention's drawn so strongly to Blake, who still hasn't moved or said a word. (And anyone who knows me understands what that means. Take my attention away from a woman? Come on . . .)

So, Blake, he's got this lazy grin on his face, and it makes me think of a sated lion. Satisfied man. I think I can guess why, though I suppose it's possible I'm wrong.

Blake raises his eyes and looks at me. He doesn't say anything, doesn't move, but the woman by his side gets the message. She doesn't so much stand up as flow to her feet. She touches his cheek with a fingertip, then drifts off, out through a door behind Blake, presumably going into the bedroom. As she shuts the door behind her, the room seems darker, as though a major source of light had vanished.

"Larson." Blake speaks the name slowly, quietly. I feel a tingle in the back of my neck. "I've heard good things about you, Larson," he goes on after a moment. "You've got supporters, people who trust you. Did you know that?"

I figure playing it chill is the way to go, so I just shrug. I'm suddenly nervous as hell that he's going to say something about Ranger, and I'm even more nervous that he'll sense my discomfort and want to know why.

But if he has any suspicions—or *more* than suspicions—he doesn't seem interested in voicing them . . . yet. "I want you on my staff, Larson," he says after another long moment. "Call it 'personal aide'." He chuckles, and it sounds like a big cat purring. "Or call it bodyguard-gofer if you like. Interested?"

Interested? Interested in becoming a member of the personal Praetorian guard for the boss of the Seattle Cutters? Interested in getting in on just about every fragging meeting of the higher-ups? Interested in knowing just where Blake is all the time—well, most of the time—and what he's up to? Well, golly gee whizzickers, let me think about it for a few minutes . . .

I shrug again, and it's one of the hardest things I've ever done to keep stone about it. "Yeah," I allow. "Yeah, I'm interested."

He nods, and there's a strange glint in his eyes. He knows something, or thinks he knows something. About me? What does he know, or suspect? That I greased Bart and had a hand in Ranger's departure? Or something else? The more I hang with Blake and the other higher-ups, the more I risk somebody figuring out who and what I am. But if I play it totally safe, I'll never learn anything worth knowing. How do I strike the balance?

I'm getting too old for this deep-cover drek.

If Blake does know or suspect I'm Star and he's just trying to suck me into a trap, he's not in any great rush to trigger it. For the next week I follow the big boss-man around like a good little gofer, sometimes running errands for him, but more often just standing around beside and behind him and looking stone. The big troll called Box is the head of Blake's Praetorian guard, it turns out. It also turns out I've sadly underrated Box all these months. Sure, he talks like he's got rocks in his mouth and crammed down his throat; sure, like anyone who resembles an escapee from a nightmare factory, he has an uphill battle credibility-wise. But I openly and freely admit that Box isn't the congenital idiot everyone takes him for, and that his warped and bulbous skull contains a prodigious amount of trivia—for example, everything you never wanted to know (and were too smart to ask) about the World Combat Cyclists League plus its past and current roster of sociopathic murderers . . . er, players, yeah, that's it. He also likes archaic, nineteen-sixties "folk" music. After Big Bad Bart, I can forgive him for that, however. He also claims he could once play the Irish whistle before he goblinized and his fingers got too big. Under other circumstances, I could get to like him, but I can't afford to let that happen. Which is probably what I hate most about undercover work.

In the first week I got to see Blake in action, in casual face-to-face meetings and more formal settings like the war council where I introduced Ranger to the wonders of escrima. I learned a lot. First off, nothing Blake does is casual—*nothing*. It's all planned out, every possible outcome, each permutation and combination worked through in that big head of his. I've seen him orchestrate a "chance, fortuitous" meeting with Bubba in the safe house hallway, disarming the cracker's defenses and setting him at his ease, then "spontaneously" dropping the point that was the whole purpose of this game into the conversation, and watching the reaction.

It's a good technique, I'll grant the man that. Ask somebody's opinion formally, and they'll react like you're forcing them to commit—publicly and irrevocably—to that position. The result? They'll weasel and double-talk and cover their hoops and spread the blame nine ways to Sunday. Trick them into letting that same opinion slip in a "casual" conversation, and you'll hear the closest thing to the truth—the closest thing to their real opinion—that you can get out of them without magical mind-probes or torture.

Blake's a master of that technique, and others. He's a frag of a leader. He listens to what everyone's saying, everyone around him—and not only what they're saying with their voices—and synthesizes it all into a kind of gestalt of the world. Nothing seems to surprise him, and he seems to know what people are going to say—me included—before they say it. He scares the fragging drek out of me. And what makes it worse is that I can't even hate him.

So in a week, I figure I've learned more about how the Seattle Cutters work—*really* work, deep down and dirty on the inside—than over the whole last eighteen months. Before I saw the execution of policy. Now I see that policy being made. If I'd known the movers and shakers were this fragging competent, I probably would have thrown this assignment back in my superiors' faces. There aren't any overt, obvious threats to my life and limb, but I can feel, deep in my gut, that I'm in more danger now than I've been for the whole last year and a half.

But enough sniveling. I was getting more real, hard intelligence about the Cutters than ever before—the deep, central, policy-related drek that I figure the Star put me here to scoop. Trouble was, it was getting a lot harder to find opportunities for getting my reports out. As Blake's "personal aide" and gofer, I was basically on duty seven or eight hours a day and "on call" most of the rest of the time. That made it tougher to get to meets where I could hand off my reports.

Frag, it was even hard making time to log onto UOL and check the message base. Who knows how many potential meets I hosed just because I didn't know about them? But I figured that would change eventually. Things would settle down as I got more worked into the schedule. For the moment, all I could do was let my handlers at the Star know I was still alive and sucking air—a simple matter of posting innocuous responses on various message bases, the actual message in the fact that I responded at all, not in the words I used. Meanwhile, I would save up all the intelligence I was gathering for one motherfragger of a report when I finally got to deliver it.

And the key burner fact in that report's going to be that the Cutters are getting into bed with some Tir-based corp.

Okay, the corp linkup isn't that much of a burner. Everyone knows—or at least guesses—that the Cutters do dirty work for various Seattle-based corps. To my personal knowledge, the gang has taken minor contracts with outfits ranging from small fry like Designer Genes to a half a dozen or so "triple-A" megacorps like Ares Macrotechnology. And those are the ones I know about.

What's interesting is that this new contract is from out of sprawl—in fact, from out of United Canadian and American States entirely. The general buzz on the street is that the Tir doesn't do much business in Seattle, except through numerous intermediaries so that the high-tone elves don't get their lily-white hands dirty. Now, I'm hearing something else. If the buzz is on the money, there's a major Tir corp that not only wants to do direct business in the plex, but is also interested in acquiring assets on the shady side of the street. Something the Star might be interested in knowing about? No fragging farce.

I don't know why the Tir corp chose the Cutters, or how

they got in contact with Blake. It's not like you can just look up "Cutters, Executive Offices" in the LTG listings. (I know how *I'd* do it, but I've got background knowledge and resources an out-of-sprawl corp wouldn't have ... I think.) Anyway, that's basically irrelevant. They did make contact, and they did carry out preliminary negotiations.

And now, there's the first official face-to-face meet between Blake and reps of the corp, whichever one it happens to be.

The meet's scheduled for the ops room in the safe house near Sea-Tac—the place where I drek-kicked Ranger—and Blake's pulling out all the stops. From what I hear, it's a "closed" meeting: only Blake and his advisors—Vladimir and Springblossom—and the reps of the Tir corp present. The ops room will be sealed tighter than a devil rat's ass, with an army of mundane and magical firepower outside. The room itself is protected by a big-time medicine lodge—set up by Springblossom, who, for the first time in our acquaintance, isn't stoned out of her head. That means nobody can eavesdrop astrally or slam some unpleasant spell into a fetish carried in by one of the corp reps (or, presumably, get in or out by sidestepping to another plane). Basically, the idea is that Blake and his advisors won't have their Praetorian guard with them, but the corp reps will know that if they do anything ill-advised (like scragging someone), they're not going to get out of the ops room alive.

(A quick digression. If Blake's got any brains—which he does—he must still be a tad edgy about security. Are the corp reps who they say they are? Or is the whole thing a setup? Drek, if I was a rival gang leader wanting to off Blake, this would be a great way to do it. Lots of possibilities come immediately to mind. Okay, so the Cutters' security is set up so the corp reps get geeked if they kill Blake. But that only happens if Blake knows he's been hit. How about a slow-acting poison or bioagent? Three days later, after the "corp reps" are long gone, Blake, Vladimir, and Springblossom convulse and die. Or maybe you don't even have to be that tricky. One of the reps could be a kamikaze, wired with explosives. Or ... well, anyway, you get the idea. All I can do is assume that Blake's done his homework on background checks and all that drek. And, of course, hope that if there is a belly-bomb involved, it's only a small one. End of digression.)

My station for all of this folderol is in the hallway outside
the big door of the ops room. Box is beside me, wearing his
finest torn leathers. We're both armed to the teeth, but that's
all for show. Our orders are to keep everything in our pants
unless and until Blake personally orders us to take action.
And yes, Virginia, even if it's a case of self-defense. (That's
one order that's going to be honored more in the breach than
the observance, you can bet your hoop on that.) I know there
are other soldiers stationed throughout the safe house, so the
corp reps are going to have to march through a gauntlet of
armed and nasty gang muscle—a reminder that they're in
deep and had better play nicely. Blake and Springblossom
are already in the ops room, waiting, while Vladimir has the
singular honor of greeting the guests (and being first on
the chopping block if their main purpose is just to blow
drek up).

So now I hear footsteps coming down the stairs. I see Box
draw himself up as close to his full height as the ceiling allows, and I do the same myself. We see four people:
Vladimir and three others. I don't stare—got to be polite
here—but I do give them what scrutiny I can via my peripheral vision. Vladimir's talking quietly to a tall, thin elf in a
corp-style suit that probably cost almost as much as my
bike. Handsome guy, this elf—young (of course), but with a
real serious air about him, like he's seen a frag of a lot in his
life. Definitely corp.

To his left and half a step back is a human I take to be the
elf's executive assistant or aide or something. Medium
height, medium build. I can't see his face—it's screened by
the elf and Vladimir, both of whom are taller than the aide.
And then my attention's grabbed and held by the third of the
corp reps.

I've seen elf women before, of course. Who hasn't? But
never one like this. She's tall—probably more than two meters in bare feet (oh, what a thought . . .)—about as tall as
me. But she looks much taller, and it's not just because of
the silver-capped heels on her shoes. She's thin and willowy
and long and lithe, and she moves like quicksilver—fluid
and effortless. Long, pale face with eyes that gleam like
bright gold. Her hair's fine and straight, so pale it could almost be white, and it falls free to just above her butt. She
wears a biz-style jacket of severe cut—black velveteen over
a synthsilk blouse of faintest jade-green. Her skirt's the same

fabric, calf-length, but slit up the side to just below the point of her hip.

Politeness be damned, there are some times you've just got to stare. I do, she notices, and she likes it. I get a speculative glance from the corner of one of those gold eyes, and the hint of something that could be a smile, and suddenly I want to run in circles howling, or dragging a wing, or some damn thing. (No, be honest, what I really want to do is investigate the degrees of freedom allowed by that split skirt.) I watch her receding rear aspect until the group is into the ops room and the door closes behind her. Then I grin over at Box.

The big troll's shaking his head sadly, apparently feeling yet another aspect of the tragedy of goblinization. I can commiserate: I'm not going to get my hands on any of that either.

It's a long meeting, and I've got plenty of time to think things over. Mainly, that means, to put the elf woman in perspective. The big question is, since there's no way I can hear what Blake and the Tir reps are discussing at the moment— what can I provide the Star that they'll want to know?

The answer is, the best descriptions I can give them of the reps. Obviously, verbal descriptions aren't as good as holos or vids—and why, I ask myself again, didn't the Star ever upgrade my headware so I could download actual images into a datachip?—but they'll be better than nothing. If the three people meeting with Blake always work together, even incomplete descriptions of all three could be enough to idee them.

Okay, so I had a good mental image of the woman, a very good image. Not as much on the elf talking to Vladimir, though, and nothing at all on the human aide (if that's what he really is). So that's my task when the meeting's over.

And finally—*finally,* thank the patron god of bladder control—it's over. The door opens with the whir-click of maglocks disengaging, and the delegation begins to emerge. Springblossom and Vladimir first, followed closely by the elf woman. We make momentary eye contact, but—biz before pleasure, frag it—I glance away quickly and focus my attention on the male elf who's walking out alongside Blake.

This time I give him the full once-over. A centimeter or two taller than the woman, similar slender build, but while she's all speed and grace, he looks like there's steel-hard muscles in there as well. Aquiline nose, dark eyes, olive skin. Black hair cropped short on top, but collar-length at the sides and in the back—a typical conservative corp style. No jewelry, no distinguishing marks that I can spot. Not much, but it's the best I can do.

Taking up the rear of the group is the human aide/ whatever. Not as tall as the other two and weighing eighty to eighty-five kilos. Medium height and medium build, basically what I picked up the first time out. He's wearing a conservative-cut biz suit in muted maroon, with black accessories and accents. Dark hair, short all over and subtly spiked. Dark olive complexion, dark eyes . . .

Those eyes meet mine, and there's a flash of recognition that hits me like a needle in the base of the spine. I've seen him before—don't know where, don't know when. I don't know who the frag he is, but I know I've seen him before— whether in person, in a holo, on the trid, or whatever.

And fragged if he doesn't recognize me too! I can see it, I can feel it—and I'll bet my last nuyen that he knows the recognition's mutual.

His eyes widen a little, and his face goes blank, totally expressionless. I'm sure my reaction's exactly the fragging same. It's like when you pass someone on the street that you know you've met before, but you can't for the life of you remember their name, where you met, or why they might—or might not—be important. So instead of making an ass out of yourself, you let your gaze just slide off them—give them the neutral scan—like you didn't really see them in the first place. It's like that, but it's worse, because we both know we both *did* see each other.

So what the frag am I supposed to do now? From the other slag's reaction, he's in precisely the same position. I know him, goes the brain, I met him—but where? And who *is* the motherfragger anyway?

We're both doing the neutral scan, trying to pretend to each other that we didn't see nothing. And we keep doing it until he's up the stairway to the main floor of the safe house and out of sight.

8

Okay, honesty time: I'm drek-scared.

Call it enlightened self-interest, call it the necessary paranoia of the deep-cover asset, call it whatever the frag you want. I just know it as a tightness around the heart, a churning, watery feeling in the guts.

Theoretically, nobody in Seattle knows who and what I really am. That's the idea, at least. That's why the Star had me transferred out west from Milwaukee. Except for my direct controls and various cut-outs within the Star—and their lovers and confidants and anybody else they happened to shoot their mouths off to—everybody in Seattle knows me solely as Rick Larson, gang-banger extraordinaire, Cutters soldier, and member of Blake's Praetorian guard.

Any attempt by official channels to dig up deep background on me would lead to Milwaukee, where the local Lone Star franchise has built me a bulletproof cover story. If the search is done unofficially—through the Milwaukee gang scene, for example—they'll run into the same cover, because Rick Larson Gang Hero was active there as well. So the only people who'd recognize my face in Seattle are my Lone Star superiors or people who've met me in my Cutters persona. Nice and logical and reassuring, right?

Yeah, well, that's in theory, and we all know what happened to the theories that man could never fly and that a nuclear chain reaction would never work. Consider the fact that I flew from Milwaukee to Seattle aboard a new generation of suborbitals launched along linear induction rails that draw their electricity from a fragging nuke plant, and you'll understand my unwillingness to depend on theories. My cover is watertight and bulletproof only as long as a single, base assumption remains correct: that nobody (except me, of course) ever moves from Milwaukee to Seattle.

Okay, granted, Seattle isn't one of the garden spots of the

universe, but have you visited Milwaukee lately? "A Great City on a Great Lake," according to the Chamber of Commerce, but in reality it's a great place to get geeked on a great toxic waste dump. But people do relocate. Hell, take Cat Ashburton, the pneumatic redhead from my meet at the kissaten. She got transferred from Milwaukee to Seattle. Sure, she's part of Lone Star and thus is no risk to me, but her transfer was totally independent of any assignment of mine, and that makes her—for the purposes of my catastrophizing, at least—just another megacorp wage slave. And if one megacorp wage slave can get bumped to the West Coast, why not another? And just as easily someone who knew me while I was going through the Lone Star Academy, before I found my way into deep-cover work.

Let's let the old overactive imagination churn away at that for a moment and come up with a worst-case scenario. Maybe the elf's aide—the guy I'm obsessing about—knew me when we were both young punks in Milwaukee. Maybe we went to school together or met over beers at some college watering hole. In a drunken stupor, I told him I was thinking about joining the Star.

No, make it worse. I met him while I was in the Academy—over the same liter of beer, probably—when I was so adamant about getting into the Star and changing the world. Our career paths thereafter diverge. I go undercover, he goes into the corporate world and ends up cutting shady deals with gangs for a Tir-based outfit. What's he going to think when he spots good old Ricky Larson, the goof who used to be an Officer Friendly wannabe flashing his Lone Star Fan Club decoder ring to all and sundry, suddenly looking like he's a top soldier for the fragging Cutters? What's he going to think? Yeah, that's *exactly* what he's going to think. He's going to be dead fragging right, and I'm going to be right fragging dead. Ah, isn't symmetry wonderful?

Yeah, well, that's the worst-case scenario. Best-case? We passed each other on the street yesterday, and for some reason our faces stuck in each other's minds. Or maybe he was one of the suits in the Coffee Bon when I was doing my gig with Cat. If that's the case, then I'm safe. When he finally places me, his reaction is going to be more, "Hey, small world," than, "Infiltrator! Call out the dogs!"

And what's the most likely case? Somewhere in between. Maybe we do know each other from Milwaukee, but met after my cover was at least on the way to being established. In which case I'm at minimal, if not zero, risk.

So what do I do now? "Grease the guy" comes immediately to mind, but that carries its own set of risks and consequences. No, obviously the smart thing to do is wrack what I use for brains to figure out who the slag was, is, or whatever. If I can beat him at figuring how and where we've seen each other before, then I'll know which way to jump. Until I get that brain wave, though, about all I can do is obsess about it, and stay drek-scared.

And I'm doing that just fine.

I'm still at it a couple of days later, and it's turning into a real pain in the fragging hoop. I still haven't placed the guy's face, no matter how hard I strain. I've tried all the little psychological tricks, all the mental judo that's supposed to help you remember. Go through your memory chronologically (Did you see him in 2049? No? Then how about 2050?). Or geographically (Remember the faces of everyone you hung with in Milo's Bar, Milwaukee. No? Try the U of W student union building . . .). Or how about associationally? (Who have you ever met who has associated closely with elves?) The only results are headaches, difficulty in sleeping, and disturbing nightmares when I do manage to get to sleep. Not productive, chummer. Not productive at all.

So, like a good little mole, I tried another channel. Using all my wiles and wits and lies and machinations, I put out feelers throughout the Cutters to find out if anyone knows anything about my mysterious Mr. X. Null program there, cobber.

Oh, sure, I got a name, but it was one Mr. Nemo. I don't think the ganger who leaked me that gem ever figured out why I looked like I was tasting something sour when he told me. Apart from something like "I. M. A. Sudonim," I can't think of anything that's more obviously an alias than "Nemo". (Doesn't anyone read the classics anymore? "Nemo" means "nobody" in Latin. Our guest had billed himself as Mr. Nobody.) Pretty fragging useless.

Well, no, let's be fair, there was something else, but it didn't do much but raise more questions. From what some of the soldiers had heard—and Great Ghu knows how they heard it—Mr. Nemo wasn't from the same Tir-based corp as the elves. That's all they could tell me. No clue as to whether that meant he was from another Tir-based corp or a corp from somewhere else in the world ... or whether he was even a corporator at all. Drek, with a pseudonym like Nemo, he could well be a shadowrunner. (But no, frag it till it bleeds, he's not a runner. I know it, and I don't know *how* I know it, and that terrifies me even more. What a bloody nightmare.)

Anyway, I've got my report all cued up and dictated into the chip in my secondary slot, including everything I know, guess, and wonder about the elven delegation. I've got verbal descriptions of everyone, but for the nth time over the last couple of days I wish I could draw worth squat or that someone had seen fit to equip me with chips for skills other than the violent.

So, yes, I've got the report ready to go, but go where? Blake's been working my hoop off as aide/gofer/bodyguard. I've been playing close-cover on him, making drops and running courier, and just basically sitting around waiting for him to figure out what he wants done next. I haven't been back to my doss in two days, crashing instead on couches, cots, or floors at one or another of the Cutters' safe houses. I've had one and only one chance to log onto UOL with my pocket computer. Of course, I took that opportunity to post the innocuous message that means, "I need a meet now. C'mon back good buddy, y'hear?" or some drek. But I haven't been able to check for replies.

Up until a little while ago, that is. About an hour back, close to 0130 in the middle of what looks like Seattle's worst overnight rainstorm of the year, Blake came out of his private doss to find me propped up against the corridor wall, catching some zees. I guess I felt his presence—or maybe I heard the door. Anyway, I popped to my feet like I was on springs, expecting royal drek for sleeping on the job.

Any other boss would surely have had my head for dereliction of duty. But Blake never does what any other boss would do. Instead of barking, he just chuckled quietly. "Take twenty-four," he told me. Then, glancing at his watch, he amended, "Well, make it twenty-two-thirty. Be back here by midnight tomorrow. Got me?"

So I told him "Gotcha," and I headed downstairs and out to my bike.

I wanted sleep, I craved sleep. But what I needed was to

log onto UOL to see if a meet could be scraped together in the next twenty-some hours. Of course, I couldn't see to that need in the safe house. Blake knew I was bagged to the bone, and what does someone who's bagged to the bone do when he's given time off? Not log onto a Matrix BBS, that's for sure. Word would get back to Blake that for some reason I ranked connect time as more important right now than sack time, and he'd start wondering why. That kind of wondering I don't need. So it was out to the bike, fire up the engine—after checking for surprises, of course. It wasn't that I was expecting trouble, but I had tended to be more cautious after seeing some grunts washing remnants of Ranger off the walls of the building. Then I cruised back toward the Wenonah.

By the time I'm rumbling onto Northeast Sixtieth Street, the sheets of rain and the wind in my face have cleared my head to some degree—and it's just enough to let me know exactly how drekky I feel. I park the bike in the back alley, chain it securely to the building's gas meter. Then I unlock the metal back door to the building, locking it again carefully behind me, and climb the narrow stairs to the second floor. The hallway—just as narrow as the stairs—is empty. The door to my apartment's at the far end, at the front of the building—I picked it specifically for the view out over the street and down to the front door of the building. Out of habit, I check the telltales I always leave around the door. Nobody's opened it since I left here a few days ago. Not that I expected anyone to have done so—Bart's uninvited visit a week back was the exception, not the rule. I unlock the door and pass into the small living room with its kitchen alcove to the right. I'm hungry, but on consideration I decide I want sleep more than I want food. Anyway, I know there's nothing in the fridge except a bottle of vodka and some yogurt that's probably quietly developing into some new form of life by now.

I turn left into the bedroom, stripping off my soaked jacket as I do so. I fling it toward the chair—miss, but what the frag—and slump down onto my bed.

My portable telecom's just where I left it, on the bedside table, jacked into the LTG socket in the wall. I power it up and hit the keystroke sequence that'll log me onto UCAS Online. While the machine's making the connection and shaking hands with the UOL mainframes—somewhere in

Virginia, I think, though of course it doesn't matter—I pull off my boots and make fists with my toes in the ratty carpet. I set my H & K with its two spare clips within easy reach on the floor next to the bed. (Again, not that I'm expecting trouble, but there are some habits you just don't want to let slide into disuse.) The telecom beeps, announcing it's ready.

On the ride over, I dictated my innocuous "get back to me quick" message into the chip in my secondary slot. So now I use a cylindrical carrier to extract the chip from the base of my skull, and slip it into the peripheral slot of the telecom. I display a directory of the chip's contents, and make doubly sure that the file I'm going to upload to the telecom, and from there to UOL, is the right one—the innocuous message, not the report to the Star that would get me a bullet in the brain. Then I check it again. I know I'm tired, and I know that tired people make mistakes. A single wrong keystroke, and the wrong file goes shooting down the datapaths of the LTG and the Matrix. Yes, it's the right file. I trigger the transfer.

A second or two later, my message is stored securely and safely on the distant mainframe, ready for my controls at the Star to view it and recognize what it means. I know I really should check the message bases to see if there's something waiting for me, but I just don't have the jam at the moment. My brain feels like it's full of spiders, and my eyeballs like they've been sandblasted. I break the connection.

The pillow on my bed is calling to me, its siren song so strong I don't even power down the telecom. I swing my legs up onto the bed—cold in the wet jeans I can't be bothered taking off—and slump backward. I feel the welcome blackness of sleep envelop me even before my head hits the pillow.

What the frag time is it?

My bedside chrono's set up to project a dim time display onto the ceiling over my bed. I peel my sticky eyelids open and look up. I see that it's 0332, which means I've been asleep less than two hours. Why did I wake up?

Then I hear the sound again, the one that had penetrated my sleeping brain and mingled with my confused dreams. The insistent chirp of my cel phone. Frag! Who the frag is calling me at fragging oh three-thirty in the fragging morning? Have they no fragging respect for the fragging dead?

It can't be the Star. Procedure doesn't allow for them calling me direct, for any reason. (And to reinforce that, I've
made sure they don't even have my number.) Blake's got the
number, as do a few other higher-ups in the Cutters. They
could be calling me, but why? I'm off duty for the next
twenty hours, and Blake didn't say anything about being on
call. Conceivably, some emergency's come up and he needs
all his Praetorians around him, but frag him and the hog he
rode in on. I'm not answering. "Get fragged," I grunt to the
phone. Obligingly, it shuts the frag up. I roll over and close
my eyes again.

Then there's a knock on the fragging door. My eyes snap
open again and look at the time display. It reads, 0333, so
no, I haven't been back to sleep.

And that's when my instincts kick in, those little warning
bells inside my skull, my belly, and half a meter lower. I can
almost hear my bag contract. Something's wrong here . . .

Instinct's important for someone who's undercover. Important? Frag, it's life itself. Supposedly I'm one of the
Star's best undercover cops—that's what my superiors tell
me when they want to stroke my ego, at least—so that
should mean mine are some of the best instincts going. All
I know is that I've come to trust those weird little feelings.
And now those instincts are telling me that something's going down.

A phone call, then a minute later a knock on my door. Un-
related? Maybe. Or maybe the phone call was an attempt to
find out whether I'm home or not. When I inconsiderately
decided not to answer, I forced my caller to use other meth-
ods. Like a knock on the fragging door.

I swing my legs—chilled and very uncomfortable—off the
bed and reach for my portable telecom. The Wenonah—
"security building" or not—never had any security for private apartments: no cameras or sensors, not even a viewer in
the fragging door. For obvious reasons, I rectified the situation when I moved in. Set into the door frame over the door
is a tiny videocam and microphone arrangement set to
narrowcast a data stream on a frequency jiggered to my
telecom. I hit the keys on the keyboard, thanking whatever
spirits—or my own laziness, or whatever—didn't let me
power the thing down. The screen lights up and I can see
what that tiny hidden videocam is seeing.

Four figures in the hallway outside my door—two men,

two women—all wearing what look like armored leathers. None have weapons out, but there's something about the way they're standing that kicks the volume of my internal alarms up a dozen notches. They're tense, they're ready— for what? I think I can guess. Frag!

One of the figures—I peg her as the leader—is right up to the door, and she's raising her hand to knock again. The fisheye lens on the videocam and the angle of view make it impossible for me to recognize anyone.

The biff knocks again. As she does, I'm up on my feet, pulling the telecom jack out of the wall. I scoop up my H & K, and let it and the wire have a little conversation. With my left hand I pick up the telecom, balancing it like a waiter carrying a tray. I move like a ghost out of the bedroom into the living room, keeping my eyes on the screen.

The woman in the image steps back and shakes her head. Three of the figures—the biff leader and the two men— reach into their jackets, and out come weapons. My instincts are deafening now, but I don't need them anymore. My conscious mind knows what's going down: a hit. Another gang trying to take out a key Cutters member? Who the frag knows, and for the moment it doesn't matter one good goddamn. Idees can wait.

In the telecom screen, I see the leader turn to the second woman, the one who hasn't pulled heat. Bonelessly, the second woman sinks down onto the floor in full lotus, eyes closed.

Shaman? Mage? It doesn't matter—it's magic, there's no other way to read it. She's getting ready to go astral so she can just sashay in through the door and take a look-see around the place. When she finds me here, the drek will really hit the pot.

The lens-induced distortion on the screen makes it tough to pick out exactly where everyone's standing relative to the door, but at least the hallway's narrow. Up comes my H & K, and I give it and the wire a split second to figure out the fire lines.

Almost too long. The mage's eyes snap open, and I know she's "seen" me. (Frag, this magic drek's scary.) She opens her mouth to say something.

And I clamp down on the trigger, a long stuttering burst right through the door. In the telecom screen I see the biff leader take most of the burst in her upper chest and throat, and down she goes spouting blood. I walk the burst into the others—tougher than it sounds when your point of view is different from the direction in which your gun's pointing. Something like trying to write while you're looking in a mirror. One slag triggers his own SMG and I instinctively drop to a crouch, his burst stitches the already-dead-or-close-to-it leader, then he's down. The second man's also going down—not dead, not yet—with a lot of his face missing. I cap off another short burst aimed lower, and see the mage's head deform under multiple bullet impacts. I drop the telecom, scuttle forward still in my crouch—Do they have support? If so I'll know in a moment—and kick open what's left of the door.

The hallway's a slaughterhouse, the air thick with the reek of blood and drek. My stomach knots and threatens to spew, and my heart feels like it's turned to ice. I want to be sick, I want to scream, but I can't let myself. I clamp down the old control and turn off the emotions. Let the brain handle things, but don't let the heart in on the party. Not yet. I can have my nervous reaction later. Icy, soulless now, I look around.

The body count's total—if the second man's not dead yet, there's nothing anybody can do to save him. I hear screams and yells of alarm from the surrounding apartments, but nobody's doing anything brainfragged like opening their own doors. Thank Ghu for small favors, but I know they're just that. Around me there's got to be a dozen fingers all punching in 911 on telecoms and cel phones, calling in the clans.

Frag, and I kind of liked the Wenonah, too.

Time's my enemy, I know that. Lone Star doesn't patrol the Ravenna area very frequently, but there *are* patrols. A cruiser might be only a couple of blocks away. Worse, the hit team might have back-up outside, already alerted by the sound of the carnage, charging up the stairs to the second floor at this very moment. And if that isn't enough, eventually somebody—maybe packing something unpleasant—is going to open his apartment door to see what the frag went down. I've got to move—now.

Back into the bedroom, sit down on the bed and pull my boots back on. Snag my leather jacket from the floor . . .

Frag, almost forgot my wallet with my credsticks—including the special one that can, if I issue the right code, access the contingency funds the Star set up for me. (That's crucial. My personal accounts are fragging near empty, as befits my cover.) Out into the living room and then through the abattoir outside, moving fast but smooth. Never run if you can avoid it; you're less likely to trip and more likely to see what's going on around you. Past the first three bodies, step over the head-shot mage . . .

Then stop like I'm paralyzed. The top of the mage's head is distinctly missing, but her face is still recognizable. And I do recognize it, and that recognition twists the knife of fear in my guts.

It's Marla, the Snake shaman who was on my team when we hit the Eighty-Eights' depot. Already knowing, deep down, what I'm going to see, I look at what's left of the other faces. I recognize them all, every one of them.

They're Cutters.

9

The engine of my Harley Scorpion howls in my ears as the glowing lines on the tach and speedo stretch upward. Wind and rain lash my face, and my drenched hair sends cold water seeping down the back of my neck. It's cold, but nothing compared to the chill that's already settled in my spine like dirty ice. I've got the bike bars in a death-grip, squeezing them so hard my forearms ache. It's the only way I can stop my hands from shaking.

The Scorpion is screaming through the night, the big bike pushing its limit, wailing south on Highway 5 at one-sixty klicks. It's not that I'm going anywhere—or that I know where to go—it's just that I need to think, and I think better when I'm moving, preferably sitting in the saddle of a high-powered speed machine. It's always been like this, even when I was growing up in Lake Geneva, before my family moved the fifty klicks or so north to Milwaukee proper. I'd wanted a trail bike, but my parents wouldn't hear of it. Instead they got me a fifth-hand Bombardier WaveRunner, a water jet-powered thing that looked like a cross between a snowmobile and a miniature boat.

I sneered at first, but after taking that puppy out on the lake and cranking it up, I felt like I was home. My folks preferred my "lake hog" to a bike, on the grounds that water was softer than asphalt if I ditched. What they didn't realize was that the WaveRunner, with the throttle cracked wide open, goes so fast that water's no more compressible than concrete. I proved that one day in a spontaneous race with a neighbor who also had a WaveRunner, when I jumped it over a ski-boat's wake, corkscrewed in, and broke my leg in three places—along with the keel of the lake hog. My folks got me fixed up, but they wouldn't—categorically would not—let me do anything but sell the WaveRunner for scrap.

I shake away the memories with a growled curse. Drek,

but it's tempting to slide into woolgathering when the present's one big Mexican frag-up. It's a good thing I'm not running the big Scorpion on a vehicle control rig. From what I've heard, if your mind wanders when you're jacked in, so does the bike. Unpleasant.

So, no more running away from reality. A Cutters team had been sent not to snatch me, but to take me out. If it had been merely a snatch, they'd have used very different tactics. A hit team composed of Cutters raised several distinct possibilities, none of them very pleasant.

First. The Team members were *from* the Cutters, but not *of* the Cutters, if that makes any sense. They could be members of the gang, but not taking their orders from anywhere in the Cutters organization. Maybe another outfit—possibly the Eighty-Eights—paid them or otherwise persuaded them to geek me. Likelihood? Minimal. One Cutters member, I could see it. A full team of four? Nah.

Next. The team was sent by someone in the Cutters, but its mission was not officially sanctioned by the gang. Perhaps there's an internecine conflict going on between factions within the gang, and the leader of one faction sent his soldiers out to eliminate a member of the rival faction. (The corollary of this is, of course, that the faction who sent the team is maneuvering against Blake, because I'm obviously one of Blake's good little boys.) Or maybe it's not even that big. Maybe it's just someone settling a score. If Bart and/or Ranger were still around, I'd give this one the big gold star. But now? As far as I know, Bart was Ranger's only loyal supporter, and Bart himself didn't have any following of his own. Sure, some people were slotted off when Blake brought in Bubba the cracker as war boss, but those people would see no percentage in having me splattered. Conclusion: likelihood minimal.

Finally—and this is the big one, folks—my cover's blown. *I'm* blown. Blake and the others have found out I'm a Lone Star plant, and they've decided to off me. A few weeks ago I'd have rated this one as unlikely. Now? After spotting and being spotted by the mysterious Mr. Neno, the odds are suddenly much higher. Yet it wasn't much more than two hours ago that I was inside the Cutters safe house, catching zees outside Blake's door. If he knew then, dealing with me should have been a matter of opening his door, leaning out with a pistol, and capping me while I slept. Or, if he wanted to make it slow and messy, using a cel phone to call down to Box and the rest of the Praetorians to come bag me. Taking me would have cost them, but they'd have been able to do it, no mistake about that.

So, this is how I figure it. Sometime between 0130 and, say, 0230, Blake gets word from some trustworthy source that I'm a mole. He whistles for Bubba—or maybe simply bypasses the war boss altogether and calls up a team of soldiers. They're given the mission and the details, and off they toddle to my doss, to arrive at 0332. The timing is tight, but definitely possible.

Okay, it's possible: now punch holes in it. That's easy. Why risk the hard option at all? Blake knew I was coming back to the safe house to resume my duties in less than twenty-two hours. Why not wait for me to jander into the safe house, straight into a crossfire or into the sights of a single sniper? Why load for bear and come visiting? (Unless he also had reason to suspect I had no intention of ever coming back and was actually heading for the hills. But set that one aside for later: one riddle at a time here.)

Also—and this might well be my own ego talking—why send just four? Why no back-up? Either Blake really underestimated my capabilities—ah, ego—or the op was a rush job (and why such a rush?), or maybe whoever set it up didn't have access to all the Cutters' resources.

By now I'm only a couple of klicks from the southern border crossing into the Salish-Shidhe nation, which means lights and border patrols and much more attention and activity than I want to face at the moment. So I slow down and cruise the bike through the next break in the concrete divider between the two sides of the highway. Then I crack the throttle wide open and head north again. Since I don't know where the frag I'm going, any direction is just as good at getting me there.

Much as I hate to think about it, I've got to admit that the most likely reason someone tried to scrag me is that my cover's been blown. Quickly, I run through my activities of the last days and weeks. I've done nothing, said nothing any different from things I'd done/said plenty of times before. If those things didn't frag my cover then, why now? The only thing that makes any sense is that Mr. Nemo finally figured out who I was and where he'd seen me, drew a few painfully accurate conclusions, and dumped the whole mess into Blake's lap.

Motherfragging slitch from hell!

Okay, okay, relax, chill. The important thing is to decide what to do right now, at this moment.

Officially, according to SOP and all that drek, I should report immediately to my controls at the Star. Use a phone if I have to, but let them know I'm blown. Then they'll call me in or give me the location of a safe house—a Star safe house this time—where I can hunker down until we're all comfortably confident that nobody's still gunning for me or until I figure out a safe way out of the sprawl. (Back to Milwaukee? Who knows?) That's the officially sanctioned thing to do, and it's also the smart thing to do.

But it involves admitting to my controls that I've failed, that I've slotted up. Frag the fact that—apparently—a face from my past made me. Frag the fact that I couldn't have done anything to prevent it, that it's just a matter of the dice coming up snake-eyes at long last. Nobody'll blame me, nobody'll censure me, there'll be no official reprimands on my record or unofficial slaps on the wrist. My controls will curse a blue streak and grind their teeth and pound their desks because the op's come to a premature end, but they know and I know that there's no blame attached to me. I'm Teflon on this one, and the drek just slides off. The point is . . .

Frag it, *I'll* blame me. I hate to frag up, I hate to lose. It makes me a snaky sonofabitch to play squash with or to spar with in the gym, but it also makes me a damn good cop. I'll do whatever it takes to win, and I'll move heaven and fragging earth before I'll admit defeat.

Translation? Frag SOP until I've explored my other options.

I can just hear you asking: What options, huh, omae? That's the thing I don't know and I *won't* know until I've scoped the situation out a bit more. Like, I've got it figured that I'm probably blown with the Cutters, but it's stupid to pull the plug on a good op until I'm sure.

But how do I go about finding out? Phone up Blake? Yeah, sure. "Hey Blakey, have you guys figured out I'm a Star undercover cop yet? No? Wiz. Chill, cobber. Catch ya tomorrow night." Boom. Yeah, right.

Then again, maybe a phone call isn't such a bad idea,

come to think of it. Not to Blake, no way. But how about to Paco? The young ganger owes me big-time—or he thinks he does, which is the same damn thing. I've saved his hoop twice in recent days. His sense of honor, that normally drekheaded Latin machismo thing, won't let him forget that. He'll cut me slack if anyone will—enough slack to talk to me, at least—and I'm good enough at "gliding" (Lone Star speak for "lying through your chops") that if he'll let me get one word in I can probably get him to listen to the whole spiel.

Plus, I know he's got his own cel phone, and I've got his number.

Of course, I don't have my cel on me. Fragging good thing, too—there's a tracer built into every cel phone. How the frag else do you think the cel network knows which cellular transmitter to send your calls to, huh? Every time your phone registers with a new cell, the system knows where you are within a couple of square klicks. Plus, I hear that a few software refinements in the cel system can let someone narrow it down a lot more than that. (Oh sure, this is real heavy-duty technomancy we're talking here, cracking into the cellular network. The Star can do it—hell, they do it regularly—but I don't think the Cutters have the resources, though I'm not willing to bet my life on it.) So, my cel phone is still sitting somewhere in my doss at the Wenonah, but only because I forgot to snag it in my hurry.

I check the next big green highway sign. I'm right on top of the next exit—South Seventy-second Street in Tacoma— and I take the ramp way too fast. Then I'm cruising east through the low-rent district of Tacoma—relatively speaking, of course, it's worlds better than fragging Ravenna, let me tell you—looking for a phone booth.

Paco's number is ringing and ringing, and I'm left with nothing to do but mutter, "C'mon, c'mon, c'mon" under my breath like some fragging mantra. The phone booth leaks, but at least all the parts of the phone itself are still where they're supposed to be, another thing which separates this part of Tacoma from Ravenna. As a sop to my rampant paranoia, I've stuck a wad of chewing gum over the optical pickup. (Yeah, yeah, I know: Paco's got a portable cel phone, audio only, so why bother? Here's why. I don't know what happens to the phone's video feed when a call is made to an audio-only unit. Maybe the feed just gets spewed off into oblivion, another data stream pouring into the old bit bucket. But maybe, just maybe, it's on the circuit somewhere, accessible to someone who's tapping into the call with a phone that *does* have a vidscreen. And maybe some feature in the vid image will let that tapper figure my physical location faster than he can actually trace the call. Yeah, I know, I'm a paranoid slot, and I admit it gladly. But I'm a live paranoid slot, which is the way I want to stay.)

A dozen rings, fifteen, and I'm reaching up to break the connection. But then there's a click and I hear Paco's voice, muzzy with sleep. (Oh yeah, it's before 0400 in the morning, isn't it?) "Whafuck jawant?"

"Paco," I say through the scrap of cloth torn from my shirt. (Not enough to spoof a full-on voiceprint recognition system, but it's better than frag-all.) "Paco, mount up!" It's what I yelled to him and the others at the warehouse when I was firing up the Bulldog to escape from the Star FRT assault. I hope he'll remember it and make the connection.

He's on it like a pit bull. "Go, 'mano," he replies, his voice clearer. "Give me two, 'kay? Call back." There's a click and he's gone. Gone looking for a quiet place to talk, if my luck's holding. Gone looking for Blake or Box, if it's not. I stare at the face of my watch, and feel rain dribbling from my hair down my neck.

Exactly one hundred twenty seconds later, I key the call in again. He answers on the first ring. "You're hot, 'mano," he says without prelude. "Melt-down hot, nova hot. What the frag d'you do, jam Blake's lady?"

I feel a chill creeping down my spine again, and it's not the rain. "What do they say I did, Paco?"

"They don't, chummer. They just say you're down by law." Down by law: Cutters talk for what the Star would call "out of sanction" or "beyond salvage". Translation: open season, teams out, maybe a bounty on my head.

"Why?"

"Got me," he says. "Everybody's sucked up tight on it, won't say squat. Just that you're out." He hesitates. "What did you do?"

"Fragged if I know, priyatel," I tell him, pouring every gram of sincerity I can fake into my voice. "All I know is that a team of hitters—including our old chummer Marla—just tried to take me out at home. Came as Great Ghu's own

surprise to me, let me tell ya." Paco chuckles grimly at that.
"Particularly since I didn't do anything to get myself
geeked." I pause. "Look, Paco . . . ," I begin.

And, like before, he's on to the idea even before I've got
it out my yap. "You're thinking setup?"

"Could well be," I tell him. "I stepped on too many toes,
or maybe Bart or Ranger got nervous toward the end and
planted a data time bomb somewhere, then weren't around
to make the regular phone call to keep it from going off."

"Yeah, that works," he says slowly. "You want me to put
out feelers?"

"Real carefully," I confirm. "If I'm really that nova-hot, I
don't want you to get burned."

He laughs at that. "I can take care of myself, 'mano." He
pauses again. "Call me back at this number at . . . make it oh
five-thirty."

"That enough time?"

"Should be," he confirms. "Keep your head down till
then."

"You got that," I tell him, but he's already hung up.

I leave the booth and swing back onto my bike, fire it up,
and cruise off slowly. Yeah, looks like I'm blown big-time.
Maybe it's time to place that call to the Star . . .

But, hey, why not wait till after oh five-thirty? Blown is
usually like knocked-up, it doesn't happen halfway. But
maybe the convincing lie I threw at Paco—that I'm a victim
of a post-mortem smear campaign by Ranger and/or Bart—
isn't a lie at all. I might do the same thing if I thought a rival
within the gang was trying to geek me. Clutching at straws,
I know, but sometimes the longest of odds pay off.

If I didn't know better, I'd say my watch had stopped. The
hour and a half between 0400 and 0530 seemed to drag on
for a least a fragging lifetime, and only the growing pinky-
red smear of the coming dawn to the east confirms that time
hasn't come to a screeching halt. My body and brain are
both reminding me in no uncertain terms that I had less than
two hours sleep before the Wenonah hallway became a
shooting gallery, but I can't let myself pay any attention.
The soykaf I'm sipping from a vending-machine cup is hot
enough to scald my mouth, and tastes like it's got enough
chemicals to ensure me a nice collection of cancers by the

time I'm thirty-five, but pain and disgust are the only things keeping me going at the moment.

After talking to Paco, I needed some way to kill ninety minutes without killing myself in the process. If I was paranoid before, I'm doubly so now. Seattle's a big fragging sprawl, but the Cutters—in one form or another—are spread across the whole fragging city. The odds are low of running into someone who knows me or who's been sent out gunning for me, but the possibility is definitely there, no matter where I go in the sprawl. So I just cruise randomly, eventually ending up in the Pier 42 area, near where we blew the drek out of the Eighty-Eights' warehouse. Safe as anywhere, I suppose, and safer than most. The Eighty-Eights could well be out in force, expecting more trouble. Sure, I might come to grief at their hands, but this is one place members of the Cutters aren't likely to show up. Anyway, there's a phone booth near the Pier 42 gate, a bus shelter with a (surprisingly) unvandalized soykaf machine—nice and dark inside, now that I've smashed the lights with the grip of my H & K—and a disused mobile office for me to stash my bike behind. I chew some more gum for the optical pickup, and find that makes me feel even more hyper.

At last the alarm I've set on my watch whines at me, and it's time to place the call.

Like last time, Paco picks up on the first ring. "Larson?" he says, and all my internal warnings are screaming up a fragging storm. Paco's only called me Larson once in all the time I've known him, and that was when he thought he was going to get his hoop shot off in the Lake Meridian warehouse.

"Yeah, it's me," I tell him slowly, thinking fast. "Got the word for me?"

"I got the good word," he tells me. "False alarm, 'mano. False alarms all round. The guns are all called back in." His voice is calm, cool—neutral and precise. And there's a message in that. I only hope I'm reading it right.

"Yeah? What went down?"

"It's like I told you last time, 'mano," he says. "Bart buried a package of lies, and when he went, there was nobody to keep it buried."

Another warning: Paco hadn't said anything about that. I was the one who had. "Yeah?" I let a hint of hope creep into my voice.

"Yeah, Larson," he echoes. "Blake and Vladimir looked into it, and they saw it's a lousy frame-job." He chuckles, but there isn't any humor in it. "Guess Box or someone popped early, sending the guns out."

And another one. Paco said "down by law". The way I've heard the phrase used, it's fragging near an official pronouncement from the gang boss. It it was just Box overreacting and sending out the Praetorians, Paco wouldn't have used those words.

"Blake wants you to come back in, Larson," Paco goes on urgently. "Come on home, 'mano. The big boys think Bart might have planted other packages—for the Star, maybe even for the news snoops, omae. Blake thinks we might be able to intercept them, but he wants you to take charge of it. Hear me?"

I hear him, all right. I let my voice drag, like I'm bagged to the bone—not a tough acting job at the moment—and tell him, "I hear you, Paco. Thanks, priyatel. I . . ." I cough wetly. "I'm burned, chummer, let me tell you. I caught one when I scragged the hit squad and I'm hurting."

"Come on in, then," he says urgently. "Come on home and the Cutters'll take care of you."

It's all I can do not to chuckle out loud. Message received five-by-five, Paco, my friend. Thanks, bolshoi thanks. "I'll be in," I lie convincingly. Than I'm off the phone, onto my bike, and back on the fragging road again.

10

I'm blown, big-time gonzo blown and no denying it this time. What Paco said—and, more important, what he didn't say—told me that, loud and clear. When he put out feelers, somehow Blake or one of the other big boys figured he'd talked to me and would be doing it again soon. Paco wasn't alone when I spoke with him this last time; other people were listening in to make sure he'd say the words that would get me fried and to make sure he didn't warn me. But he did warn me, in ways that Blake and the others wouldn't scan. And he'd done it even though everything must be pointing to me as a fragging Lone Star narc. Still he clued me. Still he saved my life. It had to come from loyalty; nothing else made sense.

So there's not avoiding it anymore. It's time to make the call.

Multiple calls, actually. There's no way the phone-drones in the Star bureaucracy are going to let a call from a street drek like me go straight through to the people I want to contact. And, for obvious reasons, those same phone-drones can't know that I'm an undercover op. In the old days, I'd probably have been given a single phone number that would connect me directly with some higher-up's office, but today that kind of direct line is too much of a risk—a datapath for outside deckers to use to penetrate a corporate official's private comm and computing system. No, these days all calls to and from Star officials have to go through switching systems with wetware components. And those wetware components—the phone-drones again—don't know Rick Larson from any other hunk of guttermeat in the sprawl. Still, there are procedures in place.

I scan the street around me. It's 0545 and the dock area's starting to come to life. I can't stay here much longer, but I figure I'm safe enough for the first call. Leaving the chewing gum in place over the optical pickup, I key the first of several numbers I've memorized.

"Lone Star main switchboard," a synthesized voice answers. "If you know the five-digit extension of the party you wish to reach, please enter it now. If you do not know the extension . . ." I punch in a string of five zeroes, cutting the voice off in mid-blather.

There's silence for an instant, then another voice—also synthesized—pipes up. "You have reached Lone Star Personnel's automated attendant," it drones. "Regular office hours are oh-nine-hundred to seventeen-hundred, Monday to Friday. Please call back." There's a click and it sounds like the connection's broken, but I know better. I punch in my five zeroes again. When I'm done, the phone beeps once, and there's more silence. No outgoing message or other voice prompt, but I know a digitizing recorder is online somewhere in the depths of "suit country" in the Star HQ building.

"It's me," I say simply, confident that the computer on the other end will figure out who "me" is from my voice pattern. "I'm blown. Call two-three twelve-hundred." And I hang up.

I hurry around back to my bike, mount up, and I'm off. I've got four and a quarter hours until I'm due to make my next phone call. (That's what the number I quoted at the end means. Yeah, it sounded like I was giving the Star an LTG number to call. Actually, I was telling them when to expect my call. The first two digits of the "phone number" were meaningless. The data content's in the last four digits: the time of my intended call, plus two hundred. Got it? Theoretically, if anyone was tapping the line, they'd keep themselves busy tracing LTG number 23-1200. I wonder if whoever owns that number might soon be receiving a visit from the Cutters . . .)

Okay, okay, why don't I just jander on down to the Lone Star HQ building, check in with a receptionist, and wait in a nice, safe office while word gets passed to the right ears—to the few people in the building who actually know about me—until someone comes to collect me? A couple of reasons. First of all, even if I'm blown with the Cutters, my usefulness in the Seattle area may not be over. I could go undercover somewhere else, on some other assignment. That wouldn't be possible if I openly showed up at the Star HQ: lots of groups with an interest in the Star—and vice versa— keep a close eye on the pyramidal building at Second and Union. Odds are I'd be marked and made, the fact that I've got Star connections spreading throughout the underworld, and my next undercover assignment would be my last. Boom.

There's another fragging good reason, too: self-preservation. For Blake to send a hit team out after me instead of waiting for me to come back to the safe house must mean he thought I wasn't *coming* back. He must have believed I was bugging out to scurry on home and spill my fragging guts to the Star. It would be a simple matter to set a few watchers around Star HQ—snipers, maybe, backed with magical talent—and hammer a bullet or a spell into my brain when I show up. Not a trick Blake would miss, let me tell you.

So if the HQ's out, why not pick another Lone Star facility, one of the "station houses" elsewhere in the sprawl? The Cutters can't possibly have a gold team watching every one of them. Well, I've also got a reason not to do that, chummer, and it's related to my cover story. A cover isn't worth squat if anybody other than your direct control *knows* it's a cover. So that means the Lone Star street monsters and patrol cops all think—if they know of me at all—that I'm a gang-banger through and through, run to Seattle to avoid the big heat in Milwaukee. I'm supposed to be a fragging cop-killer, omae! Part of my cover is that I greased a patrol car full of Lone Star Milwaukee personnel—pumped three grenades into it, then cut down the two survivors as they tried to climb out of the burning wreck. That kind of background builds credibility and rep in gangland, and it also explains why I'm not still in Milwaukee if I had such a good time there. What it doesn't do is endear me to cops.

If I were to drop in on one of the "station houses" and tell the local yokels to phone thus-and-so extension at HQ and tell whoever answers, "Larson's here," they're not going to do it without trying to idee me first. They idee me through the computer and, bing, up it comes—"cop killer," various wants and warrants out, armed and considered very dangerous, etcetera etcetera drekcetera.

So what do the local yokels do? Would they phone the extension I give them? Like frag they would. They'd simply toss me in the can for a good, long time until I could be shipped back to Milwaukee to face charges. And that would be if I was very lucky. What's more likely is that the Lone Star Seattle street monsters will live up to the rep they've got all across the continent, and arrange to have me "shot while trying to escape." I'm not farcing you, that's the way they do things. Sure, if I had a badge or idee card or fragging Lone Star decoder ring or something, it'd be different. But you don't carry that kind of drek undercover. I've got nothing to identify me but a little data that a street rat wouldn't know. But for that to work, someone's got to listen to me before trying to cap me off.

No, thanks. I think I'll go through channels, if it's all the same to you.

In the meantime I've got four-plus hours to kill, and my body's screaming for sleep. With my brain fogged like this, I know I'll start making mistakes if I don't get some rest. Right now. But where? The Wenonah's out, and showing up at a flophouse hotel might attract too much of the wrong kind of attention. (How tough would it be for Blake to spread the word to all back-alley dosses in the sprawl—there aren't that many of them, after all—saying to call such and such a number if a slag matching my description shows up, five hundred nuyen in it for you? Not tough at all.) Luckily I do have a least one contact the Cutters don't know about, and I should be able to parlay it into a doss to crash in. I find another pay phone—this one still under the Alaskan Way viaduct, but up nearer Madison—and place the call.

The phone picks up on the first ring, which surprises me. The slag I'm calling likes to get up early, I know that, but not this early. "Yes?" he says, in that clear, precise voice of his. No trace of sleep in the voice, none at all. Warning alarms go off all over again.

"It's me," I say, and hold my breath. If something's really fragged up, he'll let me know with his next few words.

"Good morning, Richard," he says, and I breathe again.

His name's Nicholas Finnigan—I don't think anybody would ever have the jam to call him Nick—and he's this dignified old fart of fifty-some, fat and balding, who carries himself through life like nothing can touch him. (The one time it did, I was there to pull his fat out of the fire, or it'd have been the last time, too.) He's a writer—a real writer, not a knowledge engineer, a dinosaur who works in linear text, words in a row, instead of hypertext. Espionage thrillers, for frag's sake. Personally I wouldn't have thought there was any market for it, but he makes out better than okay—he's got a house, an honest-to-Ghu house, near the Snohomish River and a stone's throw away from the S-S border.

I met Nicholas quite close to where I'm now phoning him—

maybe that memory subconsciously affected my choice—some six months ago. Somebody had made contact with the Cutters about buying some Gremlin man-pack SAMs, but the gang leadership had reason to believe the meet was dirty. I was leading the team whose job was to snatch the slag who came to the meet, then drag him off somewhere to sweat out of him what was really going down. (I figure Blake was suspicious that the whole deal was a Lone Star sting.)

Anyway, the meet goes down, and the slag I'm supposed to grab is this pudgy old geezer in a fragging tweed jacket, wearing *spectacles,* for Christ's sake. Nicholas Finnigan. I realized immediately this wasn't a sting, but it wasn't a clean buy either. I'd set my assets around the area, and they started moving in as soon as Finnigan showed. Apparently sensing something was going down, he was edgy and ready to bail. If he panicked and ran, I knew one of my assets would cap him.

So fragged if I didn't expose my own position and run into the open ground and wave off my troops. Then I started firing off into the dark at a whole lot of nothing, calling in the fragging clans on some innocent dumpsters. While my fellow gangers were blowing the drek out of the scenery, I hustled Finnigan out of the area and sent him on his way. When I did that—I still can't believe it—he gave me his fragging business card. Anyway, when he was clear I went back and presided over the cleanup, mocking up a cover story for Blake and crew that the meet had been dirty but the hostile overwatch team had popped early, letting the contact escape in the ensuing firefight. So sorry. Blake bought it, and that was it.

A few days later, I called the number on the business card just out of curiosity. And that's how I came to know Nicholas Finnigan. (When I reported all this to my controls at the Star, they gave me royal drek for the whole thing, of course. But frag them.)

"Morning, Nicholas," I say. I grin, and can't help adding, "Doing any more research into buying ordnance?"

He chuckles warmly. "I believe the lesson you taught me on that subject is still in force," he says. " 'Write what you know' is all very well, but I've come to accept that 'knowing' from secondary research is sufficient in some areas."

I shake my head. Finnigan always talks that way, and you've got to stick with him to the very end of his convoluted talk to know what the frag he's saying. Good guy, though. Under other circumstances, I'd enjoy him as a friend, not just as a contact. "Good to hear," I tell him. "Keep it that way, and keep out of trouble."

There's a momentary pause, and the alarms go off yet again. "Perhaps you should follow your own advice, Richard," he says slowly.

"Keeping out of trouble?"

"Yes," he says. "It seems you might need some remedial work on that."

"What's going down?" I ask, but the cold knot in my stomach is telling me I already know. How the frag did Blake or the Cutters get a line on Nicholas?

But his next words blow that train of thought off the rails. "What do you know about Lightbringer Services Corporation?" he asks me.

"What?"

"Lightbringer Services Corporation," he repeats. "I have a business card right here in front of me."

I shake my head. "Doesn't mean squat," I tell him. "Sounds like something from the Tir, though."

"The LTG number and Matrix address are local," Nicholas tells me, "yet the name does have resonances of the Land of Promise, I agree. And the rather earnest young gentleman who gave me the card was an elf."

"What 'earnest young gentleman'?" I want to know.

"The one who came here looking for you earlier this morning, Richard." His voice is casual, but I can tell he knows this is serious. "He and his two friends, who stayed in the car. He seemed very eager to learn what I knew about you." He snorts. "I think he was very disappointed to discover that was next to nothing."

"Did he believe you?" The words are out of my mouth before I know what I'm going to say.

A moment of silence on the other end, then Nicholas says slowly, "Hmm, I see. I rather think he did. Otherwise we might not be having this conversation, is that what you mean?"

I relax a little. Nicholas doesn't actually know squat about me, but fragged if I know what he's guessed. I've never told him anything, not even my cover story, and he's never asked. "What else did the elf want?"

"Well, he told me that you might find yourself in a great deal of trouble, Richard, trouble that could well be fatal. Oh, he didn't say that in so many words," he amends quickly, "but that is most certainly the inference he wished me to draw. He im-

plied that he and his friends were on the side of the angels, as
it were, and that if you were to make contact with me I should
inform them immediately. Hence the business card. I made all
the correct concerned noises, of course." He chuckles wryly. "I
really think he believed he had me gulled."

"Huh?" I blink at that. *I* know it's a setup. How does he?

Nicholas laughs again. "Oh, his lines were well-scripted,
and he delivered them very convincingly, but I've read them
before, many times. For heaven's sakes, I've *written* them.
Our elven friend was what one might call a 'blind probe'.
Anyone who's read any of my books—or any of the classics
of the genre, like Ludlum—would understand all too well. If
I were plotting this, I'd have my house watched, with sufficient assets to zero or incapacitate you should you come to
visit. I would also bug my phone, of course. You are using
a public phone, I take it?"

I blinked again. "Yes."

"Then I would suggest we keep this call short," he goes on
in the same intellectual, detached tone. "Calls are easy to trace."

He's right, and I feel my paranoia click up another notch.
But there are still things I've got to know. Normally I'd ask
specific questions, but I realize I probably don't have to with
Nicholas. "How do you read it?" I ask.

"Our friend—Pietr Taleniekov is the name on his card,
though his accent is purest sprawl—is a corporator through
and through," Finnigan states, like it's holy writ. "I would
not be surprised to find out that there is, in fact, a
Lightbringer Services Corporation in existence, and that
there is a Pietr Taleniekov on their payroll. What would further not surprise me is that the elf who spoke to me has only
borrowed that name and corporate identity.

"Still," he went on firmly, "he is a corporator with all that
implies—a 'suit,' you might call him. He and his superiors
want you, for some reason—dead or captured, I don't know
which—and they have extensive resources and sources of information, else he would never have found me. My conclusion is that you are truly in deep trouble, Richard, but I
further conclude that I have been 'compromised' as a source
of aid. I am truly sorry."

The cold fist that's squeezing my heart grips tighter.
"You're compromised again," I tell him, and my voice isn't
much more than a whisper. "You're right, they're probably
tapping your phone. They know you've warned me off."

"Very true," he says evenly, "and my only reassurance that these shadowy forces will take no action against me is that they are corporate in nature. As we all know, corporations will do nothing that has no 'percentage' for them." He chuckles again. "To quote a fine line I read somewhere, 'Revenge don't count no beans'. I wish I had written that."

"You will," I tell him. I glance at my watch—I've been on the line for three minutes and change. If there's a tap on Finnigan's line, it's time to rip this joint before the troops arrive. "Keep your head down, chummer."

"Yours also, my friend." He pauses. "Tell me about it later, if you can. It might make an entertaining book."

"You got that," I tell him and hang up. If there is a later.

There's always room for another squatter under the overpasses of the Highway 5 interchange, always another two square meters for someone else way the frag down on his luck. None of the regulars talks to newcomers, they just move out of your way—most of them, at least. With some you have to show some teeth before they back off—but you can feel the sense of kinship, the diluted, distant sense of fraternity that might almost be camaraderie if it wasn't so miserable and despairing. After my call to Finnigan, I knew I couldn't crash on his floor, just like I knew I couldn't hit a flophouse anywhere in the sprawl. I also knew I needed to sleep somewhere, and right fragging now, if I wanted to be any good to myself when I placed my next call in the sequence. The only place I could think of where I had any hope of shelter without having to worry about Lone Star patrols or curious night clerks was the squat-city under the interchange. There's always room at the bottom.

So here I am, bundled up in my leather jacket, lying on the cold fragging ground, but unable to get to sleep. There's too much drek thrashing around in my head. Pietr Talsomething, elf suit from Lightbringer fragging Services Corporation . . . like drek. Who is he and what does he want with me? Finnigan figures the elf is corp, though probably not the corp he claims, and I'll go with his reading. I don't think a Cutter, say, could impersonate a suit well enough to fool the old writer. Which corp, then?

Given one guess, I'd say the same corp—the Tir-based outfit—that met with Blake a week back, the one that sent

the delegation that included the Mr. Nemo who made my
face. Makes perfect sense that far, at least.

But how the frag did that corp track down Nicholas
Finnigan? I've never mentioned Finnigan to anyone in the
Cutters (for obvious reasons, considering how we'd met). I
did file a report with the Star, of course, describing the
aborted weapons buy, and that report did mention Finnigan
by name. (I had to do it: I had to explain why the Star
shouldn't worry about some drekheaded writer getting a little carried away
with his research into how weapons deals go down. Slot!)
But all my reports are—of course—kept very deep in the
shadows, encrypted and restricted and all that drek.

For some corp to weasel Finnigan's name out of my file
as a person I might turn to for help—frag, they'd have to be
way deep inside the Star. Very deep infiltration—deckers
digging their grubby electronic fingers into the blackest files
in the Lone Star pyramid. And that scares the living frag out
of me, let me tell you.

I've got to tell my controls at the Star. I've got to tell
them everything, from the mysterious corp contact with the
Cutters to the possibility that their own data fortress has
been compromised. (I don't know the name of the mysterious corp, but I've got to call them something. The label's
irrelevant—how about IrreleCorp?) And I've got to take into
account the possibility—no matter how slim—that this corp
might have a mole inside the Star, possibly even one of my
controls. I sigh and stare up at the underside of a highway
off-ramp, ten meters above me. If this is the kind of drek
Finnigan writes about, I'm glad I've never read any of his
books. Interlacing my fingers behind my head into some
semblance of a pillow, I close my eyes and wait for dawn.

Something whines at me and I'm bolting upright, reaching
instinctively for my H & K. Then I try to reswallow my
heart, and tell the wire to go back to sleep. The sound was
my watch alarm, which means it's 0945. It also means I actually managed to catch some sleep even though the aches in
my joints and the fog in my head seem to deny it. I check
myself over—gear and body parts—to make sure no enterprising squatter has made off with anything while I was
nulled out. Deciding that I'm intact, I hobble over to my
bike, swing aboard, and we're off again.

The rain's less now than it was yesterday, which means there are more people on the streets. Whether that's a blessing or a curse, I'm not certain. Crowds are good for hiding, but it's a knife that cuts both ways. It's harder for a hunter to spot me among a pack of people, but conversely, it's also tougher for me to make a would-be assassin before he can put a bullet into my head. Well, frag all I can do about it, so I put it out of my mind.

Another fragging phone booth, this one on Union, uphill from Highway 5, on the fringe of the "Pill Hill" region. I'm trying to grow eyes in the back of my head as I punch in another LTG number and wait. At the dulcet tones of Lone Star Personnel's automated attendant, I jam in a five-digit extension, and listen while a snythesized voice tells me, "You have reached a non-working extension." Yeah, right. It clicks at me but doesn't hang up, and I enter my five zeroes.

First comes a silence that seems to last for hours, then the phone's vidscreen lights up and I see a face I know. Shoulder-length black hair, creamy skin, eyes almost as dark as the hair—a face that you'd call beautiful if it ever showed the faintest hint of human emotion. Sarah Layton, senior manager in the Star's Organized Crime (Gangs) department, and one of my controls.

I'm a little surprised. Layton's the woman my contact sequence is intended to reach, but I'm not supposed to get her yet. There's normally one more cut-out in the sequence. She wouldn't have changed the procedure without good reason. But what the frag, I've got other things on my mind.

"What's down?" she asks, managing to cram a huge whack of cool disapproval into those two words.

I don't answer her directly, just tell her, "Get ready to receive." I slot my datachip, already prepared in its carrier, into the phone's data-access port and instruct the phone to send it. While the data's spewing through the Matrix, I scan the people passing on the sidewalk for any face that might be taking too much interest in my actions. Within seconds the phone beeps, and I know my report's been filed.

"Scan it," I tell Layton before she can say anything. "Show the others, get them to scan it too. I want a teleconference, all of you on the line." I check my watch again. "Make it eleven-thirty. That should be enough time. This relay." And I'm off the line and on my way out of the booth before she can even open her mouth to bitch about it.

11

This really isn't the kind of conversation you want to have in a fragging phone booth right out on the fragging street. But there are some times when you just don't have any choice.

Yes, *another* phone booth, this one without chewing gum or anything to cover the vid pickup. For this call, I want to see and be seen.

The phone's vid display is in split-screen mode, showing four distinct "panes." Three contain faces, and one's blank in case we need to show data or other visuals. I know all three faces, and if anyone I don't know shows up, I'm out of there so fast I'll leave a vacuum behind me.

In the top left is Sarah Layton. The slag next to her is about the same age—late forties, I'd guess—but nowhere near as well preserved: thinning, graying hair, bags under his eyes like an old hound-dog. That's Vince McMartin. Below Sarah is "the White Flash," one Marcus Drummond. He's a decade younger than the other two, a real burner of a corporate warrior, climbing the old ladder fast enough to avoid the knives constantly directed at his back. Thin and sallow, with eyes that don't miss a fragging thing. His hair's cropped almost buzz-cut short, and it's pure white. (For a moment his hair reminds me of the elf goddess with the Tir corp delegation, and I check Drummond's ears. Nope, no points.)

"I know a teleconference is unusual," I say in response to Drummond's last comment, "but it's necessary."

Sarah Layton cuts in, her voice like a scalpel. "There's nothing in your report to warrant it."

"Not everything's in my report," I tell them. "I didn't have time to bring it up to date."

"Well?" That from hound-dog McMartin.

"The Star's penetrated." I say it flatly, for maximum effect. "Your data integrity's compromised."

The three exchange glances, and by the way their eyes move I realize Layton and Drummond are in the same room, while they're talking to McMartin by phone. Their faces and eyes don't show any shock, but all three are hardened professionals who won't let emotion mar their unshakable façades.

"How?" Layton wants to know.

So I tell them. I've already described the delegation from the Tir corp in the report, but I add Nicholas Finnigan's mysterious visitors from my "IrreleCorp." I don't have to point out the significance of the fact that IrreleCorp (or whoever) knew about Finnigan and guessed I'd turn to him for help—I can see it in the combined gaze of six very steady, very perceptive eyes.

When I'm finished there's silence for a moment, then McMartin wants to know, "You're sure you didn't tell anybody else?" From the glances the other two shoot him, it's obvious they consider even this amount of confirmation redundant. Pros—definitely pros.

But I reassure him on the point anyway. "Like I said, nobody. Just you, in one of my regular reports. You've been penetrated."

"Yes," Layton says slowly.

And realization strikes like a bullet. "You know," I blurt out.

I can almost hear the steel shutters slam shut behind three pairs of eyes. Faces go expressionless, like robots.

They know. What I'm telling them is yesterday's news. If anything, it's confirming something they'd hoped wasn't true . . . or maybe proving that the penetration they've already discovered is more far-reaching than they initially feared. Frag. I want all the details, but I know better than to ask for them. These three are very much into need-to-know, and I don't or they'd have told me already.

So I set the whole thing aside, and come back to my main reason for calling. "I want to come into the light." (A hundred years back, I'd probably have said "in from the cold.")

There's no exchange of glances this time, there's no need for it. A brain-dead trog would have figured it out from the drek in my report. The White Flash nods his head slowly, and I see that he's the spokesperson for this part of the conference. "That is . . . understandable," he allows. "Understandable, but impossible at the moment."

"Why?" I ask. Not chill, not pro, but by frag I want to know.

If anything, his face goes even more cold-fish. "You know I can't discuss that with you," he tells me.

Frag this need-to-know bulldrek! That's what I want to say, but I keep it buttoned. What I actually say is, "I find that hard to accept," in a chill, steel-hard voice that sounds scary to my own ears.

But old Drummond isn't fazed in the slightest. "Acknowledged," he says with a curt nod. "Yet the facts are the facts. We can't be seen reacting to ... certain events ... in any way."

That's enough of a clue for me to fill the rest in mentally. The Star has big trouble of some kind, and these three know it. Maybe it's limited to the data penetration I thought I was cuing them to. But maybe the penetration is only a little piece of a bigger picture (charming thought). Whatever, the corp's senior suits—including Layton, Drummond, and McMartin, but almost certainly not limited to them—are doing everything they fragging can to keep the lid on. They can't let out the slightest hint that anything at all is out of the ordinary.

Hint to who? Lots of people, chummer—there are lots of people interested in finding chinks in the Lone Star armor, for whatever reason. Start with the Cutters themselves—and every other gang in the city. Ditto the yaks, the Cosa Nostra, the Seoulpa rings, the triads, the tongs ...

Toss the megacorps into the mix, too, for diverse reasons. Most corps view Lone Star as an enemy or rival. If they're into illegal drek, they'd be thrilled to find a weakness or other kind of lever against the cops chasing them. And even if some corps aren't into illegal drek, they're still in competition—in one way or another—with the big business combine that is Lone Star Security Corporation (Knight Errant comes immediately to mind).

Now check out the political ramifications. The Star holds a contract with the Seattle metroplex government to provide police services to the city, neh? How would the government—in the person of cranky Governor Marilyn Schultz, for example—react to information that the Star has some big fragging hole in its data security or anywhere else? It's business, omae. I don't know what the metroplex government pays the Star each year for services provided, but if said government can shave a couple of points off the contract because it knows the Star's hurting, it'll sure as drek do it.

Besides, Governor Schultz is a politico, and politicos have enemies. What kind of edge would it give one of Schultz's rivals if he found out—and could prove—that good old Marilyn had put the policing of the entire metroplex in the hands of a corporation that's fundamentally fragged-up? You got that, omae, a *big* fragging edge. If word of that got out, how might Schultzy react? By coming down hard and showing she's got jam, by re-negotiating the contract with the Star, or axing it once and for all.

Yeah, I think I get why Drummond and the rest of the suit squad are trying to keep the lid on the garbage can bolted down real tight. But it doesn't make me feel any better at the moment.

"I scan it," I tell Drummond, "but that doesn't mean you can't bring me in. Frag, my cover's blown, that's reason enough, isn't it? There doesn't have to be any connection—any connection at all—with the data penetration or any other drek. I'm hung out to dry out here."

For an instant I think I see something that might almost, maybe, be empathy and understanding in the White Flash's steely eyes. Then it's gone. "Acknowledged," he says again, "but still unacceptable. For reasons I'm not going to discuss on a non-sterile line. Think it through, Larson. You'll understand."

I nod slowly. I think I do understand, and that understanding makes the creeping feeling down my spine even colder and stronger.

I jumped to a big conclusion, didn't I? That Mr. Nemo made me, and that's why my cover's blown and the Cutters want my cojones for paperweights. Make sense, sure it does. And if that's the case, the White Flash has no reason not to pull me in.

But look at it from another angle, and try this on for size. My cover was blown, yes, but not by Mr. Nemo. Sure we recognized each other, but it was because he was standing in line waiting to get in the last time I got tossed out of Club Penumbra or some fragging thing. He didn't tell Blake I was a Star op, because he didn't know.

So, apart from someone who recognizes me and knows I'm with the Star, who could hose my cover? Why, someone rifling through the Lone Star secure database with his ghostly electronic fingers, that's fragging who. Makes perfect sense . . . I think. Or am I missing something here?

Frag, I'll worry about that later. Worry about all the little paranoid twists and intrigues when I'm not walking the streets waiting to see who it is who eventually gets to geek me. The fact of the matter is that the Star isn't going to bring me into the light, not right now, and I've got to work around that fact.

So, "Acknowledged," I spit back at Drummond. Understanding his reasoning doesn't mean I have to like it, or him. "When?"

Again the three suits exchange glances, and it's Layton who replies. "Thirty-six hours at the outside," she tells me. "More likely twenty-four."

"Things'll be stable by then?" I want to know.

Maybe it's a smile that quirks her lips a fraction of a millimeter, or maybe it's a bad bit in the datastream. "Stable enough," she says flatly. Okay, so they've got some counter-op going to combat the penetration, that's what it's got to mean. Go to it mightily and with a fragging will, say I.

"Keep in touch," Drummond says (like I'm not going to). "Make it every six hours, give or take five minutes."

I glance at my watch—1134—and mentally log the next callback for 1730. "Got it," I tell them. "This relay?"

Again the exchange of glances, then McMartin gives me the LTG number and security code for another relay and cutout. "It's a priority override," he tells me. "Your call will reach us no matter where we are or what we're doing."

"Got it chipped," I tell them. "Later." And I break the connection.

Six hours, from 1130 to 1730. A blink of an eye, priyatel, right? Just kick back and drink a couple of soykafs. Hit a bar and get blasted. Get a fragging massage, maybe. The afternoon's gone like *that*.

Except when you know the Cutters have every fragging asset on the street out looking for you, not to mention some unidentified corp with lines deep into the Star's data fortress. That changes the situation pronto. Every fragging move turns into a brain-buster: Do the Cutters know I've got a tendency to hang in a certain kind of place? Does my Star personnel file mention I've had contacts with thus and so fixer? If the answer is "yes," forget it. Someone could be on the spot watching and waiting, ready to blow my brains out. Makes for one long fragging afternoon, omae.

I end up spending most of the early part tooling up and down Highway 5, on the theory that the odds are real fragging slim that somebody's going to spot me there. Gives me plenty of time to think, but it feels like my brain's stuck in a groove, going around and around a limited cycle of thoughts. Like, for some reason I can't shake the thought that Mr. Nemo—the whole Tir-corp delegation thing—is an important piece of the puzzle. Frag knows why, but my gut keeps telling me that's the way it's got to be. If I can find out more about what's going down there—which corp it is, why they're interested in the Cutters, what the deal is, that kind of drek—I might better understand just what the frag is going on. That's the way it feels, at least, and I long ago learned to trust my feelings.

But how the frag do I dig up that kind of scan? I'm no technomancer—I'm more at home on the physical streets of the sprawl than the virtual highways and byways of the Matrix. Oh, sure, I can use a 'puter, who can't? But logging onto UCAS Online, instructing a telecom to transfer calls, or using a pocket 'puter or a phone with a data port to buy Seahawks tix is very different from digging up covert dirt on corp activity, trust me on that one. It takes very special talent. Since I don't have it, I've got to hire it or acquire it elsewhere.

Check the biz listings under "Research Consultants" next time you're online, and you'll find a drekload of people who claim to have that talent. Phone up one of these slags, tell 'em what you want to know, transfer cred, and just wait for them to come up with something, null persp. Works just great if what you're digging for is stuff that nobody wants to keep secret—like the current, up-to-the-minute population of Seattle, or the price of tea in China, or whatever. Hire a competent researcher and let 'em rip.

It gets more fun when the data you're after is more on the shadowy side of the street. Obviously, that kind of drek is tougher to find and takes a more talented datasnoop to snag in the first place. (Like, say, the same slag who got you a current quotation on Chinese tea futures might get himself brain-cooked trying to dig up deep background on MCT's exec veep.) Plus you've got to start worrying about the reliability and motives of the datasnoop you hire. I know for a fact that Lone Star has "personal agreements" with an indefinite number of datasnoops out there, and every other corp worthy of the name has got to be doing the same thing.

What do these personal agreements entail? It varies, probably. Some datasnoops will, as a matter of course, provide wrong answers to anyone asking questions about the corp that's got them on the string. Others will simply stall while they pass the word back to the corp that someone's asking prying questions about them. I can't believe that every registered datasnoop is on every corp's string, and there might even be one or two out there not on anyone's string, but finding someone who will give you straight answers and not rat you out to the corp you're interested in becomes a real crapshoot.

That's why personal relationships are so important in this kind of deal. If it's "black" data you're after, you don't just go to the LTG listings and pick a name at random. You go to a decker or datasnoop or researcher or whatever who you know and trust—somebody you've got a relationship with, a relationship you've built up over time. If you don't have a relationship with a decker, you go through a fixer you trust. Networking, omae, it all comes down to networking.

I've got a network, a good one: a couple of fixers, a fence or two, a decker, even a shadow doc. Or, more like it, I *had one*. Some of them I met through the Cutters, the others through the Star. And that means that one or another of the two "agencies" out to get me—the Cutters and my IrreleCorp—know about every single fragging one of them. I might get answers to the questions I ask, but is somebody paying the people giving me answers big cred to lie to me? The conclusion's simple, no matter how much it sticks in my craw: I don't have a network I can trust. Frag this paranoia drek, it's bad for the health.

But, as I rumble back and forth along Highway 5, I'm getting more and more obsessed with the idea of tracing the Tir connection. Time seems to be moving even more slowly than before. If the span from 1300 to 1330 felt more like a couple of (subjective) hours, then 1730 seems a fragging lifetime away. I can't shake the conviction I've got to do something.

So I go over it again, and again, and *again*. What resources can I use? Is there someone I'm forgetting, someone not in the Star's computer and not known to the Cutters who I can trust and who'd be willing to do me a favor?

Or maybe it could be someone who *is* in the Star's computer, but who's got the jam to conceal the fact that they're helping me. Someone like Cat Ashburton. Yeah, she could do it with one cerebral hemisphere tied behind her back.

I know I'm grinning, because the cold air on my front teeth makes them feel like they're about to split. Yeah, that's the ticket. Cat Ashburton's got the skills, the access to the necessary equipment, and the jam to hide this kind of inquiry from outside scrutiny. The one question is, will she do it? Like they say, there's only one way to find out.

I lean the big bike over and roar down the next off-ramp into the heart of South Tacoma, scanning for yet another fragging public phone.

12

I really need to sit down on something that's not a bike for awhile, and that's why I decide to take the risk and use the pay phone in this greasy-chopstick noodle house on South Sixty-fourth Street and Fife. The lunch crowd—mainly construction workers, seriously chromed and bulging grotesquely with vat-job muscle, who spend their days on the high steel of the fast-growing skyrakers—are on their way out, and I have to squeeze past them to get in. (Not *push* past them; your typical heavy-duty construction worker could reduce me to a spot of grease with one finger.) The pay phone's at the back, in a small transplas-fronted cubicle with a door and a seat.

The air's heavy with the reek of recycled frying fat. As it fills my nose, my brain gets the message, my stomach starts twisting and clenching, and I could suddenly eat one of the tables. How long since I've last eaten? Coming up on twenty-four hours, I'd guess. Considering how fast stress burns energy, I'm probably already digesting muscle tissue.

A waiter—a little Chinese guy in a jumpsuit that used to be white—approaches tentatively. "Yah?"

I glance at the list of specials on the wall. "Yakisoba and gyoza," I tell him without breaking stride. "Make that two gyoza. Back here." And I point to the phone booth. He nods quickly and scurries off.

The phone's all in one piece, I'm glad to see. I slump down in the seat and shut the door firmly behind me. There's a polarization control for the electrosensitive crystals in the transplas, and I set it for one-way. I can see out—not too well, because the calibration's way off—but (theoretically) nobody can see in. (I read somewhere that far infrared isn't affected by the crystals, but if someone packing that much tech's close enough for it to matter, I'm dead anyway.) I take a deep breath to calm myself, to slow down the pulse that's racing in my ears, and check my watch again.

Where's Cat Ashburton going to be at 1346 on a Tuesday—no, Wednesday—afternoon? She's in the Management Information System side of things, which at the Star is a round-the-clock every-day-of-the-year department. The senior suits work banker's hours—1000 to 1630, with at least an hour for lunch—but the middle managers like Cat get ground hard, doing shift-work. In other words, there's no way of knowing if she's in the office or not.

I'm gearing myself up to do battle with the Star's receptionists—all part of some conspiracy to misdirect all important phone calls, I'm fragging sure of it—when I decide to try her at home. The odds are much longer, but it's one less hassle if they pan out. I key in 114 for directory assistance, then when the synthesized voice starts yammering, I enter the "special functions" code known to all Lone Star employees (and to most of Seattle's shadow community as well). With "special functions" engaged, the directory search engine looks through more useful files than just the standard name-LTG-address drek 114 usually gives you. I key in my search string—in English, "Get me the number for one Ashburton, Catherine, age range twenty-five to thirty-five, employed by Lone Star, and make it snappy"—and hit the XQT key. A second later the screen flashes, "1 hit(s)", and asks for a second code, this one an authorization to reassure the poor machine that it's okay to give me what I want. I rattle in the character string, and see Cat's number displayed. LTG 5206 (15-2534)—that's Tacoma, Menlo Park to be exact. Cat must be doing well for herself. Dossing down in that part of town isn't cheap.

There's a knock on the transplas door. My reflexes are jazzed so high that I've got my H & K out, and damn near almost squeezed off a burst before I see it's the waiter with my lunch. He doesn't twitch or faint or go for his own heat, so at least that's some reassurance the one-way polarization works. The H & K goes back into its holster; I slide open the door and grab the fiberform tray covered with steaming food from the waiter's hands. He opens his mouth—to ask for payment, probably—but I slam the door shut before he can get out the first word. Through the one-way transplas I see him shifting uncomfortably from foot to foot, apparently trying to decide whether to knock again. Then maybe he figures discretion is the better part, and all that drek, and off he slouches.

I take a minute to cram some gyoza and noodles into my face—hot enough to scorch my tongue, but who gives a frag, it's (synthesized) food—then I tell the pay phone to call Cat's number. The vidscreen shows the normal shifting colors and patterns, supposedly designed by psych-wonks to calm people down so they don't trash the phone while they're waiting for the connection to be made. Then the status bar along the bottom of the display flashes CONNECTED. The screen clears, and there's Cat—copper hair that looks like it's polished, big round eyes, a polite if distant smile. "You have reached. . . ."

I don't listen to the rest of the spiel. Frag, a recording. I reach for the key to disconnect . . .

And the image changes. The perfect, glossy image of Cat vanishes, to be replaced by a darkened room. A head moves into the shot, too close to the pickup and slightly out of focus. The same copper hair, but now it looks like a bird's nest. Same eyes, but puffy with sleep and barely open. "Mmm," Cat says. Her voice catches in her throat. "Hoozit?"

"It's me, Cat," I say, confirming that the pay phone's vid pickup is on.

Her eyes open a little further, maybe even enough to see out of them. "Mmm," she repeats. Then, "Rick, 'choo?" I nod. She moves a little further from the phone pickup, and I see a little more of her, in better focus too. I guess she sees my grin, because she glances down and mutters, "Drek!" Then I see a pale-skinned arm reach for the phone. The screen's filled with shifting colors and patterns again, and I chuckle. Some things never change, and one of those is that Cat Ashburton sleeps in the raw.

Less than a minute later the screen clears again. Cat's got on a fluffy white bathrobe, and her hair looks a little less like a Medusa's head. Her full lips are quirked up in an embarrassed smile, but her eyes are warning me not to push things too far.

That's chill with me; I'm not in the headspace to play the double entendre game anyway. So, "Late shift?" I ask.

"Mmm, midnight to noon," she tells me. Which means she's been down less than two hours at the most. Make it an

hour. I've got to keep that in mind. She might not be tracking as well as normally.

"Twelve hour shifts?"

She nods. "It's new, some out-of-house consultants say
it'll improve efficiency." Her voice tells me all I need to
know about her opinion of that.

"Tough."

She gives the kind of low, throaty chuckle I remember and
still replay from time to time in my dreams. "Tough?
They're ball-busters, cobber." She pauses, and I see her eyes
grow a little clearer. "What's down, omae?" she asks, a hint
of concern in her tone. "You're not calling just to be socia-
ble. Or you'd better not be . . ."

I smile, but I know the expression's as tired as I am. "Not
a social call," I confirm, "I'm in some heavy drek here."

Cat runs a hand through her hair, a gesture I remember as
clearly as the chuckle. "Tell me."

"I'm blown," I admit. "Big-time, priyatel, bolshoi big."

"You got made by a random contact?"

I'm glad that's her first assumption, not that I slotted up
somewhere along the line. "Maybe, but I'm starting to
doubt it."

"Tell me," she says again.

So I do. From the start, in all the gory detail. Frag, I know
Drummond would have my nuts for cuff links if he knew,
but Drummond can eat drek. It's my hoop that's out here
hanging in the breeze, not his. Anyway, Cat's Star. And our
past history probably isn't in the Lone Star Seattle computer
system—if anywhere, it's back in the Milwaukee files.
(Does it sound like I'm trying to rationalize something? You
got that, omae.)

Cat's a good listener, but she doesn't let that get in the
way of asking what she needs to refine her understanding or
of firing out comments that force me to elaborate or look at
things from a new angle. While I'm babbling, I also manage
to cram the gyoza and yakisoba down my yam. By the time
I'm reaching the end of the story, I see the Chinese waiter
doing the old approach-avoidance thing outside the phone
booth. So I tell Cat, "Hold one," blank the screen, open the
door, and shove the empty plates out into his hands. "One
more plate of gyoza," I tell him, both to get him out of my
hair and because I'm still ready to eat my own flesh. As he
races off, I bring Cat back from limbo.

When I'm done with the story, she doesn't say anything right away. I know she's sliding the pieces of the puzzle around, trying to get them to make different shapes. Cat's good at that, always was. Eventually she shakes her head with a wry grin. "How come every time you get yourself into drek it's up to your eyeballs?" she asks.

I shrug. "Talent, I guess."

"Huh." She pauses again. "You're assuming the Tir corp and the penetration of the Star are connected?"

Again I shrug. "Yeah, of course . . ." And then I stop, because I see what she's thinking. I'd automatically assumed there was a link. An unstated, unexamined assumption, based, I suppose, on the fact that Nemo and I recognized each other and that my cover was blown relatively soon after the delegation's visit. But now that I think about it, there doesn't have to be any link at all. Frag, this kind of drek is too much of a mind-bender for a simple soul like me.

I give Cat a slightly embarrassed smile. "Search me, Cat," I say. "I don't know anymore."

She smiles back. "Zero it. I'm just playing with ideas." Her face goes dead serious again. "What do you want me to do, omae? You're not calling just to bounce ideas off me?"

"You got that," I tell her. "I need a nova-hot datasnoop, and one I can trust not to sell me out or frag me over."

"The Tir connection?"

"That's it," I tell her. "What's the buzz on the Matrix? Which Tir corps are trying to increase their presence in the sprawl? And which ones have a rep for dealing with gangs and organized crime? And what's their biz?"

Cat chuckles. Then, "You're not asking much, are you, omae? But why not just let it slide?" she asks in a different tone. "You'll be pulled in soon, and then you can do this kind of drek in sanction. Why push it now?"

Yeah, well that's a fragging good question. All I can do is shrug. "'Cause my gut tells me to, Cat," I say slowly. "That's all I can tell you. Something's telling me it's important, and anyway . . ." I trail off.

"And anyway," she finishes for me, "it's your case. Right?"

"I guess." I glance away. Looking at it logically, it doesn't make sense to do any digging now. Come into the light, then use everything the Star's got to search for the connection.

Don't waste time and effort that could better be invested in keeping my skin intact.

But just letting it ride goes against every fragging fiber of my personality (such as it is). I've always been the kind of slag who can't leave stones unturned, who's got to roll them over and poke around with a stick at the creepy-crawlies underneath.

No. That's not the whole truth either, is it? I've got to have something—some gem of data, some lead, some answer—that I can bring in with me when Layton and company bring me into the light. Something I can hand over to them with a smug grin, something they didn't know about. Something to prove I'm not just a frag-up who can't keep his cover intact.

I derail that train of thought right there. Cat's eyes are on me, and I get the uncomfortable feeling she can see the way my mind's working. So I put on a solid, emotionless biz mask, and meet her gaze directly. "Can you do it, Cat? I know it's against regs to use the Star's databanks for private drek like this . . ."

A pause as she thinks about it, then a warm smile spreads across her face. "I can do it," she confirms, "and we both know how much you really care about the regs. Have you got a time-frame for this? And don't tell me 'soonest,' or I'm going to hang up."

I don't answer immediately, my brain trying to come up with a guess about how long this could take her. After a second or two I shrug. "What can I tell you, Cat? Soon, priyatel."

She nods. "I've got two days off, so I can push it after I get some sleep. Depending on just what's going down, I might be able to give you something preliminary by . . . midnight, maybe?"

"That's better than I expected," I admit.

She shrugs that off with a smile. "I take it there isn't a number where I can reach you," she says dryly.

"Right in one," I confirm. "I'll call you."

"I might not be in," she reminds me. "I do have a life, omae." She thinks for a moment, then, "I'll log everything I find as I find it," she says. "I'll file it on my telecom under 'Special Favors.' How about that?" I nod. "I'll encrypt and lock it," she goes on. "Give me a password, something you'll remember."

A perfect opening. I stifle a grin. "Something I'll never forget," I say earnestly, then use the phone's keypad to enter the word "Mayflower." Cat blushes faintly, a factoid that I file away for future use. One never knows, do one?

13

Midnight in the sprawl. Do you know where your kids are?

A good number of them seem to be hanging out in and around Denny Park, Mr. and Mrs. Seattle, in the shadow of the Space Needle. Chipped up or gooned out, frying their brains with chemicals or electronics, trying to escape from what we laughingly call reality. Somebody once told me Denny Park was refurbished a few years back to be a kind of friendly family park, somewhere to take the kiddies of an afternoon or a lover of an evening. Doesn't look like it worked worth a damn.

Anyway, that doesn't matter to me at the moment. For the first time in a long time, I'm feeling good.

Why? I'm coming into the light, that's why. Layton and her little friends have finally come through for me. About time, too. I was starting to feel like the Flying fragging Dutchman or the Wandering fragging Jew, hopelessly roaming through the world looking for safe harbor or haven or some slotting thing.

As we agreed, I called in at 1730, and got told a big load of nothing. Still working on the matter, can't help you out, go off and play, blah blah blah . . . oh, and phone back later. So I phone back later—from the only functioning public phone on Denny Way, it looks like—expecting much the same runaround.

Surprise, surprise, surprise. "The way's clear to bring you in," Layton told me as soon as she answered the phone. "Hold for details."

Hold I did, and sure enough the details were forthcoming. Not that they made much sense, at least not from my standpoint. I guess what I'd expected was to receive the address of somewhere I could hunker down for awhile—a safe house that wasn't listed in the Star's databases—until other arrangements could be made. The fact that Layton and crew

were laying on something a tad more elaborate hinted that
there's even more to this frag-up than meets the eye. Just
what kind of drek is the Star going through? Oh well, not
my biz. I'm coming in, and that's all the matters at the moment.

Not immediately, but no surprise there. So much that has
to do with Lone Star is "hurry up and wait." I don't have to
wait long, however, and that's what counts: three hours or
so. By the time the sun's up again, I should be into the light,
even be able to sleep. (What a concept!)

In the meantime, Cat said to give her a shout at midnight
or thereabouts, and it's pretty fragging close. So I key her
number into the same pay phone I used to contact Layton,
and wait for the connection. It's not good fieldcraft, placing
two calls from the same location, but frag it. I get the recorded message again, and this time Cat doesn't break in
live. That's chill. I execute a "break" sequence and request
access to the file called Special Favors. When the system re-
quests a password, I type in "Mayflower," and I'm in.

I probably needn't have bothered. Looks like so much
drek in there; just a list of names without any kind of anno-
tation. Crystalite, Griffin, Telestrian, Marguax, and Starbright. None of the names means anything to me. What the
frag are they? Corps? Individuals? People Cat's already dug
up on or leads she's planning to pursue? Frag knows, and
nothing I can do about it. I guess it doesn't really matter in
the long run, anyway.

For the hundredth time I wonder why Layton and chummers decided to go this route to bring me in. I know they
must have a good reason, and if I can scope out what it is,
that might tell me more about what kind of deep drek the
Star seems to be in. That's how I scan it, at least. I know
Drummond would tell me I've got no "need-to-know" on
this one, but sometimes, "*want*-to-know" is enough of a
driving force. Mentally, I go through it again, trying to work
it out.

What's unusual about this whole scam is the level of personnel involvement. The way it's coming down, according
to Layton, is that I'm supposed to keep an eye on the south
end of Montlake Bridge—the single span that crosses the
Lake Washington Ship Canal between U-Dub and the
Montlake District—during the period from 0255 to 0305.

There'll be a car with a single driver who'll make contact using "generally accepted fieldcraft principles" (a high-toned way of saying "the same old drek"). I get in the car and we're off.

Layton also came right out and said there'd be at least one exchange of vehicles along the way. That surprised me on a couple of levels: one, that she thought it was necessary to say, and another, that she'd even tell me, but ours is not to reason why drekcetera. Why the pickup and why the vehicle exchange? It doesn't make any sense unless I'm hotter—*much* hotter—than I think or unless the penetration into the Star's even deeper than I figured. Frag, scary. The Star's always been the one constant in my (professional) life, the one thing I could trust and depend on when I was undercover. It rattles me that what I thought of as a solid rock foundation might actually be JelloSoy . . .

I snort, and shove those thoughts into the "To Obsess About Later" file. It's 0251 and the rain's stopped, but there's a nasty, thin wind blowing from the east across Lake Washington and Union Bay, and I'm fragging freezing. At least Layton chose a good spot for the pickup. There are a dozen good overwatch positions from which I can see the south end of Montlake Bridge without being spotted myself. (Too often, desk jockeys pick spots that offer one and only one place you can hang. If the meet gets hosed, that single spot turns into a death trap.)

I'm already hunkered down in the best of the lot, a small booth outside a restaurant where I figure the valet parking slots hang during the day. Without exposing myself significantly, I can see more than halfway north across the bridge, as far south as the overpass that crosses Highway 520, and a full block both east and west along East Shelby Street. The only kick I've got against it as an overwatch "nest" is that the fragging place isn't heated. No matter where I crouch, there's always an icy draft blowing down the back of my neck.

It's 0300 on the button—the exact middle of the specified time-span—when I see headlights coming south across the bridge. It's a single car, cruising slowly, moving not much faster than a person at a walk. As it hits the end of the bridge, the headlights flick off, leaving only the sidelights. Under the cold blue-white of the streetlamps, I see the bulbous and unmistakable shape of a Leyland-Zil Tsarina pull over to the curb at the corner of Montlake Boulevard and Shelby. It flashes its headlights once, then all the lights go out. I hear the high-pitched whine of its multifuel turbine spooling down, then a hydraulic hiss as the front and rear canopies open.

The L-Z Tsarina's a weird car, which is probably what you'd expect from an English-Russian coproduction, but I've got to admit it's a good choice for this kind of op. It's a two-seater—a pure one, not a two-plus-two or even a two-plus luggage. The passenger compartment has room for two, and only two, people: the passenger in the front, the driver slightly above and to the rear (the same seating configuration as in a helicopter gunship, a chummer told me once). The point is, with the two canopies open, there's no way or place for someone in the car to hide. Thus, no drek about someone ducking down in the passenger seat out of sight. The ambient light reveals the dark shape of one person in the car, a small figure sitting in the driver's seat. I'm not figuring this as any kind of setup, but I decide to wait and watch another minute or two anyway just because it's not chill to be overeager in this kind of situation. Then a vanity light flicks on inside the driver's compartment and I see who it is.

I rise to my feet, ignoring the way my cold, stiff, knee joints crack and ache, and I jander across the street to the waiting car.

Cat Ashburton smiles up at me from the cramped confines of the Tsarina. "Going my way, sailor?" she asks.

I shake my head with a chuckle, and swing into the front seat, trying to find a comfortable position for my long legs. Down come the canopies, the engine fires up again—little more than a subliminal whir inside the car—and we're off.

The disadvantage with the Tsarina is that you can't carry on a face-to-face conversation. I'm facing straight forward out over the short, curved nose, and there's not enough room for me to twist myself around. Cat, on the other hand, has a great view of the back of my head and my incipient bald spot. Still, you make do with what you've got. At least the car's nice and warm.

"What are you doing here?" I ask her. "Are you my official ride?"

I hear her chuckle, and I wish I could see her face. "That's me, omae," she confirms. "I got the word from

Drummond. I guess he wanted someone you'd recognize, but who wasn't traceable to you, or something."

"Maybe." A mental alarm sounds, but I don't know why.

Without meaning to, Cat distracts me from that line of thought before I can pursue it further. "Did you check Mayflower?" she asks.

"Yeah, for all the good it did me. Crystalite, Griffin, and the rest—who the frag are they?"

"*What* are they," she corrects. "And what they *are* are major Tir-based corps that have no official operations in Seattle."

"What good's that?" I want to know.

"The key word's 'official'."

"So?"

Cat sighs, probably frowning at my obtuseness. "If a corp's got no official presence," she says slowly and clearly like she's talking to a newborn ork, "it makes you wonder why they've got a security presence, doesn't it, omae? It's like, if you don't have anything to guard, why have guards, neh?"

I'm too tired to think clearly—that's my story, and I'm sticking with it. "Yeah, scan," I grumble. "And all those corps have a security presence in the plex?"

"That's what the Star files say."

"Why?"

She chuckles again. "That's the big question, isn't it?" She pauses. "It's also not something you're going to find in one single record in one single database. If there's any answer at all, you'll only find it by cross-correlating a drekload of different data in a drekload of different files."

I sigh. "No go, huh? Well, thanks anyway, Cat, I owe you—"

"Damn straight you owe me," she cuts in, "but I didn't say it's impossible. Just that it's difficult."

"Oh?" I feel a slight stirring of hope. Even if there's no way I'll have my gem to hand over to Layton, McMartin, and Drummond the moment I arrive on Star territory, it'd still be a partial victory if I could present them with something significant before they find it themselves.

"Yeah, 'oh'," she says, "and do you ever owe me. I hardly got any sleep, thanks to you."

"Didn't seem to bother you much in the past," I say innocently, then go, "Ouch, drek," as she delivers a stinging rap

to the top of my head with a knuckle. I decide I hate L-Z
Tsarinas after all.

"Why don't you think with *this* for a change?" she says,
punctuating her words with another rap to the skull. Yet
there's something in her tone that tells me she's not as
slotted off as she'd like me to think. "Anyway, as I was saying ... I whomped up a couple of smartframes and demons
and sent them out to do the dirty work and the cross-
correlation. They're at it right now."

"Huh? By themselves?"

She laughs out loud at that. "You're out of date, chummer.
You don't have to actually do a datasearch anymore. You
just write a code to do it for you."

I shake my head. Sometimes I think I'd have been better
off born in the Dark Ages, like back in 1994 or some drek.
"And what do they do when they find what they're looking
for? Phone home?"

I meant it as a joke, but she just says, "You got it. They're
programmed to log all their conclusions in Special Favors
and the raw data in a couple of other files so we can cross-
check it later. Satisfied?"

"Bolshoi satisfied."

We fall silent, and in that first instant of silence I listen,
really listen, to the warning bells that have been ringing in
my skull for the past few minutes. Cat said Drummond assigned her to pick me up because there's no connection in
our records between her and me. But if there's no connection, how did he know to get in contact with her?

Oh, drek ... I draw in a breath to tell her, but it's too late,
way too late.

At that moment I see a burst of light to the left and thirty
degrees up, from the top of a low building. Yellow-red light,
like fire. The next thing I know, that fire is streaking down
toward us, an ultra-speed comet that burns an afterimage
into my visual field.

Transition.

It's like a badly cut trideo. One moment I'm sitting comfortably in the Tsarina's front seat, the next I'm sprawled
grotesquely across something hard and jagged, head down,
hoop in the air. My face is freezing, my back's scorching
hot. There are sounds in my ears, but the horrible shrieking-
ringing inside my head's too overpowering for me to make
sense of them. When I try to open my eyes, I feel the eyelids

move, but I'm still blind. I try to move, but my body's not paying attention to the messages my brain's sending it. I feel like I'm in a fragging nightmare, which suddenly sends me into a panic. Or maybe it's the turbocharged nerve-jolts of fear that do it. My legs and back spasm, and I roll over onto my right side. Something sharp and cold lances into my left buttock.

It's the pain—precise, crystalline, localized—that seems to clear the fog from my mind. I'm lying out in the road, on top of wreckage of some kind. My eyes are open, but I can't see because there's something warm and sticky in them— blood, what else? A car crash . . . Then I remember the flaming comet.

And I'm rolling—madly, over and over to the right. Away from the direction the comet came, off the wreckage, and onto the cold, wet pavement. Frag the pain, frag the fact I've got something driven deep into my ham, frag the fact that my back feels like it's on fire. If I don't react fast— now—I'm dead. Still rolling, I drag my left hand across my eyes, trying to wipe away the blood, while my right hand pulls out my H & K.

I can see again, but I'm rolling over and over so fast I can't make sense of anything. Night sky, flames, wet pavement, flames, night sky again. The ringing in my head's decreasing, and now on top of it I can just hear the roaring of flames. And a woman screaming—high, continuous, throat-ripping . . .

Then another sound, one I've heard before, a fast-paced triple concussion. Ba-ba-bam, and my face and hands are flayed with fragments of pavement. I roll again, this time getting my hands and one knee underneath me, then, with a convulsion of all my major muscle groups, I fling myself to my feet. I'm dizzy and almost go sprawling again, but I manage to keep my balance—just. An instant later I almost trip over a curb, but I turn the move into a stutter-step and cut hard to my right. Ba-ba-bam again, and a garbage container next to me turns into shrapnel. Another stutter-step, cut left, and I risk a look over my shoulder.

In the middle of the road, the main body of the Tsarina is blazing madly, the rear of it twisted and torn into some horrible kind of sculpture. Flames are leaping merrily from inside the driver's compartment. The screams have stopped, and I know that's a blessing. The front part of the car, the

portion ahead of the passenger seat, is lying a couple of meters from the rest of the wreckage—not on fire, by some
strange chance—smashed free when the impact of the missile split the Tsarina in two right at the front axle.

There's movement on top of a low building across the
way—a single figure, I'd guess—and two more on the road,
moving cautiously toward Cat and the car that's her crema-
torium. The wire takes over and I send a couple of quick
bursts their way. Just to keep them preoccupied, not with the
expectation of doing damage. I know they're armored, just
as I know who and what they are.

All that took a split second, and fragging good job. The
Mossberg combat gun across the way roars again, and this
time the triple-shot pattern's so close I can feel it.

There's a rage inside me, a terrible, burning thing I've
never experienced before. It feels almost like it's separate
from me, with its own needs and wants and personality. Just
like the wire feels sometimes, but more so. The rage wants
nothing more than to wade out into the road, emptying my
H & K into the figures—into the killers—before I'm cut
down myself. So does the wire.

But I can't do that, I can't die. Not yet. I've got things to
do, I tell myself, and the rage inside me understands that.
I've got to find out the *why,* and I've got to confirm the *who*
(though I think I've got a pretty good fragging idea), and
then I've got to pay a few less-than-social visits. Once I'm
done with that, then whoever wants to can cut me down.

I fake right, then cut left with every joule of energy in my
body. The Mossberg devastates a lamppost a good half-
dozen meters away from me, only now the SMGs are joining
in the fun. Too late. I'm down an alley, out of the well-lit
street, back into the darkness and the shadows that I know
so well. Let the Lone Star Fast Response Team troopers
clean up the mess. There'll be an accounting soon enough.

But not now.

I run on into the night.

BOOK TWO

14

Insanity. Fragging insanity!

I'm lying on a creaky, uncomfortable bed in Room 2LR in one of the drekkiest flophouses I've ever had the bad fortune to encounter. There are honk-stains on the carpet, blood-stains on the mattress, and when the heater kicks in the reek tells me a previous occupant didn't bother making the short walk down the hall to the drekker. Still, it's the closest thing I've got to home at the moment. I needed sleep and I needed the sense of security—false or not—of a roof over my head and walls to keep out the wind and rain. If it wasn't safe crashing in a flop when it was just the Cutters out after my hoop, it's even more risky now. Maybe I could have kept wandering the streets until I got so fragging tired I started making drekheaded mistakes and didn't have the mental wherewithal to compensate for them, but dossing down for a day or so seemed like the more viable alternative.

Frag knows, I didn't get that much sleep anyway. It was just short of 0430 by the time I'd boosted a car—my bike's still behind a restaurant in Montlake, assuming nobody's managed to defeat the lock and security system yet—and rolled out to the Tarislar area of Puyallup. A major selling point for this whack of turf was that it's about as far as you can get from downtown and not be in Salish-Shidhe terri-tory, but that's not all I had in mind when I headed south. Though the Cutters are everywhere, their presence in Tarislar is only minimal. Add to that the fact that Lone Star rarely patrols this elven neighborhood, and it becomes just about the safest place for me to hunker down at the moment.

Tarislar's a hole, don't let anybody tell you any different. The region between Kreger Lake and Harts Lake, it used to be a flash place to live, or so I've heard. Sometime around the turn of the century, it suddenly blossomed from a rural area into a "bedroom community," sprouting mid-rise apart-

ment blocks like fungus. Then, of course, property rates
kinda slipped a tad when Mount Rainier erupted and spewed
toxic mud and other drek over the area now called Hell's
Kitchen. They slipped even further when the prevailing
winds shifted, bringing the reek of the Kitchen—with all its
associated toxins—wafting over it. People moved out just in
time to make space for the influx of elves pouring southeast-
ward after the Night of Rage.

So that's Tarislar today, a "temporary" haven for elves
who've never been able to move elsewhere, an area of decaying buildings filled with squatters and cities of shacks
built on parks and golf courses. Charming.

Still, as I say, it was exactly what I was looking for. I
don't know why, but the Cutters have few elves among their
ranks. It could be racism, but it probably has more to do
with the dominance of elf-based outfits in Tarislar. Non-
elven gangs aren't going to make much of a dent against
that. Lone Star, too, is mostly human, and that could well be
one of the reasons for low police presence in the area—
lower, even, than the "E" level of enforcement throughout
the rest of Puyallup. Conversely, as a human, I stand out like
a fragging sore thumb in Tarislar, and everybody's going to
take note of the *celénit*—the "unevolved monkey-man"—
walking the streets. But at least the odds are against them reporting me to anyone who cares.

So, to continue, it was about 0430 when I hit Tarislar, and
close to an hour later by the time I'd found a flophouse that
would take me. I didn't have much choice, which is the only
reason I ended up at the rat-infested flea circus called The
Promise. (Promise of what? Bed bugs, or a nice skin rash
maybe?) Into bed by 0540, call it, for twelve-plus hours of
blissful, uninterrupted sleep . . .

Which categorically refused to come. Oh sure, I did drift
off now and again—for five or ten minutes at a time, before
the nightmare woke me up. The same nightmare, every
fragging time, a replay of the ambush on Montlake Boulevard. The missile hitting the car, the FRT troopers on the
roof and advancing across the street. Cat's screams as she
burns alive. Sometimes the car ruptures under the missile's
impact, throwing me free. Sometimes it doesn't, trapping me
inside while the flames rise up around me and Cat shrieks in
my ears and I can see the satisfied grins of the troopers as
they come forward to watch the fun . . .

I shake my head, hard. Even just remembering those nightmares is unbearable. I check my watch—1300 hours, or close enough, which means I've had seven hours of something you couldn't quite call sleep. It also means the gutterpunk elf who opened the lobby door when I pounded on it, and charged me entirely too much for a room, has had seven hours to rat out the *celén* in room 2LR to anyone who's expressed an interest. The facts that my skin's unpunctured and I'm still alone—not counting the multilegged creepy-crawlies—hints that I'm safe enough for the moment.

I sit up, slide my butt up toward the head of the bed so I can lean against the wall. My gaze settles on my black jacket, hung over the back of the room's single chair. The back of the jacket's scorched, the synthleather delaminated and blistered in places by extreme heat. All I can figure is that the fireball from the exploding missile spread forward through the passenger compartment, was deflected downward by Cat's raised seat, and hit me in the small of the back to lick up toward my shoulders. Same with the shock wave, except it probably "echoed" in the space under Cat's seat, delivering enough energy to crack the monocoque at its weakest point, the front wheel-wells. Pure luck I'm still alive, then. Luck that favored me and deserted Cat.

The rage churns and twists inside me like a live thing made of hot metal, but it's under better control now. It's not going to go away—I don't *want* it to go away, not till it's satisfied—but at the moment it feels more like a useful tool. Something I can control, whose power I can channel and focus, instead of it controlling me. That's what I hope, at least. It's an extension of something they taught us in the Academy: get angry when you have to, but *use* the anger. I don't think my instructors were thinking about anything like this, but the result's the same.

The Star. Thinking about the Academy rips off the . . . well, call it the mental equivalent of a scab over a painful train of thought. My eyes burn, and my throat tightens like someone's got me by the windpipe.

The Star's betrayed me, there's no other way of reading it. They've put me "beyond salvage". Like the Cutters, Lone Star has decided that Richard Larson is "out of sanction," to be eliminated with extreme prejudice. And like them, the Star sent out the equivalent of a hit team to fry me. And, still like with the Cutters, I recognized them—after the fact. The biggest difference from the gang is that the Lone Star attempt brought with it a higher level of collateral damage than I really want to remember right now . . .

Why, frag it? *Why?* The questions parallel those I wracked my fragging brains with after Marla and friends tried to scrag me at the Wenonah. Why did the Star decide I must die? And why did it have to be an ambush? Frag, they could have brought me in, debriefed me, then fragging poisoned me, if they had a mind to.

No, wait, I'm missing something here, aren't I? I'm talking about "them" and "the Star" as if it's a definite, known group. But is it? By frag I think so. I think it's Layton, Drummond, and McMartin, that fragging unholy triumvirate who strung me along and kept me from coming into the light, then set up the parameters of the meet. Cat even said it was Drummond who sent her out to make the pickup. Doesn't that lock it in? Doesn't it prove Drummond's fragging complicity?

It's so tempting to say "yes," to pick out a nice, defined well-known target for my hatred. But it's not necessarily the case. Remember, we're dealing with someone—or some faction—that has penetrated the Star's data fortress, that has gotten in deep enough to dig up my connection with Nicholas Finnigan. That kind of penetration gives them more power and control over Star operations than I really care to think about.

Like, try this as a possible scenario. Drummond and crew want to set up a meet. They figure I'm going to be jumpy—a good guess—particularly after being kept dangling for a day, and decide to send someone I'll recognize and trust. Drummond knows the Seattle data fortress is compromised, so he accesses the Milwaukee files to find someone I know, and comes up with Cat. Unfortunately, IrreleCorp, or whoever, is in deeper than he thinks, and intercepts the data request—or maybe they've already got their hooks into Milwaukee anyway, it doesn't matter.

Now Drummond sends Cat out to make the pickup. The order will certainly be logged somewhere, but just as certainly the assignment log won't say anything about me. IrreleCorp, however, they're smart; they know Cat knows me, and they figure out what her assignment actually is. They now issue an order, through the computer network, to

an FRT team to set up on Montlake Boulevard near Roanoke
and take out the Tsarina expected to be heading south sometime after 0255. The rationale's probably something like
"magical terrorists, considered extremely dangerous, eliminate before they can get their first spell off." In other words,
ambush.

Despite the drek you see on the pirate trids, "shoot first,
then question the remains" isn't Lone Star SOP, and am-
bushes aren't just another assignment. The FRT team leader
would almost certainly have questioned the order, and
checked it out through various channels. Unfortunately,
those "various channels" would all have been electronic and
computer-mediated, and IrreleCorp could have given the
correct verifications and authorizations to set the team
leader's little mind at ease that the op was kosher. Off lum-
ber the armed and armored troopers to do their bit to save
Seattle.

Boom! Say farewell to Tsarina, Rick Larson, and Cat
Ashburton. The next morning, of course, the drek's going to
hit the pot when it turns out the orders logged and verified
as coming from Drummond's office *didn't* come from Drummond at all. Much chaos, but by that point I'm safely
scragged—mission successfully accomplished.

Frag it, it holds together. It *could* have happened that way.
With deep enough computer penetration, IrreleCorp could
have turned a nice, clean pickup into an ambush. It didn't
have to be Drummond, Layton, McMartin, and the other
suits at all. Frag, just when I thought I knew who to blame.

I shake my head again. I can run through all the paranoid
options and alternatives and possibilities and probabilities
till my ears bleed, but it's not going to do any good without
hard data to help me pick and choose between them. I need
to know something—*anything*—about what's going down.
But how to go about it?

I've still got that bee in my fragging bonnet about the Tir
corp-Cutters connection. Maybe it's got nothing to do with
anything, but at the moment it feels like the only thing I can
follow up on. Everything else seems just too big, too overwhelming. (Like, how do I get some leverage on the
fragging Star?) It's like somebody told me years ago when
I was at university: "If you don't know what to do next, do
what you can." Good advice, I suppose. With a heartfelt sigh

I swing my feet to the floor and prepare myself to face the day.

I feel naked and exposed and incredibly vulnerable walking the streets of Tarislar. It's not just the way the elves glare at me with undisguised hostility or simply pretend I don't fragging exist—though that's part of it. No, it's the realization that I don't have the wheels to bug out if trouble comes looking for me. My bike's gone, and cruising in a stolen car is too much of a risk.

If anything, Tarislar by day looks even worse than Tarislar by night. You can't see the bonfires and jury-rigged braziers burning in the vacant lots among the wreckage of collapsed buildings, but you can see the shanty-town huts and make-shift shelters on what used to be manicured lawns. There's a sense of despair that hangs in the air like a bad smell. Not the smoldering, volatile anger you'd feel in an ork-dominated slum, but a kind of dull acceptance and fatalism. It makes me sad.

After ten or fifteen minutes of walking in the cold gray drizzle, I find the public phone I'm looking for. The hinges are too rusted or jammed to close the door, but at least the booth shelters me from the rain. I sit down on the metal ledge and punch in Cat's LTG number.

Frag, I should have known it would hit me like this, seeing Cat's recorded message. But I didn't. When her face resolves on the screen—big eyes, copper hair, sensuous lips—I feel like someone's slipped an ice-cold stiletto between my ribs under my heart. My eyes burn and my vision blurs, and I have to fight to get air into my lungs. For a few moments, I don't think I can stand it. I want nothing more than to jump up and run. But then the rage reasserts itself, burning and churning in my belly. Somebody's going to pay, oh yes, they're going to pay—and then I know I *can* handle it. My emotions fade away, and I feel cold and hard and barely human as Cat's outgoing message comes to an end. With fingers that don't quite feel like mine, I key in the access code for the Special Favors file. My hands shake so much I almost can't enter the Mayflower password, but somehow I manage it.

Cat's little demons or smartframes or whatever the frag she called them have been busy little buggers. The five names—Crystalite, Griffin, and the rest—have become section headings, with paragraphs of text and blocks of numerical data after each one. Instead of a list, it's starting to look like a biz report. I quickly scan through the file, but the only one thing that catches my eye is that one entry—the one for Telestrian Industries Corporation—is much bigger, two or three times bigger, than the others. Using the phone's keyboard, I flag that section of the file for future attention.

Then, working quickly, I insert a blank datachip into the phone's data port, and key in the instruction to download the file. A second or two later the machine beeps, I extract the chip, break the connection, and head back out into the rain.

For a few moments I consider finding a good overwatch position, hunkering down and observing the pay phone. I might learn something important. After all, IrreleCorp or whoever set up the ambush must know by now I survived. If I were them, I don't think I'd miss the trick of putting a trace on Cat's phone. (But then I'd probably have remotely nuked all data files on her telecom, if that's possible. Again, I feel like I'm missing something.)

Then again, I know so little about what's going on that spotting a team responding to my call—coming to do a drive-by on the phone, for example—wouldn't help me much. More background information, that's what I need. I turn and stride off back toward The Promise.

15

There are some advantages to dossing down at a fleabag like The Promise. For one thing, you don't have to worry about maid service breezing in and disturbing your thought processes.

I'm sitting on the bed in an uncomfortable half-lotus, with a hot new pocket secretary on my lap. ("Hot" designating its origins, certainly not its performance.) My headware isn't designed for poring over a textual data file like the drek I downloaded from Cat's phone, and I seem to have misplaced my own palmtop computer somewhere along the way. Pretty careless. I really should keep better track of my toys. So anyway, I obviously needed something that could do the job, and just as obviously I wasn't going to find a Radio Shack or a Fuchi distributor in the depths of the Tarislar ghetto.

Fortunately, ghettos and their ilk have their own channels of distribution, and a blind transfer of cred to a hard-bitten elf recommended to me by The Promise's desk clerk—after another transfer of cred, of course—netted me an "almost-new" Yamaha PDA-5 that had "fallen off the back of a truck" elsewhere in the sprawl. The price was high—two-K, almost as much as I'd pay for a new one with a manual and warranty and such drek—but so was my level of need, and the elf fence knew it. We struck the deal and I hied myself off back "home" to get to work.

For the third time or so, I'm going over the file that Cat's demons put together on the five names, hoping that something will ring a bell. So far, no luck. The five names are all corps—Crystalite Environmental Research Corporation, Griffin Technologies Incorporated, Telestrian Industries Corporation, Margaux Enterprises, and Starbright Advanced Synergetics (a good dandelion-eater corp name if I ever heard one)—all more or less significant players in the Tir and, in some cases, elsewhere in the world as well. As Cat herself told me, none has any official presence in Seattle or UCAS in general. Of the five, Telestrian Industries Corporation—generally known as TIC—is by far the biggest. A big, sprawling, aggressive conglomerate, with its fingers into a hundred different pies. Annual cash flow and assets both measured in the multibillions of nuyen with corporate headquarters in a fragging arcology in downtown Portland. Into everything from genetic engineering to cutting-edge software development, with a few really weird sidelines going on in parallel.

In contrast, the others are more moderate outfits. Not small—still up in the billion nuyen range—but much less diversified and pervasive than TIC. According to Cat's demons, all of them have something in the way of "special security" forces—read "covert ops assets"—and hints that they've shown some kind of activity in the sprawl at one time or another.

And frag, why shouldn't they? Seattle's a major market, with a population density more than twice that of downtown Portland. There's more megacorporate presence in Seattle than anywhere in the Tir, and thus more biz opportunities for an ambitious, aggressive outfit trying to evade the restrictive "business practices" laws promulgated by the elven Council of Princes. Why would a corp from the Tir *not* want to diversify northward into the sprawl?

But why would all five of these corps be sending "special security" assets into the sprawl rather than doing things openly? I can think of several reasons off the top of my head. First, to avoid legal restrictions on their out-of-Tir activities (I don't know the details of the Tir biz laws, but I hear they're pretty fragging draconian). Second, because they don't want their competitors back home to know they're cozying up to Aztechnology, say, for a major joint venture. Third, because what they're planning is against UCAS and Seattle metroplex law. And fourth, from what I've seen of the biz world, corps sometimes like this cloak-and-dagger drek for the sheer frag of it, just because it's chill. Of those possible reasons, it seems that only the third one might involve cutting some kind of deal with the Cutters.

Frag it, I'm getting more pieces to the puzzle, but they're all fragging blank, with nothing at all to cue me as to how they go together. How can the espionage-counterespionage slots who do this on a daily basis keep from going round the

fragging twist? I'd last a day or two—a week at most—
before my brains started to pour out my ears . . .

Hold the fragging phone, what the frag's that?

While I was mentally shuffling all the blank pieces
around, my fingers were idly playing with the pocket secretary's mini-trackball, scanning up and down through the text
file. My eyes were on the display, but they weren't really
seeing it. Then suddenly I spotted something. Fragged if I
know what it was; I'd scanned way past it before I could react. I don't know what I saw. Not consciously—at the time,
my conscious brain apparently wasn't jacked into my eyes—
but, equally apparently, whatever my eyes snagged on meant
something to my subconscious. Meant enough to trigger an
internal alarm sharp enough to jolt me fragging near off
the bed.

Desperately, I try to re-exert control, willing my fingers to
stop trembling. Carefully—oh so carefully—I put my thumb
back on the mini-trackball and start scanning slowly and
carefully through the text. I'm near the beginning of the TIC
entry, and I'm pretty sure I was scanning backward when it
happened, so I scroll slowly forward through the text. I'm
not trying to read every word—that'd numb my mind out for
sure—but I am trying to make sure my eyes pass over every
line. If my subconscious jumped up and yelled, "Here, you
dumb frag," once before, maybe it'll do it again. Where is
it . . . where is it . . . ?

There. I lock out the trackball so I can't accidentally jog
it, and take a deep, slow breath.

I've got you, you fraggers. The first lead—oh so tiny, but
maybe oh so important—the first time you didn't tie up all
loose ends. (Why not? Were you in too much of a rush? Or
is this all just a red herring you're dragging across my path?
No, zero that, I can't let doubt in, not now.) I lean closer to
the screen and read the text surrounding the words that
caught my eye.

It's right in the middle of a long, long list of minor companies with which TIC has ongoing joint ventures, companies all across North America and around the world. All
small, so small I've never heard of any of them before . . .
except one.

Lightbringer Services Corporation. A small (as these
things go) telecommunications provider, based in Honolulu,
Kingdom of Hawaii. Offices in Tokyo, Macao, Singapore,

Palembang, Quezon City, Sydney, Quito, Mexico City . . . and Seattle.

Lightbringer. The elf—Pietr Tal-something—who visited Nicholas Finnigan said he was with Lightbringer. At the time, we'd both assumed that was a cover. A logical guess, considering neither of us had heard of Lightbringer before, and there was no hint at a tie-in between that corp and anything else that was going down. Now? There's a connection, all right, priyatel, a big fragging connection.

Or is there? Yet again, I feel like somebody's poured cold water into my soul. Just like with blaming Drummond and squad for the Montlake ambush, there are some other twisty little complexities here. I don't know that TIC's the Tir corp hooking up with the Cutters. I don't know that Pietr Tal-drek's actually a part of Lightbringer. Frag, maybe the elf who visited Finnigan just happened to pick Lightbringer as his cover, and Lightbringer just happens to be in bed with TIC, which just happpens to be one of several Tir corps interested in doing biz in Seattle. Does the Lightbringer-TIC connection mean, then, that Telestrian Industries Corporation is actually my so-called "IrreleCorp"? No, frag it. It could be pure chance, or it could be a really sly disinformation campaign designed to put me on the wrong track if I try to trace Finnigan's visitor.

Frag this paranoid drek, my mind's not built for it! Give me a gang to infiltrate—or, better yet, a troop of fragging Ork Scouts or some drek—and I'll be a happy little narc. Leave the deep, paranoid, multilayered, cerebral crap to neurotics who are so twisted they meet themselves coming round corners, that's what I say.

And hey, isn't that a thought?

I pick up the pocket secretary again and carefully save the text file. Then I start scanning through the little unit's help system. There's a trick a chummer taught me about a year or so back that might really help out here. If the secretary has the feature-set I need, of course. I wish I'd paid the extra thousand nuyen and gotten the fragging manual . . .

This pay phone's seen better days. Every exposed surface is covered with graffiti, most in English or Cityspeak, but some in that brain-fragged pseudolanguage the elves call Sperethiel—some of it actually funny ("Help your local police: beat yourself up"). The heavy metal enclosure of the phone itself is dented across the front, the impressions unmistakably made by the impact of light bullets. (I guess the calming, aggression-reducing display on the screen while a call's being placed didn't work for somebody.) All the circuitry seems to work, though—-except for the video pickup, which I broke myself.

It takes forever to make the connection. Not surprising, really. The pay phone is calling the cel unit built into my Yamaha pocket secretary, which is sitting on the bug-infested bed in my room at The Promise. The secretary is holding that call and using a parallel channel to place another call—that's multiple call capability, the feature I spent so fragging long looking for in the help files—to a number I programmed into it before I left the flophouse. When the recipient of that second call picks up the phone, the secretary patches the two lines together. Simple (yeah, right).

And the recipient does pick up. "Yes?"

There's a sequence of clicks, buzzes, and electronic echoes. For a moment I'm worried that I've asked too much of the pocket secretary, and that it's busy slagging itself down and setting fire to my bed. But then the line clears. Audio only, which means my call might have been forwarded to a cellular on the other end. "Yes?" the precise voice says again on the other end of the line.

"It's me, Nicholas," I say, and just like the last time I wait for him to clue me in.

"Richard," Finnigan replies, and I hear the honest pleasure in his voice. I relax—he wouldn't have used my name, or sounded so glad to hear from me, if he was in any kind of trouble. "Far be it from me to discourage an acquaintance from calling for a chat, but are you really sure this is wise?"

I have to grin. When I first met the old fart, I figured this overdone way of speaking was a put-on for my benefit. Didn't take me long to realize that's how he always talks, and probably how he thinks, too. "Wise enough."

"Phones can be traced," he says doubtfully.

"They can find the one that's calling you, I don't care," I state. If the drék hits the pot, IrreleCorp, the Cutters, or the Star can have the pocket secretary, and they're welcome to any fleas or other infestation they pick up at The Promise.

I can almost hear Finnigan shrug. "As you say," he accedes, but the doubt's still there in his voice. He sighs. "So, now. To what do I owe the pleasure of this call?"

"Lightbringer Services Corp for one," I tell him.

"Oh?" Now curiosity overrides the doubt, and I know I've got him hooked. "From your tone I assume you already know that Lightbringer does actually exist, that it's not a false front?"

"You got that," I agree, "it's real. And it's in bed with Telestrian Industries Corporation."

"Indeed?" he asks mildly. "Well, I must admit I find little of note in that. A great number of companies are, as you put it, 'in bed with' Telestrian. By far the most widespread and aggressive conglomerate in Tir Tairngire, with ambitions that extend far beyond the boundaries of elven territory."

"You know about TIC, then?"

"A little," Finnigan admits. "Perhaps not enough to satisfy your curiosity, however, because I take it that is where your inquiries are leading." He paused, and I know what he's going to ask.

So I cut him off. "I can't tell you why I figure the tie-in with TIC's important, Nicholas. You'll understand why."

Finnigan pauses, then, "I see," he says slowly, "yes, I really think I do see. It's not simply the fact that Lightbringer is joint-venturing with TIC—I rather imagine Lightbringer has a similar arrangement with many other organizations. It must be something else that piqued your curiosity. What, I wonder?"

"Don't push it, Nicholas," I warn him quietly.

"Hmm. ' "Curiouser and curiouser!" said Alice.' You really must tell me the complete story some time." He pauses. "I take it you have a specific request to make of me, Richard. Is that not so?"

My turn to pause. "I need someone to dig deep into TIC," I tell him at last. "Deep, Nicholas. Turn over all the fragging rocks and stir the drek."

Finnigan goes, "Hmm," again. Then, "You obviously have some level of intelligence on the corporation," he muses. "To discover the connection with Lightbringer, for example."

I shrug, even though I know he can't see me. "A chummer sent some demons and smartframes out for me."

"Preliminary research, then," he says slowly. "Autonomous data search constructs"—he rarely calls things what the rest of us do—"are of limited use for anything more extreme." He thinks for a moment, then continues, "The um, *colleague* who created the constructs is no longer available?"

The pain and the rage twist in my gut. "No," I say, and my voice is cold and emotionless—almost inhuman—in my own ears.

There's a long silence at the other end. Finally, Finnigan says, "Yes, well . . ." Another pause, nowhere near as long. "I believe I can help you in that regard," he says slowly.

"You?" That surprises me. "You write fiction."

He chuckles dryly, and I realize I've said something that would slot off just about anyone else. Finnigan's not just anyone, thank Ghu. "Yes, I write fiction. But in order to twist reality, you have to *understand* reality. You have to know the laws in order to break them." He thinks for a moment, and I can almost see him tugging at his upper lip the way he does when he's puzzling something through. "Yes," he says at last—firmly, as though he's not going to take any drek from anyone on his decision. "I have the access and the skill—and, so it seems, the motivation—to handle this for you. It's been a long time since I did any deep research in the corporate realm, and high time I took up the challenge again." Another pause. "It might take a while, you know. I assume I won't be able to call you."

I smile grimly at that one, and don't even bother answering. Instead, "How long?" I ask him.

"It depends," he says with another chuckle. "I'll get on it right away, but depending on how deeply things are buried it might take considerable time. A couple of days, probably, perhaps more."

An uncomfortable thought strikes me. "You're not planning to deck into TIC itself, are you?"

It's a full-throated laugh that comes from the phone's speaker this time. "Not even if my life depended on it. Or yours, for that matter. The sole result of even trying would be to call down whatever security assets TIC has in Seattle on my own precious cranium. No, third-party data sources only, I assure you. The effort involved and the expertise required might be high, but the danger is low. By the by, have you ever heard of Shadowland?"

I shake my head. "No. What is it, a club?"

"You might say that," Finnigan muses. "Not a nightclub, but the more traditional notion of 'club', with a very, um, rarefied membership."

"A poli?"

"Not as such. Shadowland is the name some people give to an extensive electronic bulletin board service."

"Like UOL?" I ask. "Never heard of it."

"I'd be greatly surprised if you had," he says dryly, then corrects himself, "or maybe not, at that." He pauses to order his thoughts, then goes on, "As I say, Shadowland is a BBS, with no fixed geographical location. The server hubs and nodes that make up the network 'float,' like illegal crap games. Rarely are they in the same place for more than a week at a time. So, too, the access lines—the LTG numbers and communication protocols—are highly variable."

"Why so much security? Who's after them?"

"The megacorporations," Finnigan shoots back at once. "Governments. Law enforcement agencies. Effectively, everyone."

And suddenly I know what he's talking about. "Shadowrunners," I say sourly.

Finnigan chuckles again, and I realize my reaction's given him another clue in the fragging puzzle-game he's playing—guess who/what Larson is. "Useful assets, at times," he points out.

I snort. Too many people—especially in Seattle, I've found—seem to put shadowrunners up on some kind of pedestal, viewing them as fragging "heroes of the underdog" or some such drek. Maybe Finnigan too. Who knows? Me, I think they're scum—mercenary street drek, no more heroic than the guttermeat informers and stoolies and rats I spent too much time dealing with in Milwaukee. They'd sell out their mothers for a few nuyen, and the only reason they wouldn't do the same for their fathers is that they generally don't know who their fathers are.

"Take the contact data anyway, Richard," Finnigan urges. "It might be useful." An LTG number, an extension number, and a complex string that has to be an access protocol of some kind, appear on the phone's data screen. Out of instinct, I commit them to memory. "They're current, I think," the old writer reassures me.

"How would you know?" I ask, suddenly curious.

"Stories come from everywhere, Richard," he chides me, "perhaps from Shadowland most of all." He sighs. "Unfortunately, the best ones I cannot use."

16

By the time I'm off the phone with Finnigan, the sun's going down—or it would be, if you could see it through the clouds. All sunset really means at the moment is a transition from wet, dark gray to wet, darker gray. A few streetlights fire up, and the braziers and fires I remember from last night start to flicker and smoke again.

With that, I feel the force of my rage once more. By all that's fragging holy, I'm going to find out who scragged Cat and tried to do the same to me, who ratted me out to the Cutters. I'm going to find them, and I'm going to invest a lot of time and a lot of inventiveness in making them pay. In full.

How I'm going to do it is the hard part. At the moment I've got no assets—unless you count Nicholas Finnigan, which I don't, not really. A couple of leads, but nothing solid, nothing you couldn't read a couple of different and mutually exclusive ways. My resources are limited to the few thousand nuyen on my private credsticks. Of course, I don't dare touch the contingency fund set up by the Star— not unless I want each transaction to fly a little flag saying "Geek me!" No, wait, I forgot about buying the fragging pocket secretary. That brings my monetary resources down to ... oh, something like one or two hundred nuyen. Frag! Not even enough to get out of the sprawl.

Which, I've got to admit, is starting to look like a fragging good idea. Not to get away for long, though. There's a difference between running for the hills and making a strategic retreat to regroup and plan the next battle. Seattle may be a megaplex of three-plus million, but it's a very small town when you want to hide. It'd make my life much easier if I could pull the old fade, hang for a few weeks—in Sioux land, maybe, or further south—until the dust settles some, then make my reappearance. Armed with information and resources and maybe a big fragging gun or two. The more I think about it, the better that starts to sound.

And that brings me back to resources. I *need* some, priyatel, and that's all there is to it. I might be able to get out of the sprawl on two hundred nuyen, possibly even make it out of the Salish-Shidhe lands into another nation without such tight ties to Seattle. But once I got there I'd have zilch in the way of resources. And you need money to get money, even in the Awakened world of 2054—maybe *particularly* in 2054. Ask the elves of Tarislar.

So that's why I'm jandering back toward The Promise on this cold and rainy early evening. That fragging pocket secretary. Heroes on the trid—and probably in Finnigan's books, too—never seem to worry about credit when they cut loose from their corp or government or whatever. They always seem able to buy the guns and the grenades and the ammo and the gewgaws—not to mention drinks for the biffs and a room in the hottest hotel—without worrying where the next nuyen's coming from. Me, I've got to skulk on back to my flop to pick up the pocket secretary so I can sell the pecker again—for half what I paid for it a couple of hours ago, you can bet your hoop on that.

It puts me at risk, or course, and it effectively counteracts that wiz little stunt I pulled with the relayed phone call. If anyone was monitoring Finnigan's number, a trace on my call would send them hustling off to Tarislar and The Promise. And now that's just where I'm going. No doubt things would be going very different if Finnigan were plotting this.

The one good thing about heading back for the flop is that any team out looking for me would expect to find me inside the building, because that's where the phone is. They won't be looking for me out on the street, inbound, which means I should be able to make them before they make me. Depending on who it is that might come a-visiting, I'll know something I didn't know before, maybe something important. (That's the story I keep telling myself to counteract the fear in my gut as I get closer and closer to The Promise.)

I make my approach carefully, using all the tradecraft I've learned over the years. For example, I don't come jandering east, straight down the street that The Promise is on, oh no. Instead, I jog over a block, and come swinging down the cross-street from the north, keep going through the intersection like I've got somewhere to be, all the while giving the front of the low building some solid but covert scrutiny.

No car out front. Good, as far as that goes. No suspicious figures hanging on the sidewalks either. Even better.

Now I double back to the street The Promise fronts onto. Cautiously again, of course, I move in on the other side of the street. It's dark, and maybe one in ten steetlights actually works, so there are plenty of shadows, particularly in the vacant lots and gutted buildings. I've got the moves and I'm on top of my game. I'm a ghost in the night.

I'm almost directly across from The Promise when I see him. Sprawled on the sidewalk, back propped up against the ferrocrete wall of the flophouse is a bagged-out gutterpunk elf. Looks like he was dragged through a hedge backward while trying to drink a distillery. I didn't see him when making my first pass down the cross-street because The Promise has a slightly recessed front door under the remnants of what used to be a kind of portico. He's wearing what must have been decent clothing once but has since suffered years of drek and abuse. His face matches his clothes.

It's strange about elves, that something setting them apart form all the other metatypes. Not anything as obvious as their oh-so-precious pointy little ears. No, it's more profound than that, an atmosphere or aura they carry around with them. When it's an ork or a human sprawled in the gutter, it's just plain squalid. But when its one of those rare down-and-outer elves, it's like seeing some great and noble tragedy.

But enough of the fragging sociology. Time to move in.

I'm fortunate in one sense—the streetlight right outside The Promise and the two nearest me on my side of the street are dead. The lights inside the flophouse lobby cast a pool of illumination—which could be why the bagged-out elf chose that spot to crash—but the street itself and the sidewalk in front of me are dark. I can see that the Plexiglas lobby doors are shut, which means anyone watching from outside would have to look from a brightly lit environment into a dark one. Even with enhanced optics, about all they're going to see is their own reflection in the Plexiglas door.

I take a good deep breath, and start to cross the street. Not directly in front of The Promise; I'm not that frizz-headed. No, I'm further down the block, again moving with the air

of someone whose destination is far from the rundown flophouse.

The bagged-out elf stirs. His head comes up slowly like
he's just emerging from a major drunk. He turns his head
slightly, and the light from the lobby glints off his eyes.

It's in the eyes, always in the eyes, the way the pros study
what's going on around them. Not just a steadiness of the
gaze, but more like the eyes are the front end of a sophisticated and task-designated data analysis machine. Once
you've seen it you'll know what I mean. You'll never mistake it and you'll never forget it.

I reach the sidewalk on the same side of the street as The
Promise, and I turn right, away from the flophouse. I want
to run, I want to jink left and right to make myself a tougher
target in case a laser spot is already painting the back of my
neck. But instead I keep to the same steady stride. When I
reach the intersection—a fragging eternity later, every moment of which I'm expecting the smashing impact of a round
to the head—I turn left. The moment I'm around the corner,
I flatten myself against the wall of the building and I let the
trembling in my hands run its course.

I've found the first member of the team lying in wait
for me.

An elf. Does that mean anything? The Tir connection re-
surfacing, maybe? Or is it just good tactics and asset selection? After all, this is Tarislar . . .

Okay, I know something. I know somebody had a tap on
Finnigan's line, traced the call to the cel phone built into the
pocket secretary, and sent a team to respond. (Bag or ice?
What are their orders? Take me alive or geek on sight? After
the two previous attempts on my life, I've got to assume
they want to color me dead.) Fast response time, which
means either extensive assets or just my bad luck that a team
happened to be in the area. It's not more than five minutes
since I got off the horn with Finnigan, and I don't think the
call itself lasted much more than three. Eight minutes from
the time I made the connection. Estimate a minute, maybe
two, to lock onto the cel phone and refine the locater signal
enough to pick out a specific building. Another minute,
maybe, to contact a mobile team. (You don't jack with the
cellular network from portable gear, let me tell you.) That
gives the team five fragging minutes, maybe six, to roll and
reach The Promise. Tight, tight timing, but still probably not

enough to figure out that I'm not in room 2LR at the moment.

But what does it mean that they've got a watcher out front? Especially since there's no vehicle on the street and no signs of a ruckus from inside the building. Neither of the other attempts to scag me have been what you'd call subtle: first a Cutters hit team and then a fragging missile from ambush. The equivalent response now would be to locate the room I'm in, then pump grenades in through the window. But they're not doing that. So what does that tell me?

Not a frag of a lot, other than maybe—just maybe—the mission this time is bag, not ice, after all. Best not to count on that, though.

Without really deciding to do it consciously, I'm looping back toward the back of the building. Room 2LR is at the rear, on the left as you're coming up the stairs. If there's any activity inside, I might just be able to see and hear what's going on through the window, particularly if it involves firearms or explosives. I start to make my way down the narrow, drek-filled alley that runs behind The Promise.

It's dark, but not pitch-black. The skies of Seattle always seem to glow with this sick and sullen light. Sure, it's just the clouds and the drek in the air reflecting back the lights of downtown, but sometimes it looks like the air's glowing on its own, like it's radioactive or something. It's dark enough to give me cover, but there's still enough light to keep me from running into dumpsters or tripping over rats. Of course that's a mixed blessing. Cover for me also means cover for others, and while I'm depending on meat eyes, I've got to assume the hostiles have cyber enhancements that turn night into fragging day.

The Promise is about halfway up the block. The other buildings on both sides of the alley are similar to the flophouse, low—no more than the three floors—and pretty drek-kicked. Unlike some of the other gutted buildings I've passed, all are more or less intact, dark and probably filled with squatters. The original identities and purposes of the buildings have been lost to decay, except for one across the alley from The Promise and nearer the end of the block. What's left of a sign over the rear door reads: Fi nes Que t. For a few seconds I try to puzzle it out, then the meaning hits me: Fitness Quest, it's the only thing that fits.

Then I shake my head. Frag, what the subconscious won't

do to distract the conscious mind from something it doesn't want to do—to the point of playing New Wheel of fragging Fortune with building signs. Give me a fragging break. I ghost my way past Fi nes Que t, deeper into the darkness of the alley, away from the partially lit street behind me.

Apart from the small shaded light over the flop's back alley door, the place is dark. No lights on in 2LR . . .

Or in any window, for that matter. Before the thought really has time to penetrate, I've flattened and frozen myself against the wall of the building across the alley from Fi nes Que t. I glance down at my watch. Not quite 2045, according to the faint green display. I know The Promise is full, or close to it. How likely is it that everybody dossed down here has gone out on the town or toddled off to bed before nine at night? Not likely. By all odds there should be at least one light on somewhere, right?

I feel cold all over. Whoever the hostiles are, they've secured the whole fragging building—and it's still not much more than twelve minutes—fifteen at the outside—since I placed the call to Finnigan. Frag, that's fast. The Star might be able to do it with a couple of FRT squads, and the same for any corp security force worthy of the name. But quietly? So quietly the only indication is one watcher out front and no lights in the windows? Not a chance, priyatel.

Who the frag *are* these guys?

Movement. I'm pressed even harder back against the wall, and the wire has my H & K clear of its holster even before I consciously realize it.

Suddenly I see a figure step into the small cone of light cast from over the back door. Tall, thin—an elf? No obvious weapons, hands in the pockets of a long, dark duster-style coat. Armored, natch.

I watch to see what he's doing, but the slag just keeps standing there directly under the light.

Facing directly toward me. As if he knows I'm here.

Quick as drek through a rat, I drop into a crouch behind what was once a bar fridge before enterprising souls stole the compressor and the door and other assorted odds and sods. It's lousy hard cover—anything with a decent propellant charge is going to punch right on through—but as soft-cover concealment it's the best I've got at the moment. I hunker down and wait for the drek to hit the pot.

Nothing comes punching through the fridge, or through

my body. I shift, stick my head out for an instant at about knee-level. Then pull it back and review what I saw in that momentary glimpse.

The figure's still there, hasn't moved a millimeter that I can see. No heat of any kind. He's just standing there under the light, like he's on stage and it's a spotlight. Like he wants to be seen. Like he wants me to look at him. And keep looking at him . . .

I snap my head around so fast I feel a muscle pull in my neck. The wire brings my H & K around onto the same line.

And I'm looking over my sights at two figures in the mouth of the alley. Tall, slender—again I can't tell for sure whether they're elves, but it's a good fragging bet. Moving forward slowly. With them silhouetted against the lights of the road, I can't see for sure whether they've got their weapons drawn, but it's another good bet. There's something about the way they move—slow, steady, six or seven meters apart so the same burst can't take them both—that just screams pro. Pros from what source? Not the Cutters— there's none of the ganger's swaggering machismo in their moves. The Star? Lightbringer? TIC? Or someone else— IrreleCorp, maybe?

The wire wants to cack them both, hose down the area. Burn the clip that's in the H & K, slap in another and do it again. But that would be stupid, suicidal. If they're pros, I've got to assume they're also armored. It's too far and too dark and too uncertain for a guaranteed, clean head-shot, which would be the only sure way to take them down. Even if I could cut through their armor, one of them would be returning fire and running for cover while I was geeking the other one. Not to mention Mr. Spotlight behind me, doing the same thing.

No, the Gunfight at the fragging O.K. Corral isn't the way to go here. I duck down lower and scope out my options.

Not a long process—there aren't many. Behind me is a wall. It has a door in it to my right—a heavy metal fire door of some kind—which might or might not be locked. To get to the door, I've got to move toward the two pros moving slowly down the alley, then expose myself for a few seconds while opening the door. Just a tick or two, but it's more than enough to take a few hundred grams of steel-jacketed lead. And that's if the door's not locked . . . Pass, thanks.

About a dozen meters to my left is a narrow passageway

that connects The Promise and the building next to it. Duck through that and I'm out on the main street again—and straight into the fire pattern of the elf watcher outside the lobby. If I could even make it that far. There's not a drop of cover between me and that passage, and I'd have to move directly toward Mr. Spotlight to get there. No matter what you see on the trid, running into the bad guys' guns rather than across their line of fire isn't a tactically defensible option. Pass.

Almost directly across the alley from me is another one of those narrow passageways, this one running between Fi nes Que t and the building next to it. That's probably my best bet, but it's sure as frag not a good one. To make it I've got to break from behind the fridge, cross the alley—fast, there's no cover, and I'm the line of fire of all three ops—and keep a-going. When I get to the street—one block south of The Promise, so there shouldn't be watchers there—then I decide what's next. The advantage of this option is that I'd be moving fast, at right angles to all three lines of sight. That means a tracking shot, the hardest kind, even for somebody heavily cybered up. (Again, don't let the trid tell you any different.)

I could better my odds if I had a way to distract these slags for a few instants, but fragged if I know how. Sure, if this were trid, I'd find something lying close to hand that I could turn into a diversion. A rock in a tin can, maybe, or a soykaf filter and some bleach I could make into a fragging hand grenade. Or I could just yell something like, "Look! It's Comet Swift-Tuttle!" And in the confusion stroll across the fragging alley.

Null! This is reality, priyatel. No rocks, no tin cans, not even a soykaf filter.

So I'm up on my feet before I can talk myself out of it, head down and legs driving like a sprinter exploding out of the blocks. Wildly overbalanced forward, ready to go down face-first if my legs don't keep up or if a foot catches on anything. Vision tunneled down, so all I can see is the dark rectangle that's the passageway across the alley. I give it everything I've got, every joule of energy in my body. Any moment expecting to be blown out of my boots by three bursts of autofire.

No impacts, and I'm across, into the narrow passageway between the buildings. No shouts of surprise or alarm from behind me, just the sound of running footsteps. (Pros, like I said. Pros don't have to yell, "There he goes!")

I slow down for an instant, expecting to find the passageway filled with drek and maybe squatters. But for a wonder it's empty, a clear sprinting lane for me, leading toward the light of another street. I pour it on again.

And an instant later put on the brakes. I see someone, a figure stepping into the mouth of the passageway, another tall form silhouetted against the light. Ahead of me.

I'm dead.

I skid to a stop. Up comes the H & K, but I don't fire. Same as in the alley, I might be able to cack the scag in front of me, but no guarantees. And doing it will only slow me down enough for the other three to come up behind me. I'm trapped. Unless . . .

Solid wall to the left. Windows, but four meters off the ground. To the right . . .

A door. Heavy, metal. No doorknob. I fling myself at it, slamming into it with all my weight, feeling something give in my shoulder. For a wonder, the door bursts open, and I go sprawling headlong into Fi nes Que t. As I skid on the concrete, the door hits the wall and swings back, closing almost all the way.

Where I am is a narrow hallway, black as a fragging ork's heart. Waiting for me outside are armed street ops, with one or two soon to be inside. My situation's only marginally better than it was a couple of moments ago unless I can do something to even up the odds a little. That has to wait, though, until I can get further away from that door.

I force myself to my feet and shuffle off down the hallway. It's so dark I can't see squat ahead of me anyway, so I glance back. The H & K's status lights are like little red fireflies in the blackness. First slag through the door eats thirty-two rounds of nine-mil.

And presumably the pros outside have guessed that would be the outcome, because the door doesn't open and no silhouettes appear in the doorway.

That's when I find the end of the hallway, by running into it. Another door. I take my attention off the door behind me long enough to find the knob on this one, then fling it open and duck through in a combat crouch.

Another fragging hallway, this one running left-right. That's what I guess from the ambiance and the echoes, at least. My bowels feel like they're filled with ice water, and my skin's prickling so hard it feels like I'm wearing a fragging Velcro undershirt. I still can't see, but to anyone with thermographic vision, I'm one big glowing target. Frag if I can remember if that includes elves, but if it does, not much I can do about it right now.

Which way? For a moment my sense of direction spins like a tumbled gyro. Then it straightens up. The door I barged through was closer to the front of the building than to the alley, and it was to my right. That means the street's to my left now, and that's the way I want to go.

But then comes a sound from my left. A click—a door, I think, I hope, and not the charging lever of an SMG or the slide of an auto-pistol—and the soft scuff of cautious footsteps. Decision made for me, yet again. I turn right, probing the darkness ahead with the muzzle of my H & K and my left hand, moving as fast and as silently as I can.

My left fingers touch something—another fragging door, feels like. Yes, there's the doorknob. I've got a real drekky feeling about this, but now's definitely not the time to analyze it.

I'm torn. I hate doors in this kind of situation. I hated them in the Academy when we trained in house-to-house ops. I hate them even more now. They block sound, they block light. For all I know, on the other side of the door is a fragging firing squad of elves, with xenon spots slung under the barrels of their SMGs, just waiting for me to open it.

Another sound from behind me, back toward the front of the building. Another click, and this one does sound like a weapon being cocked. I look back over my shoulder. Nothing, just blackness—no lights, no target, no options. With my left hand I grab the doorknob, turn it and push. Simultaneously I drop into the lowest crouch—eyes narrowed to slits so I (theoretically) won't be dazzled if the lights are on through the door.

More darkness. Not another hallway, though. It feels like a room, possibly a big one. I don't want to, but I duck into it, still in a tight crouch. Behind me I close the door as softly as I can with my left hand. My gaze and my H & K track back and forth across the darkness, each as useless as the other without light. I open my eyes as wide as they'll go.

And then there *is* light. A silent concussion of it, so sudden and so bright it's like fingernails jabbed into my eyes. I hear myself gasp as I flinch back. Both hands come up reflexively before I can stop them, and I rap myself in the forehead with the clip of my H & K. The pain in my eyes is so bad I want to whimper. I slump back against the door, sliding to the floor. Nothing I can do, nothing at all. Just wait for the bullet to take away the pain in my eyes. Even with my eyelids shut and hands over them, the light's so bright I can still see it.

Then the light dims. Not to darkness, but it might as well be, compared to the preceding harsh wash of light. My eyes still feel like they've got needles in them, and they're pouring tears. But I know I've got to open them. Tentatively, I take my hands away from my face and open my eyes a slit.

The light level's way down, probably lower than normal ambient light in an office, but I still can't see squat because of the big floaty blue afterimages. I close my eyes again, rub at them hard with my left fist. The wire badly wants to hose everything down—fire blindly and just get the party started—but I don't let it go.

I try to open my eyes once more, and this time I can see a little better. Everything's still blurry and the pain's just as bad. But I can see I was right: I'm in a big room, probably a gym. Nothing but bare concrete walls, floor, and ceiling now.

Except for the anomaly that's in the geometric center of the room. A table. A plain, desk-sized, macroplast table. And sitting behind it is a corp-style woman. Long blonde hair pulled back behind pointed ears, suit of severe cut. Instinctively, the wire tracks the H & K in on her, but I don't fire. She's sitting there quietly, watching me. Empty hands flat down on the tabletop in front of her. No heat, no bodyguards. Just the three of us—me, her, and the H & K. Jam, priyatel. This lady's got big brass ones.

Feeling like a half-fragged fool, I lower my gun, thumb on the safety. Then I push myself to my feet.

At last my hostess speaks. "Mr Larson," she says, her voice like silk. "I think it's high time we had a little talk."

17

I look around slowly, trying to keep chill, struggling to get myself under control. It's tough—too many shocks in too short a time. The watcher in front of The Promise, the three men in the alley, the race through the blacked-out building. And now this. My mind's spinning, like I've taken a snap to the head in an escrima sparring session.

So focus on my surroundings, on reality, until everything shakes out and comes back to normal. The table and the woman are right in the middle of the room. There's only one door—the one behind me—and no windows. Light comes from half a dozen collapsible fixtures around the room, big bulbs, diffusers, and reflectors aimed at the door and at me. No wonder I was blinded at first—it's like being the focus of six spotlights. The intensity on all the bulbs is turned down low now, with enough illumination to see clearly, but tolerable to my traumatized eyes.

I glance again at the woman. Hands flat on the table, un-moving. No obvious heat. She's almost certainly packing, but the wire reassures me I could splatter her long before she could pull anything. Yet she was able to adjust the intensity of the room's light even without obvious controls. Has to be concealed tech, probably including an internal radio or cel phone link. Either that or magic. Otherwise how could she and her goons outside have orchestrated this setup?

Yeah, that's right—and it fragging picks me to admit it—a setup. I was manipulated and channeled and played like a sap and made to dance like a fragging puppet. Every move and countermove, every option, already plotted out before-hand. This woman—or whoever she represents—knew I was coming, and guessed all too fragging accurately how I'd re-act to various stimuli. The whole thing was choreographed to get me into this room, coming face to face with this elf biff across this table. I hate being predictable.

Still, I'm here now. My bowels still feel like water and my head like it's got big targets painted on it, maybe an X-ring between my eyes and another at the base of my skull. But if this elf biff here wanted me dead, she could have arranged that early on in the gavotte, without going to all this trouble.

So I take a couple of steps forward, the H & K still in my right hand, but hanging at my side. I try to focus the last shreds of my confidence into my movements and my expression as I approach. I watch her eyes. Green, cold and hard as volcanic glass. Her face shows no expression, and her body language tells me even less. I stop about three meters away from the table and go, "Well?"

She doesn't answer immediately, just looks me up and down. I try to guess her age, but she could be anywhere between twenty and two hundred.

At last she says, "We should get a few matters clear up front, Mr. Larson." Her voice is smooth, detached. "You have a weapon, I don't. But my people are outside and I assure you that they are definitely armed. You kill me, they kill you. You hurt me, they kill you. You do anything but listen to me, they kill you. Do you understand?"

I don't even dignify that with an answer—it's not like it's the theory of fragging relativity or anything. I just wait her out.

"So," she says after a few more seconds of inspecting me, "I could, quite truthfully, say I regret the nature of this meeting, but you wouldn't believe me. Just let's say it's necessary."

"To who?" I ask.

"To both of us," she shoots back, "and again I'm speaking the truth." She pauses once more. When she speaks again, her voice is quieter, more speculative. "You're in an interesting position, Mr. Larson. Through no fault of your own, you're in the middle of something bigger than your experience and training have prepared you for."

"No drek," I say sarcastically. "Tell me something I don't know."

For the first time she smiles (almost), a minuscule upward quirking of her lips. "As a matter of fact," she says dryly, "that's the purpose of this whole meeting, Mr. Larson."

"Yeah, right," I sneer. "What corp owns you anyway, lady? Lightbringer? Or Telestrian Industries Corporation? Or maybe even Lone Star? Which?"

Her smile fades. "If you're trying to impress me with how much you know, don't waste your time," she snaps, her silky voice now lined with steel. "If your want to live through this, keep your mouth shut and listen. If you don't want to listen, you're free to leave—right now, no strings—and I'll gladly place side bets on who will get you first." She fixes me with a gaze like twin lasers. "Are you going to listen, or do I write this off as a bad investment of time and effort?"

I shrug. "My time's cheap at the moment. I'm all ears."

She nods. "I'm authorized to confirm to you that there is a link between a corporate executive called Timothy Telestrian and the Cutters gang."

"What kind of link?"

"I'm *not* authorized to tell you that," she says flatly. "But I strongly suggest you find out what it is, and why it's important. And then take whatever action you see fit."

"You don't know, then," I say just as flatly.

"We know."

"Then why the frag should I bother?" I let my frustration out, and I can hear the harsh edge to my voice. "Frag you and the hog you rode in on, lady," I spit out, then start to turn away

"Then you're dead, Larson." She says it quietly, without emotion—and it's all the more of a stopper for that.

But I can't let her see how she's scored. Slowly I turn back, and let my lips twist in a smile. "So now the threats begin?"

"Call it a promise," she counters.

"Whatever. Same thing—I play your game or you cack me, right?"

"Wrong!" And her voice is like the crack of a whip. High corp or maybe military background—someone who's used to giving orders and having them obeyed right fragging now.

"Oh?" I give her my most annoying grin.

"We're not going to kill you," she states calmly. "It wouldn't even be worth the cost of ammunition expended. There are enough others lined up to do the job. The Cutters. Lone Star. Timothy Telestrian's people. One of them will get you. Soon."

"Yeah?" I drawl. "So why tell me about this Telestrian rat-frag anyway?"

No matter how hard I try to slot her off, the elf biff refuses to be rattled. "Irrelevant," she says crisply. "All you need to know is that tracing and elucidating the connection between Timothy Telestrian and the Cutters is the only hope you have of staying alive. Following any other course will just get you killed. Believe it, Larson. I've got no reason to lie to you about this."

I don't have to answer that, my face says it all.

There's a click from behind me. I spin and crouch, up comes the H & K.

The door's swinging open, revealing two figures. Tall—elves?—but bulky with the heavy armor they're wearing. Both have machine pistols leveled at my head. I freeze, then slowly lower the H & K, opening my hand so the gun hangs from my forefinger by the trigger-guard, pivoting muzzle-down. I take it the interview's over.

Both armored goons come through the door, one sidestepping to the left, the other to the right, to flank me. They're good—careful not to get in each other's line of fire. And I mentally kick myself in the hoop. For a few seconds there when the door first opened, they couldn't have fired without a very real risk of greasing the biff. Unless she's got some kind of magical protection up, of course. I guess, on second thought, my instincts were right.

"My associates will escort you out, Mr. Larson," she says calmly from behind me. "Please don't force them to do something you'll regret."

I want to snarl some wildly improbable speculation about her ancestry and sexual proclivities, but the muzzles of the machine pistols persuade me to keep my yap shut. One of the armored slots gestures with his weapon, and I start toward the door.

"Just so you don't think I've totally wasted your time," the elf-cow says suddenly, "I'll tell you two things for free."

My little entourage—me and the armored goons—stops. I turn back. "Oh?"

"One. Your cover with the Cutters was blown by a faction within Lone Star itself. This faction told the gang leader—Blake, I believe his name is—that you were an undercover operative and that you knew too much about some plans Blake wanted kept very quiet." She grins wryly. "They told him you knew much more than you actually did, by the way. They also created a sense of urgency by telling him that Lone Star was calling you in for a full report within twelve hours. Do you understand that?"

I nod my head slowly. I understand what she's saying, and it certainly makes sense. Doesn't mean I believe a fragging word, of course. "That's one," I point out.

"Two," she says crisply. "Nicholas Finnigan suggested that you contact the shadow underground for help. I second that suggestion. It might just be the best way for you to stay alive. Perhaps the best person for you to approach is someone who goes by the handle of Argent. You can contact him through a blind relay—LTG number twelve oh-six oh-three oh-four oh-nine. Do I need to repeat that?"

"No."

"Then that's it," she states. "We won't meet or communicate again."

Don't bet on it, sister, is what I want to say, but I don't. One of the hard-men gestures again with his machine pistol. As calmly as I can manage, I slide the H & K back into its holster, and turn my back on the elf biff. Then I step through the door, hearing the two goons take up station behind me.

Lights are on in the hallway, letting me see where I'm going this time. I jander on down it, trying to stop the muscles of my back from cringing as I imagine the laser sights of those two machine pistols drifting over my spine. I keep telling myself they're not going to ice me now, not after the elf slitch went to so much trouble just to give me a message, but it's never fragging easy to turn your back on two weapons. We pass the door I came through, then continue down the hallway to where it ends with another door. This one swings open as we approach, and there's another figure framed in it. Not armored, this one. Behind him I see the lights of the street.

I jander on by him, trying my damndest to stay frosty, but I blow it and jump a couple of meters when he suddenly pulls something out of one pocket. Then I see what it is he's got in his hand.

It's the pocket secretary I left on the bed of my doss. I take it from him, and it's all I can do not to turn tail and run. I hear the door shut behind me, and I'm alone on the street in front of Fi nes Que t.

Frag, these guys are chill!

I've managed to hold it together long enough to walk a few blocks from Fi nes Que t, boost another car, and make tracks out of Tarislar. Now I'm sitting behind the wheel of a hot Ford Americar, stopped in the parking lot of a Stuffer Shack in downtown Sumner—probably an oxymoron—and I've got the shakes, big-time. Like, it's been too many shocks piled one on top of another for the past few days. To finish it off, there's the slick and frosty way the elf biff and her yobos danced me around, letting me know at just about every fragging step that they could have blown my guts out without my so much as being able to return fire. All so calm, so pro, so fragging urbane, all the way to the topper, giving me my drek-sucking pocket secretary back. If this is the level of professionalism you get from corp security assets, I'll stick with the fragging gangs. Like the lady said—or at least implied—I'm out of my league.

I drag a hand across my forehead, brush the hair back out of my eyes. My hand comes back wet. Not from the rain; I've been inside the car long enough for it to dry off. It's sweat, priyatel, fragging cold sweat.

It's not just that I was waltzed around like some greenie on the streets, though that's a big drek-eating part of it, let me tell you. A lot of it's what the elf biff said, and what she knew. She knew about Finnigan, she knew about Blake. She hinted at some really nasty fragging drek—that it was the fragging Star that blew my cover, for one thing. But who at the Star? Drummond and crew? If so, then I was on the money with my suspicions about the ambush, about Cat's death. It would have been the unholy fragging trinity of Drummond, McMartin, and Layton who geeked Cat.

But is that possible? Maybe the elf biff doesn't know about the data penetration and isn't distinguishing between official Star orders/operations and drek that's being driven by the slags who've cracked the system. Or maybe she was just lying through her chops about the whole thing, all the better to manipulate me. For all I know, it could have been she who ratted me out to the Cutters. And, for that matter, she might be the one who's got her hooks deep into the Star's computer system.

No, that doesn't make sense. Why rat me out and almost get me assassinated, then draw me into a "white contact" like the one at Fi nes Que t? Unless the circumstances have really changed, and I've suddenly assumed a lot more importance somehow . . .

Frag! I shake my head, wipe my face with my hands again. I'm just not down for this drek. Too many possibilities, too many options, too many wheels within fragging wheels for my poor little brain. Simplify things as much as possible. Either the elf biff was telling the truth or she was lying. Binary solution set, as simple as it gets. If she was feeding me a line of drek, she knew how to make it appetizing enough so I'd eat it, which implies a frag of a lot of good intelligence. So I'll assume she's on the level until something happens to indicate otherwise, but I won't put so much trust in that assumption that I'll take any chances.

Okay, that's better. As a working assumption, then, accept the existence of a connection between some slag called Timothy Telestrian—presumably the head honcho at TIC—and the Cutters. Since I've got nothing else more likely to lead to paydata, why not follow up on that?

Then comes the even bigger question of how?

Well, frag, it seems like everyone I've talked to recently has got an opinion about that. For the second time in half an hour, somebody's suggested I should try to contact some shadow-scum. First Finnigan, then the elf.

Suddenly edgy at being in the same place too long, I fire up the Americar and start cruising again.

It's been one of those days, and looks like it's not over yet.

18

Well, we all knew I'd do it eventually, didn't we?

The sun's coming up, a sullen glow to the east, off over the Barrens, and I'm cruising slowly north on Highway 5. My stolen Americar's got a fairly sophisticated autopilot, the kind that's supposed to be able to synch up so well with the traffic-control grids in the roads that it can follow a set course and not slam into anything on the way. Now's as good a time as any for a test run. While keeping my eyes on the road and at least one hand within easy grabbing range of the wheel, I'm also trying to monitor the tech and place a phone call using the pocket secretary so considerately returned a few hours ago.

Placing a call through the cel system from a moving car is the best way to avoid anyone locating me. Sure, someone decked into the phone system might be able to figure out I'm heading north on Highway 5 near such-and-such exit. But with the morning rush-hour traffic starting to build around me, I figure the resolution of any locator circuit in the phone won't be good enough to select one car from many. (Frag, I wish I'd thought of this last night . . .)

That's part of the reason. The other is that I'm heartily sick of public phones.

So who am I calling? Like I said, priyatel, we all knew I'd do it eventually. Place the call to the LTG number the elf gave me last night, I mean. The one to the blind relay that should get me in touch with the shadowrunner who calls himself Argent.

I chewed on it for most of the night, the advice I got from both Finnigan—a friend—and the elf biff—most definitely not a friend, but maybe not an enemy either. On reflection, I can see that the idea makes sense. Shadowrunners have resources that I don't—not anymore, not now that I'm cut off from the Star. They've got freedom of action, and they've

got no love or loyalty for any established organization—
Lone Star, the Cutters, or Telestrian Industries Corporation.
They're used to navigating the nooks and crannies of society, staying out of the light, and keeping one step ahead of
all the factions that'd like to see their guts ripped out. Sort
of like me at the moment. But—

But shadowrunners are the bad guys, that's what's bothering me. And no one whose gone through any kind of police
training can escape that line of thought. To a cop's mind all
people can be lumped into three simple categories: cops, civilians, and scumbags. A simple breakdown, with no excep-
tions. Oh sure, the "civilian" classification tends to drift a
bit. When a cadet first leaves the Academy, all fired up and
eager, naive and green, he might tend to rate civilians as
right up there, almost as admirable and worthy of attention
as cops. That doesn't last long, though, and soon civilians
drop way down the scale to rest only a few notches above
scumbags. Some cops—the real hard-bitten and cynical
ones—don't even bother making the distinction. If you ain't
a cop, you ain't drek, and that's all she wrote.

And there's never any doubt where shadowrunners fit into the
grand scheme. Scumbags, all of them. In fact, they represent
what I most hate about the scumbag category—amorality. Not
*im*morality—that I can live with. Frag, who hasn't gone through
one or two immoral phases in his own life?

No, it's the *a*moral route I can't handle. The amoral just
opt out of (meta)human society, totally refuse to play by any
rules. Opt out of all laws, all standards, all conventions of
conduct. Refuse to accept that there's anything more important than individual wants, desires, and impulses. Refuse to
accept that some conventions—some laws, some standards,
some social mores—are valuable to the development and ad-
vancement of society as a whole. Sure, there are some laws
I don't agree with, even some I choose not to obey and not
to enforce. But laws in general are important. I've always
believed that, and I always will. It's the same belief that led
me to the Lone Star Academy.

And it's because shadowrunners don't share that belief
that they're scumbags in my book. End of story.

Yet here I am riding along Highway 5 trying to get hold
of one by phone. It's a weird fragging world, priyatel, let me
tell you.

The pocket secretary warbles on the seat next to me, tell-

ing me it's registered with the cel network and is now dial-
ing LTG number 1206 (03-0409), the blind relay. (I'm not
sure what the frag that is, but it's probably something like
the scam I pulled with the pay phone when I called
Finnigan—though a lot more sophisticated.) As if to confirm
that, the ringing tone from the secretary is interrupted three
times by clicks and faint electronic beeps—almost certainly
transfers to different lines. Finally comes one click louder
than the others, then silence except for the ghost voices of
channel cross-talk. Disconnected? Frag, typical. Probably
one of the clicks represented some kind of notification to the
elf biff that I was calling the fake number she gave me, so
she could start laughing her hoop off at me.

I reach out angrily to shut off the phone, but freeze with
my finger a millimeter from the End key. There's another
ring tone, this one half an octave higher than the standard
cellular net tone. A private phone system? A PBX at
"Shadowrunners R Us"? Who the frag knows?

With an almost musical click, the final connection is
made, and a voice says, "Yes?" Male, well-modulated, not
harsh. Not particularly welcoming, either. Not that I expected it would be.

I key the phone's microphone on. "I want to speak to Argent," I say flatly.

"Oh?" There's a hint of dry amusement in the voice now.
"Do you, now?"

I figure there must be some kind of recognition code—
password and answer, cloak-and-dagger kind of drek—
which I don't know, and that slots me off even more than I
was a moment ago. "Yeah," I growl. "Are you him?"

"Who wants to know?"

"I do," I bark back. "The fact I know this number means
something, doesn't it?"

"Not as much as you seem to think, chummer," the voice
comes back immediately.

I let that pass. "Are you Argent?" I demand again.

A moment's pause, then, "I can relay a message," he says.
"You want him to call you, or what?"

"Tell me when he'll be back, and I'll phone him."

There's a low-pitched laugh. "You don't do this often, do
you, omae? Thanks for an amusing conversation . . ."

"Don't hang up!" I snap, my mind racing desperately. I'm
risking my hoop enough by placing this call. Giving this

slag the number for a call-back can't increase the danger
much more than it already is. "Okay, okay," I say at last.
"Get Argent to call me." I recite the pocket secretary's cel
phone number. "Right fragging quick, priyatel. Got it?"

"And who the hell are you, anyway?"

"Somebody who wants to talk to Argent, that's all you
need to know."

Another laugh, but this time with no humor in it. "Like frag
it's all I need to know. Lots of people want to talk to Argent.
Not many people Argent wants to talk to, if you get my drift."

I grind my teeth. "I'll make it worth his while," I grate.

"Give me a name, friend." The voice on the other end of
the circuit is cold and hard. For a moment the tone reminds
me of Blake, back with the Cutters. Another hard man, this,
just like the gang boss.

"Why?"

"No name, no message. Let Argent figure if it's going to
be worth his while."

The rage is back in my gut, squirming like a cold metal
snake. I want to scream, I want to kill. Not doing either one
is probably the hardest thing I've ever done, but I manage it.
"You want a name," I almost whisper.

"That's right, chummer. And make it a real one, okay?
You know Argent's going to check."

Yeah, I know it all right. Well, what the frag have I got to
lose? Anybody who's tapping into my line already knows
who I am. And if it's possible to accurately locate a particular mobile phone during Seattle's morning rush hour, it's
not Argent and his scroffy runner friends I'm most worried
about. "You want a name?" I spit out. "Tell him Rick Larson
called, browncone, and tell him I'm waiting." And with that
I hit the End key almost hard enough to crack the secretary's
composite enclosure.

So what the frag did that gain me, tell me that? Argent the
motherfragging shadowrunner isn't going to call me back. Why
should he? There's no fragging credit in it for him, and
shadowrunners don't do anything—*anything*—that doesn't pay.
That's what "shadowrunner" means—amoral, sociopathic mercenary. All I did was increase my exposure—make a call that
could be traced and then give out my fragging phone number!
Drek, what was I thinking? If I don't get my head out of my
fragging hoop, I don't deserve to live ...

What I really should do is get rid of the fragging pocket secretary. I glance out the car window. And now's probably the best time. I'm right in the middle of the Evergreen Point floating bridge, heading east toward Bellevue. Just open the window, heave it out into Lake Washington, and more fragging power to anyone who wants to trace it.

Holding the wheel steady with my left hand, I power down the passenger-side window. I've cut out the autopilot, needing to do something physical to keep myself from kicking my own hoop too long and hard. I grab the secretary and wind up to chuck it out of the car.

At that moment the fragging thing lets out a ring, startling me so much I almost drive into the guardrail. I hit the button on the dash to re-enable the autopilot, then I glare at the secretary. Do I even want to answer it now?

Do I dare *not* answer it? I punch the Stand-By/Talk key. "What?"

"You've got jam, Larson. I'll give you that." It's the same voice as before, with a strange undertone of ironic amusement.

"You're Argent, aren't you?"

There's a moment's silence on the other end. Then, "I'm Argent," the voice confirms. "And you're Richard Norman Larson, Lone Star employee number 714-80-795, highly trained and experienced deep-cover operative, Milkwaukee Organized Crime (Gang) task force, indefinitely seconded to Seattle in 2052." Another pause, then Argent goes on, "Like I say, chummer, you've got real jam." (Is that a hint of admiration in his voice?) "No fragging brains, but real jam. It's been a pleasure talking to you, omae."

I can imagine Argent's finger reaching out to break the circuit. "Wait!" I snap.

"Why?" The amusement's back in the runner's voice. "So you can trace my location? Don't waste your time."

"No." My mind's racing again. There's something here I'm not getting, something important. My subconscious is sounding all my mental alarms. It's also telling me not to lose contact with Argent. I just need time to figure out what to say to him. Time . . .

I look at my watch. Time! How long since I called the blind relay, since I left the message for Argent? Not more than about ten minutes. A horrible suspicion starts to dawn in my mind. Ten minutes . . . "You're a quick worker, Argent," I say, trying to keep my voice light. "It took you—

what?—about ten minutes to crack my personnel file out of
Milwaukee? Fast work, priyatel ... Or maybe you didn't
have to check Milwaukee. Maybe you've already got your
datahooks deep into the Seattle data fortress, huh?"

Argent snorts. "You're a paranoid frag, Larson," he says
flatly. "It didn't take any deep penetration at all. Lone Star
Seattle doesn't protect its personnel files worth drek."

"Huh?" To my own ears, my voice sounds like I've been
kicked in the gut. Something cold tightens under my heart,
like a fist. "What are you saying, Argent?"

He's surprised, and—no drek, Sherlock—suspicious.
"What do you mean?"

"You're saying you just cracked into Lone Star Seattle's
standard personnel files, and there I was?"

"Yeah, that's just what I'm ..." The runner's voice trails
off, and I know he's picked up on the same anomaly I have.
There's silence for a good couple of seconds, then he comes
back, "What kind of half-fragged game are you trying to
play here, Larson?"

"Game? Yeah, right. Like urban brawl, and I'm the flag."

"What the frag are you trying to say?"

"I don't have to say it, do I?" I snarl back. "I'm this drek-
hot undercover op from Milwaukee, right? Trained and experienced, like my personnel jacket says. And you find that
jacket in the standard employee files along with the secretaries and word-processing pool drones? Yeah, right. Come
on, Argent, grab a fragging brain here. How many other
deep-cover ops did you find in the files, huh? Tell me that?
No, on second thought, I'll tell you. Exactly fragging none,
right?"

Another silence, and I know I'm right. "If this is some
kind of reverse cover, it's not going to work," Argent
growls, but the anger's at least partially feigned now, I can
hear it.

"Yeah, right, brilliant cover," I sneer. "Maybe it gets me
closer to you, but meanwhile I'm getting chopped by the
Cutters. My file did say I was doing deep-cover on the Cutters, right? You think maybe, just fragging maybe, the Cutters might occasionally glance at the Lone Star standard
employment files, huh?"

"So ..."

"So I'm out of fragging sanction," I cut him off harshly.

"Beyond fragging salvage. You know what I'm talking about?"

"I've heard the phrases," he says dryly. "Prove it."

"You want proof? You're so hot with a fragging 'puter, check into a missile attack on a private vehicle, about thirty hours ago in Montlake. One fatality, a Catherine Ashburton—you'll find her in the Lone Star files if you dig deep enough."

"Another covert op?" Argent wants to know.

"Data processing manager," I shoot back.

"What's she got to do with . . . ?"

Again I cut him off. The rage feels like something huge within me, pressing on my lungs and squeezing off my throat so I can hardly force the words out. "I was in the fragging car." My voice is cold, like death. "Sheer luck I didn't croak too." I try to stop myself—this Argent motherfragger doesn't need to know—but I can't. "She burned. Cat Ashburton burned alive. It was a Star FRT squad pulled the ambush. They were after me. Check it out."

There's a long, heavy silence—ten seconds, maybe more—then Argent comes back. The hostility's gone from his voice, replaced now by a cool professionalism. "I'll check, Larson," he says. "Now, what do you want from me?"

"A meet." The words are out of my mouth before I know what I'm going to say. But, as I say them, I know they're the truth.

"If this is a setup . . ."

"No setup," I almost shout. "You pick the place, you pick the time. Bring friends, saturate the fragging area, I don't care. I'll come alone. If you don't like the way it comes down—if you don't like the way I'm fragging dressed—*cack* me, I need the peace and fragging quiet!"

He doesn't respond immediately. Then he chuckles quietly. "You've got your meet, Lone Star," he concedes. "Hold the line for details."

Why the frag did I agree to this? Yeah, sure, my brain knows it's the only logical next step—I'm dead-ended without more resources. But it's not my brain that's knotting my guts up so hard I want to spew. Fear? Who wouldn't be afraid walking into an unknown situation with someone who's always viewed your kind as an enemy? The other feeling is disgust, all that "to think I've sunk so low" bulldrek. Just the thought of dealing with shadowrunners leaves me feeling soiled somehow.

I force those thoughts deep, deep into the back of my mind. This meet's going to be edgy enough without Argent seeing in my eyes that I despise him and every other runner.

One thing I've got to give him, though. He does choose good places for meets. (He didn't give me the details over the cel phone, of course. That would have been little more than an open invitation for IrreleCorp and anyone else tapping the line to put in an appearance. I got the scoop via another call to another blind relay through yet another fragging public phone.) When Argent agreed to the meet, I expected he would wait for nightfall and pick a spot near the docks. That would have meant me spending the rest of the day trying to kill time, somehow, somewhere.

Instead he surprised me. An early-afternoon meet, at a place I'd only heard about in street rumors—the Hole in the Wall, a tavern out in Renton near the intersection of Maple Valley Road and Jones Road. Buzz on the street claims the Hole's a hangout for shadowrunners—mainly burn-outs and wannabes, according to some, but with a few of the "A-list" names putting in an appearance from time to time. (But if that's the case, you say, why the frag hasn't Lone Star closed the place down? Because street buzz isn't proof, chummerino. Apparently the Hole's one of the grottiest places you'd ever go a long way to avoid, but the owner—one Jean Trudel, according to the streets—keeps it just inside the limits of the health codes. Other than that? Well, frag, say the Star's after some shadow scum perp, and she ducks into the Hole. In come the boys in blue ... and everyone and their fragging dog swears up and down that the perp hasn't been here in months. Meanwhile she's bugging out the back way or maybe hiding out in the basement. Sure, you could probably put surveillance on the place, but that means diverting resources from other work. So the Hole—and other places like it throughout the sprawl—stay in business. That's life in the big city, priyatel.)

So that's why I'm jandering into the Hole in the Wall on a gray and rainy afternoon, feeling like I'd rather be just about anywhere else in the fragging universe at the moment.

The Hole's well-named, let me tell you. A small tavern fronting onto Maple Valley Road, with a wood-façade metal door and a single small window so grimed up it might as well be frosted transplast. I stand in the doorway for a few moments, holding the door partially open behind me while I let my eyes adapt to the darkness. The air's thick with smoke—tobacco and other more exotic substances—and the reek of stale beer, old sweat, and the unmistakable tang of fear. Great place, excellent ambiance. Why the frag am I here?

"Come in if you're coming," a voice growls from the shadows, "or get the frag out, but shut the drek-eating door."

Obediently I take a step forward, let the door swing shut behind me.

It takes a few more seconds before I can see worth drek. When I can, I scope the place out. The Hole's a "shotgun" arrangement, not much more than six meters wide, but stretching almost three times that in length. To the right of the door's the bar, a scarred macroplast thing with uncomfortable-looking stools in front of it. Directly to the left is what's left of a laser jukebox—you'd call it an antique if its electronic guts weren't trailing on the floor. Down the left wall are half a dozen round tables covered with terry cloth to soak up spilled beer and other fluids. Two of them are occupied, one by the hulking figure of a troll, the other by a couple of dwarfs. All three customers are giving me the evil eye, probably watching to see if I'll back down. So I give them a killer grin, jander over to the bar and settle myself down on a stool.

The bartender's down the bar, smearing the macroplast surface with a grimy rag. An ork, she's seen better decades, it looks like. Her left cheek's deeply scarred, and in the dim light of a holo beer sign, her left eye glints unnaturally. Cheap replacement, I guess. She sneers, baring chipped and yellowing fangs, and makes no move to come toward me.

I shrug. Whatever. I can play the chill game too. I wait, and eventually she puts down here cloth and stomps over to me. "Well?" she snaps.

"Draft," I reply. "And tell our mutual friend that Wolf's here." That's the code, such as it is, that Argent told me to use. Internally I cringe a little—it could well translate to "Cack me now," for all I know, but I don't let anything show in my face or posture.

The ork doesn't respond at all until she's drawn my beer, put the glass down in front of me, and slotted the credstick I hand her. Then she gestures toward the back of the tavern with a jerk of her scraggly, whiskered jaw. "Back room," she grunts. "He's waiting for you."

I nod my thanks, retrieve my credstick, pick up my beer, and jander back into the deeper shadows. There are three un-marked doors in the back wall. By the smell I identify two as cans. I take a pull on the beer—sharp tang of chemicals on my tongue—and push open the center one.

A short hallway, a closed door to my right, and a partially open one directly ahead. I step forward, and push the door open.

I'm looking into a small, cramped office—a couple of chairs, a desk with an archaic telecom, and a portable trideo box. Light comes from a single fluorescent tube mounted in a three-tube fixture in the center of the ceiling.

But I give the office itself only the briefest of scans. All my attention is drawn to the figure sitting behind the desk. Argent. It has to be.

I had no preconceived notions about this slag, but apparently I've got some about shadowrunners in general. A wea-sel, that's what I would have expected—a sly, sneaking drek who looks more like a rodent than a human. Dirty and ill-kempt, no charisma or what you'd like to think of as person-ality, the kind of slot you wouldn't turn your back on for fear he'd stick a knife into it. Maybe it's an image I picked up from the trid, then modified and filtered through my own preconceptions until it's become so deeply ingrained I didn't even know it was there until it got overturned.

And overturned it certainly is. Argent's a big man, no weasel. At a guess, I'd say he stands taller than two meters and masses ninety-five kilos, with the only fat in his body from the hamburger he ate for lunch. Broad shoulders, deep chest. Handsome, in a hard, chiseled kind of way, with short-cropped dark hair speckled with gray. Calm expres-sion, steady, cold gray eyes that glint sharply in the light. Lying palm-down on the desktop, his hands are empty, pre-sumably to reassure me, but it does just the opposite.

Argent's hands are both cyber—angular metal things, bru-tal and absolutely lethal-looking, with a smooth matte-black finish. Terrifying. I try to keep the reaction out of my face, out of my eyes, but I know I don't manage it.

The runner sees my reaction, that's for sure. Odds are he doesn't miss much, but he merely nods at me, and says, "Close the door and take a seat, Wolf."

I shut the door, but I don't sit down. I'm uncomfortable,

and when I'm uncomfortable I've got to be free to pace. "Wolf," I repeat. "What's this drek about Wolf?"

His lips quirk up in a wry smile. "You need a street handle," he says calmly. "Never use your own name if you can avoid it."

"So why Wolf?"

"Haven't you ever read any books?" he asks quietly. "Jack London? Wolf Larson ..." He shakes his head. "Forget it." He interlinks his fingers, and metal clicks on metal. I shiver. "You've got your meet, Wolf," he says calmly. "Now what do you want to do with it?"

"Did you scope out the missile attack like I told you?" I ask.

"An associate looked into it for me," he says, and I know he means a decker.

"And?"

The runner pauses for a long moment, his cold eyes steady on my face. "Interesting," he says at last. "Tell me again what you told me on the phone."

"What the frag do you need to hear again?" I ask him sharply. "Lone Star FRT set up on the rooftops. AVM into the car. I'm blown clear, the driver cooks. Need anything else, drekhead?"

Again he doesn't answer at once, just looks at me with those slightly unnatural eyes. Then he shakes his head. "That'll do," he says calmly.

I force myself to calm down—with minimal success. Will I ever be able to talk about the ambush without hearing Cat's screams in my head? "So what did your decker find?" I want to know.

"A media clamp-down and evidence of a cover-up," he tells me. "The official story is that terrorists were using the car to carry explosives, and the charge went up prematurely. That's what the Star told the media ... then told them they couldn't broadcast it." He shrugs. "Standard Lone Star procedure, as I'm sure you're aware. Under the surface, though, things are much different. There's a lot of drek going down—personnel reassignments, increased security on communication logs, that kind of thing. Just what you'd expect if the Star was trying to cover up their involvement."

I nod slowly. Yeah, just what you'd expect if they were trying to cover up the fact that they'd lost control of their comm channels ...

"You think Lone Star's put you out of sanction?" Argent wants to know.

I'm still not sure I should give up on the possibility someone outside the organization's orchestrating everything through the Star's compromised data fortress, but Argent doesn't have to know that, not yet. So, "Yes," I tell him.

He smiles humorlessly. "Then you're dead, chummer," he states. "It's just a matter of time."

I raise my eyebrows at that. "Oh? Why?"

"The corporation's got a tissue sample on deposit for you, omae," he says patiently. "Standard Lone Star procedure, part of the recruitment process, isn't it?"

"How'd you know that?"

The shadowrunner shrugs. "I heard it from a Johnson—a friend, actually—who used to be in the Star himself. Anyway, eventually they drag up that sample, they hire a mage or shaman, and they slam a ritual sending into you wherever you happen to be hiding at the time. End of story, Wolf. Nothing I can do about that."

I chuckle quietly. Argent knows more about the way the Star works than I'm really comfortable with, but at least he's wrong on this one. "No sample, Argent," I tell him.

"Did you crack in and purge it?" he asks.

"The Star purged it," I correct him. "Standard procedure for deep-cover ops, but I guess you didn't know that." I shrug lightly. "Some drek about somebody on the outside being able to take a skin sample or something from the op, then magically assensing if there's a 'contiguous' sample in the Lone Star vaults. Doesn't make much sense to me, but that's SOP. So, no sample."

"You think," he says softly.

That stops me for a moment. "I think," I have to allow. "But I've got to work on that assumption."

He nods his acceptance of that. "Your call," he says equably. He spreads his metal hands. "So you've got your meet and the meter's running, Wolf. What is it you want with me?"

I take a deep breath. I've been cogitating this for the past couple of hours, and I think I've got it refined as tight as I can. "Deep research," I tell him. "I need a decker to dig up some deep background on a corp in the Tir."

Argent smiles. "That's all?"

"It's a start," I snap back.

"You're taking some big chances coming to me if all you

want's some database search done, omae," he says quietly.
"There are some runners out there who'd geek a Star op—or
even an ex-Star op—just on principle."

"And you wouldn't?" I say sarcastically.

"I haven't yet," he points out quietly, "and I've never
been knee-jerk about that kind of thing anyway. You've got
your job to do, I've got mine. Stay out of each other's way
and we should have no quarrel with each other."

"Your job?" I sneer. "Feathering your own nest by
fragging people over?" The words are out of my mouth before I even realize it.

The chromed shadowrunner looks at me, a speculative expression on his face. I expect some kind of justification, or an
angry retort. Instead he just says quietly, "You don't know me."

Nor do I fragging want to, but this time I manage to keep
my yap shut.

Argent glances down at his hands, and I can almost hear
the intensity of his thoughts. After maybe half a minute, he
looks back up at me. "Data search," he muses. "Why?"

"My biz."

"Actually, no," he comes back immediately. "You want
me to make it my biz. Why should I?"

"I'll pay you."

"How?" He smiles grimly. "If you're really beyond salvage, the Star's frozen your contingency fund accounts,
maybe your cover accounts too."

"I'll pay you when it all shakes out," I growl.

His smile grows broader, but no less ironic, as he shakes
his head. "My people don't work on spec."

Fragging mercenary drek-eater. Why did I expect anything
else from a fragging shadowrunner? I bite back hard on my anger. He could still geek me if I push him too far. "Then I guess
we don't have anything else to talk about," I say coldly.

"I suppose not." I start to turn away, but his voice calls
me back. "Unless . . ."

"Unless what?"

"Unless you fragging open up on this, Wolf," he says, a
real hard and frosty edge to his voice. "Tell me what it's
about and give me a fragging reason why I might want to do
it. You got me, omae?"

I just stare at him.

"Come on, slot and run," he says impatiently. "Why not
just start at the beginning?"

19

So, what the hell, that's just what I do. I begin right from the fragging start, from the first moment I set eyes on that slag calling himself Nemo. All the way up to the elf biff's suggestion about contacting the shadowrunner.

Argent nods slowly at that last bit. "I wondered how you got the number," he says quietly. Then his lips twist in a faint smile. "That elf certainly danced you around, didn't she?"

I grind my teeth. "Yeah," I grate. "She certainly did."

His grin fades. "No kick against you, Wolf," he says. "I'm just admiring a pro's moves, scan?"

I nod curtly. Frag, I wish he wouldn't do that—act like a decent human being, I mean, with any kind of concern for my feelings. He did it when I repeated, in detail, the events of the Lone Star ambush and Cat's death, and he's doing it again now. What the frag right does he have?

But I push my feelings out of my consciousness. No time for them now. "Got everything?" I ask him harshly.

He raises an eyebrow at my tone, but all he says is, "I've got enough for a first pass." He leans back, and the chair creaks. "So, what do we know?"

"Squat!"

"Not quite. We do know there's some connection—of some kind, to some degree—between a corp in the Tir and the Seattle Cutters. That came out before the drek hit the pot, so I think we can accept it at face value." I nod grudgingly. "We also know that someone in the Star's put you out of sanction."

I shake my head at that. "Not necessarily," I correct him. "If somebody's penetrated the Star's data fortress—this Telestrian corp, maybe—they might be the one who ordered the ambush and who posted my personnel file in a less secure database."

Argent shakes his head, unconvinced.

"Why the frag not?" I demand.

He sighs faintly, and clasps his hands behind his head. "Maybe I can accept the ambush," he says. "Subject to confirmation, of course. That fits with the heavy-duty cover-up. But your personnel jacket?" He shakes his head again. "I can see somebody posting it there initially. But why hasn't the Star deleted it by now? And why haven't they found some way to bring you in? No," he goes on thoughtfully, "maybe Lone Star didn't put you beyond salvage initially—maybe that was Telestrian or whoever. But they certainly haven't done anything to reverse it, to repair the situation, have they?" He doesn't wait for an answer—not that he has to, he can probably see it on my face. "The only way I read it is that your superiors decided it might be better all around to color you dead as well."

I feel the chill touch of fear. "Why?"

The shadowrunner shrugs. "Because you know they've been compromised, maybe?" he muses. "It's one possibility. Have you thought how it'd hurt the Lone Star corporation if word gets out they're penetrated?"

I have to nod. Yes, I've thought about it. And bad, that's how it'd hurt them.

"So maybe they didn't issue the original death sentence," he goes on, "but it looks to me like they've decided to let it stand."

Frag. It picks me, but, "Yeah, I scan that," I have to admit.

"There could be other reasons as well," he cautions. "We should keep that in mind too."

"We?"

He flashes me a wry grin. "I mean 'you', of course."

"Of course." I slump down in the chair across the desk from him. "Well, oh high and mighty shadowrunner?" I ask sarcastically. "What's your verdict?"

Argent looks at me speculatively for a half a minute, his lips set in a tight line. For a few moments I think he's going to flare back at me—frag, that's what I'm looking for, isn't it, pushing him the way I'm doing? But he doesn't. Eventually he shrugs millimetrically. "Either way," he says calmly, "something's out of line within Lone Star. Either the corporation's seriously penetrated, seriously compromised, or . . ." His voice trails off reflectively.

"Or what?"

"Or . . ." He shrugs again. "Or something else is going on that we just don't understand. Either way, the corp's more or less out of control, and I don't like the thought of that."

"Oh?" That surprises me, deep down.

The shadowrunner gives me another one of his ironic grins. "Where do you get your ideas about runners, Wolf?" he asks quietly.

I've got no real answer for him, other than an uncomfortable shrug.

"It's not like Lone Star's the enemy, or anything," he goes on—quietly, thoughtfully, almost as if talking to himself, not to me. "Lone Star's like any corporation. Sometimes I'm working against it, most of the time I've got nothing to do with it at all, and sometimes I'm working *for* it."

I try to smother my reaction to that, but Argent's spreading smile tells me I didn't manage it.

"Didn't know that Lone Star sometimes hires shadowrunners, huh?" he asks me. "They do, you know. Not as often as some corps, maybe. But there are times when they need 'deniable' assets." His smile fades for a moment. "Sometimes expendable ones, too."

"Bulldrek," I tell him.

"I've got no reason to lie to you about this, chummer," he goes on as if I hadn't interrupted. "I've brokered maybe half a dozen Lone Star contracts in my time, and I've taken on two myself. And I've got no reason to believe I'm the only fixer in the plex that the corporation deals with." He hesitates. "There's a thought," he says after a moment. "If Lone Star has decided to color you dead, the odds are they won't use their own assets to handle it." He raises a matte-black hand to still my argument, and goes on, "I know they did the first time, but the way I scan it that was probably a rush job. Now they've had time to think it through, and if they're still out for your hide, they've probably decided to use unattributable assets." He hooks a metal thumb toward his chest. "Like me and my colleagues. Maybe I'll put out a couple of feelers," he muses, "and see if they're hiring."

"So you can take the contract yourself?"

"Give it a fragging rest, will you?" he says wearily. "It's just another way of finding out how serious they are about greasing you."

I nod slowly. I'm goading him, and I don't really know

why. It's drekheaded, it's counterproductive—he's the only resource I've got at the moment—but I know I'm going to do it again. "You were saying . . . ?" I prompt him.

"I was saying, I've got no reason to hate Lone Star. Some people have axes to grind, but the real pros—the real shadowrunners—can't afford grudges like that." He chuckles softly. "Sound mercenary, Wolf?" he asks. "Like, 'I can't hold a grudge against Lone Star because then they won't give me any more money.' It's more than that, though."

"What?" I find I'm interested, despite myself.

"Lone Star's the . . . the 'lid on the garbage can'." He smiles again, but it's a slightly self-conscious one this time. "That's about the best way I can put it. They keep things under control. Any business requires a stable, predictable environment to operate in . . ."

"So it all comes down to biz."

He shoots me a complicated look. "I've got to live here too, Wolf. Would you want to stay in the plex if Lone Star was losing control?"

I shake my head slowly. "And is that reason enough to help me out?"

"For the moment." He sits up straight. The thoughtful air's gone, and he's all biz again. The consummate shadowrunner. "I'll set Peg, my decker, on your Timothy Telestrian connection," he says, "but it might take a while. Decking into the Tir's not an easy proposition. Twelve hours minimum, I'd guess." I raise an eyebrow at that. This Peg must be nova-hot. My guess would have been more like a few days. "Have you got a safe place to flop in the meantime?"

I think about it for a moment. "Nowhere I feel particularly secure," I admit.

Argent nods. "I'll talk to Jean. She's got a doss upstairs you can probably use."

Great. A squat situated over a bar frequented by shadowscum. Yes, sir, that'll certainly make me feel fragging secure. Yeah, right.

"Wolf." The voice is quiet, close by.

I surge up out of sleep—disoriented as all frag, but too busy rolling over to snatch my H & K from beside the bed to worry about it. The wire and the smartgun are synching up even before I've got my eyes open. Then my eyes do open, and I see who spoke.

Drek, drek, drek … I let my gun hand fall and slump back onto the bed. My heart's racing at fifty-seven to the bar, and I feel like I came this close to having a foolish accident. "You slot," I gasp.

Argent the shadowrunner's sitting comfortably in a chair against the far wall of the one-room-and-drekker doss upstairs from the Hole in the Wall. I'd locked all the windows, none of which were big enough for anything more than a rat to squeeze through anyway. Which means Argent must have come in through the single door, somehow moving the wooden chair I'd lodged under the door knob. All without waking me up.

"Deep sleeper," the chromed runner remarks.

"Actually, I'm not," I counter, still staring at the ceiling and trying to control my heart rate before I have a seizure. "You fragging slot, I could have cut you down."

Argent's grinning like a fragging bandit. "Actually," he says, in what he apparently thinks is an imitation of my voice, "you couldn't."

I lift the H & K again, and this time I pay attention to what the wire's telling me about the gun's status. With a tired sigh, I drop the weapon back onto the floor and hold out my hand toward Argent. He flips something across the room to me. I catch it, turn it over and over idly in my hand. The clip from the H & K. Not only did he crack my defenses—admittedly rudimentary—to get into my room, but he also stole the ammunition out of my fragging weapon, all without waking me. I shake my head slowly. I'm getting too old for this drek.

I roll over and fix him with what I hope is a steely glare. "Okay, slot," I tell him in a cold, hard voice. "Point taken. You could have cacked me. I get the message."

His smile fades a little. "But I didn't," he points out. "And *that's* the message."

"Yeah, well, if you're trying to set me at my fragging ease, pick another way," I growl. What I don't say is that he's made his point. If he'd wanted me dead, or bagged, or whatever, I wouldn't be awake now—or if I was, it wouldn't be here.

Without looking, I slap the clip into the butt of the H & K, and let the wire confirm that everything's peachy. Then I let

my gaze drift around the dingy room. Judging by the light
coming through the tiny windows, I guess it's midday. To
confirm, I pick up my watch from the bedside table. It reads
1235, which means I've been sleeping for fragging near
twenty hours. I rub at gritty eyes as I swing up to sit on the
edge of the bed.

Argent's watching me appraisingly. "Feeling better?" he
asks.

I run a quick mental inventory and the wetware equivalent
of a Power-On Self-Test. My brain's nowhere near as
slagged-down as it was yesterday, but my body still needs
even more rest to overcome the protracted strain of the last
couple of days. Memory fragments of a dream—a nightmare, really—drift through my mind. I died and went to hell,
but hell wasn't the stereotypical pit of flames and torture. It
was a fragging parking lot—a world-sized parking lot—
where everyone lived in their cars while they waited for . . .
well, I don't know what they—we—were waiting for, and I
don't think I want to know. All I remember was that Cat was
living in the next car to me, and she was a mite bent that I
got her scragged. Understandable, and I'd probably have felt
much the same.

Wool-gathering. With a snort, I shake my head and force
the memories away. I fix Argent with another hard stare.
"So, got anything to tell me?" I demand. "Or is this just a
social call?"

"I've got something," he says slowly. "Peg's been busy.
But I think you're going to have to help me make sense of
it."

"I'll give it a shot." As I swing off the bed, Argent's already on his feet, and I join him by the large desk that dom-
inates the room.

In contrast to the room, the sophisticated telecom that sits
on the desk is in pristine condition. This year's tech, it's
right out on the cutting edge. Argent sits down in front of it
and powers the unit on while I drag up another chair and settle myself astride it, resting my forearms across the top of
the chair's back.

Argent slots a chip into the telecom port, and rattles a
string of commands on the keyboard. I watch him with interest. He's got two cyberarms and mods to his eyes—and, who
knows, maybe wired reflexes and other toys—but no
datajack. Why, I wonder? Interesting contradictions.

"It took Peg a little longer than she thought," Argent explains, almost apologetically. "She's in San Francisco, and the Tir's got extra-heavy security on the datalines from Cal Free. That's understandable, considering their situation, but still a pain in the butt. She had to relay through Seattle." He grins wryly. "Not that the security's much less on those lines, but every little bit helps in this kind of thing."

I nod wordlessly. I guess it shouldn't surprise me that Argent's decker isn't even in the sprawl—a decker can work anywhere as long as she's got datalines—but it does. I'd have thought Argent—or any shadowrunner, for that matter—would trust only people he had some physical control over. Maybe he has some serious dirt on this Peg and that's why he can trust her "remotely." I'll have to think about that when I've got some time.

The telecom screen fills with text—every second word or so highlighted, indicating a hypermedia link to other data files. I shake my head. Fast fragging work. This Peg must be one burner, I figure. I don't bother trying to read what's on the screen. Argent's scrolling and flipping around through the file. I decide to just wait until he's done.

After maybe a minute of scanning the files, the chromed runner turns to me. "This is everything Peg could dredge up on Timothy Telestrian." He shrugs. "Lots of background drek, more than you probably need."

"Summarize," I suggest.

For a moment it looks like he's about to refuse, then he shrugs. "Timothy Telestrian," he says. "Elf metatype, age thirty." A digitized image—flat not holo, the telecom's not that good—flashes up on the screen. Thin face, straight blond hair fine as a baby's, cool blue eyes, arrogant expression. Typical elf. I nod, and Argent goes on, "Son of James Telestrian III, also elf metatype . . ."

"Wait a tick," I cut him off. "That doesn't scan. Elves are born, right? They don't goblinize. And the Awakening happened in 2011. So that means . . ."

He grins. "That means James Telestrian would have been thirteen when he fathered Timothy?" He chuckles. "Yeah, that caught me, too, but I dug deeper. James Telestrian was a 'spike baby,' born before the Awakening. Rare, but it happens. James is fifty-five, born in 1999, according to Peg's research. Makes him probably the oldest elf in the world."

I sigh. "Okay, okay, forget I mentioned it."

Argent nods, but his drek-eating grin doesn't fade. "James Telestrian III founded Telestrian Industries Corporation, one of the biggest and most aggressive conglomerates in the Tir. He's still president and CEO. Timothy's his only son . . ."

"Which probably means Timothy's Senior Executive Vice President of Things Beginning with H, or some drek," I say sarcastically.

"Would have been my guess too," Argent says with a shrug. "But that's not the way it works. Surprisingly little nepotism in TIC."

I raise an eyebrow at that. "Oh?"

"Not to say Timothy's totally on his own," Argent continues. "He's a part of the TIC . . . empire, I guess you could call it, just not among the more rarefied ranks. Chummer Timothy is president of BioLogic Technologies, a subsidiary of TIC, but not a particularly large or successful one."

"And that's not nepotism?"

"Not compared to the big prize," Argent says flatly. "Bio-Logic is extremely small potatoes."

I shrug, and gesture for him to go on.

He does. "Peg doesn't think things were ever really close between James and Timothy, but they got even more distant about a year ago, maybe more. The senior suit in charge of a major TIC subsidiary called"—he leans closer to the screen—"Novalis Optical Technologies jumped ship to join a competitor, leaving the top spot open. Seems Timothy figured the corner office should be his."

"But daddy surprised him?"

"Big-time," Argent confirms. "Maybe you could call it nepotism because the slot went to family. But the slag he picked was a real hot prospect, really competent, with a solid track record. One Lynne Telestrian, Timothy's cousin."

"And Timothy didn't approve of daddy's choice?"

Argent chuckles. "You might say he was . . . critical . . . of James' business acumen. Loudly and publicly critical. Which, of course, didn't give James much incentive to change his mind." He sits back in his chair and smiles. "So Lynne got the corner officer and the stock options and the major perks, and Timothy got slotted off. So he declared war."

That makes me sit up straight. "Huh?"

"Probably not the way you're thinking of it," the runner amends quickly. "No drive-bys or geeked suits or blown-up facilities. No, this was corp warfare—stock manipulation, industrial espionage, and one of the nastiest proxy battles you've ever seen.

"Seems young Timothy wasn't quite the frag-up daddy imagined," Argent goes on, seeming to warm to the role of storyteller. "As soon as the drek hit the pot, James tried to can Timothy from his position as prez of BioLogic."

"Tried?" I blurt. "James is head honcho of the whole fragging Telestrian empire, isn't he?"

Argent nods. "True, but the various subsidiaries have some degree of autonomy. That's the way he set them up. They're under the TIC umbrella, but they've got their own boards of directors, their own shareholders, and all that drek. What happened was that James went to the BioLogic board of directors and told them to turf Timothy. The board told James to go frag himself."

I nod slowly. "Timothy's got some kind of lock on the BioLogic board."

"At the very least. It seems that James got a little twitchy at this point, and checked out the . . . the political reliability, I guess you could call it . . . of other parts of his empire . . ."

"Only to find Timothy had the fix in with them, too," I finish.

"Bingo. Not enough to give Timothy control—not as such—but enough so that daddy didn't have complete control himself. I understand he was a tad slotted off."

"Wonder why." I ponder for a moment, then nod again. "Okay, proxy fight between father and son. Where does cousin Lynne stand?"

"Firmly in James' camp. In fact, she's his expediter and honorable hatchet-man. James either has other fish to fry, or he judges Lynne is better than he is at this kind of drek. She's his Saint Michael, fighting off Timothy's incursions."

"What kind of incursions?"

Argent shrugs again. "Proxy fights, like I said. Intimidating shareholders, undercutting contracts . . ." He refers to the screen, pointing to a particular paragraph with a metallic finger. "Yeah, here it is. As one of the oldest elves around, James Telestrian has a megahuge rep in the Tir, which he's managed to parlay into a partial lock on the business community. That means if Timothy wants to increase his market share—and trust me, he does—he's got to do it outside the Tir." He looks at me expectantly.

I nod. Yeah, it makes sense, doesn't it? "And since all's fair in love and war, he'd have no qualms about dealing with the Cutters if it suited him." Then something else strikes me. "Got a picture of Lynne?"

He blinks, then rattles in a command on the keyboard. Another image appears in a secondary window. Long blonde hair pulled back behind her ears. Cold green eyes. Aloof, almost arrogant expression. "Pleased to make your acquaintance, Lynne Telestrian," I say quietly. "Again."

"The elf biff?"

"That's her." I pause. "Unless it's someone magically impersonating her . . ." Then I shake my head with a snort. "Nah, that's just getting too complicated, too paranoid."

Argent is scrutinizing the image on the display. "Lynne Telestrian. Interesting." Now he glances my way again. "So what does that tell us?" he asks.

I don't answer immediately. It tells me a few things, but I'm not sure why the frag I should share them with a fragging shadowrunner. Then I shake off that thought. He's treated fairly with me—so far, I amend—and there's no reason—again, so far—why I shouldn't level with him. His eyes are steady on my face, and it's not the first time I get the feeling he's making much too fragging good a guess about what's going on in my mind. I break eye contact, studiously examining the image of the elf woman. "It tells us we can put more faith in the Timothy Telestrian tie-in," I muse. "What would Lynne gain from sending us after a Timothy-Seattle connection that doesn't exist?"

Argent nods brusque agreement. "Anything else?"

"Maybe." What was it Argent called her? "If she's James Telestrian's Saint Michael, it means that the Seattle connection is important—to both sides—otherwise she wouldn't be wasting her time dancing me around." I shrug. "That's about it."

"There's something more," the shadowrunner says quietly. "*You're* important, Wolf."

I snap my head around so fast I almost sprain my neck. "Huh? Bulldrek." The word's out of my mouth before I realize it isn't bulldrek after all.

"It's the same logic," Argent says firmly, reinforcing what I just realized myself. "You must be important, or else she wouldn't be wasting her time dancing you around. She'd ignore you or geek you. But she hasn't done either."

"Yeah," I agree unwillingly. "All right. But why?"

"My guess is you should be putting some serious skull-sweat into figuring that one out," the runner says. "She must figure you know something—or can do something—that could frag up whatever Timothy's got happening in the plex. Any ideas?"

What fragging danger could I be to some ambitious elf suit? Unless Timothy were to get caught in the crossfire when the Star and the Cutters try to geek me, I can't see I'm of any significance to Timothy fragging Telestrian. "Not right at the moment," I say mildly.

Argent chuckles. "Well, give it some thought, omae. For your own sake, if for no other reason."

"No drek, Sherlock." I rub at my eyes. Frag of a thing to have to deal with when you first wake up—trying to figure out how you fit into some elf-corp infighting. "Did Peg dig up anything on Mr. Nemo?"

"Nothing under that name," Argent says, face twisting wryly. "No fragging surprise. And it's not as if your description was worth much."

"It's not as if there was much to fragging describe," I snap back, feeling suddenly defensive. "Brown and brown, olive complexion, medium height, medium build, no distinguishing features, age twenty-eight to forty. Not a frag of a lot to go on, you know what I mean?" Translation: I'd like to see you do any better, hotshot . . .

For an instant, Argent's modified optics narrow and take on a frosty glint. I know he scanned the last message just fine, and I think maybe this time I've pushed him too far. But the tension lasts only an instant, then the hard lines of his body relax and he nods. "No kick against you, Wolf."

"None taken," I lie back, and honor's satisfied. Frag this Alpha-male, ¿Quien es mas macho? drek. It just gets in the way. "Too bad."

"Shoganai," the runner says. "Jap for 'drek all we can do about it.'"

I'm silent for a moment, then, "You know, sometimes no distinguishing features can be distinguishing enough. Like, neither of us qualify. I'm too tall, you're . . ." I don't finish the thought.

Argent gives a feral grin, and there's a metallic snick as he clenches both fists. "Point taken."

"So assume Nemo's in the TIC empire somewhere," I go

on. The runner nods in acceptance. "Personnel jackets have photos. Could Peg pull up shots of everyone who's male and plain vanilla, no distinguishing features? I'll do the mugshot route and see if I can spot him."

Argent's not convinced. "You know how big the TIC empire is, omae?"

"Then limit it to Timothy's bloc," I say impatiently.

"Maybe."

"Can you think of a better way?"

Eventually the shadowrunner shakes his head. "No," he admits. But he's not giving up totally. "You figure Nemo's worth the effort?"

"Fragged if I know, but he could be. We marked each other, remember?"

"I also remember you don't know from where or when."

"Frag, I know that, okay?" I bite back on my impatience the best I can. "I don't know if it's important. I only know it might be important. Got any better ideas" . . . butthead?

Argent doesn't say a word, but his steady gaze gets the message across just fine: Yeah, kick your sorry hoop out of here back onto the street, and go back to hoopfragging the corps for major nuyen like a good little shadowrunner.

For maybe fifteen seconds we sit like that, giving each other the old stare-down, and the wire starts really wanting to scrag Argent. But it's the shadowrunner who looks away first, with a minuscule nod. "Okay, it's another possible lead," he says quietly. "I'll pass it on to Peg."

And I realize I've just won an argument with a shadowrunner.

20

Which leaves me with the question, just what the frag am I supposed to do next? I'm a nullhead, so I can't do squat to help the datasearch. And with a death-mark on me—courtesy of the Cutters and the Star and who knows who else (Timothy fragging Telestrian, maybe?), going out to work the streets is an invitation to get myself geeked. And where would I go and what streets would I work anyway? I feel about as useless as tits on a fragging bull, and I don't like it.

The moment Argent leaves to go relay the Nemo lead to Peg the decker, I feel like a caged fragging animal. I have to do something—anything. I jander on down the stairs that lead into one of the back rooms of the Hole in the Wall and I look around for something to occupy my time and my mind. I'm still looking for it in the office where I first met Argent, when I hear the door open behind me.

Pull the H & K, spin and drop into a crouch . . .

And wind up looking over the sights at the crabby old cow of an ork-woman who was tending bar yesterday. Jean Trudel, the owner of this place, according to Argent.

If staring down the muzzle of an SMG fazes Trudel in the slightest, she's too hard-bitten to show it. She just glares at me out of her mismatched eyes, and snorts. I don't know whether the sound is one of disgust, amusement, or both, and don't really want to know.

Trying not to show my chagrin, I make a production of safing and returning the weapon to its holster and standing back up. "You startled me," I say mildly.

She makes a disgusting phlegmy noise I tentatively identify as a laugh. "Big man with his little gun," she chortles. "Lone Wolf, hah?"

I don't need to put up with this drek. I head right past her for the door without giving her so much as a glance. I'm just about out of the office when she says, "You want a car?"

That stops me, just like she knew it would. I turn slowly. She's smiling, giving me a better look at her chipped tusks than I really want at the moment.

"Argent said you'd want a car," she says again, as unfazed by my hard-eyed appraisal as she was by the H & K. Tough old bat—either that or too dumb to know when it's smart to be scared.

"He did, huh?"

"Surprised it took you so fragging long."

I decide to leave that the frag alone, and go along with the game. "Where?" I ask.

She's got one hand deep in a pocket of her baggy jumpsuit, and now it comes out. I have to overrule the wire to keep from dragging out my weapon. I look down at her hand. Hanging from a stained and callused forefinger is a keyring with an electronic codekey hanging from it. "Parked out front," she says.

I snag the key as I brush past her. She chuckles, and my stomach twists at the sound. "It's red," she says helpfully to my retreating back.

"To match your fragging eyes," I mutter under my breath. Her hearing's better than it has any right to be, because she barks with laughter. Frag her and the hog she rode in on. And frag Argent too for knowing I'd want to hit the streets and for letting Trudel in on it. Serve them both fragging right if I took their car, slipped the border heading north— I've always liked north—and sold the pecker for a starting stake in, say, Vancouver. Let Lone Star, Timothy Telestrian, cousin Lynne, the Cutters, and the shadowrunners of Seattle frag each other's hoops till they bleed, and good riddance say I. Pleasant daydream, but everyone knows I'm not going to put it into practice.

Trudel-hag spoke truly: the car is red, and it's parked out front. Right out front, in a taxi-only zone. Either somebody's got a much better handle on predicting my actions than I'd really like—all odds say it's Argent—or I'm under surveillance, electronic, meat, magical—or all three. Can't say I like either option worth drek. The car, however, is enough to make me feel marginally better. It's a Eurocar Westwind 2000, the 2054 model. A rag-top, which means it's got the turbo engine and performance suspension package. Just short of 150-K nuyen worth of high speed and high performance—and somehow I get the feeling Argent bought the fragging thing instead of boosting it. Once again I find my image of shadowrunners isn't exactly on the money.

I trigger the codekey, hear the doors unlock and the engine—smooth as silk, like music to my fragging ears— light up instantly. I slide into the driver's seat, which is low to the road and contoured like something from a fighter plane, and run my hands and eyes over the instrument suite. I blip the gas pedal, and watch the low-intensity orange symbology of the analog instruments respond instantly. Yes, even though I'm not exactly sure where I'm going, I get the feeling I'm going to enjoy getting there. I close the door—a whoosh-click, not the clunk you get from your typical Americar—drop the transmission into gear, and pull out.

The Westwind's got a sophisticated entertainment system installed, and I put it to good use as I head north on 405 through Bellevue. At first I scan the bands for some music hot enough to blow the cobwebs out of my brains. Classic Mercurial, maybe, or the latest by Marli Bremerton and the Shadows. Anything but Darwin's Bastards. The music is fine but it gets old pretty fast, and I start feeling the need for a serious data fix.

I've always been a news junkie, a tendency repressed but not extinguished when I got into undercover work. How long since I checked in with what's happening outside the tiny little sphere that's my own existence? Too fragging long—three days at least. I wander the bands again looking for a newsbreak, then I'm in heaven when I hit something I recognize as the NewsNet feed—audio only, of course—out of Atlanta. The Westwind's pilot and handling package are so smooth the thing feels like it wants to drive itself, so I give it free rein while I concentrate on Ted Turner's spiritual descendants.

Nothing much new or earthshaking, at least not at first. Among the NAN states, Salish-Shidhe and Tsimshian are still slagging each other off in council meetings, and threatening war over some new resource-allocation scheme. Pueblo doesn't like Ute now, while Sioux—the old enemy— seems to be the flavor of the week. In Europe, the Serbs and the Croats are at it again, and everybody still hates the Israelis. Three universities are holding celebrations of the one-hundredth anniversary of some slag named Tolkien publishing the first book in some trilogy or other, and an At-

lanta Neo-Anarchist group wants to declare a "Day of
Shame" about the activities of someone called McCarthy,
also from a fragging century ago. (Get with the present, will
you?) The biz news boils down to the megacorps still giving
it to the consumer up the hoop. No mention of TIC, Bio-
Logic, Lightbringer, or Novalis Optical Technologies, but
that's no big surprise.

The local news—from some sprawl-based NN affiliate, I
assume—jars me, makes me realize how out of touch I am.
NewsNet has a better rep for sticking to the facts than any
competing organization, including the Catholic Church. According to this report there's some kind of nasty viral infection cutting a swath through the underclass of the Seattle
metroplex. Sure, this is NN, but the network's still concerned with ratings, so cut back the level of hype and hysteria by a factor of ten. If the announcer's on the money,
then this is something a little more disturbing than the latest
outbreak of Shanghai P super-flu. I slow down and punch up
the volume.

"City health officer Dr. Ken Blatherman describes the
mini-epidemic as a novel species of retrovirus, showing limited infectivity, and spread by an unknown vector," the talking head announces, hardly stumbling over the big words at
all. (This *is* NN . . .) "The fact that, so far, the viral infection
seems limited to the city's underclass indicates more that the
conditions faced by the under-housed and underemployed"—
translation: squatters—"lead to increased expression of the
disease than that the source of the infection is somewhere on
the streets of Seattle, Dr. Blatherman states. The doctor also
takes pain to contradict the reports from irresponsible media
sources"—translation: NN's competitors—"that fatalities
have, so far, been limited to the metroplex gang subculture.
He also states—even more vehemently—that this is not similar in any way, shape, or form to Virally Induced Toxic Allergy Syndrome. This is not, as has been previously—and
irresponsibly—reported by others, an outbreak of some myth-
ical strain of VITAS 4.

"In other local news . . ."

I reach out a finger and hit the Scan key, and the talking
head's voice is replaced by the assembly-line blast of some
neoindustrial hit. Christ knows, I'm not one of those
drekheads who look back on some mythically ideal "good
old days," some Camelot golden age when everything was

fragging peachy and everybody loved everybody else, but sometimes I can't shake the feeling that some evil drek's started going down recently. Maybe it's just my Lone Star background, but whenever someone officially and vehemently denies the truth of any rumor, I start taking fragging precautions. VITAS 4? Just fragging wonderful. How many people did VITAS 3 take down forty-some years ago? One-plus percent of the world's population. Something like fifty million deaders—if I haven't slipped a decimal point somewhere.

Then again, maybe something like this putative VITAS 4 is just what Seattle needs. A super-bug that takes down only gangers, and maybe add the shadowrunners into the mix while we're at it. Some of my old Star colleagues would just love that, and I surely wouldn't shed any tears along the way.

Ah, it's just hysterical drek anyway. How many outbreaks of "VITAS 4" have the news media ragged on about over the last decade? Three or four that I can remember, and none of them turned out to be the great apocalyptic pandemic. One round was unpleasant—that new strain of meningitis that cacked a dozen school-kids in Chicago back in 2045—but the rest were just non-starters like nuevomycin-resistant strains of herpes and syphilis. No scare as long as you took basic fragging precautions. It only makes sense; throw enough antibiotics and wonder drugs at bugs and all you're doing is selecting for tougher and more resistant bugs. Isn't that how evolution and natural selection work in the first place?

Forget about it. I don't have the bug, nobody I know has the bug, and it wouldn't make much difference anyway. I'm still out here cruising the highways and byways of the sprawl, without the slightest fragging clue about what to do next, a fact not changed an iota by news of a killer bug that happens to be going after the local gangs.

I take the next exit off 405, cut over onto 520. I kick the throttle as I hit the floating bridge, and the Westwind howls with feral joy all the way across Lake Washington. I hang a right into Montlake and rocket onto Montlake Bridge, the car fragging near painted onto the road, even taking the exit at almost twice the posted speed. I keep my eyes fixed straight ahead, trying to blot out all glimpses of the area. It's no good, though, and I know I'm going to relive the ambush in my nightmares again tonight. Onto the U-Dub campus past the cantilevered nightmare of the new stadium, through University Village and into Ravenna. And that's when I cut way back on my speed and start to wrestle with whether I might actually have thought of a way to handle this whole thing or whether I just want to call it a bust and blast on back to my hidey-hole in Renton.

Like, it's just the most unformed idea possible, nothing concrete enough to merit the name of a plan. It was the "super-bug" report that got me thinking about the Cutters, you see. The gang is the one angle I haven't been paying much attention to lately. Instead, I've been wracking my fragging brains about the way the Star's been acting, while Argent and Peg are presumably digging up the dirt on Timothy Telestrian. But we seem to have forgotten all about the Cutters, the other end of the Tir-Seattle connection. (Well, "forgotten" might not be the right word. It's kind of hard to totally forget about people who've put a death-mark on you, but maybe I could say something like "failed to give adequate attention.") The connection's there, though. Nemo and the elf contingent, who I'm assuming are linked with Timothy Telestrian, did meet with Blake, and it only makes sense to follow up on that angle. But how?

And that's the question. The Cutters did try to geek me, and there's no good reason to believe they've changed their opinion of my continued existence. That means I can't very well just march into one or another of their safe houses and ask, "Hey, chummers, what's down?" Not if I don't want to suck hot lead, at least.

But maybe I could learn something important by observing the activity around one of the safe houses. Frag knows what that might be. If I had the answer to that question, I probably wouldn't be looking in the first place. Who knows? Maybe I'd spot Nemo again or another member of the contingent—spot, follow, bag, and interrogate. Now what you'd call a likely outcome, but remotely possible.

Sure, it's a risk to go anywhere near Cutters activity, but I figure it's a calculated one. Even if the gang's still looking for me with intent to scrag, the last place they'd be expecting to see me is the street right outside one of their safe houses. Also, the Westwind represents excellent cover and concealment. The car's windows are nicely tinted, letting me see out clearly, but making it a cast-iron bitch to see in. Besides, nobody who knows Rick Larson, ganger, will expect him to come cruising by in one hundred-fifty-K worth of Eurocar Westwind 2000 high-performance automotive technology. Or, that's the line I keep trying to feed myself, with limited success.

Well, if I'm going to do it, let's fragging do it. I cruise east on Northeast Fifty-fifth Street, then hang a right onto Thirty-sixth Avenue Northeast. The safe house is in the middle of the block, on the east side of the street. I figure a pass right in front to scope out the overall situation, then from there I'll decide what to do next. I punch up the Westwind's autopilot so I don't have to split my attention between surveillance and trying not to hit parked cars. I lock in the speed at forty-five klicks—slow enough to give me a reasonable view but not so slow it'll attract unwanted attention—and we're off.

But something's wrong, I see that at once. The safe house is just that—a safe place for Cutters gang-bangers to hang, a place for them to doss when they need to, that kind of drek. It's not going to remain safe if it's got a lot of activity around it, particularly such obvious gang action as knife-duels and such drek. Predictably, then, all Cutters safe houses are more or less quiet places—unobtrusive, not memorable.

But there's a difference between quiet or unobtrusive and totally fragging dead—which is how the Ravenna house looks as I cruise by. Front door open—that door's never left open—with not the slightest sign of movement inside or outside. Yeah, sure, everybody could be out doing biz or maybe attending some major gang meeting in the basement. But they wouldn't leave the front door open while doing it. And that doesn't explain my unshakable gut sense that the place is dead as the Calvary Cemetery a block away. (Deader, maybe, considering the rumors of ghouls in Calvary.)

Before I can have any second thoughts about the wisdom of my actions, I've disabled the Westwind's autopilot and pulled over to the curb. I open the door and get out, sliding my hand under my jacket to grip the butt of my H & K to let tech and gun handshake. Still no movement in or around the safe house. I cross the road to stand in the partial cover of a drek-kicked van that's up on blocks. (This is Ravenna, after all . . .) And I stare at the building until it feels like I'm getting segs on my eyeballs.

Nothing, priyatel, not a fragging thing.

So what now? Something's gone down with the Cutters, something significant. I think. But am I certain enough of my conclusion to put my hoop on the line? Think about it—even if Blake hasn't actively sent out any more hit teams after me, I'm still known among the gangers as a Star mole. Chances are that if I should happen to jander across somebody's gunsight, that somebody would cack me for sure. Strolling into a Cutters safe house is just an invitation to trouble, right?

But it's too late to turn my back and play things safe now. No fragging way. Who knows, maybe this is some kind of clue to the Telestrian-Cutters link I was babbling about on the way to Ravenna. Curiosity may have killed the cat, and maybe it'll kill the Wolf as well, but right now I can't seem to turn it off like some fragging light switch.

Okay, I've been standing and watching long enough. If I'm ever gonna move, now's the time. For the benefit of any neighbors or pedestrians who'd probably be all too glad to hit the PANICBUTTON and report the presence of an armed man in their street, I keep both empty hands at my sides as I jander frostily up the front steps and in through the open door.

The minute I'm into the hallway, out comes the H & K and jander turns into combat crouch. My back against the wall in the corner, I hold my breath and listen. Again, nothing—no running water, no muffled trideo, no footsteps. Nothing. The place is empty, the feeling hits me again even stronger than before. It's a chill, creepy sensation. Scanning with the H & K muzzle, I move deeper into the house. At the back, looking out over the optical-chip-sized yard, is a lounge where gangers hang, watch the trid, and generally blow the drek. Usually the place looks like a grenade hit it, with pizza boxes, beer cans, and similar drek thrown and scattered everywhich where. There's a phone, too, next to a patch of the wall scrawled over with notes, LTG numbers, and such. If I'm going to get a quick indication of what's gone down, and when, the garbage lying around might be where I find it.

I pass the staircase, then the kitchen—check both of them out quickly, finding sweet frag all. I reach for the door to the lounge . . .

Then instantly freeze in my tracks. I can hear something

now. Breathing—a steady, bubbling, phlegmy noise that reminds me of Jean Trudel's laugh. Like the sound of somebody snoring—an old man, maybe—but not quite that.

I study the situation. The door to the lounge is closed almost all the way but it's not latched, which means I don't have to slot around with doorknobs. It opens away from me, into the room—the perfect deal for kicking the door open, going in low, and hosing down anything that moves.

Which in real life is rarely the best tactic in a tight situation, no matter how many times you see it on the trideo. The snoring—or whatever—is steady and deep. There's a kind of hitching sound—more like a bubbling click, actually—after the exhalation and before the inhalation, and from way out of left field the thought suddenly strikes me that that's exactly where the breathing's going to eventually stop. Breathe out, click . . . and nothing at all, ever again. I shove that thought away violently, and slowly open the door with my left hand. The H & K's ready and the wire's humming, ready to pop anything that threatens me.

There's nothing threatening inside the room, not immediately threatening at least. Drek everywhere—chip carriers, empty flash-pak food containers, beer cans, the usual—piled on the two low tables and the handful of chairs. Everywhere except on the single big couch under the window and across from the trideo set.

And that's because there's a figure on the couch who's the one doing the snoring. But with the door open now, it doesn't sound so much like snoring anymore as someone trying to breathe through scuba gear clogged with porridge. More than disconcerting. I feel claustrophobic and smothered just to hear it.

The figure looks small—not a kid, but a small-framed adult human, I guess—and it's so bundled up in coats and stained blankets and the lounge's curtains, for frag's sake, that I can't tell who or even what sex it is. The most important thing at the moment is that nobody else is in the room, so I move forward on cat's feet. The H & K's leveled at the center of the figure's forehead, just in case, but that's more out of habit than because I'm really worried about facing any problems here.

There's no change in the breathing—none at all—as I get close. I get a whiff of something unpleasant—biological, kind of like rotting meat, but not quite. And a whole bunch of different ideas all fall into place with an almost-audible click, and I don't like the picture they make. Not one little fragging bit. Using the H & K's flash-suppresser, I push a fold of curtain back from the figure's head so I can see the face.

It's Paco, and he looks like drek. His skin's not so much white as a faint tinge of blue, except for two big, dark smudges under the eyes. I could almost convince myself those smudges came from somebody blacking the young ganger's eyes for him, but the truth is those marks didn't come from external trauma. His lips are cracked and peeling, showing fissures here and there so deep they're down to pink meat. There's thick, yellow-white mucus trailing from his nose, and now I know why his breathing's got that underwater sound to it—his lungs must be full of that drek. He stirs and coughs, and his breath on my face is thick with that rotting-meat reek. "Frag!" I mutter, backing away, stifling an impulse to retch.

His puffy eyes blink, then slowly open. They're so blood-shot I can barely see any white at all. They roll wildly, blindly for a moment, then they settle on my face. "Larson." Paco's voice is a tortured, horrible thing, bubbling like a man being drowned in a swamp. "Larson, 'choo?"

Oh Mary Mother of fragging God. I move closer—if whatever this drek is gets transmitted by breath, I'm already infected. "It's me, Paco," I tell him softly.

"I'm sick, 'mano," he says. "I never feel this bad. Help me, huh?"

I nod—I don't trust myself to speak. "I'll help you," I tell him, though I haven't got a fragging clue how to go about it.

"Help me," he says again, like he hasn't heard me. "I got the bug, 'mano. I think I'm gonna die."

21

I've never liked doctors, and I've never liked hanging in places where doctors are around. Sure, I've dragged chummers, comrades, perps, and strangers into more emergency rooms than I really care to count, but I've always hated the experience. I suppose because some irrational part of me is drek-scared I'm going to catch whatever the other guy's got—even if he's not diseased, but shot, cut, broken, or otherwise injured. Frag logic. I can tell myself a hundred times that bullet wounds are not contagious, but I still want to get the frag out into the open air as fast as I can.

So, imagine how I feel when the other slag actually *is* diseased? Infinitely worse, priyatel. And if that weren't bad enough, it's not a real hospital where I'm hanging, and that motherfragging Argent is fragging late . . .

Nothing to do but pace, my boots clicking dully on the scarred linoleum floor. (Linoleum! Tells you how old this fragging place is.) There's a tattered vinyl couch in the waiting room, but I'm not in the mood for multiple puncture wounds from the springs. Sit on the couch and you suddenly become another patient for the doc to patch up and charge you a hundred nuyen for doing it. I keep finding my gaze drawn back to the ancient twelve-hour-style digital clock on the wall. It reads six oh-three, which translates to 1803 in real time, only a minute or two since I last looked. Time fragging flies when you're not having a drekky time.

Okay, so I'm probably not having as drekky a time as Paco. The shadow doc has been working on the poor slot in the operating room or clinic or whatever ever since I got him here three hours ago. The fact that the doc hasn't come out yet probably means that Paco hasn't snuffed, but that's about all I can say. Not a fragging clue about how serious the situation is or what the diagnosis and prognosis are. The doc told me—ordered me, more like—not to so much as touch

the OR door, and that's one order I've got no real desire to buck.

Looking around at the decaying shadow clinic, I feel kind of guilty about bringing Paco here. Sure, the kid's Cutters, and according to the Lone Star canon that makes him a scumbag. But I always kind of liked him, on a personal level. He always dealt straight with me. Frag, he was the one to warn me when my cover was first blown. He put personal loyalty to me—a chummer, a comrade—above loyalty to the gang. That's got to count for something. It surprises me, but I'm feeling like Paco's a friend, and I don't have too many of those. Like, none, if he bites it, and that's a sad fragging thought.

So, all in all, I'd be much happier if I'd dragged him off to Harborview Hospital. Out of the question, of course. Paco never mentioned it, but I'm assuming he's SINless. Harborview wouldn't touch anybody without a System Identification Number. Plus there's always a major Star presence in the Pill Hill area. Dragging Paco into the lobby would probably have only got him booted out, and me bagged or geeked. That, of course, left a street doc, a shadow cutter, as the only option.

The one I picked—one Dr. Mary Dacia, known to the street as Doc Dicer—had a good rep among the Cutters, and was even mentioned as a "resource of last resort" in my Lone Star briefing when I was transferred to Seattle from Milwaukee. Apparently a real-and-for-true M.D., specializing in trauma cases, with publications in the academic literature and everything. (So, why the frag is she working as a shadow cutter and not a real doc? Got me hangin'.) Doc Dicer works out of a defunct restaurant on Blanchard, within sight of the Space Needle. A small, well-built woman with short red hair, she's tough, competent, and has a real frosty edge. And yet I sense a caring human being under that street-hard façade. Best I could do for Paco, and maybe good enough.

The door from the alley—Dicer's "front door"—swings open, and out comes my H & K. I put it away when I see it's Argent. "Took you long enough," I grouse.

The chromed runner shrugs. "Jean told you I was busy when you called," he says reasonably. "I only got the message"—he glances at his watch—"twenty minutes ago." He crosses to the couch and slumps down wearily. Hitting the treacherous springs doesn't make him jump back up again. Either he's too tired to react to multiple puncture wounds or his hoop's as armored as a tank. "You said it was important," he notes.

"Maybe." And I tell him about my visit to the Cutters safehouse.

From his expression I can tell he's not too thrilled to hear about my decision to go to Ravenna, but he keeps listening, then nods as I explain the rationale. "Risky," he says, "But I'd probably have done the same. Go on."

So I do, telling him how I brought the Westwind around back, dragged Paco out of the house wrapped in curtains, and blasted downtown to Doc Dicer's establishment, whereupon I called him. When I'm finished, he nods slowly. "Interesting," the runner muses quietly. "I've heard about this super-bug. You can imagine the wild rumors on the street. But it's all been 'friend-of-a-friend-of-an-acquaintance' kind of thing. Nobody I know has caught it, or even knows anyone personally whose got it. I just wrote it off as this-year's-model flu epidemic and a huge whack of hysteria." He glances toward the door. "Maybe it's time to re-evaluate."

"No drek," I growl. Now that Argent's here, I'm not completely sure why I called him in the first place. It seemed like a good idea at the time, but now? Do I want to be cooped up in here with the shadowrunner if all he can do is help me wait?

As if in divine response to my doubts, the door to the OR-or-whatever-it-is swings open, and Doc Dicer appears. She's scragged—I can see that in her face and the sag of her body—but she's also worried. Not a good sign.

"How is he?" I ask.

She doesn't answer immediately, instead turning to Argent, who's already on his feet. A broad smile spreads over her face, and she suddenly looks a decade younger. They embrace, the petite woman dwarfed by the burly runner. His matte-black cyberarms hold her gently, almost tenderly. After a moment they separate.

"Long time," says the doc.

Argent shakes his head slowly as he looks around. "Quite a change."

She shrugs. "I can make a difference here," she says, "and that's a change worth making." She raises an eyebrow as she looks pointedly at his arms. "Some changes on your side, too."

"Can we, like, postpone old-home week?" I put in dryly. Both turn suddenly cold gazes on me, but I don't back down. "How's your patient, Doctor?"

"Dying, maybe," she shoots back. "Every time I think I've got him stabilized, the retrovirus does this funky antigenic shift and he's on the greased slope again." She pauses, and her hard expression softens slightly. "A friend?"

"Yeah," I say, and it's the truth. "Yeah, a friend." A new thought hits me. "Would he be better off in a real hospital?"

"Maybe, but it's not a sure thing," she replies. "Might just be a better-decorated place for him to die in."

I nod. "Can I talk to him?"

She wants to say no, I can see it in her eyes. But after a second or two she nods. "I'll give you two minutes," she says sharply, casting a glance at Argent as if recruiting the big runner to help keep me in line.

"Two minutes," I say, and Doc Dicer opens the door.

Paco looks small in a bed surrounded by high-tech monitors and other drek. He's got wires and sensors and other crap attached to his head and his wrists and also disappearing under the covers to reach his chest. He looks like a little fragging kid. The smudges under his eyes are darker and more pronounced, and his lips still look like hell, but at least there's not any of that yellow drek pouring from his nose, and his breathing sounds almost clear. His eyes themselves and his cheeks are sunken, though, and it looks like he's gotten thinner in the three hours since I dragged him in here. I feel cold.

"Is he contagious?" I ask.

The doc smiles humorlessly. "About time you asked that question," she says. "He's surrounded by laminar-airflow isolation, which should keep any bugs right where they are. Without that?" She shrugs. "I don't really know, and I'll tell you more about that in"—she raises her watch—"precisely two minutes. Mark."

I move closer to the bed—not too close, I don't know how far out that laminar-airflow drek extends. "Paco." Then again, louder, "Paco."

His eyelids flicker, then open. The eyes fasten on my face immediately this time, and I'd have said that was an improvement if not for their glassy, unnatural sheen under the white lights, and the fact that one pupil is dilated maybe twice as much as the other. "Larson," he says, his voice sounding like he's got gravel in his throat. "You didn't leave me, 'mano."

"Only long enough to get you to a doc, chummer," I tell him past a lump in my throat.

"Yeah . . ." His voice trails off.

"Paco," I say sharply, "stay with me, chummer. Don't drift on me. Okay?" He nods, and I glance over at Doc Dicer. She's pointedly watching the display on her watch.

No time for the gentle, subtle approach. Small she is, but I get the feeling the doc could chase even Argent out of her clinic if he broke her rules. "What the frag happened, chummer?" I ask him. "The house was empty. Why?"

"Sick," he mumbles. His eyes flicker, then shut. I'm losing him.

"Yeah," I say hurriedly, "I know you got sick. But what about the rest of the gang, huh? What happened?"

He shakes his head. "No. Not me." He takes a deep breath, and the bubbling's back. "Yeah, I mean, yeah, I got sick. But not just me. Others."

What? "How many others, Paco?"

"Seven, eight. Ten, maybe. Thought it was food poisoning. That's what they thought at first, thought we ate some bad drek. But that's not it. People who got sick didn't eat the same things. Sick. People got scared. It got real bad."

"Yeah, I can imagine." Frag, there's so much I need to know. Much more than I can get in two minutes, but it's a sure thing Doc Dicer isn't planning to give me any extensions. I've got to cut to the fragging chase, and fill in the details later, or just let them hang. "When did this go down, Paco? When did it start?"

He doesn't answer at once. His eyes are shut, he's breathing porridge through his regulator again, and I think he's gone. But then he twitches, and says, "Couple days. Couple days back. Day after the meeting."

"What meeting?" Dicer's eyes are telling me I'm on borrowed time here. "What meeting, chummer?"

Again there's the long delay, and I desperately want to tell the doc not to count dead air against my total. Then he says, "The elves, 'mano. The elves, like the last time."

"The elves from the Tir?"

"Yeah. After that." His voice is fading so much I start to

lean closer to hear better. Out the corner of my eye I see the doc's warning look, and I freeze. Oh yeah, laminar-airflow isolation drek.

"Okay, Paco, I scan it—the elves. Then what?"

Long pause, and I think he's drifted off totally into oblivion. But then his cracked lips move again. "Panic," he whispers, "get out of there ... people run ... leave me. I'm sick, 'mano ..." And then, with a long sigh, he does fade away. There's that click again between exhalation and inhalation, and I feel sick.

Dicer grabs my arm in a firm grip. "Right," she snaps. "Out."

Like before, I don't want to buck her order.

Argent and I don't talk as we hang in the waiting room. I've got too many thoughts rattling around in my skull for conversation, and the runner's eyes tell me the same thing's happening in his head.

Elves. Elves from the Tir. Then this disease—frag, ten people down in two days, it *does* sound like VITAS. Is there a connection with the elves—a real causal connection? Or is it just coincidence? From out of the deep black depths of the past, I flash on something from a freshman philosophy course. One of the common logical mistakes—*post hoc, ergo propter hoc*—"after this, therefore because of this"—the assumption that because event B follows event A that event A somehow caused B.

Frag, I know I'm emotionally burned when I start remembering fragging Latin ...

The OR door opens, and Doc Dicer emerges. "No, he's not dead yet," she says haggardly, answering my question before I can ask it. "He's sleeping—probably the best thing for him at the moment—and I think he's stable ... but I thought that before." She leans against the wall, and rubs at her eyes. What's she feeling at the moment? Scared, maybe? I can't see how that laminar-airflow drek could protect her while she's actually working on Paco. There are magically based isolation schemes that are supposed to block out every bug known (and unknown) to man, but I've seen none of the fetishes and talismans and other drek associated with that kind of thing around here. Somewhere in the back of her mind Doc Dicer must fear being exposed to VITAS 4 or whatever it is that Paco's got, but she agreed to treat him and she's still working on him. It's one thing for me to risk dragging him out of the safe house and schlepping him across town; he's my chummer. I don't know whether I'd put my hoop on the line for a stranger.

"Any joy?" Argent asks.

Dicer nods slowly. "Something major. Whatever your friend's got," she says, turning to me, "it's not contagious."

"Huh?" say I, or something equally cogent and compelling.

She shrugs. "I don't fully understand it," she admits, "but it's not contagious, not at the moment. It might have been at some point, like when your friend first came in with it, but I'm not totally convinced." She sighs. "It's got this trick of pulling a really profound antigenic shift. That's the best way I can describe it, though it's not exactly right."

"In English," I suggest.

She shoots me a nasty glare, then seems to repent, and nods apologetically. "Antigenic shift," she says, starting again. "It's like . . ." She closes her eyes as she searches for an analogy suitable for bonedomes like me. "As part of the immune response, the body produces these things called antibodies. You can think of them like cops, okay?" I glimpse Argent's faint grin, but I ignore him.

"The cops get this report to stop a red Jackrabbit with tag thus-and-so," the doc goes on, "and the car's the virus. Okay?" I nod. No-brainer so far. "In an antigenic shift, it's like the red Jackrabbit keeps changing its tag and its color," she continues. "The cops keep getting updated reports— now it's a black Jackrabbit with out-of-sprawl tags, that kind of thing—but they're always one step behind. That's antigenic shift, and that's what this virus is doing." She frowns. "Sort of."

"Why 'sort of'?" Argent wants to know.

Dicer shakes her head, and her eyes flash with anger. Not at either of us, I suddenly realize, but at herself maybe. "It's an antigenic shift, but it's more than that, too. Let's go back to the car analogy. It's like the Jackrabbit suddenly changing into a Westwind instead of just changing its color and tag when the cops start getting too close. And then maybe into a city bus. And then a Merlin V/STOL. And then a suborbital. And then a fragging cruise-liner." She snorts. "That's why I said it might have been contagious when your friend got it, but it's not now. It can change that profoundly. It's not

precisely like anything I've ever seen. And there are even
more disturbing characteristics . . ."

Argent holds up a matte-black hand. "Let's take this
slow," he suggests. "You say it's not precisely like anything
you've seen before. Is it *vaguely* like anything else?"

The street doc smiles wryly. "I hear you," she says, "and
yes, the thought had crossed my mind, believe me." She
pauses, as though she doesn't want to voice her conclusion.
"It *is* similar in some ways to VITAS 3. In *some* says," she
stresses again.

"VITAS 4?" The question's out of my mouth before I can
stop it.

She scowls at me. "Meaningless label," she snaps.

"But it says it, doesn't it?" I shoot back.

"To the uneducated," Dicer ripostes, and the battle's
joined . . .

Or it would be, if Argent doesn't raise another metallic
hand. Both the doc and I shut up instantly. "We're both uneducated when it comes to this kind of thing, Mary," he says
softly. "How about giving it to us in words of one syllable?"

Her hard expression softens, and she nods. "This is a
retrovirus," she says after a few moments. She glances at
me. "Like VITAS 3, yes, I'll admit that. But there are other
retroviruses too. Some are nasty—HMHVV causes vampir-
ism, for example—one causes a kind of meningitis, but then
there's the retrovirus that causes recurrent dandruff in trolls,
and one that seems to convey a severe allergy to peanuts.
Popular media to the contrary, 'retrovirus' doesn't necessarily mean 'global pandemic,' okay?"

"Okay," I agree. "But is this particular retrovirus like the
particular retrovirus that causes VITAS 3?"

"Sometimes," she says grudgingly. "I've seen some
modes where it looks remotely like the VITAS 3 virus. And
I've seen some modes where it looks nothing like it. It's this
damn antigenic shift thing."

"Yeah, moving target, I get that." I pause for a moment.
"You're saying that *in this mode*"—I hit the words hard,
earning me a scowl from the doc, but what the frag—"it's
not contagious. But it may have been, and it might get that
way again. So even if it's not a—what did you call it?—a
global pandemic, it can still get pretty fragging nasty?"

Dicer doesn't want to, but she nods. "Theoretically," and
she hits the word pretty fragging hard herself. "And, also

theoretically, it might antigen-shift itself into something totally harmless . . ."

"Or something that causes recurrent dandruff in trolls . . .
Yeah, right."

Dicer looks at me curiously. "Why do you want this to be
VITAS 4?" she asks quietly.

That shuts me up for a moment. It's sure as frag the way
I've been sounding, I realize, reviewing my last few comments. Then a new thought hits me. "Hey, wait a tick," I say
suddenly. "It had to be contagious at one point, right? Paco
caught it, nine or ten other people caught it. That's contagious, isn't it?"

Both Argent and Dicer are shaking their heads, but it's the
doc who answers. "Not necessarily. Not necessarily at all.
'Contagious' means you can catch a disease from someone
who's already infected. But there are lots of other vectors—
that's 'ways of transmitting a bug'," she amplifies. "Off the
top of my head, I could list you a dozen diseases that are
nasty as drek but aren't strictly contagious."

"I don't get that," I admit.

"There was a nasty bug that decimated the hemophiliac
population in France back in about 2037," the doc explains,
her voice taking on a dry, lecturing tone. "A virus with a
long latency period—decades, in some cases. You couldn't
catch it from someone infected, not normally. You could
suck face with them, jam with them, share eating utensils,
whatever. But if you get a blood transfusion from them,
bingo, you've got the bug." She pauses. "Okay, that's still
contagious, strictly speaking, because you can catch it from
someone who's got it, even though only through special circumstances."

"Tsimshian two-day fever," Argent suggests, and the doc
nods.

"Good example," she agrees. "That's a kind of bug you
find in certain streams in the Queen Charlotte Islands in
Tsimshian—or whatever they call those islands now. The ex-
perts think it might be a retrovirus, but nobody's sure because the Tsimshian government has outlawed research, for
some wrong-headed reason.

"Anyway, if you drink the water, you get the bug, you get
the fever, and you're probably dead in forty-eight hours. But
even while you're honking up your stomach lining," she
goes on, "you can't infect anyone else. Not by breathing on

them, spitting on them, honking on them, drekking on them, bleeding on them ... nothing. The sole vector for the bug that's ever been found is the water of those particular streams. If you don't drink the water, you'll never get the bug. Got it?"

I nod. Explained that way, it's an easy enough concept to grasp. "So what's the ... the vector ... for what Paco's got?" I want to know.

"Yes, that's the sixty-four thousand nuyen question, isn't it?" From her expression, I figure Doc Dicer's got an answer, but I also figure it's one she doesn't like at all.

"Go on, Mary," Argent prompts, his voice quiet, and I know he's scanned it the same way I have.

The woman nods and makes a grim face. "This is all tentative," she starts, "without more study ..."

"Received and logged," Argent interrupts gently. "We're not holding you to anything here."

Her smile combines gratitude and embarrassment, as she goes on, "Okay, I'm assuming this isn't contagious, and it wasn't when the subject ..."

"Paco," I correct.

Her gaze meets mine for a moment, then she glances away. "Sorry. It wasn't contagious when Paco was infected. Granted, it could have been, but I think the odds are small.

"So that means some other vector," she goes on. "I'd guess it's either airborne or ingested."

"Lots of mucus," Argent points out.

Dicer nods. "His GI tract's a nightmare too," she says, "though I don't know which is primary and which is secondary."

"Paco said they thought it was food poisoning," I say.

"He also said they all ate different things," she comes back fast. Then she relents, "Okay, it's possible ... Maybe something in the water. But I still put my money on airborne. I think the ... I think Paco breathed it and it got into the bloodstream through the lungs."

"So the question becomes, where did it come from? Right?" I press. "How did it get into the air, or the water, or the food, or whatever." I glance at Argent, see his frown. From somewhere I get the feeling he's wondering the same thing as me—a connection with the elves here?

Dicer nods, but slowly, like she's not totally convinced. "What?" I ask.

She doesn't answer immediately, and I feel a kind of cold twisting in my gut. Suddenly I don't want to hear what she's got to say. Just keep me comfortably and reassuringly ignorant, thanks all the same. "Yes," she says finally, "that is important. But there's another question. What triggered it?"

Argent and I go, "Huh?" in unison.

"Some viruses and bacteria are infective all the time," the doc explains slowly, as though it's something she doesn't want to think about either. "They get into your system and they make you sick, end of story.

"But then there are some that act differently." The dry lecture-tone's back, and I get the sudden strong feeling she's using it to numb out her own emotions. And that's even scarier. "Some bugs—viruses and bacteria—can get into your system," she goes on, "and just stay there for months or years or decades . . . sometimes your whole life. They're totally latent—they're there, but they don't do anything. Until something happens to trigger them. Then they start to replicate, and they start to make the body sick. AIDS was like that before the T5 phage treatment was discovered. HMHVV is like that. Harmless until triggered, then they go on a rampage.

"You can have all kinds of triggering conditions. Some are internal—the body's immunological response to another infection can trigger a latent form of viral meningitis, very nasty. Some are external—like a certain chemical or combination of chemicals in the diet, for example." The doc's voice trails off.

"And this bug has a triggering agent or condition?" Argent prompts quietly after a moment.

The shadow cutter nods. "Magic. A spell."

"Impossible," Argent counters.

"Why?" I demand, and they both look at me. "There's Awakened animals," I explain hurriedly, "and insects, and even fragging plants that are sensitive to magic, or resistant, or can use it—or all three. What do they call it?"

"Paranatural." It's Argent who answers.

"So why not viruses?" I finish.

Dicer looks at me, and her expression seems to hint she's decided I'm not a congenital idiot after all. She nods. "Why not?" she echoes. "Okay, granted, this isn't quite MIT&M or Berkeley, and I'm not exactly Dr. Derek Maclean either." (Who? I want to ask, but I keep my yap shut.) "But it certainly looks like there are several sections in the virus' RNA almost directly analogous to the magic-sensitive introns in the DNA of Awakened species."

"Which means?" Argent asks.

"Which implies," she responds, "that this particular retrovirus is latent—no, more than that, totally inert—until it's triggered by magic."

The shadowrunner clenches his metal fists. This is worrying him a lot more than it is me, and I don't understand why. Frag, at the moment I'm still dealing with the relief that I'm probably not going to kick off from VITAS 4. "How certain are you of this?"

"Not certain," she replies, "not certain at all. I can't be, based on one case, and with the limited resources at my disposal. But," she emphasizes, "I'd definitely say it's indicative. Strongly indicative."

Argent nods soberly, and I remember he knows more about her background than I do. He seems to consider that as serious drek.

In contrast, I feel like I've missed the fragging meeting. "I don't get it," I blurt. "What's so fragging important? It's an Awakened virus, and its triggering condition is magical activity nearby, right?"

"Wrong." The doc turns a cold and steady gaze on me. "The trigger isn't just background magical activity or magic use in the vicinity."

It hits me then. I glance at Argent, and he's nodding again. He's got it, too. "You said the trigger was magic," I say slowly, "a spell. A spell. A specific spell."

"A spell specifically tailored to the particular RNA subsequence of this particular retrovirus," Dacia confirms. "Until the virus is in the area of effect of that specific spell, it's totally inert."

"But that's impossible, isn't it?" I say, and my words sound lame in my own ears.

"Evolutionarily speaking," she amends, "I'd agree. This retrovirus couldn't have evolved naturally. Which means . . ."

"It was engineered." It takes me a moment to realize the voice is mine.

22

Doc Dicer's eyes are steady, locked with mine. For a moment she doesn't say anything or react in any way, like she's trying to stare me down.

She's the one who blinks first, then looks away a little uncomfortably. "Maybe," she says. "There's a whole lot of 'ifs'. If I'm right that the trigger is magical. If I'm right that it's only a specific spell and not just generalized magical activity. If, if, if . . ." She tries to smile, but there's no humor in it, the expression ending up more like a grimace. "If I had a real lab, with a trained staff, and all the bells and whistles . . ." Her lips twist back from her teeth, and she spits, "Frag it!"

Argent and I both react. It's the first time the doc has cursed, which adds immeasurably to the impact.

"But you said it was 'strongly indicative,' " the shadowrunner points out, echoing her own words back to her.

She glares at him for an instant, then her hard expression softens. "I did say that, didn't I?" She takes a deep breath, and I'm momentarily distracted by what that does to the lines of her white jumpsuit. "I stand by it, too. I could be wrong. But I don't think so."

Argent sits back down on the couch, and again he seems immune—or oblivious—to the grievous bodily harm it tried to inflict on me earlier. "Okay," he says slowly, his voice even more tired than it was when he first arrived at the shadow clinic. "Let's assume you're right, Mary. The virus is genetically engineered—whether from scratch or just tweaked doesn't really matter at the moment—and only a single, specific spell will trigger it, presumably developed in tandem with the bug itself." He glances at the doc, and she nods confirmation. "Then where does that lead us?"

Nobody speaks immediately, and the silence grows heavier and more tangible. Finally I have to say something just to break it. "It's the perfect murder weapon, isn't it?" I ask. "Unattributable. Silent. Fragging elegant, almost. The victim doesn't even know he's dead until later."

"I don't see it," Argent says thoughtfully. "It's a two-step process. You've got to get the bug into the victim's system, then you've got to hit him with the spell. Too complicated, too much to go wrong." This from someone who's probably got some hands-on experience at assassination.

But I still think I'm right. "The first step's easy, because you don't have to worry about nailing collateral targets," I insist. "Infect as many people as you like . . ."

"The entire Cutters gang?" he puts in.

". . . a whole fragging city, if necessary," I override him. "It doesn't matter, they're not going to get sick, are they? Then, as much later as you like, you nail the victim with the spell. He gets the bug, and keels over."

The shadowrunner shakes his head firmly. "No good, Wolf. You've got to get a mage or a shaman within range of the target. And if you can do that, why not just cook him in his boots or turn him into a tree or something?"

"It's a good way to keep your assassin alive," I say doggedly. "No manhunt, 'cause there's no murder . . . not one that's obvious at the moment."

"Okay, point," Argent concedes. "But it still doesn't scan right. To trigger the bug, you've got to hit it with a spell, right?" Dicer nods. "Which means the spell's got to get through any magical resistance or shielding or whatever the target's got up. A serious target's going to have that shielding—because if he didn't, you could get the same effect by acquiring an astral link and slamming some nasty ritual sending into him from the other side of the world. And if the target's too inconsequential to have serious astral security, this is just way too much technological overkill. Just hit 'em with a power bolt. Or better yet, knife 'em in an elevator if you really want them gone."

Which leaves me grinding my teeth. The fragger's right, and that slots me right off. "Then how do you scan it?" I snap.

To my surprise, it's Doc Dicer who answers. "It seems to me it's the perfect terrorist weapon," she says quietly.

We both turn to look at her. "Why?" we say, almost at once.

For a moment it looks like she's going to back down in

the face of our scrutiny, but she visibly grabs some guts and soldiers on. "Several reasons." She ticks them off on slender fingers. "One. Maximum impact, maximum penetration. Terrorists have tried bioweapons in the past, but they've never had full impact. Mainly because some people always come down with the bug before everyone's been exposed to it, which cues the authorities to what's going on, and leads to precautions to stop the spread. With something like this? Drop some into the water supply or wherever, and wait a few days—weeks or months, if you feel like it—until a large percentage of the target population's been exposed."

She shakes her head. "Hell, you could even wait years, couldn't you? Then, when you're ready, you hit the group with the spell—some area-effect thing, probably—and that's it. Okay, sure, important people—the people who go around with serious astral security—aren't going to get sick, because the spell won't get to the bugs. But what percentage of the population is that? Pretty small, I'd say.

"Two." Another finger. "It's not a quick kill, which has all sorts of advantages from the terrorist's point of view. First, there's the hysteria. Panic, xenophobia, scapegoating of various groups—all the stuff you read about with every plague in history. You'll probably end up with lots of casualties among people who weren't even exposed to the bug or the spell, and much greater demands on a city's or country's infrastructure.

"And then there's the medical load. Terrorists kill somebody, and he's dead. Put him on ice until the ruckus is over, then incinerate him. But this way isn't anywhere near that clean. This bug doesn't kill people, it makes them very sick. They go to the hospital or to a clinic, where they tie up a bed, the time and energy of doctors and staff, and other resources, for as long as it takes them to get better or die." She looks really sour, and I don't blame her. "If the bug has a high fatality rate, if there were an epidemic, the logical thing to do would be triage—simply don't treat bug victims, because they're going to die anyway. But no society could do that. And if a society got to the point where it could, the terrorists have basically destroyed it anyway."

She sighs, a deep, heartfelt sound. "And there are other advantages, too," she goes on steadily—dully now, almost mechanically, as if suppressing her emotions. "Theoretically, you could spread the bug in advance, years before you even start your terror campaign, whatever it is. The society or government doesn't know it's in trouble, so its security is low. After you start your campaign, security's tightened up, but it doesn't matter—you've already infected the victims. Then, when the time is right, you trigger the bug. Hell, you could even withhold the epidemic if you get what you want by other means, and nobody would ever know about it." She shudders. "You could bring down a government with this."

I exchange glances with Argent. Neither of us say anything—there's not much that needs to be said. Doc Dicer's right, her analysis makes perfect sense, and I can't punch any holes in it. I find myself shuddering too. The perfect terrorist weapon is right. Except . . .

"Why's Paco got it, then?" I ask. "And why the other Cutters? It's not like it's something you can pick up from a fragging toilet seat, is it? You've got to get the bug—ingest it, breathe it, whatever—and then get nailed by the spell. Why do that to the Cutters?"

"A rival gang?" Dicer asks tentatively, then she scowls and shakes her head. "Erase that. Too complex. Too high-tech for gang war, right?"

The shadowrunner and I nod. Then we exchange glances again, and I get the strong feeling he's scanning it just the same way I am. And he doesn't like it either.

It's me who voices it first. "Field test?"

"Yeah," Argent rumbles deep in his chest. "That tracks."

The street doc looks back and forth between the two of us. Obviously it doesn't track for her.

"You're going to try out something like this before you base a whole terrorist campaign on it," I explain. "Pick some limited social group that's as parallel as possible to the society you're eventually going after, then put the scheme through its paces. Work the bugs out early." I shrug. "And why not a gang? It's a tight-knit but socially heterogeneous group—the Cutters are, at least—and best of all, mainstream society's not going to pay much attention."

"If they hear about it at all," Dicer concludes quietly. She's obviously heard the news media's attempts to downplay the "gang plague" too. "A field test, then?"

"Military and paramilitary organizations always test drek before they put any trust in it," I say, and Argent nods agreement.

A new expression spreads across the doc's face. "So do marketers," she says, so quietly I can barely hear her.

I don't know how Argent got to the clinic, but he's happy enough to ride back to Renton with me in the Westwind. Being in close proximity to the shadowrunner still gives me the creeps, but I've got to admit I welcome the chance to bounce ideas off someone else, someone who knows more of the background than I figured was wise to tell Doc Dicer.

Maybe Argent is reading my mind. "How do you scan it?" he asks as we howl up the ramp onto Highway 5 southbound.

I shrug. "The doc's probably right," I say slowly. "A bug like that is the perfect terrorist weapon, but terrorists aren't likely to be the ones to develop a bioweapon, right? Just like terrorists don't make their own C9 plastique. They buy it from Ares Arms or whoever."

"Or they steal it," the runner puts in.

"Whatever. It's the same thing. What they're getting is a fully developed, fully tested product."

"Frightening."

"No fragging kidding!" I almost snarl back.

We drive on in silence for a couple of minutes. We're wailing past the gray-black stained Kingdome when Argent speaks again. "So who?"

I shoot him a glance. His face is locked in a grim expression, the same kind of tight control you see on the faces of point-men in Desert Wars gun-cam footage—and again I know he's thinking the same thing I am. Well, frag, somebody's got to say it. "The fragging elves, who else? The Tir Tairngire contingent, including chummer Nemo. Too much of a coincidence otherwise." I shrug again. "Anyway, they had the best opportunity to set it up. Two meets with Blake and the others—at least two—in a Cutters safe house. The first meet to release the bug into the air, or get it into the food, or whatever. The second to cast the triggering spell." A new thought hits like a nine-mil hollow-point, and I feel suddenly very, very cold. "I was around for the first meet . . ."

Argent's grinning tightly, but it's not an expression of humor. "I wondered if you'd catch that," he says quietly.

"I could have that drek inside me, too."

"You could," he stresses. "But you weren't in the area of

the spell effect at the second meet—if that's actually what went down."

True, but not as reassuring as it might be. If my whole chain of logic is right, I've got a biological time bomb in my lungs or in my guts, and whoever put it there can set it off with the casting of a single spell. Only with a major effort do I stuff those fears deep down into the mental swamp. They'll bubble up again, sure—and probably at the worst possible time—but at least they're out of the way for the moment. What I tell myself is that, okay, maybe I've got the bug in my system. But activating it means the bad guys— whoever they are—have to target me with the trigger spell. Which requires them knowing where the frag I am and that I've been infected with the virus in the first place. Chances of that? Pretty fragging slim, or at least that's the way I choose to look at it. Who knows? Maybe I avoided infection in the first place.

The chromed runner's still watching me, so I slap a frosty expression on my face. "Yeah, well, doesn't make much fragging difference, does it?" I say. His lip quirks ever so slightly, and I know he scans the truth, but isn't calling me on it. At least he's got the decency to leave a man to his own fragging paranoia.

We cruise on through the gathering dark for a few minutes more, then again it's Argent who breaks the heavy silence. "Who?" he asks.

He doesn't have to elaborate. "Timothy Telestrian and his faction," I say flatly.

"You don't know that," he points out.

"The Telestrian angle's there," I stress. "Lynne Telestrian and Lightbringer establish that. And if it's not Timothy, we've got frag all else to go on. I say we stick with what we've got until something else comes up to prove otherwise."

Argent nods slowly. He doesn't argue because he knows I'm right. If one lead is all you've got, you follow it up even if it doesn't seem one hundred percent germane, hoping it'll break something else loose. The only other alternative is to sit around waiting for something to fall into your lap, and that's a bulldrek waste of time.

"Timothy's prez of BioLogic, isn't he?" I muse. Argent nods confirmation. "BioLogic sounds like it might be into genetic drek, doesn't it?"

"A gengineering firm? Could be. I'll have Peg dig into it."

"Go after any gengineering activity under the TIC umbrella," I say. "The link might not be that obvious."

He nods again. "I'll get her on it." He's silent for a moment, then, "It might take some time. Maybe you'd best stay low profile in the meantime."

I find myself thinking about the smears under Paco's eyes and the sound of his breathing, and my skin crawls. "I think I'm down for that," I say quietly.

23

Paco died that night at about 0230. Doc Dicer phoned me with the news, through the same kind of blind relay I'd used to contact Argent in the first place. (The runner had resisted the idea of giving the doc the number, despite their apparent friendship, but I held my ground, and eventually he caved.) She didn't say, "He went peacefully," or any of that feel-good drek doctors usually feed to the families. She didn't have to tell me anything, I know how he went—inhale, exhale, click . . . and then nothing.

The news slotted me up so much I couldn't get back to sleep until the thunderclouds were starting to lighten in the east. Another friend gone. And of course it didn't help to know the same fragging bug might be lurking in my own system. When I did get back to sleep, the dreams weren't pleasant. I was back in the parking lot that was Hell, but this time everyone around me was breathing like Paco, and I could feel the start of the bubbling mucus in my own lungs. Just fragging peachy.

When I finally got up to face the day at about 1030, I decided to take Argent's advice to heart and keep my head way down low. Like, as low as it's possible to get, leaving the room only to visit the drekker. Apparently Argent had clued Jean Trudel in, so I found meals—greasy bar food, no surprise there—delivered to me upstairs. Breakfast—and lunch and dinner—in bed, if I wanted it. All three meals Bavarian-style soy-smokies sitting in buns the texture of styrofoam packing material. Yum.

While I wasn't cramming grease down my yam, I took some time to check out the capabilities of the room's telecom. Extensive, in a word—more extensive than my ability to take full advantage of them. For a couple of hours I wrestled with a nasty case of ESO—Equipment Smarter than Operator—until I stumbled across the interactive online help, and got my hand electronically held as I scoped out what the machine could do for me.

Not that it would help particularly. Sure, having a slick and wizzer telecom's all very well, but you've still got to know how to go about researching databases and accessing the drek you need. Like, you can have the hottest car on the road, but if you don't know how to drive the puppy, it's not going to win you any races. So I spent a good whack of the day getting bounced by the security around systems like Lone Star's basic personnel files—security that any decker worthy of the name could have sliced through without missing a beat. Frag, I couldn't even crack into the local Stock Watch service—a nominally open system that wouldn't give me the time of day because I haven't paid a subscription fee—to see if TIC stocks were moving up or down. (I don't savvy much about that kind of biz, but I've heard often enough that you can scope a frag of a lot about what a corp's up to by catching what's happening to its share prices.)

So eventually I was relegated to scanning the newsfax databases—those at least I could access without some kind of fragging subscription. I ran an even dozen searches, using different parameters, key words, and Boolean operators—every reasonable combination of "plague," "epidemic," "infection," "retrovirus," and "gang" I could come up with.

Coming up with one huge whack of nothing. Nothing at all, not even a denial of the report I'd heard on the NewsNet feed on my way to Ravenna. No retraction, or apology, or explanation for claims of a new VITAS epidemic. No comments from Dr. Blatherman. Nothing. It was as if the original reports had simply never occurred at all. Total media blackout. Fragging scary, chummer.

And that's how I spent the day after Paco's death. And the morning of the next day as well, and part of that afternoon. By the time Argent walked in the door, I was on my way toward a good dose of cabin fever.

"What the frag kept you, Argent?" I demand. The chromed runner doesn't respond to my polite greeting, but only crosses to the armchair and slumps down in it. He's tired, again, but fragged if I know why. It's not as if he's the one doing the datasearches; he's passing them off to Peg whatever-her-name-is, the SanFran decker. Makes me wonder if he's doing other biz on the side, and it's that that's scragging him out so bad. Yeah, that would be typical, wouldn't it? Got to get some cred flow happening, or the International Federation of Shadowrunners will pull his union card as an accredited mercenary bastard.

Or maybe he just hasn't been getting any sleep, worrying about this terror-bug drek. Frag, I probably don't look much better. "Got anything?" I ask.

He tosses me a chip carrier. "Slot this."

I do, slipping it into the telecom's data port. Argent gives me the access code, which I type in. The screen immediately fills with text and organizational charts that look like circuit-path diagrams or maybe webs spun by spiders jazzed up on overdoses of electric lady. "What the frag is it?"

"That," he says, "is the TIC umbrella—or maybe 'empire' is a better word. Two dozen major divisions. Twice that number of wholly owned subsidiaries. Major equity positions in maybe a hundred other corps, and joint-ventures and strategic partnerships with at least as many."

I purse my lips in a soundless whistle. "Impressive. I didn't think there were any real Tir megacorps."

Argent chuckles wryly. "TIC's a decent-sized conglomerate," he says, "but it's nowhere near being a megacorporation. Not yet. MCT or Yamatetsu or any of the triple-A megas could buy the whole TIC network out of contingency credit."

I don't really want to think about that at the moment. Instead, I gesture at the complex drek spread over the screen. "Talk me though this, will you?"

"Where do you want to start?"

"The gengineering angle, remember?"

He chuckles grimly. "As I said, where do you want to start?"

Uh-oh. "Lots of gengineering activity?" I guess.

"You could say that." His voice is dry, ironic. "Peg estimates that forty-seven percent of the empire's entire cred flow is related to gengineering, either directly or indirectly. Less than a quarter of the business entities are into gengineering, but they tend to be the more profitable ones."

I nod slowly, taking that in. "Then what about the . . . the 'business entities' in Timothy Telestrian's sphere of influence?"

"Peg's already broken that out," the runner tells me. "Go to Bookmark One."

I key in the command, and the display changes. Still a twisted spider web, but at least the spider was less ambitious. I shake my head in frustration. "Why so much focus on gengineering?" I want to know.

Argent chuckles again. "It's the Tir, chummer. Don't forget that. Biotech's their big thing. If they can modify things without using techniques as . . . inelegant . . . as implants"—he clicks his metal fingers together—"that's what they'll do. They're gengineering everything down there. Food crops, algae, bacteria, animals, plants, even themselves."

I think about it for a few seconds. "Okay, then how about limiting it by outfits that gengineer viruses?"

He shakes his head. "Don't know much about gengineering, do you?" he says rhetorically. "One of the most dependable techniques uses tailored viruses to insert plasmids into target cells."

"In fragging English," I growl.

"Everybody uses viruses, chummer. No joy there."

I grind my teeth. "Okay," I say, "how about backgrounds in bioweapons?"

"Bookmark Two," he directs, and I key in the command.

The display shifts, and now we're down to something I can almost understand. A dozen or so companies—all still interlinked, but the network's much simpler and more straightforward. "What's their . . . " —I search for the right word—"their allegiance?" I ask.

The shadowrunner grins, and I know we're finally starting to get somewhere. "Most of them are loyal to Lynne Telestrian, and through her to James," he says. "But there's one particular outfit that's firmly in Timothy's camp, and I scan them as real scary. Check Bookmark Three."

I do, and read the text header that's displayed. "Nova Vita Biotechnologies." For the second time in as many days—or thereabouts—I find myself dredging through the Latin I learned too many years ago. "Nova Vita—'new life'. Good name for a gengineering outfit." I pause. "And Nova Vita's got background in bioweapons?"

"That's the buzz on the Shadowland BBS," Argent confirms. "They've got a major facility out in a place called Christmas Valley—maybe eighty klicks southeast of Bend—that does bioweapons research for the Tir military."

This time I whistle out loud. "Serious drek." But then I realize this doesn't make sense.

The runner sees my frown, and cuts in, "There's more. Nova Vita Biotechnology's got a subsidiary, Nova Vita Cybernetics, with a research facility right on the Columbia—Salish-Shidhe side of the river, for a wonder—at a place called Pillar Rock. An isolated facility, by the way, not connected to the Matrix." He chuckles. "Which slotted Peg off something fierce."

No skin off my hoop what slots off Peg: my attention's on

his earlier statement. "Oh? Why's a Tir outfit got its research on S-S Council turf?" Then I shake my head. "What's it matter anyway? The Christmas Valley outfit's the one that's important. We're after the gengineering and bioweapons connection, not the cyberware side, right?" Argent doesn't say anything, just sits there grinning. "All right, fraghead," I snap, "tell me what I've missed."

He shrugs mildly. "Peg just found it interesting that there've been some personnel transfers between Nova Vita Biotech and Nova Vita Cybernetics over the last year or so."

Oh-ho. "Gengineers, by any chance?"

"Coincidentally," Argent confirms with a nod. "Chimeric gene-splicers, a couple of hotshots at viral tailoring. Not the kind of skillsets you'd expect to be recruited by a cyberware outfit, neh? Makes you wonder if NVC hasn't broadened its horizons a little."

"Makes you wonder," I echo. "And I don't suppose NVC's assumed any military contracts from NV Biotech?"

"Peg thought of that and checked, but actually, no." Argent's wearing a real poker-face now, and I know we're getting close to the punch line. "You might want to check a list of the outfits NVC has signed contracts with in the last two years. Bookmark Four."

I jump to the new place in the text, and quickly scan the list that appears. A long list, populated by some of the major megacorps like Mitsuhama, Yamatetsu, Fuchi, even Aztechnology. NVC is either a significant player in the cyberware field or else these corps are looking for gengineering expertise. I'm about to turn to Argent and ask him whether he or Peg knows, when a name near the bottom of the list catches my eye.

Lone Star Security Services (Seattle) Incorpoarted.

"Interesting, huh?" Argent asks quietly.

I nod slowly, but don't say anything. The runner's poker face has turned into a grim mask. He's really intense about this. But why? Okay, sure, it kind of creeps me out to see the Star linked to a corp that might be developing terrorist weapons, but NVC must also be working on a lot of other, innocuous projects as well. "Tell me," I say flatly. "You know something else. Tell me."

"It's funny the way things work sometimes," Argent says, his voice calm, almost emotionless. "Just like you asked, I had Peg scan as many personnel files as she could in the

Telestrian 'empire' looking for your Mr. Nemo. No luck, by the way. Apparently the Telestrian outfits are pretty adamant when it comes to hiring only metahumans. Less than five percent of its employees are humans, and none of them meet the criteria she programmed in for the graphical search.

"Anyway," the runner goes on, "then Peg came across NVC and got distracted. She ended up running a full newsbase search, looking for any media reports on NVC and what they might be up to. That newsbase search extended to the news media's image banks as well."

I'm getting the faintest hint of where Argent's going with this, but I keep my yap tight shut.

"When she was browsing the image banks," he continues, "it turns out she hadn't purged the search criteria from her deck." He indicates the screen with a matte-black finger. "Bring up Bookmark Five."

There's real tension in my chest and my gut as I do. The screen fills with a full-color image, a newsfax-type shot of some kind of corporate ceremony—a ribbon-cutting for a new building or some such drek. In the foreground are two slags in high-tone four-piece suits who've got drek-eating grins plastered on their faces as they cut a ribbon with an oversized pair of scissors. Both elves, one of them's friend Timothy Telestrian. "Who's the other guy?" I ask.

"David Margeson," Argent answers immediately. "Prez and CEO of Nova Vita Cybernetics. One of Timothy's little puppets, that's how Peg scans it."

"Yeah?" I say, but I'm thinking, so what? We already know NVC's in Timothy's camp. Argent wouldn't attach so much significance to confirmation of a fact that doesn't really matter. Which tells me there's got to be something else. I scan the background of the image. A small knot of undifferentiated dignitaries behind Telestrian and Margeson, a couple of rows of them, but with only the front line clearly visible. Probably veeps and other suits from NVC. I give them only the most superficial scan, trying to concentrate on what little of the building shows behind them. If this is the Pillar Rock facility, maybe there's something significant to be seen . . .

"You missed it," Argent almost whispers. "Enhance the image centered on coordinates five-twelve X, fifteen-fifty Y. Try four-X enhancement, for starters."

Assuming a two-K-by-two-K grid—the current standard— that's the upper left-hand quadrant of the image. Frowning,

I key in the command, and watch as the image zooms in. This is a newsfax file, the graininess of the enlarged image shows that clearly enough.

But, graininess or not, I immediately spot what Argent's on about. A face in the second row of suits and execs. Not even partially hidden, but with half of it in shadow from something overhead and out of the frame. The only human among a passle of elves. I recognize him instantly.

"Nemo?" Argent asks.

"Nemo," I confirm. I lean closer to stare at the grainy image. Unbelievable—fragging unbelievable—that Peg's search software would pick up on something like this. Frag, for a moment it totally slots me that tech can do something like this.

But of course it doesn't matter how we've found Nemo, only that we have—and that we've discovered some connection between him and NVC, and from there to Timothy Telestrian. "Who the frag is he?" I demand.

"It took Peg a while," the shadowrunner says quietly. "He's not part of NVC, and like I said, he's not part of any Telestrian organization."

"Then who?" My patience with this fragging Socratic method is wearing real thin.

"When Peg dead-ended there, she cross-referenced this image with the rest of the newsfax image banks she could deck into. She found another holo—a really good one, a professional portrait. Apparently taken about a year ago when he got a corporate transfer to Seattle."

I snap my head around to stare at the image of Nemo. The feeling of familiarity, of impending recognition, is even stronger than when I first saw him in the Cutters safe house. I *know* him . . . Thoughts come together with an almost audible click. "He's from Milwaukee, isn't he?" My voice is barely louder than a whisper.

"His name's Gerard Schrage, but you probably haven't heard it before. He was a senior veep in Corporate Services, Lone Star Security Services, Milwaukee."

"And his transfer?"

Argent's next words bowl me over. "Gerard Schrage is executive veep in charge of Lone Star Seattle's Military Liaison Division," he tells me.

24

I slump down onto the desk chair. That last one hit me like a knee to the pills. I feel like I've walked right into the middle of a play with the wrong fragging script.

Argent is watching me, evaluating, probably wondering how long it's going to take the Lone Star dork to get his legs back under him. I steeple my fingers in front of my face, pressing the palms together to still the shakes. Unmodified eyes wouldn't spot it, but my state of mind is probably blatant as all drek to the runner's modified optics. I take a deep breath, then exhale fully, trying to blow the tension out of my chest and the fog from my mind. "Maybe I'm just out of touch," I say as levelly as I can, "but I didn't know the Star even had a Military Liaison Division."

Argent chuckles at that and relaxes a little. I get the feeling I've passed some kind of test, maybe because I didn't say "we" when talking about the Star. "It's new, at least in Seattle," he allows. "I didn't know about it either. Apparently Schrage is the first veep, and it's his job to build it up."

"Build it up to what?"

"I assume to the same level as other Military Liaison Divisions across the continent," he says. "And yes," he adds, answering the question I'm about to ask, "there are others. Not in Milwaukee—I suppose that's why you haven't heard of it—but in DeeCee, and a big mother in Atlanta."

"And just what the frag are they supposed to do?" I want to know.

The shadowrunner's smile fades slightly. "That's the big question, isn't it? Officially"—and he hits that word real hard—"its job is just what the name implies: liaison between Lone Star's constabulary duty and the local military. It's the ML group that's supposed to coordinate crisis planning—civil defense crap, natural disasters, and all that. Should martial law ever be declared, the ML team is supposed to make sure Lone Star assets work with the National Guard or the army or whoever to prevent any overlap that would let anything fall through the cracks."

"That's officially," I say.

"What the official mandate doesn't explain," Argent continues, "is why the existing Military Liaison Divisions are so fragging big and well-funded. Going just by the official mandate of their operations, the Military Liaison outfit in Atlanta could get by with a couple of managers, a drekload of low-level data clerks, and some fancy computer systems. But what they've actually got are comm specialists, logistics people, weapons and tactics teams, and just shy of a hundred officers . . . all of whom have been seconded to ML from SWAT and FRT outfits."

"Sounds like a fragging private army. . . ." The touch of outrage in my voice draws an amused grin from Argent. That makes me realize I shouldn't be so surprised that Lone Star has some kind of private army. Every megacorp has its "extended security assets"—or whatever the euphemism du jour is at the moment—whether they openly enter them in Desert Wars or not. So why should Lone Star Security Services Corporation be any fragging different? It's just another mega.

But what's slotting me up is my belief that the Star *should* be different. I can scan why MCT and Ares and Shiawase and the rest use private armies to protect and promote their biz interests around the world—either by kicking the snot out of other private armies or by overthrowing national governments who have the temerity to get in their way, or whatever. That's just the world we live in today, priyatel. So why not Lone Star?

Because it *is* Lone Star is what my emotions answer. Maybe it's just some kind of illusion I want to maintain, some drekheaded belief that I don't work for a greedy, grasping megacrop—I work for *Lone Star*, chummer, for the good of my fellow man. Yet how different is Lone Star from the other megacorps? When you get right down to it, isn't law enforcement just another product or service? The Star doesn't keep the peace and enforce the law because doing so is a Good Thing. It does it because a variety of governments pay it good nuyen to keep the peace and enforce the law. The Star is just another corporation making profits by meeting a demand in the marketplace.

So why wouldn't the megacorporation that is Lone Star look for other ways to make money, to promote its biz? And if those other ways require a private army, would the corp shy away from them because fielding a private army goes against some moral or ethical stance? Not fragging likely.

Glancing at Argent, I see him still watching me closely, but with a hint of something new in his expression. Something that might be understanding, or sympathy. Pity, even. And if there's one thing in this whole fragging world I don't need, it's pity—or even sympathy—from shadow-scum like fragging Argent. So I bury my reactions as deep as I can, and do an internal check to make sure my expression's frosty, just this side of outright aggro. "Yeah," I mutter, but still loud enough for Argent to hear. "Yeah, makes sense. I always figured cleaning the drek off the streets and out of the shadows can't pay well enough to keep a big corp going."

"The way I scan it," Argent says, not reacting one way or the other to my attempt at nonchalance, "Military Liaison is a resource Lone Star hires out to national governments, corporations, other organizations—frag, maybe even policlubs—to act as a more or less unattributable force to slot with and destabilize rival countries, corps, societies or whatever."

"Kind of like shadowrunners, huh, priyatel?"

Again, I can't read whether I've scored or not. The man just shrugs his muscular shoulders and gestures vaguely with his metal hands. Maybe he doesn't mean the gesture as a threat, but it's a good reminder to me of what might happen if I push him too far. "Similar concept, perhaps," he says mildly. "Unattributable assets, with skillsets you don't want to get caught having on-staff. But from what Peg's dredged up, it's quite a different animal from even the best-trained, best-equipped team of shadowrunners."

"Why?" I want to keep scoring points off him, but my curiosity's too strong on this one.

He grins, and again I think the big runner's reading me like a fragging trideo listing. "It's the military connection, Wolf," he explains. "Full-on military, and that's the big difference. You take a good shadow team—like my old squad, the Wrecking Crew. We'd be like a Special Forces fire team.

Tough as snot for infiltration, sabotage, and hit-and-run actions. But pin us down in a toe-to-toe, stand-up fight with a single squad of army regulars, and we're fragging rat-bait, and that's all she wrote."

"Why?" I ask again. "Lack of military discipline?"

Argent gives me another slow, speculative look, and this time I scan the message in those modified optics just fine. Are you going out of your way to slot me off, or are you just a natural drekhead? those eyes are wondering. "In the Wrecking Crew—and in any first-tier runner team— discipline's just fine," he says quietly, "Don't believe what the trideo shows to the contrary, particularly when the programming's sponsored by corps who'd like to stamp out popular sympathy for shadowrunners before it even gets started." I nod slowly—that's an angle on the trid's treatment of runners I hadn't really considered before, but it makes a lot of sense.

"No," Argent's saying, "it's resources and logistics. The Wrecking Crew was four people . . . and that was including Peg, so cut it back to three guns, one of them a shaman. A standard UCAS light infantry squad is ten riflemen and a sergeant—eleven guns, and one of them a mage. On a mission, we're usually limited to as many rounds as we can hump in on our backs. The squad's probably got logistic support—a bunch of guys in an APC or scout panzer whose sole job is to deal out replacement magazines to people running low.

"As for weapons, we're limited on most runs to only what we can more or less conceal." He grins wryly. "Your comrades tend to take a dim view of people packing belt-fed GPMGs around the streets of the plex, trust me on that one." His humor fades. "So that means SMGs, mainly, maybe assault rifles if the circumstances allow it, and once in a fragging blue moon, a light machine gun.

"The squad? Assault rifles all around, probably with all the toys . . . including grenade launchers. Depending on the mission, maybe one or two are packing assault cannons, and there's always one slag humping along a heavy machine gun or maybe a fragging minigun if they're feeling really militant." The runner shakes his head. "As I said, it's a big difference, Wolf. And that's the Wrecking Crew stacked up against a single squad. From what Peg dug up, the ML outfit in DeeCee can field a platoon—that's four squads, with a combat mage for astral support."

Argent shrugs again. "Face it," he says quietly, "there are some missions where a shadow team's the only way to go. But for big-time destabilization, or staging a coup, or something like that, you need the milspec weaponry and the military communications channels and force coordination."

Again, what the runner's telling me makes perfect fragging sense. And again, it disturbs the drek out of me. "Are you saying this . . ."—I reach for the name—". . . this Schrage . . . Are you telling me he's got a platoon of regulars he's hiring out to any takers?"

"Not to just any takers," Argent corrects. "He'd be very selective about whose cred he takes. Probably not for any moral or ethical reasons, but I'm sure ability to pay's a big criterion. And also whether he can do it without getting made."

"Yeah, yeah, sure," I growl impatiently, "whatever. So, does he have that platoon?"

"Not that Peg could find out," the runner replies. "There are about sixty names officially assigned to Seattle ML, but I don't think they've got the same special training background as the guys in DeeCee. I'd guess most of them are managerial or clerical . . ." He pauses, visibly shifting to another train of thought. "Maybe you can confirm that, Wolf."

"How?"

"Recognize some names, maybe. I'll get Peg to run off a list." And, just as abruptly, he switches back. "So the answer's no, he doesn't seem to have the same kind of force together, not yet." He shrugs. "Maybe it takes more than a year to organize a private army."

"No," I say quietly. Argent looks at me questioningly. "No," I repeat, a little louder, but still more to myself than to him, "I don't think that's it."

"Then what?"

"Maybe he's not going the same route," I say, thinking out loud, the ideas as new to me as they are to Argent. It's like I'm listening to another part of myself, deep down in my subconscious, that's already worked out a lot of this drek, and now I'm just repeating it to the shadowrunner. It's a weird, schizoid feeling, and I hope my subconscious isn't going to make a fragging habit of it.

"What do you mean, Wolf?" the big runner presses.

"I'm not quite sure," I admit. "But if I wanted to set up some kind of fragging army—and keep it secret from the general public—I sure as frag wouldn't want to do it in Seattle. Much too small, priyatel, let me tell you." Sounds funny talking about the sprawl as small, but for drek like this it is.

Argent shakes his head. "Doesn't scan," he announces. "Other corps have got private armies in and around the plex and it doesn't slot anybody up or cramp their style."

"It's different, Argent," I insist. "This is Lone Star."

"Which we all know is oh-so-different from all the other megacorps," he almost sneers.

"No, it's not different," I concede, and it grinds me to do it. "But for frag's sake, does Jane Q. Public on the streets of Bellevue see the Star as different from MCT or Fuchi? You bet your hoop she does, chummer. The Star's the cops. MCT's a megacorp. There's a big fragging difference in the way they're perceived, the way they're treated by the news media . . . everything." I glare at him, and he gets the kicker that I'm not about to articulate in words: That's the way I always saw it, priyatel, and I was in a better position to scan the truth than your general-purpose civilian. But did I see the truth? Uh-uh.

He doesn't move for a few seconds. Nothing. Not even a blink. Then he nods unwillingly. He scans the logic of what I'm telling him, but seems unwilling to accept it. He doesn't like who I am or what I represent any more than I like him. I'd rather gargle with toxic waste than accept anything he says without a struggle, so why should he be any different? "Lone Star does it in DeeCee and Atlanta," he points out, but his heart's not in it.

"Yeah, well, that's DeeCee and that's Atlanta," I fire back immediately. "They're both national capitals, with all that implies. More corporate presence than Seattle, with more private armies. Who's going to pay much attention to just one more private outfit?"

Then a new thought hits me. "Also, ML's supposed to be liaison with the national military, right? If there's already a major military presence, and ML's in tight with it, it's hard to spot the distinction, neh? Who's going to notice an extra platoon at a full-blown army base? Only the real higher-ups know that Zebra Platoon—or whatever the frag—is actually on the Star's payroll. But what have they got for camouflage here in Seattle? The fragging Metroplex Guard. Yeah, right."

Argent's nodding slowly. If I keep hitting him with enough arguments, he's got to go along. Then yet another idea strikes. "And maybe Schrage and his little chummers don't need a fully geared-out platoon," I point out. "Clients who want that heavy a hammer can hire it out of DeeCee. Maybe Schrage is after clients who want something a little less blatant. Still military, but not regular ordnance."

Argent gets it too. "Bioweapons?"

"It's a possibility," I say, even though I'm convinced it's more than that. "Let's say Schrage wants to expand his repertoire with this retrovirus. Maybe some client's asking for the capability, or maybe he's going to use it as a big selling point in next year's marketing campaign—it doesn't really matter. He approaches Nova Vita Cybernetics, which just happens to have a jim-dandy little number for sale. On the Tir side of things, friend Timothy Telestrian's got this big proxy fight thing going on, and cutting a major deal with the Star would earn him big credit and big face." I shrug. "Who knows, maybe he's thinking of putting pressure on the Star after the fact, to help him out directly with daddy James . . .

"Problem is," I go on, "the 'bug' hasn't gone through field testing yet . . . or maybe Schrage isn't into taking NVC's word about what it's supposed to do. So some NVC reps and Schrage himself—this has got to be much too big to leave to drones—make contact with the Cutters under some cover story, and they've got their field test." I look at Argent. "How does that scan?"

"It scans all too well, omae," he says softly.

"Did Peg happen to find out whether ML's got any major clients on the go at the moment?" I ask, and the sudden look in the runner's optics answers that one clearly. "Tsimshian." He speaks the word flatly, coldly. "Peg says Military Liaison-Seattle cut a deal with some outfit in Kitimat, the Tsimshian capital."

"When?"

"Two months back." Argent smiles grimly. "The time-frame's about right, isn't it? Two weeks of research to find a good bioweapons supplier, two weeks of negotiation, then about a month for the field test."

"What's the deal?"

The runner snorts. "Peg's good, but she's not that good.

Trust me, omae, the grim and gritty details are buried so deep no decker's going to lay mitts on them." He shrugs. "If I were Schrage, I'd have all that secret drek on an isolated machine, not part of the Matrix. You know, Tempest-shielded so you can't even get it through induction or influence-scanning or anything."

"Any guesses? You probably know more about the background than me. You've been in Seattle longer."

He chuckles. "All my life, chummer. The sprawl's my home. I was born here, and when it's time to die, it's as good a place as any." He's silent for a moment, and I can see him getting his thoughts in order. "The Tsimshian nation's just basically bad news," he says finally. "Intertribal squabbles tearing it up, the Haida and Kwakiutl underclass against the Tsimshian and Tlingit power bloc. Maybe it's the national government wanting to finish off the 'Haida problem' once and for all. Or maybe it's the Haida National Front wanting to geek the government. Or maybe it's not tribally motivated at all.

"Tsimshian seceded from the NAN Sovereign Tribal Council in . . . what was it? Twenty thirty-five . . . ?"

"Twenty thirty-seven," I amend.

"Whatever. Since the secession, Tsimshian and Salish-Shidhe have been *this close* to border wars on a dozen occasions, mainly over some major ore deposits and industrial facilities that are just close enough to the border to be in what you could call 'disputed territory.' Maybe Kitimat figures it's high time to settle things with the S-S Council." He shrugs eloquently. "As I said, chummer, Tsimshian's bad news. You need a fragging menu to find out who's on their hate list for the day."

Just fragging wonderful.

Argent's looking at me with his steady, ironic gaze, like he's waiting for me to figure something out.

The realization finally comes. "Yeah," I growl. "It's all speculation because we don't know for sure that NVC created the bug. It could be that Schrage cut a deal with NVC for something innocent like implant technology. And we don't know for fragging sure that Schrage had anything to do with the Cutters getting hit by the bug. But how else can you scan it?"

"That's almost beside the point, isn't it?" Argent says quietly. "I could tell you I'm all the way, one hundred percent gonzo convinced, but what the frag? What difference does it make?" He gives a single bark of humorless laughter. "It's not like we can take our suspicions to Lone Star and have the cops look into it."

"So what the frag do we do about it?" I snap.

Argent's humorless grin fades into that cold poker-face I've seen too many times, and I think I know what his answer's going to be. "Why should I want to do anything about it? Corps frag people over all the time. Why should I get bent out of shape about one more case?"

Frag, I fragging knew it! He's a fragging shadowrunner, and there's no credit in this for him. The familiar rage against runners has been keeping a low profile for the past few days, but now it starts twisting and writhing in my chest again. I draw breath to say something poisonous . . .

Which is just what the cybered-up fragger is waiting for, of course. Before I can get out a word, he says, "But I'm curious about what NVC's up to. Curious enough to maybe hum on down the Columbia River to Pillar Rock and have a little look-see." I stare at him, and he gives me an innocent, drek-eating smile in response. "Want to come along?"

25

Frag that Argent anyway! The miserable son of a slitch must have known what was going through my mind, what I was thinking about him. And he fragging let me think it, let me get all morally superior and deeply into hating the ground he walks on.

And then, just when I was ready to tear his fragging head off, he basically said, "Hey, I want to do the right thing too, chummer," and let me know he was just yanking my chain. Lousy son of a slitch.

In no time at all he's got our transportation arranged and all that drek, and we're in the car heading for Sea-Tac. Meanwhile I've been getting more and more cranked up, while doing my fragging best not to show it.

I don't care if the runner knows I'm slotted off, priyatel. It's me who's bothered. Argent was yanking my chain to make a point, feeding me a line that matched perfectly with my preconception of shadowrunners, the one I've picked up from cop talk and what I heard in the Academy . . . and, yes, that I'd probably sucked up from the fragging trideo. Fragging Argent knew that, and decided to make me eat my cherished ideas. By playing perfectly in synch with them, then doing a high-speed one-eighty and taking off in the opposite direction. And of course what I'm supposed to learn from this is that shadowrunners aren't the mercenary, empty-hearted slots I always believed them to be. I hate being proved wrong even at the best of times, and definitely not by some holier-than-thou scumbag like Argent.

And that's why I'm sitting, fuming, in the passenger seat of the Westwind as Argent tools west, then south, through the southern end of downtown toward the part of Sea-Tac airport where private planes are kept. I start getting the creeps as we pull up to the guarded security gate that leads

to the plane-owners' parking lot, but Argent doesn't show the slightest sign of tension.

The sec-guard's eyes glint unnaturally in the watery afternoon sunlight, and I see the fiber-optic cable running from his datajack to the 'puter pack on his belt. As he looks at us, our images are being transferred from his cybereyes to that pack, and probably relayed from there to some analysis/ recognition system in a nearby building. The best outcome is that neither of us match up with the database of people authorized to use this gate. The worst, of course, is that my image triggers all kinds of watchdogs, and then things just kind of slide downhill from there.

I might as well have saved my stress for something that mattered—like the impending flight, for example. The sec-guard scans the two of us, focuses his eyes on infinity for a moment, then nods to Argent with a lot more respect than he'd shown a moment ago. "Head right on through, sir," he says. "You know where to park."

Argent smiles in response—the perfect image of some high corp suit accepting respect that's only his due from a subordinate—and rolls on. I wonder what ID the 'puter came back with when it scanned Argent's image, but I'm not going to humble myself enough to ask. I figure I've been humbled enough for one day.

Earlier, when the runner was telling me he'd arranged for a plane, I imagined some thrashed beater of a single-engine prop plane about as old as I am, if not older. A Piper Club, maybe, or a fragging Comanche dating back to the turn of the century. (When I was a kid, I used to read everything I could about planes, old and new. Not really as a hobby, but trying to eradicate the irrational fear I've always had of flying. Didn't work worth a frag.) As we cruise past the aircraft parking area, I see enough of those ancient planes, death-traps looking like they're held together with chewing gum, baling wire, gaffer tape, and positive thinking.

But Argent doesn't stop here. Instead, he keeps driving, and we start to pass planes that are clawing their way up the socioeconomic, chronological, and reliability ranks. Cessnas and Fiat-Fokkers from only a decade or two ago begin to replace defunct De Havillands, and I start to feel a little better about the whole thing.

And still he's not stopping. Instead he takes a right, and now the planes that we're cruising by are a year or two old, if that. Lear-Cessna executive turboprops and Agusta-Cierva "Plutocrat" rotorcraft sit cheek-to-jowl with drek I've never seen before, most of the birds sporting corporate livery of some kind. The runner hasn't cut some kind of deal for this kind of transport, has he?

But no, ahead of us I can see what we'll be using, and my anxiety's back in the pit of my stomach. Not that it's an old beater of a plane. Not at all. It's a brand spanking new McDonnell-Douglas Merlin, a small, slick cousin to the Federated-Boeing Commuter. It's a tilt-wing with two long-bladed turboprops, apparently based on a nineteen-eighties' design called the Osprey, a V/STOL that switches from horizontal flight to vertical by pivoting its wings, effectively turning props into helicopter-style rotors.

Frag, everybody in any city in North America has seen the F-B Commuters do their thing. And, similarly, everybody knows how unreliable they are—manufacturers' claims to the contrary, of course—and how vulnerable to loss of power during the transition from horizontal to vertical or vice versa. I promised myself a long time back I'd never fly in a Commuter, and now here I am faced with riding in the smaller—and even more unreliable—Merlin. Just fragging wonderful, and I really want to thank you for that Argent, from the bottom of my heart.

Again, of course, I try to hide my discomfort. I focus my eyes on the blue and white craft, trying to pay close attention to two jumpsuited techs or mechanics or whatever they are dicking around inside open access covers. To get my mind off crash and fatality statistics, I try to recognize the livery and the angular logo on the fuselage.

"Don't worry about the corp affiliation," Argent pipes up, going back to his old mind-reading routine. "Yamatetsu sold it to a chummer a while back, and she never got around to repainting it." Uh-huh. And I wonder if she ever got around to changing the radar transponder to read civilian instead of corp?

Argent pulls up next to the Merlin, and we climb out. I see movement in the open hatchway, then a figure emerges. An elf, but shorter and broader than the typical metatype. At first I scan her as fat, but I quickly revise that as she comes down the ladder to the apron. "Comfortably well-upholstered" might be a better description. Her face, too, is broader than the elf standard, and her eyes and buzz-cut hair are dark instead of light. But she's got the elf ears, and there's something I can't quite label about her smile at the sight of Argent that confirms her metatype as far as I'm concerned. She's wearing a shapeless black jumpsuit with altogether too many pockets and stuff apparently crammed into every one of them.

"Hoi, Argent!" she calls, and her voice and broad smile remind me of a kid with a new toy.

"Hoi, Raven." He takes her offered hand, and they shake like old chummers.

Seeing her close up now, I try to guess at this Raven's age. Judging by her voice and the way she moved, at first I had her chipped at about twenty. Now, though, I kick that up by ten years, maybe fifteen. Her face is weather-tanned, with networks of deep crinkles around her eyes. I hadn't spotted her mods before, but now I see three datajacks, one in each temple, and a third that looks relatively new because of the faintly pink and tender-looking skin just above the joint of her jaw on the right side. Presumably, she's jacked for a vehicle control rig. You don't find many deckers buying and flying cast-off corp planes.

"Long time," Raven tells Argent, her smile not fading in the slightest. "You gotta come see me sometime when it's not biz, okay?"

Argent smiles back, and his eyes are more relaxed than I've ever seen them. Old chummers for sure. "Okay, I promise." He remembers me, and gestures me over. "Raven, this is Wolf."

The elf sticks her hand out, and I take it. Firm grip, cool, and the texture of the skin—not quite right—tells me the datajacks aren't her only mods.

"You've picked a good day," she announces, glancing at the sky. "High overcast, good viz." She grins at me. "Ready to do some flying?"

Raven's a slick pilot, I'll give her that much. Every maneuver the Merlin makes is smooth as synthsilk, perfectly controlled, without any sense that she's fighting the machine or forcing it to do anything. On the contrary, it feels more like the plane's doing everything naturally because that's what planes do, and we're just along for the ride. Even the transition between vertical and horizontal flight—when the wings pivot to turn overhead rotors into turboprop air screws—was so smooth and steady I didn't notice the event until a few seconds later when I realized our flight regime had changed. For the first time since I spotted the Merlin, my anxiety level has begun to shade down a bit.

Not that watching Raven at work was all that reassuring. Oh sure, I've flown on planes piloted by riggers—everyone who's ever hopped a commercial suborbital, semiballistic, or HSCT has—but that doesn't mean I've been on the flight deck to watch them at it. And now I'm glad I wasn't. I tell you there's something disturbing, something just fragging wrong about watching the pilot—the person who's got your life in her hands—jack into the control board of the plane and then promptly fall asleep!

No drek, that's just what it looks like. Raven looks totally boneless, slumped there in her flight couch. Only the four-point safety harness and the special headrest with forehead strap keep her upright, stop her from sliding like a corpse down into the well under the panel. Her eyes are shut, and her mouth is hanging slightly open. And she's fragging drooling. Just a little, but it's enough.

Argent looks over at me and grins. He's sitting in the co-pilot's chair, to Raven's right, while I'm squatted down on a jump seat just back of the gap between the two front seats. I've never liked being relegated to the back of the bus, and this time's no different. The Merlin's got incredible visibility, though. From where I'm sitting, it looks like maybe seventy-five percent of the small plane's nose is transplast, which means I've got a better than one-eighty-degree field of view in the horizontal plane, and more than ninety in the vertical. It feels like being in a fragging bubble hanging eighteen hundred meters in the air.

To take my mind off the mild case of agoraphobia I didn't know I had, I concentrate on the jump seat I'm strapped into, and the tech-drek around it. First I notice a tiny swing-out console that shows a set of repeater displays matching most of the sensors controlled from the main panel. They're not labeled worth a drek, of course, but they're interesting nonetheless. I think I've scoped out a few of them—ECM and ECCM tell-tales here, threat display over here, and a display of consumables carried over there. (I note with grim interest that the Merlin's got a full load of chaff and flares on board. Why, I wonder? Because Raven just doesn't take any chances, ever? Or because she's expecting to have to use them in the near future?)

"Don't like flying, Wolf?" the runner asks mildly.

Frag. I thought I was hiding it better than that. I shrug in response.

"I used to hate it." He chuckles. "Of course, that was back when going up in a plane usually meant I was going to jump out of it at some point." I file that fact away for future reference—paratrooper training and experience. Just what is Argent's background, anyway?

"Then I figured, why not just sit back and enjoy the view?" he goes on. "Why worry? We all have to go when our number's up, and it doesn't matter where we are—in a plane, in a firefight, or in a nice warm bath—when the time comes."

"Yeah," I grumble, hooking a thumb toward Raven. "But what if it's her number that comes up?"

The Merlin's a fast plane, a blessing because it means we'll be back on the ground all that much sooner. Within minutes after dust-off, we're at eighteen hundred meters and cruising south. The demarcation where the sprawl ends and the Salish-Shidhe nation begins is obvious, even though we're too high to see the walls and fences and guard posts. On one side of the demarcator there's city; on the other, countryside. It's like God took a hand razor and sculpted a sharp edge along the urban area that would otherwise be spreading south toward Portland.

I'm a little anxious about crossing that line, the invisible boundary dividing UCAS airspace from S-S airspace. Even though I've never tried it myself, I've heard enough about how fragging difficult it is to slide "over the wall, out of the sprawl"—that is, slip the border into the Amerindian territory surrounding Seattle. I can't believe the S-S Council's going to be any more amenable to us scroffy "Seattlites" encroaching on their pristine fragging country by air.

But the grief's not as bad as when Argent drove onto the Sea-Tac private apron. I've got to assume Raven is in contact with ground controllers and all the usual drek, but her meat body didn't shift a millimeter, and she didn't bother to patch whatever communication she had through to the cockpit speakers. Or—who knows?—maybe she didn't have to talk to anybody. For all I know, the transponder in the Merlin might still be squawking the idee for a high-level Yamatetsu exec transport. Whatever, we just blow on through into S-S airspace without the slightest hassle. Thank Ghu for small favors, say I.

As soon as we're clear of the sprawl, the sound of the engines changes. For a split second, I think we're in trouble, then I realize Raven's goosed the throttles. As the big engines spool up to full power, I scan the repeater displays in front of me for something that might be an air-speed indicator. Eventually I see numbers reading out in the right range. If I'm right, the air-speed's fluctuating at about six hundred klicks per hour. Not bad. We could be in Portland in about half an hour. Pillar Rock—the location of the NVC facility—is on the other side of the Columbia from Portland, maybe sixty klicks to the west, toward the ocean.

Before long I can see the glitter of water ahead of us. I lean forward, craning my head between the two front seats, to see the satnav map Argent's brought up on the co-pilot's main display station. Yep, the water ahead is the Columbia, just like I guessed. According to the little point of light that's the Merlin, we're ten klicks to the east of Pillar Rock, passing over the town of Skamokawa. We buzz over the town—a small, spotless-looking community—and Raven banks the plane right, westward. Judging by what I think is a radar altimeter, we're down to five hundred meters or so. Speed's cut back too, down to about three hundred klicks.

"Two minutes." The voice is Raven's, but it doesn't come from her mouth, which continues its drooling down the front of her jumpsuit. No, the voice sounds from the small speakers mounted over the main console.

"Got it," Argent responds. I see him clear the satnav map from his screen and call up a new one. It takes me a moment to realize it's a magnified real-time image of the terrain ahead, presumably picked up by some external vidcam. The image tracks and zooms in and out as the runner tests out the sensitivity of the controls. Then I notice a small cross-hairs reticule in the center of the screen, and I start to say, "Um, Argent . . ."

He turns to me, then sees the direction of my gaze and chuckles. "Null sheen, chummer," he tells me. "It used to be a chain-gun rig, but Raven replaced it with a vid setup when she bought the bird. I just figured we might want something a little more vivid than memories."

I nod my head, cursing myself. Yeah, pictures, that's the

fragging ticket ... I should have thought of it myself. I get the feeling I'm thinking less and less, recently.

The Columbia's wide here near the mouth, at least a klick across, I'd guess. The Merlin's hugging the northern shoreline, a hundred meters or so out over the water, and we're steady at about two hundred and fifty meters. I look out the left side of the cockpit. Over there, a klick away, is Tir Tairngire. The terrain, which looks exactly like that on the north side of the river, is basically flatlands with grass and small trees, the whole area looking kind of wet and swampy. Somehow I'm disappointed—the mucho mysterioso "Land of Promise" should look different, maybe covered with faerie glamor out of kids' stories or some such drek. From this distance, there's nothing special at all.

Raven's voice sounds from the speakers again, making me jump. "I've got the target," she announces. "Argent, give me the camera."

The runner hits a couple of keys on the panel—slaving the camera setup to Raven's rigger controls, presumably—then sits back and crosses his arms. On the co-pilot's screen, the image shifts sickeningly as the camera slews to train out to the right. It zooms in on something, a small cluster of buildings. Even at maximum magnification, we're too far out to see anything useful.

"How'd you make it so far off?" Argent asks curiously.

Raven chuckles. In contrast to her voice, which sounds natural, her laugh strikes me as horrible and inhuman, coming disembodied through the electronics. "Couldn't hardly miss it, cobber," she announces. "It's got one serious nav beacon, it's got permanent glide-paths delimited with radar beams, and even the backscatter from the surface-scanning radar reads just fine on my sensors."

"Surface scans," the runner echoes. "Landward, or on the river?"

"Both."

"Serious drek," Argent mutters. "Permanent glide-paths mean controlled airspace, right? So any guesses as to how far out?"

"Tough to say," the rigger admits. "In the plex, private facilities are limited to a diameter of half a klick. But this is tribal land, and I don't know the relevant ... Hel-lo," she interrupts herself. "They're interrogating our transponder."

"What the frag does that mean?" I demand.

"An electronic version of, 'Who goes there, friend or foe?'" Argent throws over his shoulder, then turns his attention back to Raven. "What's the scoop?"

"We're squawking as a Yamatetsu air ambulance," she replies.

"Tell me if they try and raise you by voice," Argent suggests.

I still can't see the site by naked eyeball, but the visual on Argent's display is getting bigger and clearer. The place looks more like a fragging prison than my image of a research lab. Four major buildings and a couple of little outbuildings, all surrounded by a wall. From this distance and angle, it's impossible to tell how tall it is. We can probably analyze it later from shadow angle and such, but my first impression is that it's high and solid. And those things at the corners—architectural elements, or watchtowers? What the frag is this place anyway?

I glance down at the repeater console in front of me. Telltales and displays are flickering all over the section I've tentatively identified as dedicated to ECM and sensors. Probably the first fringes of the air-control radars and designated flight paths Raven was talking about. "How far out?" I ask.

"Five klicks," she replies. "I'm swinging out a little further from shore, just not to make them too nervous." Even before she's finished speaking, I feel the Merlin slip into a shallow bank to the left.

Wheep! A shrill warning tone sounds through the cockpit, and a handful of red lights light up on my repeater panel. "What's that?" I demand.

"Pulse-mod radar, tight arc," Raven shoots back. The words convey precisely dick in the way of data, but the tone of her voice, which comes through the datajack speaker link just fine, is tight. A fact conveying entirely too much data. We're in drek.

"Kill the transponder," Argent snaps.

"Done," replies the rigger. "No joy, we're close enough, and that beam's beefy enough that they already have a skin-paint on us." The bank gets suddenly steeper, and the engines howl as the rigger cracks the throttles wide open. She's diving, too, probably to pick up speed faster or to get under the radar (if that's still relevant these days). The camera loses lock and Argent's display goes dead, but at the moment nobody gives a frag.

More displays light up on my panel, including two little annunciators marked Lck and Lnch. A raucous buzzer sounds, painfully loud, until Argent punches a button on the console and stills it.

"What?" I yell.

It's Argent who answers. "Radar-homer," he barks. "Incoming missile."

The engines scream louder, and I guess Raven's kicked in emergency power. I'm thrown against my harness as she snaps the wings level. The Merlin's still got a steep nose-down attitude, and all I can see ahead is the gray-brown water of the Columbia River, rushing closer every second. I tear my eyes from that hypnotizing sight and check the radar altimeter. Thirty meters, and dropping fast. Then the plane starts to lift out of the dive, pulling enough gees to feel like I've got Argent sitting on my chest. The water's almost close enough to touch, whipping by at fragging near seven hundred klicks below the cockpit. I figure Raven must be trying to lose us in the surface effect. A good idea in theory, but from what little I know, flat water—like a river—isn't the best place to try it. Your chances are much better over rough terrain. Not that we've got that much choice, of course.

I'm hurled against my straps again as Raven snaps us into another steep bank. Out the side of the cockpit, it looks like the left wing tip's only centimeters above the water. If the rigger misjudges and plants the wing tip, it's game fragging over. My imagination's easily vivid enough to visualize the Merlin cartwheeling across the river, tearing itself apart before it vanishes in a red-black fireball.

"Read me off the radar characteristics," Raven's voice orders. "I'm kinda busy at the moment." I can believe it. Even with vehicle control rigs, there's only so much "band width" a human brain can handle, and flying something like a Merlin this low, this fast, has to take up a lot of the processing "horsepower."

Argent loosens his straps and leans forward for a closer look at his panel. "Gen six, pulse width class B, pulse freq class 4C," he reads out the stats. "It's got a hot lock on us. The launcher's still painting us, too. Do you care?"

"Not right now," the rigger replies. We snap over into as steep a bank in the opposite direction. "With that radar profile, we've got us an Ares Type Four seeker."

"Is that good?" I ask.

"It could be better," Argent remarks.

I grab onto the handholds on either side of my jump seat as Raven wrenches the Merlin through a sequence of ever-tighter turns. Twice every second, there's a hollow boom from the back of the fuselage, and the plane jolts. I've got to assume the rigger's punching out chaff—at least some of it probably active chaff with radar-emitting microchips incorporated into the mylar foil.

"Still locked," Argent announces. "A thousand meters out, inbound at a thousand relative."

"Echo that," answers Raven. "Hold on tight, boys. Make-or-break time."

Two more booms, then the chaff dispenser falls silent. The Merlin's nose pulls up, engines screaming and airframe complaining. I let out a whoof! as the gees land on my chest. All I can see out the front of the cockpit is the gray overcast a few thousand meters above us. If this is the last thing I'm going to see, I'd have preferred something a little more interesting.

Displays change on the repeater panel in front of me. Good news or bad?

"Missile's lost lock," Argent announces, his voice totally steady despite the fact that he currently weighs twice as much as normal. As if to punctuate the comment, there's an incredible concussion from behind us. The plane shakes, and I hear myself squall in fright.

I feel the Merlin roll, and I think we've been hit and we're going in. But a second later I realize it's just Raven completing the maneuver, something like a split-S. Within seconds the wings are level and we're heading due east at the Merlin's full emergency speed. I wipe my forehead, and my hand comes away very wet.

Argent turns to me and remarks conversationally, "The missile locked onto the chaff and augered in. Pretty impressive detonation, huh?"

Yeah, right. I look over at Raven. She's still just sitting there, jaw sagging spastically. Great company I'm keeping these days. The runner glances at his displays again and announces, "The launcher's stopped painting us."

Damn fragging good thing, too. "Time to head for home?" I suggest hopefully.

Argent nods. "We've got a home vid to watch."

26

It's late evening by the time we're back in Renton, and I'm feeling like it's been a frag of a long day. I'm twitchy as all frag. On the drive home on the freeway, a car next to Argent's Westwind had to jam on the brakes, its brake shoes letting out a squeal that sounded all too much like the Merlin's radar-lock annunciator. I think I managed to suppress my reaction—enough at least to keep from going through the fragging roof—but it was a sure sign of how far outside my comfort zone we've been operating. Recon flights and missile attacks? Give me a nice friendly knife-fight or gang shoot-out, please.

We hit the Hole in the Wall and head upstairs to my doss. (Why always my doss? Obviously because Argent doesn't want me to know where he crashes, and I don't really blame him.) The runner slots the chip with the Merlin's vidcam data on it, and we bring up the best image we've got of the Pillar Rock NVC facility.

Seeing it in better detail now, I realize my first guess was right on the money—it does look like a fragging prison. Based on shadow-angle calculations, the telecom's (surprisingly sophisticated) image-analysis software estimates the walls to be eight meters high. Even with maximum image-enhancement, we can't see whether those walls are topped with anything, but judging from the overall look of the place I'd expect a few strands of razorwire (at best) or monowire (at worst), supplemented by sensors of some kind. What I thought were guard towers *are* guard towers, or at least something remarkably like them. There's a single gate to landward, and a couple of boat docks—outside the wall, of course—on the river.

After a minute or two of close examination, I encapsulate my analysis. "It's a fragging fortress."

Argent nods slowly. "An interesting design for a lab, I'd

say," he agrees. "I've seen corp facilities with serious security before, but it's never this obvious, this blatant."

Something that's been bothering me for a while chooses this moment to surface. "If NVC's a Tir-based corp, why's this place on the north side of the river? That's S-S-turf."

The shadowrunner shrugs. "I'd guess it's because the Tir keeps such a close watch on corporations operating in the nation. And remember that James Telestrian has ties with the government and the conservative biz community. If Timothy T. is using this lab for something dark and nasty, he wouldn't want it anywhere within his father's sphere of influence, would he?"

"I thought the S-S Council came down hard on corps," I point out.

"Some corps, yes," Argent confirms. "But I know of two or three that have managed to curry favor with the council." He snorts. "Probably through hefty bribes, but that's just a guess. I'd say this proves you can number Nova Vita Cybernetics among those corps."

I turn back to the telecom display. "We still don't know anything, do we?"

Argent shrugs again. "I think the fact that somebody hosed off a missile at us is somewhat indicative," he points out dryly.

"Indicative that NVC's up to something they want to keep in the shadows, yes," I correct. "It could by anything, though, couldn't it?"

The runner's not convinced. "I'd say that the missile, combined with the Schrage connection, plus the fact that Nova Vita transferred gengineers to Pillar Rock, tells us something."

I shake my head firmly. "To use your word, it's indicative, but it's sure as frag not conclusive. It's circumstantial evidence, not proof. There's nothing we can take to the authorities, and what authorities would we trust with this anyway?"

Argent starts to argue, but a new thought comes hurtling out of nowhere to slam into my mind like a bullet-train. "Hold the fragging phone," I snap. The shadowrunner shuts up, and watches me curiously.

I'm silent for a good minute or two, then feel my face crease in a smile. Yeah, that hangs together.

"What?" Argent asks, referring to the smile.

"I'll give you the details later," I tell him. "In the meantime, there are some things I'm going to need from you and Peg. Maybe you should take notes . . ."

Argent didn't go along with me immediately, but then I didn't expect him to. I've got to admit, though, that he wasn't anywhere near as adamantly opposed to my plan as I'd expected. (Or, possibly, as adamantly opposed as I'd have been to a plan of his. I'll have to think about that . . .) When he saw what I was driving at, he went along. Sure, he pointed out a few holes I hadn't noticed, but he also suggested ways to fill them, and the scheme ended up stronger as a result.

So, now here I am, sitting in front of the telecom, trying to relax, trying to slow my heart rate down to something even approaching normal. I've got to be frosty, I keep telling myself. If this were some kind of combat situation, I could at least try to depend on my training to see me through it. But this is so different. If I don't handle it right, I'm going to be on the run from the Cutters and the Star and anybody else who's in on the game until somebody finally scores and manages to blow my brains out.

I glance over at Argent. He's straddling a chair nearby, but out of the vid pickup's field of view. He's watching me calmly, almost detachedly. Easy for him. It's not his head with a death-mark on it. Frag him anyway. I turn back to the telecom and enter the code-string Peg supplied.

Placing the call seems to take forever. The screen remains totally blank at first, but the speaker's alive with hums and clicks and faint beeps as the utility I've triggered has its way with the LTG grid. Eventually the screen fills with the familiar shifting patterns, and the status line at the bottom of the display reads Establishing Connection. The status line changes, and from the speaker comes the familiar "ringing" tone, but with a strange echo to it. No fragging surprise; this call is going through a seven-node relay—the most complex link-up Peg can handle with any reliability—as opposed to the two-node relay I used to reach Argent. If the recipient of the call can trace through seven intermediate nodes, I don't even want to know about it.

The phone keeps ringing. No answer. I start to worry I've got a bogus number, or that the only way to put the call through is via some kind of pre-process handshaking.

Argent's told me Peg had the fragging devil's own time getting this number, and the odds of reliability—the chance that the number's right, that it's still in service, and all that drek—isn't much more than fifty percent. As the screen keeps flashing Ringing, I get the nasty feeling those odds just haven't come up. Frag! It might have worked. I reach out for the End key . . .

And that's when the status bar flashes Connected, and the screen clears to show a face. "Telestrian," the figure says briskly. The elf-woman's eyes narrow, and I know she's looking at a blank screen. "Who is this?"

I flick on the telecom's vid pickup, and I see Lynne Telestrian's hard green eyes narrow millimetrically in surprise. Then the same steel-edged control I saw in the deserted Fi nes Que t is re-established. "Mr. Larson," she says slowly. "I must say I find this . . . unexpected."

Too fragging right, it's unexpected, is what I don't say to her. The direct-connect LTG number to Lynne Telestrian's private office was almost as tough to deck out as nuke launch codes, according to Peg. I just smile, and say, "I figured our conversation wasn't quite over, Ms. Telestrian. Last time we talked, I didn't ask the right questions. I decided it was time to rectify that."

She raises her eyebrows in a mixture of disdain and curiosity. "Oh? And what makes you think I have any intention of answering your questions?"

I shrug. Out the corner of my eye, I see Argent gesture with metal fingers. He's keeping a timer on the conversation, and I've already burned twenty seconds of the two minutes we've budgeted as safe. "Maybe the questions themselves would change your mind," I point out. "Like, 'How would the stock market and business community react to the revelation that a Telestrian company is testing biowarfare agents in downtown Seattle?'" I grin. "Sure, there are some mitigating factors, but I don't think your average eager shadowsnoop's going to care too much about them. Or the news media either."

"What? That's nonsense," she snaps. "Nobody would believe that."

"Don't be so sure," I say mildly. "The stock market's notoriously skittish, isn't it? Even if you proved later that your faction had nothing to do with it, the short-term damage would still be done. The big question is, which faction would get hurt the worst in the short run, yours or Timothy's? Worth thinking about, isn't it?"

She doesn't respond at once. Her gaze is cold and steady, green and unblinking, more like a snake's than a woman's. Again Argent gestures—one minute down. The seconds are ticking away, and I start wondering how much safety margin Peg built into her estimate that I could talk for up to two minutes without the risk of being traced.

"You've been busy, I can see that," Lynne Telestrian says at last. "If your aim was to get my attention, consider it all yours." She sits back, and the telecom automatically refocuses to keep her features crisp. "Now that you have it, what would you like to do with it?"

"Last time we talked, you gave me some advice and I took it to heart," I tell her, feeling more comfortable now. This part of the conversation, at least, I was able to script out mentally before placing the call. "I've looked into Timothy Telestrian's involvement with Seattle, and I don't like what I've found. I don't know how much you already know or what you intend to do about it. But let me tell you, Ms. Telestrian, unless we can come to a meeting of the minds, everything I know is going to every shadowsnoop, reporter, muckraker, and news correspondent I can track down ... with particular attention to the pirates. Do you scan me, Lynne?"

She doesn't answer with words, but the look in those green eyes is expressive enough. Not for the first time, I'm real glad I'm on the other side of a telecom link.

"Get ready to receive a datafile," I tell her. "It's a compilation of everything I've found out and everything I can guess. What you do with it is your business, but I suggest you *do* do something with it. Drag your hoop on this one, and like I said, the same report goes straight to the shadowsnoops.

"I also want you to call me back in precisely one hour," I go on quickly, before she can reply. "The number's at the end of the datafile. For obvious reasons it's a multi-node relay, but don't try tracing it. The relay will only be active for two minutes, starting precisely sixty minutes from my mark, so you'll be dead-ending yourself. If you don't call me back within the time-span, the file goes to the snoops. Scan me?" Again I don't wait for an answer. "Open your capture file, here comes the data. Oh, and ... mark."

With that, I kill the vid pickup and execute the preprogrammed utility to spew my report on everything I know and can guess about the Telestrian-NVC-Star connection down the phone line. Transferring the compressed file takes five seconds. The instant the telecom beeps completion, I break the connection. The screen goes blank, but again the speaker beeps and clicks to itself as Peg disassembles the seven nodes of the relay.

I sit back in my chair and look a question at Argent.

"Hundred and twenty-one seconds total connect time," he announces. A rather feral grin splits his face. "I think a one-second overrun's acceptable performance on this one." He's silent for a moment, but I know he's got something more to say. I wait.

"Nice moves," he says at last. "You glide well, Wolf. You're too good for Lone Star." And then, like he's embarrassed because his praise is too effusive, he pulls out his own cel phone to coordinate the next step with Peg, leaving me effectively alone to chew on what I've heard.

27

Waiting has always been intolerable for me, and this time is no exception. Before I placed the first call, Argent and I hashed through how much time to give Lynne for the callback, and we settled on an hour. Long enough to read through and digest my "report," and long enough to at least begin to corroborate anything she didn't already know. Not long enough—or so we hoped—to stage some kind of counter-op. (The fact that we couldn't come up with any convincing ideas about what counter-op she might stage didn't make us breathe any easier on that score.) So we settled on an hour, for all the nice, sensible, logical reasons.

What we didn't take into account was what it would feel like for us to wait out that hour. I was pacing the floor within the first fifteen minutes, cranky enough to bite someone's head off for so much as speaking too loud. Argent just sprawled on the bed, lost in his own thoughts. At first I thought he was totally unaffected by the waiting, and hated him for it. But then, somewhere around fifty minutes into the span, Jean Trudel waltzed in the door with a plate of sandwiches and a couple of cold beers—and the chromed runner had leaped halfway off the bed before he could stop himself. A little jumpy, Argent? I wanted to say, but kept a tight rein on my yap.

At T-minus-two I settle myself down at the telecom, with Argent in the same spot as before, out of the field of view. I run the self-diagnostics on the telecom twice—growling "Frag off" at Argent when he chuckles—and then I've got nothing to do during that last, endless minute. The timers on both our watches go off within a second of each other, and I can imagine that, somewhere in SanFran, Peg the decker's busy patching together another seven-node relay, this one to handle an incoming call. The telecom's flatscreen lights up with a calibration grid, the signal that we're hot and tracking, waiting for Lynne Telestrian to place her call . . . assuming she *does* place the call.

In a trideo show, we'd have to sweat out fragging near the whole specified time before the call comes in, just to artificially crank up the tension. I guess, deep down, I expect reality to work the same way, so I almost go through the roof when the trid beeps with an incoming call less than five seconds after going online. I take a deep breath, and hit the Standby/Talk key.

Lynne Telestrian's ice-maiden face fills the screen. "I commend you on your diligence, Mr. Larson," she begins, her voice cool, detached. "When I suggested you investigate Timothy's activities, I really didn't expect this kind of result."

I can't help asking. "What did you expect?"

She shrugs thin shoulders. "Honestly? I expected you to provide a minor irritant, a minor diversion, to Timothy—something to distract him momentarily, before he killed you."

I nod. That's basically the way I'd figured it—send the Star bonehead crusading into the fray, and then learn something from the circumstances and manner of his geekage. "Sorry to disappoint you, *leäl,*" I grate, using a very indelicate Elvish word indicating extremely close acquaintance. (No, I don't speak Sperethiel, but I long ago discovered the utility of being able to insult people in as many native tongues as possible.)

If I'd been hoping to get a rise out of Lynne Telestrian, I'm not getting it . . . although I'm fragging sure she's filing my rudeness away in some ice-cold corner of her brain. She just watches me steadily for a few moments, and then says, "Message delivered, Mr. Larson. If that's all . . ." An arm enters the frame, and I know she's reaching for the End key.

"Hey, wait!" This isn't going the way I wanted or expected it to. "What are you going to do about it?"

She shrugs. "I don't see why that's any concern of yours."

"It's my fragging concern because I say it is," I snarl. The rage is twisting in my gut again, and I'm starting to realize how much I hate Ms. Lynne fragging Telestrian. Not only for who and what she is, but for what she represents. "What the frag are you going to do about Timothy and his fragging killer bug, huh, Lynne? What?"

For the first time a smile—thin and nasty—appears on her face. "That's none of your business, Mr. Larson."

"Well, I'm making it my business." In my peripheral vision, I see Argent indicating fifty seconds gone. I flip him the bird, and focus back on the Telestrian slitch.

"Oh? How?" Her tone's amused, which only further feeds my rage.

"The file, you fragging bat! The file I sent you. You tell me what you're going to do about it—right fragging now—or the instant you're off the phone, I'm going to spread this little gem around to all the news media, and let the blue chips fall where they may. Maybe it'll distract you from your little proxy fight, having to prop up your own stock prices. And who knows, maybe you'll have fun dodging legal response as well. I'm sure the metroplex government will be just thrilled to learn that the Telestrian clan's using Ravenna as a bioweapons lab. Maybe the federal government would be interested too. And how about the Salish-Shidhe Council? Tribal lands are downwind of Ravenna, aren't they? And does the Tir government know what's going down? Using bioweapons on another nation's territory might be considered an act of war . . ."

I pause to take a breath, and she jumps in. "All right, you've made your point . . ."

"I'm not done," I roar. "You tell me what you're going to do, and we're steady for the moment. But if it turns out you don't do what you say you're going to—like, if you just back off on the whole thing—you can bet that shapely little hoop of yours that NewsNet, ABS, NABS, and the rest of the boys are going to be getting a package that should kinda pique their curiosity . . . If you scan me."

She doesn't reply at once, nor does her expression shift in the slightest. But I can feel the anger and the hatred, like palpable waves, coming off her image. Well, frag her too. Eventually she asks quietly, "Is this intense interest only because of the death of that ganger, Paco?"

"That's part of it," I snarl back, "but only part."

"And the rest is because Timothy's actions transgress some moral code you hold particularly dear?"

"Timothy's, and Lone Star's, and that's still only part of it, and it's none of your fragging business!"

In person, my blast would have blown her hair back. On the flatscreen, her only reaction is another ironic smile. "To paraphrase you," she says calmly, "perhaps I'm making it my business."

"Why?"

She shrugs. "Because it's a way of gauging your level of outrage," she replies, "your level of commitment."

Argent's signaling again—I flip him off again. "Commitment to what?" I ask.

"To . . ."—she pauses in thought— ". . . to 'seeing justice done' might be the best way of putting it."

I start getting a real nasty feeling about this. "What are you talking about?" I ask suspiciously.

She smiles again, and real fear starts to twist with the rage in my gut. "It just occurs to me we could help each other," she says. "We both want some action taken concerning Timothy's bioweapons. You can trust me on this," she adds. "Our reasons aren't that different, in all probability.

"You want confirmation that action is taken," she goes on. "You also have some other needs, but you probably haven't connected them to this issue."

"Like what?" I demand.

"Like clearing your name with Lone Star," the elf-slitch says quietly. "An order's still out for your execution, by the way. I've checked. Officially issued by one"—she glances to the side—"Marcus Drummond, but actually instigated by Gerard Schrage, of the Military Liaison Division." She gives me an executioner's smile. "Apparently Mr. Schrage has tight ties with certain other executives within Seattle Lone Star. Ties of which the rest of the Lone Star establishment is unaware."

No drek, Sherlock. Like Sarah Layton and Vince McMartin, for starters. One nice, cozy, happy little fragging family. "You've got proof of that, I suppose," I sneer.

"Of course," she says simply.

I just wait for the other shoe to drop, and sure enough it does.

"I can pass the proof to you, Mr. Larson. Or, if we come to an agreement, you can leave it entirely up to us."

My skin crawls. "What kind of agreement?"

Her smile grows broader. "Yes, that's the question, isn't it? We both have problems, Mr. Larson, and each of us represents an answer to at least some of the other person's problems. You, for example, want to see something done about the bioweapons, and you also want your name cleared . . .

preferably at the expense of Schrage, Drummond, Layton, and McMartin. Am I right?" I don't even bother answering. "I, on the other hand, need a leader for the surgical strike I'm planning against Nova Vita Cybernetics' Pillar Rock facility."

I just stare at her, not caring that I must be gaping like a gaffed fish. Argent's eyebrows have shot up almost into his hairline, just about the most unrestrained emotion I've seen from the chromed runner. "You move quick, lady," I tell her, in honest respect.

She accepts the compliment with a tilt of her head. "The strike planning is underway," she reiterates. "My people are recruiting forces as we speak. But the slot of strike leader is open, and I'd like you to fill it."

The woman's brass is unbelievable. "No fragging way," I say with a grim laugh. "Find another fragging pigeon, *leäl.*"

Her expression becomes harder and I know I've stung her at last, but her voice retains the same smooth control. "Think about it, Mr. Larson," she says calmly. "We can both benefit if you accept."

"Yeah? Like how?"

"On our side, I should think it's fairly obvious. The . . . I believe 'assets' is the correct word . . . The assets performing the raid don't have to know the mission's purpose. All they need know is their specific assignments and the fact that they'll be paid on completion. They don't have to know the central objective of the raid—and, for obvious reasons, that's exactly how we want it." I nod. Yeah, that's obvious— Lynne-slitch wouldn't want anyone to know that Timothy's playing with bioweapons.

"The strike leader's another story, of course," she continues. "He has to know the purpose and all the background."

"So?"

"So," she continues smoothly, "the ideal situation is for the strike to be led by someone who's already aware of the issues." She smiles coldly. "We would be most satisfied if we could keep the number of people who are, er, in the know as small as possible.

"And then there's the issue of your knowledge, Mr. Larson. You know a lot that could be very damaging to my concerns. I'd very much like to—shall we say—defuse the threat you represent."

"By putting me in the front line and getting me geeked? No thanks, lady, I've played that game once before."

She shakes her head. "You misunderstand. You're a professional, Mr. Larson. I understand that. And a professional always takes precautions. A data time-bomb, for example. That file you've been threatening me with, stored in a secure system, with a broadcast utility and a distribution list. If you're not alive to send the system a password every day, the utility sends the file to all the news media you've mentioned. Isn't that the way it works?"

I nod. I haven't set up something like that—not yet—but you can bet your hoop I would if I figured I was stepping into harm's way.

"The best way to defuse that threat," the elf woman goes on, "is to arrange things so it's no longer in your best interests to use the data while you're still alive. If we happen to kill you, yes, certainly the file will get distributed. But if we . . . link . . . you to the events in some highly negative way, you'll never be able to use the data for blackmail. Do you understand?"

I think I'm starting to, and it's certainly an elegant idea. Okay, I've got evidence that some faction within the Telestrian empire is doing the dirty with bioweapons. But if Lynne-slitch has proof I've become voluntarily involved in something highly illegal—like a paramilitary raid on a private corp facility, for instance—I can't release my dirt without incriminating myself. My data still retains its value as a life insurance policy—if I'm dead, I won't care whether I'm incriminated in the raid or not—but it's no longer grist for the blackmail mill. "Smooth move, lady," I tell her, and again my admiration's sincere.

She accepts it as no more than her due. "Sometimes the best way to negotiate is to lay all your cards on the table," she allows. She pauses, and shifts mental gears. "Those are the reasons why your participation benefits us. But you're wondering what might be in it for you." I think I can guess where she's going, but I keep my yap shut and let her tell it. "First, the obvious. Because you're in command, you'll know the job's been done right. You'll know appropriate action has been taken. Second, in return for your aid, I and my associates"—meaning James Telestrian III, no doubt—"will use our influence to eliminate Schrage, Drummond, Layton, and McMartin as threats to you, and to lift the 'sanction order' filed against you."

Yeah, I'd read that right. I let a faint cynical smile show on my face. "Is that it, *leäl?*" I ask with a sneer.

Her eyes flash, but her expression doesn't change. "I'd hoped I could convince you merely by describing the carrot," she says coolly. "Brandishing the stick is so inelegant. Still, if you insist . . ." And now her face looks pure predator. "If you don't agree to my suggestion, I'll enjoy issuing my own sanction order against you, Mr. Larson. Trust me, the operatives I select will be much better at their job than anyone you've ever faced before—than anyone you've ever had nightmares about facing. If you're very good, you might be able to hide from Lone Star's executioners. You will never be able to escape mine. Trust me on that."

I do. If there's one single, solitary part of the slitch's entire proposal that I believe—wholeheartedly, right down to the core of my soul—it's the gravity of this threat. I force myself to ignore the sick knot of fear that's settled in my gut, and struggle to keep my face expressionless. "You've got an interesting negotiating style," I tell her as smoothly as I can.

"Does that mean you accept?"

I sigh. "Yes." I studiously keep myself from glancing at Argent.

For a few seconds, at least. Lynne Telestrian's next words break that resolution. "I assume Argent is with you, am I right?"

The runner's eyebrows shoot up again, and his metal hands click as they clench into fists. For a moment I think he's going to ignore her. But then he rises slowly and crosses into the field of view of the telecom's vid pickup. "I'm here," he says, his voice like oiled metal.

"My . . . *invitation* . . . extends to you as well," she says with a faint smile. "Your skills would be of great value in the strike."

Argent smiles. "I think my comrade put it quite succinctly. No fragging way. Find another fragging pigeon, *leäl.*"

She looks mildly surprised. "You don't even want to hear a business offer?"

The runner doesn't react for a second or two, then he shrugs. "I'll listen."

I grind my teeth. Of course he'll fragging listen. He's a fragging shadowrunner, isn't he? And now you're talking his language—biz and credit. Just flash enough nuyen signs and Mr. fragging Argent will jump frosty and do any little thing you say. That's what being a shadowrunner means.

"I'm willing to offer you a sum of thirty thousand nuyen in bearer share certificates," the elf-woman says crisply, then smiles faintly. "Telestrian Industries Corporation stock, of course. To give you extra incentive to keep certain matters quiet. Desert Wars veteran and shadowrunner or not, I think you'll agree that's fair payment for a single day's work."

I shoot a glance at Argent, but don't say anything. Desert Wars veteran? No fragging wonder he's such a tough bastard.

The runner's smile broadens. "Thirty thousand? No way, lady." He pauses, and his smile fades. "And don't even bother coming back with a counter-offer."

Lynne-slitch frowns. "You said you'd listen."

"Just long enough so I could laugh in your face, scum," he says lightly. The elf starts to cloud up big-time, drawing breath to say something that's bound to be poisonous. But Argent cuts her off. "Give me a reason, chummer. Give me a good fragging reason why I should want to come along."

That knocks her off balance; I can see it in her eyes. She doesn't answer for a moment, and I can almost hear the thoughts churning wildly. Then she nods slowly. "I think I see," she muses. "Try this, then.

"Do you know why no magically activated viruses are currently being used commercially or have even been developed?" she asks, her voice deceptively calm. "At first blush, it would seem to be an incredibly rich and useful technology. For tumor treatment or control, perhaps. Or control of other diseases. The virus is insinuated into the body, but triggered only at the opportune moment—when a symptom manifests itself, perhaps, or when the virus is concentrated in the cancerous tissue." She shrugs. "Those are only a few possibilities, ones that came to my mind over the last hour. I'm sure any viral geneticist or medical researcher could come up with thousands more. So why aren't we seeing this technology in widespread use?

"Because of the risks," she answers herself. "All attempts to insert mana-sensitive introns into genetic material have led to a drastic weakening of the DNA or RNA chain. Obviously, if the introns are already there—as they are in species subject to Awakening—there's no weakening ... or very little, at any rate. But in all attempts to ... er, retrofit the introns, the results are totally unpredictable."

"Weakening." The word's out of my mouth before I know I'm about to speak. "What kind of weakening?"

"It manifests itself in terms of vastly increased susceptibility to micro- and macro-mutation," she says flatly. "The genetic code is very unstable, and can shift drastically from generation to generation."

"Antigenic shift," I murmur, remembering Doc Dicer's description of the virus that killed Paco.

I didn't think I'd said it loud enough for anyone to hear, but Telestrian picks up on it. "Yes, antigenic shift is one consequence, but more drastic changes are also possible. The reason magically activated viruses aren't used is that nobody knows what they're going to turn into." Her voice is cold—or maybe it's just my reaction to what she's saying. "The antitumor virus, tailored to attack cancerous cells exclusively, shifts and starts attacking only those cells that *aren't* cancerous.

"Think of the potential consequences," she goes on. "As you stated in your report, Mr. Larson, the virus that infected the Cutters is closely related to the VITAS 3 retrovirus. Not VITAS 4 ... not yet. I'm no viral geneticist, but it seems to me the transition between non-infective and infective— between targeted bioweapon and lethal pandemic—isn't a particularly big one.

"The raid will go on, with or without you, Argent. But I'd say the chances of success—of blowing the lab and destroying all stocks of the virus—are much greater with you along.

"And that," she concludes, "seems to me to be a good enough reason."

Silence. Nobody moves, nobody talks. It stretches longer and longer—probably only seconds, but it feels like half a fragging hour. Finally Argent nods once, briskly. "I'm in," he says.

"Good," Lynne Telestrian purrs. "Hold for details."

28

Fragged if I know what to make of it. I'm starting to get the uncomfortable feeling that the whole fragging world is conspiring to take my preconceptions and cherished attitudes and drop them into the drekker. Like, "The Star's different from other megacorps." Wrong! And like, "Shadowrunners care about squat except money." Wrong! They're both hard to swallow, but I think I'm having more trouble with the second one.

Well, actually that's not true, since the second one's connected to the first. Here's how it scans out in my mind. As a Star undercover op, I'm working out of the light to further the ends of the corp that pays my salary. Kind of like a shadowrunner, neh? The only thing that sets me apart is that I'm doing what I'm doing for reasons other than improving my cred balance, and runners don't do that ... Except that Argent, the quintessential shadowrunner, is taking on something because it's important to him even though it won't net him any cred at all. So where, then, do you draw the line between me and Argent, tell me that? It's a tough fragging question, and one that's twisting up my guts.

Okay, yeah, that's not the only thing that's twisting up my guts. There's a healthy dose of pre-op tension as well. And why not? I'm sitting on one of the rear benches of an assault-rigged GMC Riverine, crushed between Argent to my left and the boat's gunwale to my right, wearing a suit of medium body armor that feels half a size too small, holding a smartgun-modified assault rifle. Ironically enough it's a vz 88V; I wonder if Lynne Telestrian bought it from the fragging Cutters. On top of all that, I'm trying to bend my mind around an unfamiliar datachip in my skillwire chipjack. Beyond Argent, and across the rear deck area, are the other elements of Assault Team Able—eight hard-bitten

merc types, wearing the same kind of armor as mine and packing a frightening assortment of weapons.

It's just like those few minutes in the Bulldog with Paco, Bart, and Marla—all dead now—as we're coming up on the Eighty-Eights' warehouse by the docks. Like, but unlike, too. There's the same level of tension, but it's much more focused here and now. The quantity of chatter is a lot less, and and so is the forced bravado. All the slags sitting around me—most with their face-shields down, looking not quite human—have done this before, many times, and probably under worse conditions. Sure, there's some degree of checking out weapons and sharpening knives, but it's not for show like it was among the gangers. These slags—men and women, humans and other metatypes—have gone through enough drek that they've got nothing left to prove to anyone, even themselves. That's the way I read it, at least.

I glance over at Argent. Like me, he hasn't yet lowered his face-shield. There's going to be plenty of time to stare through that transplast plate, breathing in my own exhalations, and hoping I don't fog up the heads-up display that's ready to synch up with the wire in my head and the circuitry in my rifle. The wind—sharp and cold, chilled by the gray water of the Columbia River—helps keep me focused on the present, prevents my mind from drifting into catastrophic imaginings.

Argent's facing straight forward, his cyber-modified eyes shut against the wind and the intermittent spray. But he seems to feel my gaze on him. The eyes open, and he turns to me. He's got a Panther assault cannon held vertically between his knees, his matte-black hands lightly gripping the cooling vanes on the massive barrel. His expression's totally calm, almost detached, more like he's on a day-cruise to a fragging picnic spot instead of headed for a bloody firefight. But of course he's done this drek before, I remind myself. He's military—corp military, that's what Desert Wars is, but military just the same—so this is just old home week for him, a return to his fragging roots. Suddenly I feel very much alone. I'm no merc, I'm no soldier, and no new optical chip in my slot is going to change that.

"How'd you get into undercover work, Wolf?"

Argent's low-voiced question catches me by surprise. I shoot a hard glare at him, but his eyes are clear and his expression mild.

I'm so surprised that I answer him—wheeling up the standard response I've gotten down pat after hundreds of repetitions, of course. "At the time it seemed like the best way of making a difference," I tell him.

The runner's lips curl in a smile. Not scornful, but definitely with a hint of irony.

"Why not?" I snap.

He doesn't answer me, just keeps smiling.

I could just dust him off. His opinion doesn't matter to me, I tell myself firmly. When this drek's out of the way, the only time I'll ever see him again is if I happen to arrest him. The answer I gave him has satisfied everybody I've told it to—colleagues, acquaintances, even my superiors at the Star. Who the frag does he think he is to dig any deeper into the dirt, huh?

So it's a total shock when I hear myself bringing up the secondary justification, the one I've never had to mention to anyone. "Okay," I growl, "it's for the rush. The fragging excitement. Okay?"

His smile doesn't fade in the slightest, and the rage is twisting in my gut. Or is it the rage? At the moment, it could just as easily be fear.

"Really?" Argent asks mildly.

"You're so fragging good at asking questions, why don't you answer one?" I growl. A couple of the mercs around us turn toward us, their semi-mirrored face-shields reflecting distorted images of me and the runner. But I don't care. "What happened to your fragging arms, Argent?"

The words are out before I even faintly consider their possible effect on the chromed runner. I guess part of me is trying to get a rise out of him, but just what kind of rise am I looking for? An assault rifle isn't worth squat in close combat, and even though the escrima chip's slotted and hot, the cyberarms I'm grinding him about could tear out my throat before I could react at all.

Yet, still, his expression doesn't change. "Voluntary replacement," he tells me quietly.

You can bet your hoop that sets me back big-time, priyatel. Voluntary replacement? I'd always figured it was a matter of his meat arms being blown or shot or chopped off. When Lynne Telestrian mentioned Argent's Desert Wars background, I figured for sure he'd gotten too close to an exploding grenade or some drek.

But voluntary replacement? Chummer, that means jandering into a cyber clinic and telling the doc, "Lop off my arms and replace them with machines." How the frag could anybody even consider that? (Yeah, yeah, okay, I've got cyber mods myself, to the tune of skillwires and chipjacks. But that's augmentation, priyatel, addition to the meat, like bolting a turbocharger onto the engine of your bike. Very different from the route Argent took.)

If he'd wanted to shut me up, he couldn't have come up with a better way of doing it. He stays silent for a moment, and I don't think I could talk if I fragging tried. Then he goes on idly, musingly, "I used to know somebody who was a deep-cover infiltration agent. Nobody knew his real name—sometimes I wonder if *he* knew it—but we called him Steel back then. He was good, chummer, he was really good. But . . ."

He pauses. "But it didn't take me long to realize *why* he was good," he continues, voice softer now. "The same reason he got into it in the first place, I guess. Steel was a loner, the absolute lone wolf. Never had any friends, because he never wanted any, because he couldn't let anyone in. He couldn't drop the guard long enough to let anyone close." The runner chuckles wryly. "He had lots of acquaintances. Don't get me wrong, he wasn't a hermit or anything. Nova-hot with the ladies, too. Dozens of people considered Steel a friend, and thought he felt the same. But he didn't. They were just there, they didn't mean anything to him one way or the other, even though he always gave off all the right cues to keep them thinking he cared about them."

Argent shrugs. "I don't know what made him that way. Yeah, sure, I could guess—all that facile psychobabble about family of origin and that drek—but it doesn't really matter. He was a . . . a social chameleon, that's the best way I can put it. Drop him into a group—*any* group—and in a hour he'll have the best-looking woman in the sack and everybody else thinking he's their best chummer ever and that he respects and cherishes them. All without him ever giving the slightest flying frag about a single one of them.

"And I always figured that's why he went into deep-cover," the runner concludes. "That's the way he was, and deep-cover was the only job in the world that actually rewarded him for that kind of behavior." He turns his slightly silvered gaze on me. "Neh?"

My gut twists—it's got to be the rage, what else could it be? "You're saying I'm like that?" I demand.

He shrugs millimetrically. "How many people do you trust, Wolf?" he asks. "How many can you *bring yourself* to trust?"

"None," I shoot back. "Just like a shadowrunner."

"Wrong." Argent's voice is firm, but there's no anger in it. "I can trust my chummers. Like Peg, and Jean, and Sly, and Dirk." I only recognize half the names, but it doesn't matter. "And there are the ones I used to trust before I lost them—Hawk, and Toshi, and Agarwal. Not many, Wolf, but some. Shadowrunners don't have many friends, that's true. But we cling to the ones we've got."

"Frag you," I snarl. It's the only answer I can give him. "Just frag you, okay?" I snap down my helmet's face-shield, and concentrate on the HUD's symbology.

"It's gotta be lonely, Wolf." The closed shield muffles the runner's voice, but not enough so I can't hear it.

A voice sounds from the button earphone built into my armored helmet, sharp and tinny. "Point One."

And again I feel like time's just this big wheel that keeps turning, round and round. For just an instant, I believe I can shut my eyes, then open them again, and I'll be in the Bulldog with Paco and the rest, about to bust through the gate of the Eighty-Eights' warehouse. I force Argent's words—and the strange effects they've created in my gut—deep down into the swamp, to deal with later. Strange time to play the psychobabble game, I think ... but then I realize that those few minutes of conversation kept me too busy to get freaked out about the upcoming op. Was that why he did it?

Who the frag knows, and who the frag cares? More important things to think about at the moment. I stand up, gripping the gunwale to steady me.

The Riverine's boring west, downriver from our staging area halfway between Skamokawa and Cathlamet, at its cruising speed of about thirty-five klicks. From what Argent told me, it's water-jet impellers can boot it up to three times that speed at full emergency power, but at the moment anything more than cruising would draw a lot of attention we just plain don't want. Standing, I can see over the combing that leads to the upper deck, built on top of the main cabin, past the gun position. The gun—a Vanquisher minigun, very nasty—is currently unmanned and safed, its multiple

Gatling-gun barrels pointed at the sky, but I know there's a crewer poised to put it to use at a moment's notice.

The whole Riverine is painted a vivid green, with yellow-gold trim—the livery used by most companies in the Telestrian empire, including Nova Vita Cybernetics. The transponder is also ready to identify itself as a Telestrian asset to any radar beam that interrogates it. (The livery and transponder aren't some kind of scam, at least not at this level. The Riverine—and every other vehicle involved in the assault—is a Telestrian asset, owned by some portion or other of the Telestrian empire. The key issue is which portion . . .) To our right—starboard?—and slightly back, I can see another Riverine just like the one I'm aboard. Assault Team Baker. Beyond our sharply raked bow is the gray water of the Columbia, and maybe a klick-and-a-half ahead, the shore and the dark, blocky outlines of the NVC facility. This is where it's going to get nasty.

I reach down and run my fingers over the tiny keypad mounted on my left hip. The keys control the more sophisticated features of the "commander-style" HUD and comm package built into my armor. (I've also got a tongue-activated version on the chin-guard for those times when both hands are busy, but I'm just not comfortable with it.) The HUD symbology changes, giving me a schematic representation of the forces under my command.

My command, it is to fragging laugh. Yeah, sure, Lynne fragging Telestrian insisted I take nominal command of the strike, for all the twisted reasons she laid out during our phone call. But that's got exactly zero relationship to reality. It's Argent and a couple of the other mercs who've worked out the assault plan, logistics, and contingencies, based on the assets Lynne's willing to commit to the op. Damn fragging good thing too, say I. I'm not military, I'm not a merc, and I'm not fragging competent at this kind of drek. Leave it to me and I'd probably hose it up big-time, get everybody killed, and not do a speck of damage to the lab complex. No, priyatel, this is one for the pros. I'll play figurehead if that's what the elf-slitch wants, but nothing more.

There are some advantages to being figurehead, of course. It was the reason Argent and his "advisors" actually explained the overall plan to me, rather than keeping me in the dark along with the individual mercs on the various assault teams. (Maybe he'd have told me anyway, figurehead or not, but at least this way I don't have to sweat about it.) The plan's a wiz combination of pure brass and deception, using some capabilities I'd never heard of before in the tech we got from Lynne.

The basics come down to a modified Trojan horse ... or some drek like that. Two Riverines with transponders identifying them as Nova Vita supply vessels and arriving at the time the NVC facility is expecting supplies. A small but well-armed ground-assault force. And the cavalry ready to come over the hill—a detachment of Yellowjacket rotorcraft, currently sitting on the ground at the staging area, all systems shut down, invisible to the target's radar and other sensors. Cruising five hundred meters overhead, fragging near visible to view and to radar, two Aerodesign Systems "Condor" stealth drones, relaying realtime surveillance to the various forces. And, ready to be committed at the appropriate moment, three Wandjina RPV combat drones, currently loitering a couple of klicks back of us, less than a meter above the river's surface, packing some nasty surprises tasked to take out the specific defenses we've spotted through earlier recon. Biggest damn op I've ever been on ... or ever want to be on. Everybody else just seems to take it in stride.

We're a klick out, and I feel the Riverine's motion change as the helmsman gooses the throttles. The Baker craft kicks up onto the step as well. Yeah, we're attracting attention to ourselves, but the time for stealth's almost past anyway. Any moment now, some radio operator at the NVC facility's going to be calling for a password or recognition signal we're not going to be able to give, and then the drek hits the pot. When that moment comes, the closer we are to the shore—and the faster we're going—the better all around. That's the plan, at least.

And the moment's now. A blinking text message on my HUD tells me to listen in to a particular short-range comm channel. Clumsily, I punch in the requested frequency with my left hand.

I come in on the middle of the conversation. ". . . escorts coming out. Identify, please." I don't recognize the voice, but it's easy to guess it's the NVC facility's radio operator.

Escorts, huh? I strain my eyes to spot them.

It takes me a second, they're smaller than I expected. When I recognize them, I feel my cheeks stretch in a drek-eating grin. Four of the little shapes are buzzing out across the river toward us, presumably to take up station flanking us. They're Suzuki Watersports, or at least watercraft very much like them. Up-engined brethren of the Bombardier WaveRunner on which I used to tear up the lake as a kid. Yeah, it makes sense—they're probably the perfect high-speed high-maneuverability river craft. Slap on a little armor and equip them with a firmpoint or hardpoint, and they could even be decent weapons platforms.

"NVC 1, we're bringing in supplies, transfer authorization Zulu-Kilo-Tango One-Five." That's the Able Riverine's "talker," using the authorization code Lynne Telestrian was able to dredge up from frag knows where. It's not nearly enough to get us through unscathed—we all know that—but it should buy us a few more seconds. "Thought you boys might be getting a mite hungry in a couple of days," the talker goes on.

Apparently the guy on the other end of the link has left his sense of humor in his other suit. "Requesting recognition code, One-Five," he says calmly.

I tap another key, sending a preprogrammed message to the helmsmen of the two Riverines. I'm almost knocked off my feet as the Able boat kicks in full power. Alongside us, the knife-edge bow of the Baker boat rides up higher out of the water as it too increases speed.

"Recognition code . . . lessee . . . ," our talker mumbles, "I know I had it around here a minute ago . . ." Lame attempt to gain the Riverines the extra second that would let them get an extra ninety meters or so closer to the target.

It doesn't work. My HUD lights up with warning symbols, much too much information for a greenie like me to integrate. But strip away all the pulse modulation and amplitude data, and what's left is the news that some fire-control radars have just kicked in. None of them is painting either of the boats yet, but that won't last. I tap another key, launching another preprogrammed macro, and a raucous warning tone bleats from the speakers of both boats. General quarters, man battle stations, and all that drek. The gunner leaps to the minigun mount and powers up, strapping himself into his harness while the multiple barrels spin up to speed.

A teeth-splitting wheep-wheep-wheep in my ear, and I know we've been painted. Instantly, a brilliant yellow-orange lance of light reaches out toward our boat from somewhere along the riverbank. I know what it is, and I was expecting it, but even so I just barely keep control of my sphincters. Probing out across the river toward us, making the water boil and spray where it touches, it looks for all the world like a "death-ray" from out of some bad sci-fi trideo.

No death-ray, this, but something as deadly. It's the stream of fire from a Requiter minigun, a terrifying display of high rate-of-fire. We know they're there—two of them mounted in hardened auto-turrets flanking the facilities's docks—and we've taken them into account in our planning. (Correction: *Argent's* taken them into account in *his* planning.) From what I read of the specs, a Requiter is even more lethal than the Riverine's Vanquisher, with a rate of fire listed at something like two thousand rounds a minute. Of those, only one in six is usually a tracer, but that's enough to make the stream of fire look like a slightly flexible bar of glowing optical-plastic. Terrifying.

Even more terrifying if that stream—and the other one that's now reaching for the second Riverine—touches its target. The only good thing is that even with radar fire control, scoring with a minigun like that is a touchy business. We've only got a few seconds—if we're lucky—but we're poised to use that grace period.

"Do it!" I snap into my throat mike.

"My" troops don't even need to hear the words. Even as I was issuing the order, the first of the two infantry mortars on the bow deck of the Able boat coughs, echoed by both tubes on the Baker boat. The whine of the Riverine's engine is too loud for me to hear the projectiles in flight, but I certainly do hear them detonate. Perfectly timed airbursts, about twenty meters above the river, maybe fifty meters offshore, between us and the guns. Way too far out to damage armored auto-turrets, of course, even if the warheads had been straight high-explosive, which they weren't. Instead, when they went boom, they sent up a big floating cloud of drek that glittered and twinkled in the watery afternoon light.

Some of it's metal, or, more precisely, metallicized mylar, chaff cut into strips whose exact dimensions are tailored to best frag up any typical fire-control radar. Mixed in with the mylar is the same kind of active chaff that Raven the decker-pilot had used to spoof the SAM off our hoop in the Merlin. And if that wasn't enough, there's a special concoction of "smoke" containing living microscopic blue-green algae cells in a water suspension. The cloud of dispersing water droplets makes it fragging difficult to see clearly, and the fact that there are living organisms in those droplets extends the effect to magical sight too. (All Argent's idea, I happily admit. He remembered shells like this from his Desert Wars days, and asked Lynne if she could get any. An idle request, we'd both thought at the time—this stuff is hardly the kind of drek you find off-the-rack. But Lynne-slitch hadn't blinked an ice-green eye when she agreed, and the shells were waiting for us when we arrived at the Columbia River staging area. Fascinating, and fragging scary. Maybe we should have asked for a couple of heavy panzers, or maybe a Main Battle Tank or two . . .) And while I'm going through all this in my mind, the mortar tubes are delivering more of these ever-so-wiz loads, the wired-up mercs laying the weapons while adjusting for the boats' motion between shots.

And it's working. Again my HUD display changes, telling me—I think and hope—that the targeting radars have lost lock. Radar or not, the streams of light are wavering aimlessly now, drifting further away from us as both Riverines maneuver.

The four Watersports that were on their way out for escort duty are between us and the chaff cloud. The drivers know that serious drek is going down, and they're honking their machines round in the tightest turns they can manage. Even from this distance, I can see the curtains of water the hulls are kicking up as they carve. The Baker boat's Vanquisher opens up—a sound like an amplified fart—and the stream of fire turns one of the Watersports into a fireball. Then the three survivors are through the chaff, which protects them as effectively as it does us.

Time for Act Two. "Bring up the Wandjinas," I order, simultaneously switching my HUD mode to window in a view from the Condor stealth drones drifting overhead. In the grainy image, I see the three Wandjina combat drones—looking like miniature fighter planes with two-meter wingspans—pop up from where they've been loitering, and bore in toward the NVC facility at full military power. The clouds of active chaff and other drek are between the Remotely Piloted Vehicles and the target, so I know the riggers who are "flying" the drones from afar aren't getting squat from the Wandjinas' on-board sensors. But it doesn't matter for the moment; they can fly them just fine using the overhead view from the Condors.

The combat drones burst through the chaff cloud. I know they've suddenly appeared on the target's fire-control radars, because both miniguns suddenly train out to engage the new bogies—sensible, since they're the only thing the gunners can "see" clearly. But high-speed, high-maneuverabilty drones are much tougher to hit than Riverines. (Which is just the way we like it, you can bet your hoop.) One of the Wandjinas gets grazed and disintegrates, but the other two race in toward their targets, the auto-turrets. They fire their weapons, and pull up. I zoom in the overhead image, and see both weapon loads strike home.

Query: How do you destroy an auto-turret well-armored enough to shrug off a round from a panzer's main gun? You take out the intelligence controlling the turret, that's how—at least that's the way Argent approached the problem. Our recon and Lynne's intelligence both confirmed that the auto-turrets themselves were too small to fit anything but the Requiter miniguns, which means the gunners have to be elsewhere. And who would those gunners be? Riggers, priyatel, slags like Raven, jacked into the fire-control radar and the servos that manage the guns themselves. Sitting in revetments too well-hardened to be cracked by anything less than a tac-nuke, but with nice fiber-optic cables running directly into their skulls.

And that's how you take out the auto-turrets. The weapons the Wandjinas were bringing to bear aren't bombs or rockets or missiles or napalm. They're larger versions of taser darts, pure and simple, big beefy capacitors capable of delivering the biggest fragging jolt you've never wanted to experience. Just like the "zappers" the more militant sprawl gangs use to take out Star drones, the theory is if you pump a high enough voltage spike into the hardware end of a rigger circuit, you can set up brain-frying neural feedback in the wetware end—in other words, the rigger. The light show's impressive as the zapper darts hit home and discharge, creating myriad bright blue arcs from turret to ground. One minigun shuts down instantly, the other slews around to spray a stream of fire directly into the sky. Then it too shuts down.

The Condor overhead-view shows me the two surviving

Wandjinas cutting back, pulling more gees than any meat pilot could ever take, and lining up for coordinated strafing
runs over the main compound with their machine guns. That
should take the edge off the concentration of anyone inside,
particularly when those slags figure out that the coordinated
fire missions are going to have them under a drone's guns
every ten seconds or so.

And so comes Act Three. "Bring in the Yellowjackets," I
order.

Again, I doubt my troops actually waited for their fearless
commander to give the order. When I shift HUD modes once
more, the radar display shows eight bogies inbound from the
east, flying nap-of-the-earth following the shoreline. Here
comes the cavalry.

And just in time, too, as it turns out. Our own chaff frags
up our radar view of the NVC facility, and the smoke-mist
drek puts normal vision out of the running too. But that's at
ground level. When something gets high enough up, we've
got line-of-sight over the intervening crap. So that's how I
spot the half-dozen Yellowjackets taking off from inside the
compound, then climbing to altitude. The light-attack choppers on both sides kick in full power and dart forward to mix
it up like . . . well, like yellowjackets. (I'm just fragging glad
I'm not up there, priyatel. All fourteen or so choppers have
the same Telestrian green and gold livery because they're all
Telestrian-owned birds, and their transponders will all be
squawking more or less the same thing. That reduces the
value of all that oh-so-wiz Identification Friend-or-Foe tech
they're no doubt packing to precisely zero. You interrogate
any bird up there with your IFF rig and it's going to come
back as "friendly," no matter who's flying it. Nasty and chaotic, and leave it to the flyboys.)

The Baker boat disappears into the chaff cloud—
dissipating now—and then a dozen seconds later we're
through as well. There's sporadic small-arms fire from the
shoreline, and I even hear a couple of rounds slam into our
Riverine's armored hull. But this limited resistance doesn't
last long as the Vanquishers on the two boats sweep the
shore clear of opposition.

I inspect the docks while the gunners finish off the last
pockets of resistance. There's a Samuvani-Criscraft Otter
moored to one of the quays, a small five-meter design with
a single medium machine gun on a pintle mount. Next to it

sits an Aztech Nightrunner. Tied to the second quay are a couple of Watersports. That reminds me: where's our "escort" gone? If they're smart, to California, but we can't depend on that. And *that* reminds me . . .

I turn, and kick in my helmet's electronic binoculars. Less than two klicks away from us is Tir Tairngire territory, can't forget that. The helmet's built-in optics bring the opposite shore closer. There are planes over there, planes and rotorcraft. For a moment fear wrenches my gut. I think we can take the NVC facility. We sure as frag can't take the NVC assets plus Tir air support.

But then I make a little better sense of what I'm seeing. There's lots of air power up there, but all of it's staying very carefully on the Tir side of the river. Nothing's ranging out over the Columbia toward us. Not that it's overly reassuring, of course. A couple of klicks is pointblank range for any full-on military "smart" missile.

It is demonstrative, though. The Tir military might be showing its teeth, but so far it's more a warning that if we don't keep our scrap on our side of the line, they'll be kicking some hoop. I flip them an ironic salute. Scan that one, priyatel. Corp-equipped mercs scare the drek out of me quite enough without getting full-on military into the game.

When I turn back to the main event, the Baker boat's already backing away from the dock, its contingent of troops ashore and heading for the reinforced gate I can see ahead of us. I look up. Yep, like I'd expected, it's absolute fragging chaos up there. There's less than a dozen Yellowjackets still in the sky, and they're mixed up real tight. Nobody's using rockets or missiles, everybody's in the aerial equivalent of a knife-fight, almost getting close enough to recognize individual pilots before cutting loose with their chain-guns. Doesn't look like anything important's going to get settled up there, but I seriously doubt anybody's going to have a free moment to pound at the ground assault. Which is just the way we planned it.

Way over on the other side of the facility, I see a big beefy fireball roiling up into the sky. That tells me our ground assets are hitting the landward side of the compound with everything they've got. (Not much, to be honest, but hopefully enough to distract even more attention from the Able and Baker assault teams.)

Now it's our turn. The Able boat takes the other's place,

bumping hard against the construction composite of the quay. The water-jets race, holding us in place with their thrust.

It's time. I grab my assault rifle, giving the wire a split-second to synch up with the weapon's circuitry. Safety off, gas-vent recoil compensation at nominal one hundred percent, thirty-five rounds in the clip, one in the pipe. Ready to rock. Most of Assault Team Able are already over the side and running toward the compound by the time I've moved. I sense a presence next to me, don't have to look to identify Argent.

"Cranked up?" the chromed runner asks, cradling his assault cannon in his metal hands.

I give him a feral street grin. "Out on the pointy end," I shoot back.

He slaps me on the armored shoulder, and we vault over the gunwale together.

29

There's nothing left to oppose our advance. Covering us from behind, the two Riverines are positioned to annihilate anything with their twin Vanquishers before they pull back to a safe distance. (Wouldn't want our best way out of here to get sunk . . .) Overhead, the Yellowjackets are still mixing it up in a chaotic fur-ball, while the two surviving Wandjina drones continue their coordinated fire-missions. Time to change that.

"Do the gate," I growl into my throat mike.

A rigger somewhere hears my order and honks one of the combat drones around in a turn that would pulp a meat pilot. It races out over the river, its engine screaming, then pulls an Immelman that looks as tight as a hairpin, boring right in toward the gate.

"Cover!" Argent bellows beside me, and both assault teams hit the deck.

Not a moment too soon. The Wandjina's nose is pointed dead center at the gate, its machine gun pouring rounds into the reinforced composite with no obvious effect. It doesn't matter. The drone slams into the gate, and the shaped charge installed in place of some of its more advanced sensors detonates.

I don't see it, of course, because I'm on my face sucking mud with my arms protecting my head. Even through my armor, I feel the heat pulse. And then the pressure wave drives the air from my lungs and bounces me a hand-span off the ground. I land hard, my head bouncing inside my armored helmet, and I hear fragging bells. I try and shake it off.

Then a hand grabs my arm—hard texture, surprisingly gentle grip—and helps me to my feet. "You all right?" Argent asks.

I consider shaking off his hand, but the way my equilibrium's still spinning I decide against it. "Chill," I tell him,

and we both know it's one of those little white lies. While
I'm still waiting for my brain and the law of gravity to agree
exactly which way's down, I look toward the gate.

Only to see there isn't a gate there anymore. Team Baker
and most of Team Able are already through, and over the
ringing in my ears I hear the ripping of autofire from inside
the compound. Typical, considering the situation—the assault troops are tearing things up while their supposed "commander" is still trying to get his brain in gear outside the
area of battle. I pick up my assault rifle—which I'd
dropped—and grip it in a kind of sloppy port-arms. "Let's
do it," I tell Argent. And together we dog-trot forward.

There are a couple of corpses inside the gate, or what's
left of them after the RPV's jury-rigged warhead did its
thing. At least our armor's different from the defenders', letting me know it's NVC troops that are down.

Inside the prison-style walls, the facility's just like I'd
have expected from the vid we shot from Raven's bird. Four
major buildings set around the perimeter of a square, with a
handful of smaller structures. As we enter the compound
proper, a half-dozen firefights are going down around us.
The single remaining Wandjina drone has given up its random strafing because the rigger has no way to tell friendlies
from targets. It's still in the fray, however, pouring autofire
into the guard towers (or whatever the frag they are) at the
four corners, apparently against the possibility that the occu-
pants have weapons that can be trained on the inside of the
facility. Doesn't strike me as likely, but I can't think of a
better way to expend that ammunition at the moment.

Assault Team Baker has fanned out, and they're basically
blowing the drek out of anything that moves. My comrades
on Team Able are doing pretty much the same thing, except
for the four lighter-armed troopers—combat deckers whose
job is to find the lab complex's computer, crack into it and
download anything and everything they can lay their electronic mitts on. (It's a serious drag that Lynne Telestrian's
intelligence couldn't tell us exactly which building con-
tained the computer core, but those are the breaks.) As assault leader, my job's basically to oversee what's going
down and not get myself geeked in the process. Apparently
Argent has taken upon himself the task of bodyguarding me
around, which is fine with me. At the moment I feel totally

out of my depth, wandering around like a half-fragged fool, trying to figure which way to go next.

At the moment I decide to go left, toward what looks like the biggest building and also the one with the most firing going on around and inside it. I head that way, Argent dogging my steps.

Movement, in my peripheral vision. For a horrible moment, I'm back in the Tsarina, cruising through Montlake. Movement above me and to the left, on top of one of the smaller buildings. Then I snap back into the present. Without thinking, I drop to one knee and bring up my rifle. The link between the tech in my head, the smartgun in my hand, and the armor's circuitry brings up a display from the rifle's scope onto my helmet's HUD. A single figure, wearing light armor different from the gear my troops are wearing. Swinging around like he's just spotted me too, bringing some kind of weapon to bear. The Czech assault rifle and the new chip in my head—the one supplied by Lynne Telestrian—synch up, and I squeeze the trigger.

The tech tracks the fire, and where the bullets actually go is a good meter from the projected point of impact. Frag! That's the difference between data you get on a chip and the muscle-knowledge that comes from practicing enough with the tech to integrate it and make it yours. I've done that with the escrima and the H & K chips, but not with this new one. Even with gas-vent compensation, a long burst on full-auto equates to fierce muzzle-rise. I struggle to bring the rifle back on line, but I'm too late. I try to fling myself aside . . .

Fire bursts from my target's muzzle, and half a dozen impacts on my armor drive the air from my body. The sheer force of those impacts is frightening, sending bolts of pain through my chest. Fractured ribs? Quite possibly, but now isn't the time to worry about it. I fight the rifle back onto line, and squeeze the trigger again.

An instant too late. There's a dull whomp from beside me, and my target is blown apart by an assault cannon round. I release my own trigger, but not before I've hosed a couple of rounds through the carnage on the rooftop.

Argent's looking down at me. "You okay?"

I glance down and see the bullet-impacts stitched across my chest armor. The reinforced composite of the armor is cracked and deformed by the impact, doing its job of absorbing the kinetic energy of incoming rounds by crushing

and compacting. I take a deep breath, and it feels like somebody's worked me over with a baseball bat. But that's much
better than I'd be feeling without the armor . . .

With a groan, I push myself to my feet. "I'm okay," I tell
him, and that's another little white lie.

He scowls. "Your armor's compromised."

I nod, looking down at the buckled macroplast again. No
drek, Sherlock. Which means if I wade into the middle of incoming fire again, the armor's not going to protect me ade-
quately. Definitely something to keep in mind.

But on the other hand, I can't just hunker down and wait
for it all to be over. (Why not? part of my mind wants to
know. Simple drek-headed macho pride?) Forcing those
doubts away, I grip my rifle tighter and try to look frosty. I
think I see Argent shrug as I move forward again, but it's
hard to tell under all that armor. There's a door in front of
me, and I kick it open, ducking into the shelter of the door
frame after I do it.

No burst of fire from inside, so I spin around the frame in
a crouch, scanning with eyes and with the barrel of my
weapon. It's pitch-black inside, and the light from outside is
enough to illuminate only the first half-dozen meters of the
hallway that stretches away from me. What the frag happened to the lights? Did some of our troops blow the power,
or have the defenders decided that darkness is more a disadvantage to us than for them? Cautiously I move forward
again.

And for the second time in as many minutes, I find I'm
flashing back to the past. It lasts only a split second, but this
time it's to the darkened concrete corridors of the Fi ness
Que t in Renton, where Lynne Telestrian's troops waltzed
me around like a fragging puppet. This time is different,
very different. First, because my helmet's circuitry has automatically kicked in light-amplification and thermographic
sensors, projecting the composite image onto the HUD of
my face-shield. And second, because I can sense the comforting presence of Argent and his assault cannon behind me
and to my right.

Somewhere deeper into the building, I hear the character-
istic ripping of an Uzi on full autofire, getting louder. I don't
think any of our troops are carrying Uzis, so I tense and
ready my weapon.

Ahead of me, at the end of the corridor, a door bursts open

and a figure backs through. In thermo, the muzzle plume of his Uzi as he fires back through the doorway is a meter-long lance of brilliance. The composite image is grainy, and its false color doesn't match the actual color of the armor either side's wearing. So it takes me a second to confirm that this is a bad guy.

In that instant, he spots me in his peripheral vision. Inhumanly fast, he spins and fires. Thank Ghu his marksmanship's nowhere near as jazzed as his reactions. His burst goes high, smashing concrete chips from the ceiling, and sending ricochets whining off behind us. I fire my own burst a second later—starting low, like the chip in my head tells me, and walking the burst up into his body.

Or trying to, at least. His juiced reflexes kick in again, and he's back through the door so fast that, by comparison, my attempt to walk the burst looks like a causal stroll. Beside and behind me, Argent sends a Panther round through the open door. The flash of the explosion is dazzling even with the HUD's flare compensation, and the overpressure wave in the enclosed space pummels my ears. Above the sound of the detonation I hear a shriek of agony. Argent got somebody. The Uzi gunner? No way to know, just like there's no way to be sure he's out of the fight. No way except to go and look. I move forward again.

In the lower-right corner of my visual field, the HUD flashes a message. Signaling for Argent to wait, I key on the radio circuit that links me with one of our "spotters," a rigger watching the fun from the vantage point of the Condor stealth drones overhead.

"Strike Leader," I announce myself.

"Eye One. We've got a break-out, Strike Leader." The woman's voice sounds either bored or drunk, but I know she's neither. The sluggishness of her speech has to be from trying to split her attention between so many tasks at one time that getting her mouth to work right is way down on her current priorities. "Four bad guys on foot. I don't know where they came from, they just suddenly appeared. Magic maybe?"

"Where?"

"Down by the docks," she answers.

The boats. Yeah, it makes sense. With a ground force to landward and pure, pluperfect hell in the skies above, the river's the only escape route.

"Armed?"

"No heavy weapons visible," the rigger says. "Only one's wearing armor; the other three are in soft clothes. Corp suits, maybe."

"Got it," I confirm, and kill the frequency. Corp suits, huh? I want them. I turn to tell Argent, but he's already heading back toward the outside. He must have been listening in on the conversation too. All the better.

For a big man, Argent moves like a fragging sprinter when he wants to, and I have a frag of a time keeping up with him. As we race through the compound, it looks like the fighting's starting to die down. Then I'm proved wrong as a magical fireball bursts among a knot of my troops on the other side of the compound. They go down like tenpins—stunned and wounded, but not toasted like the enemy mage obviously wanted. The few combat mages we've got among our force apparently are earning their keep by effectively providing the rest of us with spell defense. I can't stick around to see how the exchange turns out; Argent is darting back out through the blasted gate, vaulting over the twisted bodies lying in the opening.

One of the boats is missing from the dock—the Samuvani-Criscraft Otter. I look around quickly, and see it almost a hundred meters offshore, already up on the step, its stern buried and kicking up a healthy wake. I see Argent bringing his assault cannon on line, but I snap out a "No!" before he can fire. He shoots me a doubtful look, and I tell him, "I want them alive. See if you can whistle us up some air support."

He thinks about it for a moment, then nods brusquely and begins to get busy on the radio. While Argent is doing that, I run out to cast off the lines securing the Aztech Nightrunner to the dock.

But I stop in my tracks at the sight of it. The interior of the Nightrunner is a mess of shattered plastic and composite, some of it still smoking and smoldering. Somebody— obviously the slags in the Otter—tossed a grenade into the craft before taking off. The concussion, confined by the partially enclosed cabin, was enough to crack the hull, and already the sleek boat is starting to settle in the water.

Argent's beside me so suddenly I don't hear him come up. "Well?" I ask.

He shakes his head, and through his face-shield I can see

a humorless smile. "The word is that our air assets are 'fully engaged'," he says.

I glance up. The air battle's still going on, but only a half-dozen Yellowjackets are still in the air. I understand what he means.

What about the surviving Wandjina? I scour the skies for it, don't spot it. Either some antiair defense has taken it out, or it's burned all its fuel and augered in. No joy there.

Frag it! The Otter's two hundred meters out at the moment, heading west. Our two Riverines are east of here, out of harm's way but also totally out of the action. Without air support, and with the Nightrunner crippled, the slots in the Otter are going to get away. Unless . . .

My gaze shifts to the two Suzuki Watersports moored at the next dock over. Why the frag not? "Come on!" I bark at Argent and the two of us sprint on over.

30

The low-slung, sleek-hulled vehicle looks something like a water-going combat bike, with the same fairing and twin-firmpoint arrangement as an assault-rigged Harley Electraglide-1000 armed patrol bike. The basic layout may not be much different from my old Bombardier WaveRunner, but that's like saying Raven's Merlin isn't much different from an Eagle assault fighter because they've both got wings. This Watersport—painted a mean black—has a different geometry. In fact, everything about it is more raked and streamlined than my old toy. Even moored to the dock it looks slotting fast.

Fast enough to catch the Otter? We'll see.

I sling my assault rifle and swing myself astride the Watersport. "Hop on," I tell Argent as I start to cast off.

"On that?"

Any other time, I'd find the expression on his face humorous as all hell. Not now. "Poor widdle man too scared to get on the widdle fragging bike?" I growl.

The runner still hasn't moved. "You know how to ride one of these things?"

"Fragging right I know," I snap. "Now get the frag on!"

I hear him sigh and he slings his cannon. The stern of the Watersport settles alarmingly as he seats himself gingerly on the back of the seat. "There should be handgrips on either side of the seat at the stern," I tell him without turning around. While he's trying to find them, I'm scanning the control panel. Very different from my old WaveRunner, let me tell you. This thing's got gauges, for frag's sake—a speedo, oil pressure, temperature, and fuel. On my old toy the only way to judge speed was by how hard the thing jounced when you hit a wave, and the only way to tell you were running out of gas was when the engine started to sputter. At least the steering and throttle arrangements are the

same. All I've got to remember is to keep my fingers off the triggers for the firmpoint-mounted weapons—medium machine guns, they look like—until I'm ready to rock.

I hit the starter and the engine catches instantly, a smooth, turbine-like whine from somewhere under my hoop. I scan the gauges—everything in the green—fuel tank nearly full—and check to see I haven't missed casting off any lines.

"Hang on," I tell Argent, and I grab a handful of throttle.

Too big a handful. The Watersport lunges forward so hard my head snaps back on my neck. I grab the handgrips wildly to keep from getting thrown off, and one finger hits a trigger. The right MG cuts loose with a short burst, chewing the drek out of the other Watersport moored a couple of meters ahead of us, while I feel two metal hands grabbing onto my shoulders in a death-grip. I release the throttle and the thrust fades. "Sorry," I mutter.

Argent's grip on my shoulders loosens slowly. "You said you knew how to ride this thing!" he snarls.

"I'm fragging rusty, okay? And use the fragging handgrips!"

This time I give it some throttle more cautiously. The small hull surges forward, kicking up onto the step almost immediately. Small waves slap against the hull, and I raise myself a little off the seat, taking the shocks in my thighs rather than in my hoop. I glance down at the speedo. Already we're doing forty klicks—pretty fragging near top speed for my old WaveRunner—and the throttle's only half-open. Either the tech's advanced drastically since I was a kid, or this is a specially jazzed mil-spec model I'm riding—or maybe a combination of both. Whatever, it doesn't really matter. I crack the throttle wider open. The wind lashes at me and the spray mists my face-shield. Suddenly I realize I'm grinning like a fragging bandit. "Yeeeaah!" I howl into the wind of our passage.

The Watersport's going like a bat out of hell—fragging near seventy clicks, according to the speedo—and it feels like a live thing under me. I do a couple of quick turns, just to scope out the maneuverability. This baby's way more nimble than anything I've ever ridden before, but that's no surprise. Just the slightest shift of weight and millimetric adjustment of the steering makes the hull carve deep and hard, slashing up a high curtain of water to the outside of the turn. It's all coming back to me, all the techniques for squeezing maximum performance out of the machine. My muscles seem to remember like it's yesterday. Shift the weight forward to drive the leading edge of the hull deeper, maximizing the carve. Shift it back to kick the bow a little higher, getting it to plane better over the waves. Argent's weight is like a sack of fragging potatoes behind me, a hindrance even though he's starting to get the hang of it, leaning into the turns with me rather than fighting them. It probably doesn't matter that much, though. The little beauty's screaming now, skipping across the water, catching a half-second of air off even the smallest wave.

Up ahead I can see the Otter. We're closing the gap, maybe only a hundred meters back now. But just as I realize that, I see the stern of the boat sink lower as the driver pours on more power. I think we're still reeling them in, but the rate of closure's dropped drastically. Frag it!

Yet maybe it's not going to matter much. To my right, I can see a Yellowjacket breaking away from the dogfight and now skimming toward us low over the river. I turn my head slightly and yell back to Argent, "Is that our air support?"

I feel him shrug, then hear him mumble into his throat mike. If he can raise the small rotorcraft, we've got this whole thing chipped. The Otter's got a machine gun, but that style of pintle mount doesn't let you elevate the weapon enough for antiair actions. The Yellowjacket can fire a burst of chain-gun fire across the boat's bows and order it to stop. We'll catch up with the rotorcraft playing overwatch, and it's game over.

If, that is, the Yellowjacket's one of ours . . .

The thought hits me with shocking suddenness, and my gut knots. Argent's still muttering into his mike, but it doesn't sound like he's getting the response he wants. The small rotorcraft's hurtling in closer, and it's lined up with us, not with the Otter. I throw my weight to the right and drive the leading edge of the hull deep, honking the Watersport around in the tightest possible turn. Only sheer luck keeps us from catching a wave and going over. Equally sheer luck keeps Argent from ripping my arms off as he grabs my shoulders again.

Just in time. The Yellowjacket's chin-mounted chain gun sparkles, and the fire-stream churns the water where we were a second ago. The pilot tries to correct, slewing the micro-turret, but he's coming in too fast on his strafing run

to compensate. Then he's over and past, already swinging up
in an arcing bank.

I carve us around in another tight turn as the Yellowjacket
sets up for another pass. The pilot seems to have learned his
lesson. This time he's cut his speed way back and is cruising
in slowly instead of going for a high-speed pass. The
rotorcraft looks dead level, a perfect solid weapons platform.
I carve again, and his first long burst misses by ten meters.

Behind me I can hear and feel Argent wrestling with his
assault cannon, trying to bring it to bear. Tough job; there's
just not enough space back there to move around much without going swimming, and my hard maneuvers aren't helping.
Another burst of chain-gun fire, this one only a couple of
meters astern of us.

"Hold us fragging still!" Argent barks.

"Like frag I will!" I shout back. The Yellowjacket's hov-
ering now, the pilot tracking us entirely with the micro-
turret. Another longer burst almost right on the money, and
it's sheer luck we're not dead.

"We're dead if you don't," the runner snarls at the back of
my head.

"We're dead if I do."

But he's right, of course, the Yellowjacket's going to score
eventually. So I grit my teeth and crack the throttle as wide
as it'll go, tearing off perpendicular to the chopper's line of
fire to give the pilot as tough a tracking problem as possible
without any more wild maneuvers. The chain gun fires
again, the bullets slashing into the water meters behind us.
The pilot checks his fire, I see the micro-turret slew, and I
know what's coming next.

Sure enough, the water churns wildly ahead of us, as he
tracks the stream of fire toward the racing Watersport. In a
second or two we're going to intersect, and that's all she
wrote. "Do it, Argent!"

The Panther cannon roars, the recoil almost enough to put
us out of control. Perfect shot—the high-explosive round
impacts dead center of the Yellowjacket's canopy. It staggers
in the air, then a secondary explosion blasts it into fragments
and the greasy fire of burning fuel.

The relief's enough to make me want to yarf, but I've got
to stay frosty a little longer. While we've been playing
games with the Yellowjacket, the S-C Otter's been opening
up the gap, boring forward at full speed. We've got to play

catch-up, but I'm starting to think we're not going to make it.

"Will this thing go faster with just you aboard?" Argent asks.

I nod.

"Then this is where I get off," he says. "Catch ya later, Wolf."

And then he's gone, just dumping himself overboard. I wince at the thought of the impact he took. At the speed we're going, water's about as compressible as concrete. Good luck to you, priyatel, I tell him silently. Hope you don't break any bones.

And I hope you can swim.

Free of the extra weight, the Watersport picks up like the engine's turbocharged. The speedo bar creeps up to just below eighty klicks, and the impact as the little craft skips over small waves is almost enough to knock my teeth loose. The exhilaration's back, but it's coupled with real fear. A Watersport's like a bike in some ways, but water isn't like a nice smooth highway. Waves and boat-wakes are real dangers, and if you hit them just the right—or wrong—way, they can send you cartwheeling across the surface.

Those fears are starting to increase as I close with the Otter. The open boat's kicking up a good wake, making waves high enough to throw the Watersport into the air at the speed I'm going. I've got to be real careful how I shift my weight as I come back down.

Now that I've cut the gap to less than fifty meters, it's time to check out what my firmpoint-mount machine guns can do . . . and, more important, how using them will affect my handling. I squeeze both triggers, carving a slight turn to rake the stream of fire across the Otter's stern. I can feel the Watersport shift and shimmy with the recoil—disturbing, but not critical. Firing only one of the guns would probably be more risky, but as long as I balance the recoil I think I'll be okay.

And that's all fine and good, but I'm not the only one who's got weapons. I see the muzzle flashes as the Otter's medium machine gun opens up. This isn't a chain gun with a grotesque rate of fire, so I can't see the stream of fire, which makes the whole thing all the more frightening. If the Otter's gunner gets a dead bead on me, the first indication I'll have of it is when I start taking hits. I cut left, catching

a good second and a half of air as I cross the wake, shifting
my weight desperately to stop the Watersport's tendency to
corkscrew. Almost immediately I cut back right again, jump-
ing the wake a second time. Then back to the left.

I'm like a water-skier cutting back and forth behind the
boat, getting closer with each crossing. This is starting to
feel suicidal, but it's the only thing I can think of. The gunner aboard the Otter can traverse his weapon to track me—
with limited success so far, thank Ghu. Not so with me. My
firmpoint-mounted weapons are fixed, so if I want to hit
something, first I've got to point the nose of the Watersport
at whatever it is. Meaning, in turn, that I can put my imag-
inary sights on my target at only two points of my zigzag-
ging, and those make for maximum-deflection shots anyway.

Meaning, still further, that my odds of scoring serious hits
are next to squat, while the chances of the Otter's gunner being able to blow me into scrap get better and better the
closer I come. For about the millionth time in the last minute, I seriously consider simply giving up the whole mess as
a bad fragging job. But then I remember what Eye One, the
drone spotter, said: three corp execs. Would execs bail out
without taking as much incriminating drek with them as they
could? Not fragging likely, priyatel. Even if the combat
deckers crack the lab's system, there might not be anything
left to find because all the dirt might be downloaded onto
chips now aboard the Otter.

Before I have time for second thoughts, I lean into a hard
turn to the right, and just keep on going until I'm eighty or
ninety meters off to the right of the Otter. Then I straighten
up my course until I'm paralleling the boat. Cutting back
left, I point the bow of the Watersport at the center of the
Otter, crack the throttle, and clamp down on the twin triggers. I can see where my fire's falling, chewing up the water
a dozen or so meters short of the Otter, so I shift my weight
back until my arms are fully extended. Up comes the bow—
not much, but enough—and it's like I'm walking my fire
onto the Otter. Meanwhile, spray from the other gunner's
fire is kicking up all around me. But at the speed I'm going,
and the way the Watersport's skipping around on the waves,
I'm a frag of a tough target. The way the bike's moving is
just splattering the stream of MG fire every which way, sat-
urating the volume of space occupied by the Otter. At least
that's what I'm hoping for. The boat is looming bigger and

bigger—thirty meters away, twenty. Something goes spang off my hull, and another round punches clear through the right fairing. I've got to break off . . .

But then I see the gunner blown backward, the pintle-mount gun spraying fire into the sky before it falls silent at last. Without the MG to worry about, I chop the throttle, jump the wake again, and I'm right in the "slot," directly behind the Otter and about fifteen meters back. I squeeze the triggers again, and watch the twin MGs chew the living drek out of the boat's stern. There's a flash of fire, a plume of oily black smoke as I drive a dozen rounds into the inboard engine, and then the Otter's down off the step and slowing so fast I almost plow into its stern. I chop my own throttle right back, and squeeze off two more short bursts right into the open cockpit.

It's a matter of maybe ten seconds to come alongside. I'm driving the Watersport with my right hand, holding the assault rifle in my left. That's my off hand, but with an autofire weapon it's not going to matter worth squat at this kind of range. I swing my butt onto the Otter's gunwale, pivot my legs over and I'm aboard.

And suddenly in the middle of a charnel-house. Of the four people aboard, three are messily dead, chewed into dogfood by machine gun fire. The fourth is still alive but only just, and not for long. His right arm's damn near off, and he's pulsing bright arterial blood all over the boat's bottom. He's conscious, his eyes glazed and dulled with agony and shock. His face is streaked with blood, but I have no trouble recognizing him.

"Hello, Mr. Nemo," I say quietly. "Or do I call you Gerard Schrage?"

The Lone Star suit looks up at me blankly. He recognized me the last time we met, but I suppose he's got other things on his mind right now.

There's a war going on inside me. Schrage is a motherfragger—the one who put me beyond sanction, the one who pushed Drummond and the others to set up the ambush that killed Cat Ashburton. The one who cut the deal with Timothy Telestrian to acquire the magically triggered bug as a tool for use in his Military Liaison projects. The one who killed Paco and the other Cutters as part of a fragging field test. But no matter how much I hate him, it still slots me to see him lying there bleeding to death.

Frag, how many times over the last few days have I imagined putting a bullet through his lousy head? But each time I pictured it, it was a matter of pow, over. Cap him and that's it. Clean, with no lingering aftereffects.

It's different with me suddenly faced with the consequences of my vengeance. I may not have known he was aboard, but it was my bullets that maimed him. His blood's spreading over the decking, and I'm standing in it. This is reality. I should be feeling satisfied, feeling some sense of completion and closure at Schrage's death. But all I feel is sick.

I turn away. There's nothing I can do to save him, even if I could bring myself to do it, but that doesn't mean I can watch him die. I suppose I should search the boat for any datachips or other material Schrage and his chummers have taken from the facility, but I'm just not down for it. Frag it all anyway, if Schrage's death doesn't put an end to the whole nasty pile of drek, I don't want to know about it.

The fire in the Otter's engine is out, but the engine is totally dead. While I'm standing there staring at it, I finally spot a secondary drive, a small, low-power electric motor. I stand there in the blood a moment longer, then feel a grim smile spread across my face. Yeah, that's the fragging ticket.

I cross to the gunwale where my Watersport's floating, and take a couple of moments to secure the small craft with a line. Then I go forward and fire up the Otter's silent electric drive. I put it in forward gear at dead-slow, less than walking speed. When I'm confident it's going to keep running—that I didn't frag it with my gunfire—I swing overboard and straddle the Watersport. I cut the line loose and fire up the Suzuki's water-jet. Using my own craft, I nudge the Otter onto the course I want. Roughly south, toward the Tir Tairngire shore of the Columbia. Frag knows what the Tir border forces will make of the trashed boat and the bodies, including a senior suit from the Star. But if James Telestrian's links with the Tir military are as strong as his ties with its business community, the evidence aboard the boat should become a big enough club for James to beat son Timothy into fragging oblivion.

Once I'm confident the Otter's rudder is amidships and the boat's not going to veer off, I crack open the throttle and turn north toward where the flames and black smoke are rising into the sky from the Nova Vita compound.

Epilogue

I'm a few minutes early for my late-afternoon appointment, and the weather's about as good as it ever gets in the sprawl, so I decide to walk the last few blocks. I hit the Override key on the autocab's control pad, and the dog-brain autopilot pulls over to the side of the road, fragging near greasing a young woman pushing a baby stroller.

As I climb out and pull my credstick from the charge slot, I look at the street sign on the corner. First and Union. The Charles Royer Building—otherwise known as Metroplex Hall—is at Fourth and Seneca, which is a five- or six-block hike, including the stiff slog up the Seneca hill. Well, like I said, it's a good day for a walk. I swing into my stride.

It's freaky how everything feels back to normal—on the surface, at least. I don't know exactly how she did it, what strings she had to pull, or what bodies she might have threatened to unearth, but Lynne Telestrian followed through on her promise to lift the Star's out-of-sanction order against me. I can walk the streets again with at least some assurance that I won't get geeked at any moment. The Cutters might still want my blood, but from what I've been able to dredge up on the street, the gang's now history, at least as an organized force to be reckoned with. Maybe that'll change, but the deaths and the panic and hysteria created by the killer virus seemed to rip the vital social structure of the gang apart. An organization like a major gang depends on a very precarious balance among various social dynamics, and the bug episode seems to have knocked that balance to hell and gone.

I don't know what effect the destruction of the NVC facility had on the Timothy versus Lynne internecine battle— whether it's still going on or whether it gave James the leverage he needed to oust Timothy totally. The Telestrian empire's still in existence, but they're definitely not airing any dirty laundry in public, and I honestly can't make myself care enough to try and dig it up. If they want to frag each other blind, let them go to it with a will, say I. Just keep me out of it.

I also don't know what effect, if any, the arrival of Schrage and the other deaders on the Tir shores might have had. Again, I could probably find out if I cared enough, but at the moment I simply don't.

Apparently, some people are concerned about Lone Star's involvement in this whole mess, people in high places. When Peg put out some electronic feelers to discover my status with the respectable world a few days after the raid, she found that Governor Marilyn Schultz was very interested in meeting with me—at my convenience, of course—to "enlist my aid in evaluating the ongoing contract between the metroplex and Lone Star Security Services" or some such drek. The way both Argent and I scan it, some serious shakeup is in the works, and Marilyn wants to hear my fix on things.

So that's why I'm slogging up Seneca on this warm afternoon. I hit Third and check my watch—still ten minutes early—so I decide to go around the block and enjoy what serves for sun in Seattle. I hang a left on Third, and find the street blocked off by Lone Star barriers about halfway down the block. The barriers are lined with spectators. Curious, I drift on over.

It's the fragging Lone Star motorcycle drill team, practicing and demonstrating their precision riding for an appreciative crowd. Yeah, that makes some sense, the fair and show season's coming up, and the drill team puts in appearances all over the sprawl and even elsewhere in the Salish-Shidhe nation. So they're out here today on Third between Seneca and University, all shiny and proud in their blue and gold dress uniforms, riding Harley Electraglides so polished they look almost mirror-finished, demonstrating their precise maneuvers, laying those big bikes so far over that the chromed pipes are scraping the pavement.

The Star had a team like this in Milwaukee—has one in every major city—and when I was at the Academy and afterward it was chill to ridicule the people in it. They're all volunteers, so you've got to be a prima donna to sign up, but then you've got to be accepted by all the other prima donnas already on the team. Anything to get out of doing real police work, I guess, Or so went the joke.

No matter how much I ridiculed them publicly, though, deep down I guess I always felt some sense of pride when I saw them show their stuff. Sappy and sentimental, maybe, but it's true. Pride stemming from the sense that there was a kind of grand tradition behind the whole Lone Star operation. That was then. Now I know what this kind of show really is—a marketing display for a megacorporation selling its wares. Feeling empty inside, I turn my back on the spectacle, and continue to walk on up Seneca.

The Metroplex Hall's a striking building—thirty floors sheathed in dark green glass—but at the moment I'm in no mood to appreciate it. I climb the stairs, pass the statue of Chief Seattle, and walk into the lobby. At the reception desk, the functionaries confirm I'm authorized to be here and give me a pass keyed to my destination—including a circuit that will beep warningly if I stray off course. A minute later I'm on the way up to the twenty-ninth floor. Other people are in the elevator with me, but for some reason they seem to stay as far away from me as they can, leaving an invisible wall of empty space around me. Fragged if I know why, but it fits with the way I'm feeling—detached, empty, not part of any of this, just going through the motions. The elevator disgorges me on the right floor, and I stroll into a plush waiting room.

For ten minutes I sit in a leather chair staring through a vid screen on the opposite wall. When a biz-suited functionary comes to get me, I can remember precisely squat of what I've just been watching. The functionary leads me down a hall to an oak-grained macroplast door, knocks, then flashes me a model's meaningless smile, turns her back and vanishes. The door opens before me, and I walk in.

Into an office bigger than the place where I used to doss in Ravenna. One whole wall's a window, providing a spectacular view southwest toward the massive high-tech ziggurat that is the Renraku Arcology. I give it maybe one second's worth of attention, then focus on the two figures waiting for me. Neither one's Schultz.

The slag behind the desk—a glossy exec-type with a face that just screams PR flack—stands and extends a hand to me. "Good afternoon," he says, "I'm Alphonse Baker."

I just stare at his hand until he drops it back to his side. "I understood I was to meet with the governor," I tell him.

His eyebrows rise—I've committed a major breech of etiquette, but I honestly don't give a frag. It takes him only a split-second to compensate, though, and a warm smile— precisely as insincere as the one the other functionary just gave me—spreads across his face. "That's true, Lieutenant Larson," he says smoothly, using the official rank I haven't bothered with since I first went deep-cover. "But you'll understand, of course, that Governor Schultz is an incredibly busy woman, and various . . . um, exigencies . . . arise from time to time that require her immediate attention. I thought that we might be able to achieve the goals of this meeting without her presence, just you, me, and Mr. Loudon here."

I slowly track my gaze to the second figure in the room, standing to the left of Baker's desk. I've never met him, but I recognize his chiseled face. William Loudon, Division Head of Lone Star Seattle. My putative boss.

Well, frag, that settles that, doesn't it? Maybe Schultz was serious about investigating the Schrage-Telestrian connection when she first contacted me. Hadn't Lynne-slitch told me that Schrage had unofficial ties with the unholy trinity of Drummond, Layton, and McMartin, implying that they were playing some kind of game behind Loudon's back? Everything else the elf-woman told me had turned out to be true. Initially, Schultz might really have wanted to hear what I had to say.

That's obviously not the case anymore. Loudon must have gotten in first and cut some kind of deal with Schultz and the metroplex government. Maybe Lone Star offered to reduce its rates in return for Schultz keeping the lid on the nasty drek that was going down. Or maybe the governor realized the simple truth that threatening to axe the Star's contract with the plex wasn't a viable club to use against Loudon. Cut the contract, and who would police the city? There's no other corporation out there capable of taking the contract, not immediately, and the Metroplex Guard certainly can't handle it on their own.

Whatever the specifics, the fix is obviously in. Loudon and Schultz have come to some agreement they could both live with, and anything I might say would now be an embarrassment to both sides. I'm sure Schultz's failure to show isn't because of some "exigency" but a way for her to cover

her own hoop. If I do decide to make public what I know,
Schultz can claim ignorance of anything the "deranged undercover operative" might babble. Yeah, it all makes perfect
sense.

It should frag me up to realize this, it should trigger the
rage in my gut. But there's nothing there in my gut
anymore—nothing. I'm empty. I feel hollow, like a cold
wind's blowing around inside. Too much has happened, too
fast. Maybe I've dissociated. Maybe it'll all come back at
some point in the future, a huge fragging tidal wave of emotion that will turn me into a raging mucker, I don't know.
But at the moment I can't feel anything.

And the absence of emotion gives me a clarity of thought
I don't think I've ever experienced before. Which is why I
turn to Loudon and say calmly, "What's it going to be,
then?"

He's nowhere near as smooth as Baker. He blinks, and it
takes him a second or two to find his voice. "What do you
mean, Lieutenant Larson?"

"What's it going to be?" I repeat simply. "A citation for
performance above and beyond the call of day? A commen-
dation? A promotion, maybe? All on the understanding that
I'm going to keep quiet about what I know?"

You don't make it to the top of Lone Star Seattle by being
stupid. Loudon is back in control by the time I'm finished.
"A citation has been discussed, yes," he tells me calmly. "As
to the rest . . . What exactly do you know? Mr. Schrage is
dead, so his motivations are dead too."

Yeah, this is all playing out according to the script. "And
what about Drummond?" I ask. "And Layton? And
McMartin? Shot while trying to escape?"

Loudon's totally unfazed by the fact that I've just accused
him of murder, which tells me how deeply all this drek is really buried. "A tragic car accident, Lieutenant Larson," he
corrects mildly. "These things do happen, you know."

I know, all right. Everything's wrapped up in this little
morality-play package for the news media, should it ever become necessary to discuss it at all. Like, if I decide to shoot
my mouth off. It's got the formula-story structure of your
typical corp-sponsored trid drama. Several corporators stray
from the true path and get into shady dealings with "unsa-
vory elements" of society—in this case, an "evil corp" from
the Tir and the Cutters gang—which lead them ever further

from the path of righteousness. The corporation starts to investigate infractions in procedure, and the wise chief
executive—let's cast Nicky Sato as Loudon, why the frag
not?—senses that some trusted members of the flock have
gone bad. The investigation puts pressure on the
malefactors—who are, as everyone knows, basically unstable, irrational, and dangerous, as befits their attempts to jack
with the status quo. Pressure leads to mistakes and to back-
biting and infighting. One faction within the bad guys attacks another, killing one of the central figures. The others
panic, pile into their waiting getaway car and head for the
hills. In their flight from the forces of light and righteousness, they lose control of the car, wrap it around a lamppost
at two hundred klicks, and that's it—fade to null and roll
credits. Like I said, perfect plot structure. I wouldn't be surprised to see NBS running something like it during the next
sweeps week.

Loudon's still looking at me. His expression is mild, but
his gaze is hard as steel. "Yeah," I mutter. "These things do
happen."

Loudon relaxes visibly. "The past is gone," he says, "and
we've got the future to be concerned with. As to your career
path, Larson—you were right, a citation is in order for your
work in breaking the Cutters gang." He pauses significantly.
So that's the way it's going to read in my jacket, and he
wants confirmation that I'm going to play along. "And of
course a promotion," he goes on magnanimously, "with con-
comitant rise in pay. Plus your pick of your next assignment.
I think that's only reasonable in return for the stellar police
work you've performed." He glances at Baker, and the flak
nods in confirmation—a strange show of good-cop-good-
cop. "What do you say to that, Larson?" he asks.

What do I say to that? What *can* I say? This is life in the
corporate sector, I know that now. Right and wrong aren't
the issue—it's deniability and culpability that matter. Lynne
Telestrian thought that Schrage was operating without his
superiors' knowledge or consent, but now I can see that
things would have played out pretty much the same whether
or not they knew. The moment the scam broke open, the
Star's executives—Loudon in the lead—only had to point at
the perpetrators, all now conveniently dead, and howl in
shocked outrage. Any shadowsnoop interested enough to dig
for documentary evidence will find plenty—all manufac-

tured, all bullet-proof, and all pointing to the "fact" that Schrage and the rest were working entirely on their own against the greater good of the corp and of the populace at large. End of story. Justice? Null program, priyatel. Expediency is all.

There's only one thing I can say and still be true to the beliefs that led me into Lone Star in the first place. The beliefs that lead you to do certain things just because they should be done. The beliefs I haven't found anywhere recently except in the shadowrunner Argent. "Frag you," I say quietly. "Frag you both."

I don't wait for their reaction. I just turn on my heel and walk out of the office, out through the waiting room and into the elevator. I half-expect someone to follow me, to stop me from leaving. But they leave me alone, again creating around me the invisible wall. The elevator takes me down to the lobby and out onto the street, and I'm feeling so empty, my last words to Loudon still echoing around in my gut.

What do I do now? Where do I turn? I'll think about that later.

The barriers and the Electraglides and the spectators are gone. A cold breeze chills the back of my neck, and out over Elliot Bay the rain is beginning to fall. Overhead, the leading edge of a black storm cloud covers the sun as I move into the shadows of early evening.

YOU'VE READ THE FICTION, NOW PLAY THE GAME!

WELCOME TO THE FUTURE.

Magic has returned to the world. Man now shares the earth with creatures of myth and legend. Dragons soar the skies. Elves, dwarves, trolls and orks walk the streets.

Play **Shadowrun** and **you'll** walk the streets of 2053. When the mega-corporations want something done but don t want to dirty their hands. it s a shadowrun they need. and they ll come to you. Officially you don t exist. but the demand for your services is high. You might be a decker. sliding through the visualized databases of giant corporations. spiriting away the only thing of real value—information. Perhaps you are a street samurai. an enforcer whose combat skills make you the ultimate urban predator. Or a magician wielding the magical energies that surround the Earth.

That's exactly the kind of firepower you'll need to make a shadowrun…

AVAILABLE AT FINE BOOKSTORES AND GAME STORES EVERYWHERE!